DECANUS

Quintus Roman Thrillers
Book Two

Neil Denby

SAPERE
BOOKS

DECANUS

Published by Sapere Books.

24 Trafalgar Road, Ilkley, LS29 8HH

saperebooks.com

ISBN: 978-0-85495-033-1

To Jen and Em, with love and pride in your achievements

ACKNOWLEDGEMENTS

It would be remiss of me not to acknowledge the input of family and friends, and also those who provide constructive criticism in their reviews. It is much appreciated.

A shout out once more for Mary Beard's excellent *SPQR* and for Guy de la Bédoyère's *Gladius*. Both were invaluable to me and highly recommended for fans of this period. In addition, I found extremely useful James J. O'Donnell's crisp new translation of Caesar's *De Bello Gallico, Julius Caesar: The War for Gaul*.

I: DECANUS

Jupiter was not just angry, he was furious. Fuming against the earth and the sky, and especially against all the beasts and birds that inhabited these places.

Neptune was just as full of rage, angry with the waters and the waves, the sand and the shore — and he was just as powerful as Jupiter. Between them, they made the heavens shake and the miserable humans tremble. Pluto, the third brother, rubbed his hands in anticipation in his own realm of Hades, ready to welcome the shades of storm-wrecked seafarers and lightning-seared landsfolk to his halls.

The mighty crack that rent the heavens was deafening, a demonstration of Jupiter's power, echoed by the crashing of the huge waves that Neptune sent to rise up and meet it. The light that followed it was as a spark from a forge, a flare of fierce fire, as if noonday sunlight briefly blazed — then at once the flash was extinguished and it was instantly dark, as black as the slopes of Vesuvius.

Julius Quintus Quirinius, legionary soldier of the Old Legio Nine Hispania and now decanus, leader of his squad, clapped his hands over his ears in an attempt to shut out the brutal noise. It did no good. The thunder was too loud, shaking both him and the boat he was in, whilst the sheet of lightning burned his eyes before darkness fell again. The flash made him blink desperately, hot salt tears mingling with the cold salt sea.

Quintus, restricted by the ropes that bound him, was now certain that his end had come. The rain, driven sideways on the fierce wind, stung his face and the back of his hands, like a thousand tiny metal arrows. Though Quintus was wrapped in his cloak, it was soaking wet and provided little protection. He felt bruised all over, having been battered against the timbers of the ship.

He had not chosen to take this voyage. He would never have set foot on board ship if he had control of his own destiny, but his cohort — his twice disgraced and much diminished cohort, now spread across more than thirty ships — had been ordered on a mission for the general and emperor, Augustus Caesar. They were journeying from Hispania — which was just leaving the coolness of spring and entering the long heat of summer — to Britannia, a land of mist and mystery, of bleakness and cold, across Ocean, the encircling sea that bounded all known lands.

'Jupiter and Mars and Neptune!' The shout would be heard by none but the divine above the pounding of the waves, the roaring of the wind and the incessant hammering of the rain, but Quintus shouted it anyway. Jupiter and Neptune were at war around him, and Mars was the god of all soldiers. The shout, the prayer, was carried away, whipped into oblivion by the tempest.

He knew now why the ship's boy had insisted he tie himself to something solid, for if he had not been bound to the housing for the tiller (the tiller and its helmsman having long since left their company) he would have been flung over the side into the angry waves, waves that carried the image of Neptune's horses, their long jaws snapping at him beneath flowing manes.

When Quintus had joined up with such enthusiasm that spring day on the Campus Martius, he had expected to fight in heroic battles and take part in triumphs; he had thought women would throw themselves at his feet. He did not care that his father — his father who had also served, who was spent from the incessant wars of the old republic — wanted only to see the back of him so that he could lavish all his attention on Quintus' younger brother. He thought he would be picked first due to his great height, his reach, his stamina, but instead it was those youths with wide shoulders, deep chests and solid thighs that had been the first to be chosen. He was fair, lithe and supple; they, it seemed, wanted squat, wide and strong. He was intelligent — he could even read and write — and he did not think those that went before him were. When finally chosen, his new companions had immediately named him 'Macilentus', 'lofty', and referred to him often as a streak of piss, but there was no malice in it.

He had gained a friend, Crassus, mocked for his serious demeanour rather than his height, a dark and curly-haired blacksmith recruited with him who had proved loyal and steadfast. His entry into the legions had been more of a forced decision than a choice; he had been running from a violent war-scarred father, a mother afraid of him, the fire and the forge of his trade. And the ghost of a kidnapped brother.

For now, he did not know if his friend, or any of his contubernium, had survived this tempest.

The waves lifted the boat and tossed it from crest to crest — a bigger, heavier ship would have plunged bow first into the valleys between the mountainous waves; it would have sought the seabed with its pointed prow. Their boat, however, was light, and whilst it was hurled into the air, it turned and tossed, pirouetting and dancing, splashing water out of its sides at much the same rate as it was coming in.

For a full day — and maybe even a full night, for it was impossible to tell the difference — the boat was tossed and battered. The rain veered between incessant to a gentle curtain, soft as a summer shower. Sometimes, when it relented, it seemed to Quintus as if he might touch the ghostly white cliffs of Britannia he could glimpse to the north. At other times they hung impossibly in the air, unreachable.

Even if he had the means to steer the crippled craft, to fight the wind and waves, they could not have landed. The cliffs dipped their ivory claws into the sea at their base, whilst the foam crashed and complained at the lack of beach. Jagged rocks stood up, some visible, others half submerged, appearing only when the trough of a wave reached them. Any one of them would have ripped the boat apart.

The wind veered from north to west and back again, making the craft buck like an unbroken stallion. From time to time he was able to glimpse the rest of the boat. He couldn't make out much detail, but at least he knew that some of those in his charge were still on board, lashed to parts of the hull or the mast. Whether or not they lived he could not tell.

The ship's boy in just his loincloth, his body exposed and battered, was lashed to the mast. Near him, tied to the hatch, was Publius, his helmet gone and his face moon-white. His nickname of Lux suited him more than ever as his bright blond hair flew madly around his head. Further down the deck he could see the back of dark-haired Cato, Publius' closest comrade, Nox to his Lux. He was definitely alive, but his head was also uncovered, and he was trying to shake his curls free of the rain. With him was Rufus, still helmed, but identifiable from his long moustache, its bright red colour darkened by water. Quintus saw the shadowy figure of another, one he took to be Sextus, rocking behind him. He thought that maybe, for once, Sextus was no longer smiling his knowing half-smile, no longer seemingly aware of all that had been and all that was to come. Yet he hoped that he lived still; he would be sad to lose him, irritating as he was.

Quintus could not tell whether the body that appeared now and then from behind the open hatchway was alive or dead, or whether it was one of the veterans, Marcus or Tullius. The scarred and ear-ringed Tullius had completed his service twice over, yet still marched with the legions. He was burdened with the weight of loss and blame, and spent all his spare time relentlessly polishing every item of kit and buckle and blade. Marcus, once decanus, once optio and once centurion, had been demoted, shamed, and slated for a flogging or worse — all of it Quintus' fault. The two of them had brawled, and the centurion had been demoted to the ranks.

Marcus carried the will of Ursus, who had been his primus amicus or first friend. Ursus had been killed by his friend's own hand as part of a brutal punishment, in which the cohort had been forced to slaughter a tenth of its men. Ursus' shade would forever haunt Quintus, for he had failed in his solemn promise — he had not protected these men scattered across the deck.

Crassus, Quintus' own amicus, the staunch and strong son of Vulcan, he could not see. The legs that came into view were a stark white, so they must have belonged to someone else. They were shod in *caligae*, so they belonged to neither of the slaves, Maxim and Jovan. Whilst he could be sure that it was not the dark-skinned blacksmith that was being pitched from side to side, he also knew that worse might have befallen him.

The two slaves he could not see at all; the last sight of both had been below deck, before the worst of the tempest. Maxim had been hugging the body of the dead mule, it's neck broken against the hull, as if he might bring it back to life. Jovan had been fussing over the wet contents of the satchels. Quintus thought that the two cousins might still be in the belly of the ship, but did not dare to untie himself to look.

As he felt himself reaching the end of his endurance, he realised that not only had the torrent of rain lessened, but this time so had the wind. The rain fell downwards rather than driving horizontally, and it was softer. Individual sounds could now be made out — the creaking and groaning of the hull, the flapping of the remaining tatters of sail, the slap of the timbers against the water.

Suddenly, Quintus found it difficult to breathe. He opened his mouth, gulping as the taste of sulphur overpowered the acrid bite of the salt. The rain ceased and the air became warm. He felt dizzy and tugged at the ropes that bound him, but he was unable to undo the knots and began to panic that he would die from lack of air. His eyes began to close and darkness surrounded him; then, just as suddenly, the air returned, rushing in fast enough to choke him. He took great gulps although it burned his throat.

The crack of thunder that followed echoed along the water, but there was a gap between it and the fork of lightning that broke into a dozen branches from the bolt thrown by Jupiter at his brother below. The gap between the thunder and the lightning signalled that the worst of the tempest was over. The farmer in Quintus knew instinctively, and with great relief, that the centre of the storm, whose passing had caused the air to fail, had moved away to the east.

As part of Jupiter's last spiteful act, a gust knocked Quintus' head against the ship's side and he lost all consciousness.

Had he been able to listen, he would have heard the mighty crack as the ship, irrevocably pushed beyond its limits, broke in two, its back finally succumbing to the power of wind and wave, the power of Jupiter and Neptune. It divested itself of its mast, which wheeled away into the distance, and of its cargo, through a rent in its side. What remained of the ship was reduced to matchwood in the churning water. The other men, the members of Quintus' contubernium, were scattered, vanishing as the two halves of the ship spiralled away from each other.

The hurricane finally died down, its roar tailing off into the east as it chased the last of the rain. Heavy dark clouds rolled ponderously after the wind, giving way to smaller, whiter clouds, riding higher in the sky. Patches of pale blue emerged. A single seabird dared to call plaintively, though there was no answer.

Quintus, unconscious and still lashed to his timber, became just another piece of flotsam, bobbing on the water.

II: CAUDEX

'Thank Jupiter and Ceres,' Quintus mouthed, including his own family god, the god of the farmer and herdsman, in his prayer to the one who was most responsible for the storm and the shipwreck. He would need to find a bull to sacrifice, a white bull. He was not sure where he would find such an animal, but he knew that Jove would accept no less. 'Thank the gods of whatever land this is, too,' he remembered to add, feeling the sand beneath his palms.

The ground felt solid beneath him, the sea had withdrawn, and the light was fresh and clear. Quintus realised that, against all odds, he had survived the tempest, the wrath of the gods, and would not be crossing the Styx to the world of the dead yet.

Jupiter, for his part, seemed to laugh at what he and his brother had wrought, as the clouds parted and sped away, edged in scarlet and gold, streaming tails of white fire behind them. Neptune, too, seemed to have tired of the game and had withdrawn to his palace deep in the ocean, leaving behind a gentle sea. Pluto, Father Dis to the soldiers, turned his attention back to the relentless stream of arrivals ferried across to him by Charon.

All at once, it was as if the storm had never been.

Coughing seawater from deep in his gut, Quintus rose to his knees, gripping the sand and pebbles between his fingers. It was not like the soil of the farm on which he had been raised, not cool and full of life, but dry and salty. It had wormed its way under his eyelids, so that when he rubbed his eyes, it made them sore, and it was in his armpits, between his toes and in the creases of his groin. When he tried to move, it scratched and stung his grazes. He would have cried out in frustration, but his throat was too dry.

His tunic clung to him in the cool breeze, a salt-encrusted dampness. His helmet he had finally managed to pull off, letting it lie in the sand as he shook salt from his hair. When he tried to rise, he was confused by the weight attached to him, pulling him down. He looked down in wonder at the thing that had saved him. Though his hands were free, his waist was still tied to the carved oak that had been part of the ship, his sodden cloak protecting him from the worst of the ropes cutting into his midriff.

The bonds that he had so carefully tied needed to be unpicked, which his sore and swollen fingers managed to do eventually, with difficulty and much cursing. The remnant of the wood to which he had been lashed fell away as he bit through the last strand of the final knot. He then undid his cloak and let it fall. He offered up another prayer, to the dryad of the tree that had kept him from Charon's boat. Finally, still wearing his *lorica laminata*, the segmented armour that he did not have the strength to remove, he managed to stand.

The effort was enough to make him draw breath, and he almost fell back to his knees. But safety lay in the line of green that he could see far from the gentle lapping wavelets at the water's edge. He knew that he needed to find water — fresh water — both to drink and to wash the irritation from his eyes and ears and nose. His hair, long, brown and fine, was almost white with salt. The skin on his face was raw, flayed by spray and wind, his knees scraped and sore. He had to reach the line of green before the sea reached him, though he had no idea whether the tide was rising or falling.

As his head cleared, Quintus found faint hope. He could definitely see trees — and trees meant water. They looked to be a long way off, but his heavy caligae, his hobnailed sandals, were still bound to his feet and he knew he could walk there. His belt was still fastened, the protective leather straps, the *baltea*, dangling from it. His gladius — wonder of wonders — still hung at his right-hand side, and his pugio, the sharp two-edged dagger, was at his left. Stupidly he had not thought to use either to cut his bonds — *idiot*, he thought, *caudex*, *blockhead!*

As he stood, dizziness overcame him and he swayed, reaching out for a non-existent support before finally managing to right himself. What he saw through his still half-closed eyes did not fill him with joy. He appeared to be in a little bay or inlet, presumably carved out by the waves. The wind was robust and bitingly cold, catching at his tunic with eager fingers and making him shiver where it touched his skin. The sea was calm now, stretching out flat to the horizon. The sun was riding high in an almost cloudless sky, hurting his eyes and causing him to shade them with his hand.

A thought struck him and, in panic, Quintus scrabbled beneath his tunic, sighing with relief when his hand closed over the bulge at his hip and he realised that the package was still in place. An ingenious pocket, sewn into the inside of his undershorts, contained the oilskin-wrapped treasures pledged to him by Ursus, poor Ursus who had been executed as part of the cohort's punishment for cowardice and desertion, though he was neither coward nor runaway. The package contained Ursus' will, faded and tattered now, but still legible, the sacred vow that Quintus had taken to protect his tent-mates, and to protect and cherish Ursus' family, and the copper armband that Ursus had won for valour, that sealed the promise. He had no idea how he might fulfil the oath now — his comrades were missing, probably drowned, and he had almost no chance of ever getting back to Rome. But he lived. And while he lived, he believed there was hope.

Behind him, at the top of the slope, the dark line of green was punctuated by tall trees in full leaf, with thick undergrowth beneath them. In front of them were big rocks, white and round, at their base a line of seaweed and broken shell that showed where the highest tide had reached. As if in answer to his prayer, issuing from a spot between two of these boulders was a tiny stream making its way to the sea, rushing down the slope in two gullies then spreading into a mini-delta as it reached the flattest part of the beach.

His bones and muscles aching, Quintus knelt down by the deeper of the two rivulets and carefully cupped his hands, lifting water first to his parched lips, then washing the salt from his eyes. He blinked rapidly and the haziness gradually fell away. He used the water to take the sting from the grazes on his arms and legs, splashing it on his face and hair. To his surprise, his chin bore stubble — he had been away from a razor for longer than he had realised. The bruising and red weals where the rope had been would have been worse had he not been wearing armour. He cleaned them of salt and sand as best he could.

Now that he could look about properly, the wreckage of the storm could be clearly seen. Scattered in the crook of the little bay were the remnants of his ship, spars and timbers, ragged sails, frayed lengths of rope, broken boxes, shattered and unrecognisable matchwood and, amongst them, as if arranged by giant hands, the goods and equipment that had been so carefully stored in the hold.

Quintus judged that there was barely enough timber for a single ship, so the rest of the fleet must be elsewhere. He presumed them either wrecked on the wicked cliffs, sunk without trace, blown onto the southern shore, into the arms of fierce Germanic and Frisian tribes or, beyond all hope or expectation, safely landed somewhere, either here in Britannia or on one of the shelving shores of Gaul in lands controlled by Rome.

A jolting movement caught his eye. By the water's edge, a strange grey monster seemed to writhe and struggle, apparently trying to escape the waves. A closer look revealed it to be the remains of the mule, with at least one person still clinging to it, but now trapped by its wet weight.

As Quintus watched, another man emerged, grunting and retching. With joy, he recognised the dark figure of the slave, the Macedonian Jovan, his black hair and black beard wild about his head and face. The man battled from under the animal's body, then turned to try and lift it where it pinned the other man. Quintus could see that Maxim, the contubernium's other Macedonian slave, was still trapped under the beast, hugging it as he was wont to do when it was alive. Quickly, he moved to help, for this man was both cook and husbandman and, Quintus might have admitted in private, sometimes friend.

Reaching the water's edge he stooped to grapple with the dead weight of the carcass, helping Jovan, who, though Quintus knew him to be literate, a factor in his former life, was also an ex-soldier, broad-backed and strong. It was difficult, and Maxim could not help, seeming to be alive but without his wits, his fingers needing to be prised from the fur of the beast to which they were locked. After a struggle and much expenditure of energy, the two of them finally managed to loosen his grip and roll the mule from him, the animal subsiding into the waves. Quintus pulled Maxim up onto the beach, where he lay on his back, eyes shut, not moving. But he breathed still, and Jovan put his ear to his chest.

'I hear his heart beating,' said Jovan, 'but he has been battered terribly.' He reached up and lifted an eyelid, but the eye beneath was dull, and stared back at him without a flicker. He shook his head.

'There is fresh water,' said Quintus. 'A little stream runs here. We need to force some between his lips. He will have swallowed much salt and needs to be rid of it. Then he might wake.' He stretched his arms wide. 'Welcome to my little world, seafarer. I am delighted to see that you live.'

'And I, you, master.' Jovan attempted a bow, but instead Quintus grasped his wrist and the two men embraced, though slave and master should not show such feeling for one another.

'Come,' said Quintus, 'let us see if we can save your cousin.'

The two of them dragged Maxim up the beach and deposited him next to the trickling stream, using their hands to splash water on his face. Jovan tried to force water between his lips, which made him half choke. Quintus turned Maxim's head quickly as he heaved and threw up a quantity of seawater flecked with blood and bile.

'That will help,' Jovan said, as he turned his cousin onto his back again, 'but I do not think it is enough.'

'I learned this from a battlefield physician,' Quintus said as he pressed a thumb into Maxim's arm. The print showed in the dark flesh, and then blood flowed back to it, restoring the colour. 'It stays pale if life has fled,' he explained. 'He also told me the difference between sleep and unconsciousness, but I forget.' He lifted one of Maxim's eyelids and looked. 'It flickered. There is life there yet; he just needs to rest.'

So saying, he flung himself down on his back and breathed heavily, Jovan doing the same. The three of them lay for a while under the sun, which was already halfway towards its rest. Quintus and Jovan were exhausted, but glad to be alive — and glad to have each other. Neither of them had spotted any other movement that looked like life.

Quintus caught himself just in time before drifting into the sleep that his body so desperately needed. He sat up — too quickly, making his head spin — but steadied himself and spoke.

'We need a better camp than this.'

Jovan turned his head to listen, then sat up himself. His thin, plain tunic was ripped in places and clinging to him.

'You need better clothing,' Quintus continued, 'and we need food and fire, and shelter should that storm return. I also think the tide has turned and is creeping towards us once more.' He pointed. 'That line of seaweed shows where it is heading to. We need to move.'

Jovan nodded. Between them, they half carried, half dragged Maxim's body up the beach, away from the water and, eventually, into the shade. The undergrowth beneath the trees was matted and knotted, but it flattened easily enough. They lay him down in an area of shadow that was protected from the breeze.

'I will stay here and watch over him,' said Quintus. 'You need to forage. Collect what you can from the beach — clothes, weapons. You should be armed yourself.'

Jovan started at this, for he knew others of the contubernium would not approve of a slave — and a Macedonian — with weapons.

Quintus saw the movement and recognised the sentiment. 'They are not here,' he said, 'and we do not know whether they are alive. If you were going to kill me whilst I slept, I am sure you would have managed it by now. I left my cloak and helmet behind and the contents of the ship are scattered. There could be tunics for each of you, and satchels that may have food or other useful things within. Be quick. The tide has turned, and it will sweep away much that is useful.'

They both watched the water already destroying the marks that their rescue had made in the sand, swiftly rising up the flat beach. Soon the rising sea would reach some of the other wreckage, including Quintus' cloak.

'Look!' Jovan exclaimed as an apparition rose with the rolling of the waves. 'The ship's boy!'

III: CASTRA

The ship's boy was indeed still with them, lashed to a spar, part of which now stuck out of the water. He had a smile upon his face and waved to them, his arm jerking with the swell, his tattered loincloth flapping to and fro in the rhythmic waves. His head was nearest to them, out of the water, lying as if in repose, the rest of him still grasped by the greedy sea.

As the mast and its captive turned, Quintus realised with shock that the boy's legs were missing, cleanly sheared off above the knee, a whipping rope or sharp spar having crashed into him. He was not smiling, but gaping, his mouth open in death. He was long dead. The sun, already well down the western sky, shone eerily red on what was left of his body.

'Publius,' exclaimed Quintus hoarsely, 'I am sure he was near to the boy. Where is he?' Neither the slave nor the boy could provide an answer — something which the legionary realised at once. 'Go,' he urged. 'Be quick. Before we have more visitors such as this one.'

The boy's arm waved at them once more before his corpse rolled over in a wave, bobbing up and down with the piece of wood. Seabirds stalked up and down the beach, and would have pecked at Quintus had he not thrown stones at them.

As dusk drew in, the birds, big black and white things that hopped and squawked and squabbled, flew off to find other pickings. Quintus thought of his comrades and shivered. He was used to death — and to blood and butchery — but the idea of birds such as these taking out the eyes of his friends with their great sharp bills, made him shudder.

In the morning, we will bury or burn whatever is left of the boy — and any others — at low tide, he promised himself, though he was not sure he would have the energy for such an enterprise. He had been half hoping to make a meal from the mule, but it was already submerged, and anyway, it had been as much a friend as a worker. Nor did he know if the meat was edible — as a farmer, he had never been in the position where he had to eat mule. Working animals that died were boiled down, but not by him, and not for food.

For the moment he was happy enough to have fresh water, but he knew that they needed fire and food. Fire, in particular — but how could they make fire when all was so damp?

The evening air did not hold any of the heat of the sun, but quickly became as cool as the wind. He shivered, missing the warmth of his cloak.

As Jovan made his way down the beach, hoping to rescue at least some of the gear before the sea took it, Quintus did his best to make Maxim comfortable. He beat down some of the prickly growths to create a sort of grotto, open on the seaward side, but sheltered on the other three from the wind and any further rain. It even had a roof of sorts. The ground on which he laid Maxim's head was covered in a crisp carpet of dead brown leaves — damp on the surface, but still dry further down despite the storm, the close-knit branches above having protected the ground from rain before the torrent came.

Quintus made a makeshift bed out of small branches pulled from the lower reaches of the ash trees, along with a pillow of bracken and moss. He arranged Maxim on his back, arms at his side, legs straight. He would have liked to cover him, but had no cloth to spare, and he decided that a covering of leaves would be inadequate. He straightened Maxim's thin tunic, which at least was now dry, and took another look beneath his eyelids, lifting each of them gently and peering within. The eyes were bright now, not dull, and the man's breath came regularly, and Quintus hoped for a recovery.

Though he did not know what land he was in, he was glad that the trees at least were familiar to him — not only ash, spreading wide above him, but also oak and blackthorn, the latter growing low and providing much of the undergrowth, the last of its white flowers fading. There was also holly, providing protection on the landward side. However, there were no trees that might have provided food. No olives, no lemons, no oranges. The air was crisp, and the sun seemed to hold no warmth — perhaps they had been blown so far north that summer did not reach here. If summer did not, then nor would autumn, and there would be no fruit.

As the sun set in a blaze of reds and oranges, only thin clouds remaining in the sky, it was as if the storm had never been. Even the evidence of the wreck was being rapidly eaten up by the tide.

It took Jovan three journeys to bring back everything he had foraged, rescuing Quintus' cloak and helmet first. He worked quickly. Though his body was battered and bruised, and his strength waning, he knew that here could be many objects that would help them to survive. His haul included two satchels and a heavy sack. He piled all of it at Quintus' feet.

'Is Maxim back with us yet?' he asked.

'Not yet.' Quintus shook his head, moving carefully around the supine body to pick up his cloak, still heavy with seawater. 'Well done for retrieving this.' He hung it in the trees, where it would both dry and serve as a windbreak. The helmet had his initials, 'JQQ', carved inside, while those of its previous owners had been scratched out.

'Should we perhaps shake him awake?' asked Jovan.

'I don't think it would work. And, if I remember rightly, it could bring more harm to him. Let nature take its course.' Quintus turned his attention to the pile of formless wet things that Jovan now dragged forward. 'What else did you find?'

Jovan separated the two satchels and the sack. 'If I am right, the sack contains grain. It is poor stuff, food for the mule.' He allowed himself a smile. 'I do not think that he will need it. But if I can make a fire, it could feed us, at least until we find something else — fruits or roots or berries, perhaps.'

Quintus nodded, though he was doubtful. He did not think that they would be able to light a fire and, even if they could, he did not know if he could stomach eating animal feed that was clearly spoiled by seawater. 'I have no great hope of finding food — the season is wrong,' he said. 'There is much green, but no sign of fruit.'

'If there are people here, they must live on something.'

'Are those blankets?' Quintus asked, looking at the dark entanglement.

'I think so, and another cloak, and perhaps some tools,' said Jovan. They stepped away from Maxim and the trees and, with much effort, they separated out two blankets, a torn but otherwise serviceable cloak, a short-shafted sapper tool and a shallow cooking pot, its handle bent, both part of the equipment that all soldiers carried.

'These, at least, will be useful.' Quintus brandished the pan in one hand and the sharp-edged spade in the other. 'What about the satchels?'

Jovan opened each with difficulty, their ties being wet and tight. In the first were papers, sodden and virtually destroyed, probably the wills of comrades; some dried dates which, once washed in their little stream, were edible and welcome; a little phial of olive oil, still sealed; a broken flask; and a few coins in

27

a leather purse. This seemed more likely to be a collection belonging to one of the veterans than the younger men. These were the little luxuries that legionaries allowed themselves, and which veterans learned to hoard — but hardly sufficient for a feast.

'This is better!' Jovan exclaimed, holding aloft a small metal box taken from the other satchel. 'A flint and striker — we shall have fire!' He handed the box to Quintus excitedly. 'Look, it is still sealed.'

Quintus prised it open with a fingernail. Inside it was dry; it had indeed survived the storm and the wreck. To whom it belonged he had no idea, but he silently thanked them, and Vulcan of the forge. That it might be the pack of the blacksmith, Crassus, his amicus, was a thought that distracted him, but only temporarily. If Crassus' bag had survived the tempest, then perhaps so too had the man.

'We have the makings of a camp,' Quintus said as, between them, they hung the blankets and the cloak from the trees so that the little area was now enclosed by fabric on three sides, and Maxim was properly protected from the breeze which, with the coming of evening, had dropped to a cool whisper. They also fetched large, round stones from the beach to construct a fire pit. The sea had reached the line of seaweed and rocks that marked its limit, and appeared unlikely to come any further. The work, carried out in an efficient silence, served to warm their limbs and dry their tunics. Differences in status were all but forgotten as Jovan and his erstwhile master found dry kindling and built the beginnings of a fire. Quintus handed the box to Jovan. 'You do it,' he said.

Jovan took the flint and made a spark, gently blowing on the dried leaves. As the last light of the day faded, and stars began to appear, a small flame began to crackle. More leaves, twigs and thin branches confirmed their success. They smiled at each other with pride as they sat with their backs against the undergrowth, the fire in front them.

As they watched, a bright half-moon rose and cast a silver light over the little bay. There was no evidence of the previous tempest. Quintus thanked the gods once more for his rescue, giving them gratitude quietly, fighting the urge to sob with relief. He could not allow himself to show any emotion before the slave, though Jovan was also holding back tears, lest his master think him weak.

They stared out at the bay, the sea and the moon, before deciding, almost simultaneously, to be practical.

'Food,' said Jovan, reaching for the sack and knocking against Maxim as he did so.

Maxim grunted, turned, and opened his eyes. To start with they were round with terror, then, focusing, they took in first his cousin, then his master. When he opened his mouth to speak, no words came out; instead he made a sound like the moan of the wind passing between two mountains. Jovan quickly bent over him with concern, but his cousin just sighed and closed his eyes again. Jovan made to shake him, but Quintus stopped him.

'No,' he said, putting a hand on Jovan's arm. He leaned across and peered beneath Maxim's eyelid. 'Now he truly sleeps. He will wake again naturally, in good time.'

'I hope you are right,' said Jovan, standing up. 'Let me wash the grain to see if I can remove the salt, then I will try to make it edible. Will you take some of it, sir?'

Quintus smiled. 'Of course.'

IV: LIBERI

Inside the sack was a mixture of grains and oats. The grain was not wheat, but barley, so poor fare — in fact, a punishment meal for legionaries who had transgressed, but it was better than nothing. Jovan took it out one handful at a time, and using the water from the stream, he washed some of the salt out of it. He then set it to boil over the fire in the little pan. All he could do was make a type of gruel, one that was still salty despite his best efforts. But at least it was food, and it was hot.

Though both men were exhausted, Quintus instructed that they took it in turns to keep watch. They were in a strange land and there could be wild animals, or the storm could return. Such caution, such discipline, had been hammered into him during his basic training. He took the first watch himself, encouraging Jovan to sleep. At this time of year he expected warm nights, perhaps even to be troubled by insects, but here it was cool and insect-free. He found himself marching up and down the beach, blowing on his hands to keep them warm.

As he walked, Quintus marvelled at the change in the weather. Jupiter and his brothers had clearly settled their argument, at least for now, and the moon shone in a peaceful sky. He looked up at the stars and tried to remember the constellations, but these skies did not seem familiar. He wondered what his comrade Sextus — who could read the stars — would make of them, what future he saw here. It was Sextus who had forced him to fling the last of his gold nuggets — nuggets he had brought all the way from Hispania — into the heart of the tempest, claiming that they were cursed. He had been sure that the action would quell the storm, but it only seemed to make it rage more fiercely. Now, Quintus could not rid himself of the idea that perhaps he still carried the ill fortune with him. He sighed as he moved to where Jovan slept.

The Macedonian woke easily when Quintus roused him and gave him the second watch of the night. He was used to being roused at all hours, to work, to serve.

As the risen moon cast soft light on to the beach, he sat with the pugio, Quintus' long bladed dagger, watching the waves lap the shore. The wind had dropped completely and, as the moon rode down the sky, all but the endless song of the sea was quiet.

Quintus pulled the damp cloak from where it hung and draped it over his own shoulders. To begin with the material was cold, but soon his own body heat warmed it and he began to nod off by the dying fire. Though he had intended to stay alert, as soon as he closed his eyes exhaustion overcame him and he fell into a dreamless sleep.

His training ran deep, and he woke automatically in time to take the last watch of the night. Jovan was used to working before the first light of day, so he did not go back to sleep. Instead, he busied himself, as much to keep warm as anything, and found chores that needed doing. The fire was all but out, just a few embers remaining, on which he blew as he added small twigs and branches. The result was a thin spiral of blue smoke and a small tongue of flame that flickered, unsure whether to live or die.

'Leave it,' said Quintus dismissively, watching his efforts in the half-light. 'It needs drier timber.'

Jovan nodded, then went to check on the blankets and the torn cloak to see if they were yet dry, wanting to use one to cover his cousin. One of the blankets, thinner than the other, was now damp rather than wet, so, glancing at Quintus for approval, he took it down and placed it over Maxim before returning to sit with his master. Jovan also returned the dagger with diffidence, knowing that slaves should not be armed. Quintus accepted it without comment.

They watched the rising dawn together, each lost in his own thoughts.

Suddenly, a noise made them both sit up. Instantly alert, the two men looked at each other in surprise at the sound of voices somewhere in the undergrowth behind them. An argument, by the sound of it. Quintus silently gripped the hilt of his gladius, having neither helmet nor shield to protect him, the first still by the fire, the second not being amongst those things rescued from the beach. He cursed as he realised that in his weariness he had left himself with little protection, only his skill with a sword and dagger.

He drew his pugio from his belt and handed the wicked blade, hilt first, to Jovan. Each had known instinctively not to make a noise

They observed a number of shadowy shapes moving across the beach in the dim light of early morning, the first glow of dawn just discernible in the east. There was enough light to glint off the spears that the figures on the sand carried. The tide had retreated once more, leaving behind debris, one dark mass being the half-buried mule.

Seeing the beached treasures, the visitors had quickly run down to them, their voices carrying excitedly on the morning wind. They were lithe and quick, hopping from one piece of wreckage to another. There were no more than a dozen of them; clearly they had witnessed the storm and presumably the wreck, and had now come to see what booty they could find. Quintus and his Jovan had made no attempt to hide either the wreckage or themselves, although their little camp was at least concealed from the land by thick trees and bushes, if not from the sea. It was a foolish oversight, thought Quintus bitterly.

It was no surprise that the wreckage had been found. Now it was only a matter of time before someone looked up and saw them.

The visitors danced around the body of the mule, poking it with their spears, then drew back in a chattering and laughing knot. Their complacency was abruptly shattered by something out of Quintus' line of sight. There was shock and fear in their voices as they turned and ran back towards the trees, dropping some of the things they had picked up. He stood, prepared to defend himself both from them and from whatever had spooked them. But in their flight, the natives, whom he could now see were adolescent boys, failed to notice him as they careered off in the direction from which they had come.

Quintus looked to see what it was that had struck fear into their hearts, and started himself as a figure rose from the water, waving its arms. A monster indeed.

The ravaged face and wild tangle of wet hair whipped by the wind belonged to the ship's boy. His arms jerked with the motion of the waves, his mouth hung open in a silent scream, and his eye sockets gaped empty. Some trick of the tide had lifted the corpse, still lashed to the spar, upwards, so that he appeared to be emerging from the ocean; some trick of the wind had created an unearthly howl as he rose. Some trick of the gods had combined to frighten the boys away.

Quickly, Quintus crouched back down again, in the hope that the boys would not return. There were too many for him to fight — even with the help of Jovan. It seemed that his prayers were answered, for the voices calling to each other diminished and died. All was once more silent, only the footprints on the sand bearing witness to the brief sojourn of their visitors.

As the sun rose, and the body of the ship's boy subsided once more beneath the waves, Quintus and Jovan each breathed a sigh of relief. They still did not speak, instead signalling to each other to stay down until they were sure the boys had gone.

But Maxim could not be urged to silence; he was, after all, not yet in this world. It was not his fault, therefore, that he let out a low moan as the morning sun touched his face, as the wind tugged at his hair and beard. Quintus' forefinger rushed to his lips and Jovan quickly bent over his cousin, in an attempt to silence him,. They froze, listening hard, unsure whether or not they had heard movement in the undergrowth to their left.

As they watched, the blanket that still hung from the trees was slowly pulled aside by a careful hand. A pair of dark eyes, lit with curiosity, took in the scene, Jovan with his hand over Maxim's mouth, Quintus crouched in silence, then quickly withdrew. Quintus and Jovan tensed, waiting for an attack.

Suddenly, three figures jumped out of the undergrowth, all shouting in their own language, all brandishing spears.

Quintus and Jovan were both soldiers, and reacted as such, instinct and training taking over. They automatically moved to stand side by side, weapons raised, to protect the defenceless Maxim at their back. A thrust, a swipe, a stab, a plunge, and it was all over.

At the sight of Quintus in his armour and cloak, the last of the boys paused in his charge and turned to run back. But it was too late for the other two. Both gladius and pugio had struck.

'Are there more?' Jovan asked, looking at the area from which the boys had emerged.

'I cannot see any,' replied Quintus.

They moved carefully out of the shadow of the undergrowth, watching all the time to see if the larger group would return. Quintus turned one of the bodies over with his foot and let out a curse as lifeless eyes stared accusingly at him from a smooth-cheeked face. This was a young boy, lean and slender-limbed. His chest was marred with a deep wound, a fatal stab to the heart. His death had at least been swift.

'They were children, *liberi*,' Quintus said quietly.

'They were armed,' said Jovan, kicking at the spear dropped by one of the attackers, although on closer inspection it looked more like a sharpened stick than a *pilum* or javelin.

'Someone brought them here; one of these fools must have encouraged the attack.'

'Perhaps the one who ran?'

Quintus was at once angry with himself, and took it out on Jovan. 'Whoever led them, they were children. This one has seen no more than eleven or twelve summers. This one even fewer.' He tapped the other fallen boy, who lay face down and was smaller than the first. 'They are barely old enough to hold a weapon, let alone wield one.'

Jovan accepted the rebuke in silence; then a groan escaped from the smaller body.

'He lives,' he said.

V: CHARON'S OBOL

Quintus bent down and gently turned the boy onto his back. He looked at the young features, the hurt on the boy's face obvious, the soft moan escaping from his lips accompanied by grey and red spittle. His wound had not been clean, and his hands were clasped across his belly. His guts had been spilled, and he was trying to push the mass of tubes back from whence they came. He whimpered, with no strength in the effort, nor did he have strength in his hands, and his innards were slipping and spilling despite his attempts.

'He will not live,' said Quintus sharply, shaking his head. He bent over the boy and thrust his gladius into the scrawny neck, upwards and deep into the boy's brain. The boy's eyes thanked him mutely before the light died from them. Quintus looked to the heavens. 'The gods indeed are cruel,' he said, then turned to Jovan. 'He could not live with such an injury, only die in agony.'

'Yet we might have saved him,' Jovan dared to argue, looking around nervously for any sign of the boy's companions.

Quintus shook his head firmly. 'You have grown bold for one of your status,' he said. 'You should know your place.'

'I do not believe you mean that,' Jovan said under his breath, but still loud enough for his master to hear.

Quintus ignored him, though he knew that he was right. 'He would not have survived, but he would have taken a long time to die,' he said. 'If nothing else, we have made an enemy here. We need to collect what we can carry, and quickly. We need to move.'

Again, Jovan dared to argue. 'We cannot leave the dead like this,' he said, looking down at the two pathetic forms sprawled on the sand. Though clad in loincloths made of some rough woven material, their chests were bare and hairless and their thin arms and legs betrayed their youth.

Quintus was brusque. He had intended to leave them, but now thought better of it. 'Before we leave, we show them respect. We send them to whatever and wherever they believe they go when they die.'

'But…' began Jovan.

'I know,' interrupted the legionary. 'We have no idea to what gods these natives pray, what barbarian customs they follow. Yet we must try to show them honour.' There was a military reason behind the decision — he looked around, in particular at the treeline. 'I think that we are being watched. We can only try to treat them with reverence.' So saying, he bent over the fallen boys and straightened their limbs, placing them so that it looked as if they slept in peace, though he could do nothing to tidy the sprawled guts of the smaller one.

'The Egyptians, I have been told,' mused Jovan, 'inter bodies in great stone tombs, preserved in spices and wrapped in bandages.'

'We are not Egyptians,' snapped Quintus. 'Some entomb, others bury or burn. These people might even leave fallen warriors for the sea to take. We do not know. I do not even know the customs of *your* people.'

'We…' Jovan was about to enlighten him but stopped, as it was clear that the death rites of Macedonians were of no interest to Quintus.

'We can only trust that their own gods will escort them to wherever their people go after death without the need for ritual or ceremony.'

Jovan was unconvinced, but said nothing. The boys' gods had hardly looked after them this morning.

'We have fire,' said Quintus, pointing at the thin wisp of blue smoke that, despite Jovan's best efforts, still escaped their poor hearth, 'so we burn them. We would do no less for one of our own. Let us build a pyre. There must be dry timber in these trees. But we cannot take long. Curious boys may stop to watch what we do, and they will then fetch their parents. They may have sent for them already.'

'The ship's boy, too?' Jovan's question was tentative. He pointed to the shoreline, where the mangled body still lay, tangled up with sail and spar.

'He, too,' agreed Quintus. 'Cut him away from his ship and he can join the others. They are of an age. Perhaps they will find Hades, or wherever, together.'

Jovan still held the long knife. 'Should I use this?'

Quintus nodded. 'Then we will see if we can find dry timber.'

They worked quickly, first to cut the ship's boy from the spar and lay his truncated corpse with the others, hoping that this showed no disrespect to either tribes or their gods. He then pulled branches from the trees and gathered thin, wooden debris that had been thrown up by the sea and was drying quickly in the wind and the sun. Quintus and Jovan then built the pyre until it seemed large enough.

'Take his feet,' said Quintus, pointing at the first body. Though he could easily have lifted the corpse on his own, he thought this would show greater respect. 'I will take his head. Lay him on it gently.'

They lifted the two children in turn onto the stacked wood, arranging them with what they hoped was reverence. They even placed with them the spears that they had dropped, in case some sort of weapon was required for entry into their afterlife. Jovan said he thought it was a custom of the Gauls. They then laid the remains of the ship's boy between these two with difficulty, trying to cover up the white stumps of his legs with leaves. There were no flowers or fragrant oils, but at least it all looked proper.

'Where are the coins we found?' asked Quintus.

'Here,' said Jovan, rooting around in their little pile of treasures for the leather purse and dropping the few coins into Quintus' palm.

'A denarius,' said Quintus, picking out a small silver circle, 'will serve as Charon's obol.' He placed it in the ship's boy's mouth. 'Perhaps the others will be allowed to embark with him. These look appropriate.' He picked out two other coins, small and bronze, with a ship's prow on one side and on the other an unrecognisable head which he knew to be Saturn. He placed them in the mouths of the native boys. 'Fetch a flame from our fire.'

Jovan ran back to their camp and soon returned with a bundle of twigs that he had set alight. 'Maxim is awake!' he called joyously. 'He is whole, I think.'

'Good,' said Quintus as he took the brand and lit the leaves and kindling at the base of the pyre. It smoked and fretted, but finally a flame appeared, and the fire spread. 'I am glad. I did not wish to leave him here, but we could not carry him. I hope he can walk — the sooner we leave here, the better.'

Sadly their hurried efforts did not meet with success. The fire was not hot enough to consume the bodies, nor big enough for three. As they watched, the remains were charred and twisted, but not turned to ash. They tried to feed the fire, but the wind and sea spray hindered their efforts and smoke swirled around, stinging their eyes.

'We should leave it,' Quintus decided. 'The sea will claim it after all. Fetch your cousin, if he is fit enough. We need to collect what we can from the flotsam, then leave this cursed place. We take only what is useful and what we can carry.'

There were many things that might have been useful but which, without a cart or pack animal, they would not be able to haul. Amongst the timber, rags of sail and coils of rope were shields, spears, and foodstuffs that were mostly ruined, though Jovan rescued some and they were able to eat. There was also a skin, which they filled with fresh water, and some tools. Another satchel yielded more olive oil and a twist of salt, which made them smile. They had tasted nothing but salt since they were flung onto this shore. Maxim responded to his cousin's shout and came to help, though he looked pale and unsteady on his feet and held the blanket close. He had looked with horror at the charred remains on the smoking fire and retched at the smell of burning flesh, before trying to gather some of the goods. But his strength was gone, at least for now, and he could carry little.

There was far too much for them to take with them, although enough to kit Quintus out as a legionary once more. Now that he had a shield and spear to go with his sword and helmet, he felt better. He felt Roman again. They cached the remaining items in the place where they had camped, covering it with twigs and leaves, partly in the hope that they might return, partly in an attempt to deny equipment to their attackers. Quintus had his own gear, and Maxim and Jovan would bring as much of the rest as they could carry, wrapped in a cloak or blanket and slung over their shoulders.

The sky was a pastel blue and the sun was bright, already clear of the horizon. Fair-weather clouds were high in the firmament, though the breeze still had an edge to it. Quintus, with some misgivings, allowed Jovan to don the torn cloak, now dry. It was something to which he was not entitled, and allowing him to wear it was an action for which, under normal circumstances, both he and the slave would be punished. Maxim sat with his blanket, envious of the honour bestowed on his cousin, but keen to learn all that had happened since he had been knocked on the head as the ship foundered.

Whilst Quintus hid equipment, Jovan produced a makeshift breakfast of bruised fruit, grain and water, something that could be eaten as they marched.

They had to decide whether to follow the coast or go inland. Quintus argued that they should keep the sea in sight, while Jovan wanted to move away to try to find food. Maxim stayed quiet for a while, then intervened in support of his cousin. 'I think we are right to go towards where food might be...'

Quintus exploded with frustration, shouting sharply at both of them. 'Do not add your voice. I do not know which way to go. All I know is that we should get away from here. Those children had parents, and they will not be far away. Food, people, settlements — we are not going *towards* anything, we are going *away*, far away from this thrice-cursed beach. First the shipwreck, then the attack, then a pathetic fire that will not honour the dead. We go from here by whichever way is easiest. Gather what we can carry.'

Maxim did not answer, but cast his eyes to the ground and wrapped the borrowed blanket tighter around him, as if the chill of the wind had suddenly increased. Jovan looked at him, but stayed silent.

Quintus felt no remorse for his outburst. He would brook no further airing of opinions. He had decided that coastal villages or settlements would be easier to find, and that harbours — with ships that might return them home — would of necessity be by the sea. The choice then was west or east, a decision made by the stiff breeze that still blew from the west, which he would put at their backs.

They climbed upwards from their campsite, the trees crowding around them, until they came to a clearing where they could look out to sea. Foam beat against jagged rocks, and pieces of their ship — or someone else's — still floated on the surface. A great oak stood here, its canopy wide, welcoming all manner of bird and beast, whilst beeches and birches fought each other at its margins, growing tall and slender in their search for light. A rowan tree, almost as large as the oak, had been toppled by the wind. Next to its fallen body a track had been made by many small animal feet, wending its way through fern, bracken and bramble, and it was along this that the trio trudged.

On a dead birch grew mushrooms as large as the round shields of the cavalry, with which they might have supplemented their meagre breakfast had Jovan not recognised them.

'They will not kill you,' he said, 'but they are not pleasant to eat.'

He broke one off, and it was cracked and woody. As they climbed the rise, the guilty smudge of smoke from their pyre marred the sky, showing all from here to the middle of the sea where they had been. In time the waves would claim it, and all the evidence of their short occupation of the bay would be scoured clean. But for now it was a danger to them. It revealed their presence. They needed to get away.

They were heavily laden and Maxim was still weak, so they moved slowly. The ground was broken and uneven, beset with cracks and clefts, some of which were so wide that they had to go around them. In places, though, they found summer fruit

— small wild strawberries in particular, not especially sweet, but at least not salty.

They had continued to climb until, with surprise, they realised that they were well above the sea, and could no longer even hear its gentle rhythm. Looking out over its expanse, they could see no land other than that on which they stood. Quintus had half-hoped that they were not far from the coast of Hispania, or even Gaul, but clearly it was not the case.

VI: AUCISSA

As the sun reached its zenith and began to dip, they had thoughts of stopping to rest, perhaps to eat. Maxim kept dropping back, even though both Jovan and Quintus had relieved him of some of his burden. As they crested yet another ridge, several columns of smoke appeared before them.

For an instant, Quintus thought that they had somehow managed to march in a circle and return to their own fire, but then he shook the thought from his head. Not only had they kept the sea on their right all the time, but also the tide would certainly by now have extinguished the pyre.

The legionary called a halt. 'Quietly,' he said softly, signalling them to drop down.

He crawled to the top of the slope despite the brambles and nettles and peered through the long grass. Below him was a small settlement, three or four households, probably sharing the farming of the land or the fishing. A long inlet snaked in from the south, where it spread to form the delta of a river, at this end terminating in a wharf where a couple of boats — fishing boats, most likely, he thought — were tied by a plain stone bridge.

There had been a dozen or more youths exploring the wreckage on the beach. The youngest would have been eight or nine, the oldest perhaps sixteen. Quintus did a swift calculation. By his reckoning, there were not enough families here to have produced so many youngsters. He prayed that he was right, for he had decided — as soon as he saw the boats — to approach these people for help. He shuffled back to where Jovan was fussing over his cousin, who was lying flat on his back and panting.

'There are people down there, families. I do not think they are the fathers of those that attacked us. I think they are peaceful farmers and fishermen, not warriors.'

'I was a peaceful farmer before the Romans came,' muttered Maxim.

Quintus overheard him, but chose not to respond. Now was not the time for politics.

Jovan gently kicked his cousin in remonstration. 'You were a soldier, like me,' he mouthed.

Quintus was trying to decide who should go down. He was glad to have his sword, shield and spear, but he could see that this would more likely frighten than reassure the people in the settlement.

'We will all go,' he finally decided. 'You will walk as my attendants. Leave everything we do not need here. We can come back for it.' He put his shield, helmet and spear down, then wrapped the cloak around him so that neither his gladius, pugio nor chest armour were visible. Though still armed and armoured, he could have passed as a traveller.

Maxim and Jovan dropped their burdens with relief. Jovan, with his cloak pulled tight, could have passed for a companion of the legionary. Maxim, with the blanket around his shoulders, looked like another traveller.

'That will not do,' said Quintus sternly, as he inspected them. 'You will arrive as what you are: my slaves. Take off the cloak and blanket. You will come down behind me, in tunics.' As he set off, he instructed them further, 'Do not come empty-handed. Look like you are of some use to me.'

Maxim decided to carry the blanket, and a small cooking pot. Jovan decided to carry the cloak, hoping that he could don it again — he now thought of it as his, and perhaps a small step on the road to his freedom. The bandana he habitually wore to hide the slave tattoo on his forehead had been lost in the wreck, but he had quickly made another from the material they had rescued. Now he did not know whether or not to take it off. He waited to be told, but Quintus said nothing, so he left it on.

They were ready to risk contact.

Quintus made another decision before the three of them set off down the slope. 'You should be armed,' he said. 'It would not look out of place if you were armed for your master's protection.' He sounded like he was trying to convince himself. 'Maxim, take the spear. Jovan, you have already handled this; look after it.' He handed him the long dagger from his belt. He knew that there were many who would have disapproved, but they were not there to witness it.

They approached the little group of huts slowly. Maxim held the spear awkwardly in the same hand as the cooking pot, while Jovan had the pugio in his belt. Quintus was seemingly unarmed, with his gladius hidden beneath his cloak, unable to predict what they would meet. Unconsciously he bent his knees, making himself smaller. He prayed that his calculations were correct, and that the boys they had killed had not come from this place, for if they had, the others would have returned with the ill news, by faster roads than he and his companions.

They were spotted by the villagers, several of whom came out to meet them, carrying stout sticks. They did not look as if they were coming to attack, or to bring murderers to justice. Their skins were dusky, closer to that of the Macedonians than the Romans, and their countenances seemed open and welcoming. They seemed small, certainly in comparison to the legionary, but then Quintus knew that he was exceptionally tall.

As they descended, the trio saw that an outcrop had blocked their view of the settlement and that the collection of huts was bigger than Quintus had thought, with a large round building in the centre and several others hiding in the lee of the cliff. He felt bile begin to rise in his throat as he realised that, had he been able to see these huts, his calculation would have been different. This settlement was indeed large enough to have produced the number of boys who had come scavenging on the beach. But it was momentary — he realised at once that a few boys of the same age as their attackers were standing and discussing the visitors, but with no sign of anger. With a gulp he pushed back the fear and straightened his shoulders.

Now he was at the base of the cliff he could see that the settlement was not just based on the land, but in caves that ran back into the rock. To the other side, the wharf looked big enough to hold many more ships; the river was wide at that point, its banks high, with a long narrow stone bridge spanning the water beyond where the ships were beached. Quintus guessed that when the tide was in, it filled the inlet and allowed the ships to sail into it. Immediately he thought like a Roman — the channel should be dug deeper, or the wharf moved nearer the sea.

The far bank was dotted with flocks of large birds, along with a number of ponies. He could not tell whether these people farmed the land, fished, kept beasts or hunted their food.

A pace apart, each party halted. Quintus offered his open palm in what he hoped was the universal gesture of peace, though in so doing, he revealed the sword at his side. To his surprise a small woman stepped forward, the men seeming to defer to her, and grasped his forearm in the Roman fashion.

'I am named Aucissa,' she said. 'I have comrades of yours here.' She welcomed them in heavily accented Latin. When Quintus' expression revealed his surprise, she explained, 'I recognise the cloak and the sword, though you tried to hide it. I also recognise the dagger your man carries. I hope you come to us in peace — though we can defend ourselves if we wish.' She indicated the men with the sticks. 'I think your countrymen will be pleased to see you. Come.'

As Quintus followed her, her companions parting to let them through, she gave further details. 'There are two of them, who arrived in cloaks like yours, clinging on to a large piece of timber. Foolishly they were still wearing armour, as are you, though it could have drowned them. They were fortunate to be washed up, and they were pulled from the water like bedraggled rats, only just alive. One seems naturally idle, the other naturally industrious. One smiles and does nothing, but somehow persuades others to serve him, while the other growls but is willing to work. One is smooth and pale, endlessly grooming himself and preening like a cat; the other is dark and curly-haired — a Celt, I would think, from the west somewhere, or from far to the south. Do you recognise them from my description?'

'I think I do,' said Quintus, grinning broadly and scarcely believing his good fortune. Surely this could be none other than Sextus and Crassus; a more accurate description of Sextus would be hard to come by. 'Where are they?'

'Come.' The woman was beckoning them forward. He made to follow, then turned to make sure that the slaves were with him. Maxim and Jovan were hovering — they were not sure if their presence was still required. He motioned to them with his hand and they closed the gap quickly, both still armed, both still unsure whether they were slave, servant or bodyguard.

'We will all go,' said Quintus to the cousins. 'I am sure that our friends would like to see you too.'

The woman pointed to a gap in the huts, towards the cliff face. 'Through there,' she said.

Sitting by a small fire outside was Sextus, talking to a dark-haired woman crouched before him, her back to them. Their entrance made her turn, and Quintus realised that she was both young and pretty. Her face was round and honest, with a snub nose, long eyelashes and big inquiring eyes. Her long black hair was plaited down her back. She did not look afraid.

Quintus looked past her, delighted to see Sextus and making no attempt to hide his pleasure. Sextus had been told that there were strangers coming down the cliff path, but he had not allowed himself to hope that it was his compatriots. He, too, had thought it more likely to be others — Centurion Antoninus, perhaps, whom he knew would have soon put a stop to his life of ease. He rose quickly, gesturing for the young woman to stay where she was, and strode towards his comrade. Quintus, as ever, bent his knees to make himself smaller to receive his friend, although he was not conscious of the action.

As Sextus embraced Quintus, he looked behind him, hoping to see other familiar faces. Noticing Maxim and Jovan, he greeted them with a crooked smile. 'Survived then, did you?' he said, as if they had somehow conspired not to be drowned.

Quintus looked behind Sextus, searching for his own primus amicus, the blacksmith who fought at his shoulder, who was his 'first friend' both on the battlefield and off it. In vain he looked for the tall dark figure with the broad shoulders, curly black hair and serious demeanour that was Crassus Malleolus. Behind Quintus were the slaves, behind Sextus, no-one.

'Ursus' charge, do you have it still?' Sextus whispered urgently.

'I have it,' said Quintus. 'It is safe, and I still mean to carry out his will.'

'And the gold?'

'It is gone.'

'Then perhaps our luck will hold.'

The two men separated and stood at arm's length, hands on each other's shoulders. Sextus was smooth-cheeked, his hair somehow combed, while Quintus was rough-jawed and dishevelled, his hair a salt-streaked rats' nest.

'Is it just you and the slaves?' Sextus asked. 'Or are there others? Please tell me there are others.'

'Just I,' said Quintus sadly, 'and our Macedonians. We are yet to find any others. But the woman told me that you had a companion. Who is it? Who survived with you?'

Before Sextus could answer, the broad figure of the blacksmith appeared around the back of the hut, carrying a bundle of freshly hewn firewood. The young woman ran to take the faggots off him, pointing at the new arrivals.

Crassus looked over, and a rare grin cracked his face. Still he did not rush to drop the wood, but carefully transferred it into the woman's arms, making sure that she could manage. He then walked towards them, opening his arms even wider than his smile, and enfolded Quintus in a bear hug.

'We thought you lost,' he said, as he held his amicus by the shoulders.

'*You* thought him lost,' said Sextus, laughing. '*I* told you that he was a survivor.' He smiled that half-smile that his comrades found so infuriating. 'I told you that he would ride out the storm. I saw it in the stars.'

Crassus did not put much faith in Sextus' fortune-telling abilities, but was glad that he had been right on this occasion.

'You are whole?' Quintus asked. 'Both of you?'

'My wound pains me, but yes. Apart from that, we are whole.' Crassus rubbed his lower back, where an injury inflicted by a Spanish tribesman in the hills of Hispania had almost killed him

'I am as you see me,' said Sextus merrily, opening his arms wide and doing a little twirl. 'These people are open and friendly.' He seemed unmarked, his tunic fresh, his weapons in place at his belt, the leather straps of his apron whole, though he wore no armour. Crassus, too, was dressed simply, in a tunic too short for him, and caligae. He had clearly been working, for his front was dust-streaked and sweat-stained.

'Where are we?' Quintus asked. 'Do you know?'

'We at least reached our intended destination,' said Crassus with a laugh. Quintus saw that the laughter pained him, as he grasped his back unconsciously. 'We are on the island of Britannia — the misted isle that lies across the Ocean Stream.'

'Which means that we have left the world as we know it,' said Sextus, shaking his head.

Crassus ignored the interruption. 'This is the land that the general visited all those years ago, though I fear that the three of us are insufficient to complete our mission.'

'Unless the rest of the fleet has somehow escaped the storm's power, Emperor Augustus will not be getting a bridgehead any time soon,' Quintus observed with a wry smile.

'Unless it is a very small one,' chuckled Sextus. He called to the woman who had taken the wood from the blacksmith. The others were unable to comprehend any of what he said other than 'Annaig', which they took to be her name. They understood when she arrived with a skin of water.

'Settle yourselves. I will crick my neck if I have to talk to you as you stand, Macilentus,' said Sextus, making Quintus smile at the use of his nickname.

Sextus passed the skin around, offering places for the legionaries to sit and ignoring the presence of the slaves. 'I have been learning some words in their language, though for some reason they seem to know a lot of ours. I think they may have met Romans before.'

VII: AQUILO

Annaig knelt on the floor so that she could pass the skin from one man to another.

'She is pretty,' remarked Quintus, glancing sideways at the Macedonians. 'Is she a slave?'

'She is not,' replied Sextus. 'She is of this tribe and serves of her own free will. But that reminds me...' He spoke to the woman quickly, nodding towards Maxim and Jovan, who stood awkwardly on the edge of the conversation. She took the cue and, leaving the skin with Sextus, rose and ushered the two slaves away. 'She will make sure that they are fed and watered. She understands their status, but they will be looked after, I assure you.'

A brief exchange out of earshot brought Jovan back to Quintus. 'Sir, this is yours,' he said deferentially, holding out the pugio, handle first. 'I do not think I will need it.'

'Nor this,' said Maxim, joining him and laying the spear on the floor.

Sextus raised his eyebrows and looked in query at Quintus; slaves should not be armed. Quintus ignored him and instead addressed Jovan and Maxim.

'Good,' he said, pleased with their loyalty. 'When they allow you, you should go and retrieve our belongings. We are amongst friends.' He dropped his voice, 'though I think we may have already made enemies on this island.' As the two slaves followed Annaig, Quintus turned back to his comrades. 'Tell me your story, and I will tell you mine.'

'We were tossed and turned by Neptune's mighty hand and Aquilo, god of the fierce north wind, blew mightily upon our little ship. Jove's thunderbolts came down upon us from a black sky, and his lightning rent the heavens with terrible power. The waves were high as mountain peaks, their crests as white as marble, and all around trumpeted a great noise of wind and spray and…'

'There is not much to tell,' Crassus cut in, 'certainly not enough for poor poetry.' His bushy brows drew together as he looked at Sextus. 'We both know that we were unconscious for most of whatever happened.'

'But that should not spoil a good story,' Sextus complained.

Quintus laughed. 'Come now, Crassus, you tell it. Tell it plainly. How did you survive?'

'In truth, I do not know. Sextus may even know more than I,' he admitted. 'For myself, I was thrown about the ship until, inevitably, I cracked my head and fell into darkness. When I awoke, I was lying on a raft of sorts — I think it was part of the deck, sheared off — upon a shingle beach, many strange faces looking down on me. My hands had to be prised from the edge of the timber, I am told, for I would not let it go. Then all was blackness again. I awoke on a cot in this place, covered by a blanket. I had been stripped of all I wore, even my undershorts, though they did not manage to untie my caligae. I was given a sort of loincloth — hard to tie comfortably — and this tunic, which was clean before I started working, though barely big enough. They are not a large people.' Crassus was tall, bull-necked, muscular, a blacksmith with the frame of a wrestler. 'Where everything else is, I do not know. I think I wore my armour, my helmet and my cloak when I tied myself to the ship, but it is hard to recall.'

'Your weapons?' Quintus asked.

'With my cloak, I assume, though again I do not know.'

'And you?' Quintus turned to Sextus. 'Tell me without the intervention of the poet in you.'

Sextus pouted theatrically. 'Much the same,' he admitted, 'though I do not even remember being on the beach. I just remember waking here, with Annaig looking over me.'

'The dark-haired young woman? The pretty one? The one with the eyes of a forest deer?'

'You noticed, then,' he said, smiling. 'Yes, she. She helped me into my tunic and has stayed to help us both, trying to teach us some of her language and learning some of ours. She would have taken my belt and weapons, but I stopped her.' He raised a finger. 'There was no malice in it, I felt. They were being taken for safekeeping. I think yours are safe, Crassus. She also tried to discover what food we would eat.'

'Milk,' spat Crassus in disgust. 'They offered me hot milk, and it seems that I may have drunk some of it during my recovery.' He shivered, for it was not part of a Roman's diet. It was a drink for babies, slaves and animals.

'And they eat even their evening meal sitting upright on stools at a board, or squatting by the fire, as if they were permanently on campaign,' added Sextus. 'They have no benches, no proper way of taking food.'

'Pleasant as they are,' Crassus muttered, looking around to ensure he was not overheard — although it was doubtful that their hosts would understand him — 'they are barbarians.' He said it with finality, Sextus agreeing with him with a firm nod. Crassus gestured to Quintus. 'Now your tale. How do you come to be cloaked and armoured?'

'I have a shield and helmet too,' he replied quietly. 'I left them outside the village. Jovan and Maxim will fetch them soon. And there are other useful things that the sea has given up.'

'The people here have collected much that has appeared on the beach, and have put it in a hut. I will ask them to show you later. But none of our comrades' bodies have been found, nor the ship's master. In fact, it would seem nothing has washed up from any ship other than ours.' Crassus sighed. 'I think we may be the only ship blown to this particular shore.'

'We found the ship's boy,' Quintus said, 'or at least a part of him. He did not survive. We took him from the sea and tried to send him to his gods, but the fire would not burn. I think we failed.'

'At least you tried,' said Sextus.

'There were others,' Quintus admitted. 'Whilst you have made friends, we may have made foes.'

'How so?' Crassus asked.

'*Fortuna mala*,' came the reply

'*Fortuna mala*?' Sextus asked. 'I thought you did not believe in the fates?'

'Sometimes I wonder,' said Quintus quietly. He then told them most of what had passed, including the failure of the pyre. He hid only the extreme youth of those they had killed.

Sextus and Crassus were not shocked. They too would have defended themselves against attackers. They shrugged at the news of the ship's boy, but could not feel sorrow. He was not a friend, probably not even a countryman. Sextus appeared to be more shocked that Quintus had given a blade to Jovan, but he stayed his tongue.

'It was not far away,' said Quintus, 'no more than a day's march. They may be allies of this tribe.'

'Or a branch of the same tribe,' said Sextus, as he finished the last of the water.

'Or even relatives,' said Crassus.

'Whatever they are, we can only hope for the best. Either they are friends or family of those you slew, or they are not. You did nothing in malice or rage.' Sextus was sanguine. 'There is little we can do about it.'

'If they are friends, you might at least be able to explain the accidental nature of their deaths, and the effort that you were making with the fire,' offered Crassus.

'*If* they are friends...' Quintus mused. 'One thing is certain. We are Roman, not of this island, guests — and we have already made enemies.'

Their conversation was interrupted by the small woman who had greeted them on the cliff path, and had introduced herself as Aucissa. She returned with two men, who seemed to Quintus by their age to be counsellors. Judging by her position between and before them, he took her to be a chieftain or leader of some sort.

Quintus and his companions looked at the three who approached their hearth and, as one, they rose to greet them.

'No,' Aucissa said, laughing, 'sit, sit. I am not royalty!'

'But you seem to be a leader...' said Quintus.

'A leader I may be, but no more,' she said, then indicated her comrades. The two men were in the autumn of their lives but still stood straight and looked at the Romans with clear eyes. 'These men are elders of my tribe. They have as much right to speak as I. They are here as much to translate as anything. Tincomarus, here —' she pointed to the first of the men, who bowed his head in acknowledgement — 'he speaks both your Latin and our own language.' She spoke a few words to the other man in a rapid and staccato tongue. He nodded to acknowledge the visitors, his long drooping moustache fascinating them. His face had many lines of wisdom, and was framed with long brown hair shot through with grey and tied at the neck. The woman continued her explanation. 'Commios speaks only the tongue of the Atrebates, our people — I have just told him what I am telling you. He carries a great store of knowledge and history on which we may wish to draw.'

'Both are welcome,' said Crassus without thinking. He was left feeling somewhat awkward, as it appeared he was inviting someone to sit in their own home.

Aucissa smiled again, accepted the offer with good grace, and sat with them, the two men squatting to either side. Quintus noticed that none of them appeared to be carrying a weapon and was impressed by this level of trust. He and Sextus were still armed, and the spear lay near them on the ground. If there were other members of the tribe waiting out of sight, his furtive glances could not detect them.

'You are guests,' she said, following his eyes and guessing his intent. 'Surely you have rules for guests in your own home?'

'We do,' said Quintus, 'but we would still disarm them at the door.'

'Or they would lay down their weapons of their own accord,' she mused.

Sextus at once made a move for his sword, intending to offer it to her, but Quintus put a hand on his arm. Crassus, already disarmed, had not moved.

'We are trained to keep them with us,' Quintus explained. 'We sleep with them nearby, or even wear them in case of attack. They are a part of us, as familiar as our own skin. I can tell you that my companion —' he nodded towards Crassus — 'feels naked without his belt and blades.'

Crassus smiled weakly and nodded. 'It is a punishment to be deprived of our belts.'

'You should have said,' Aucissa answered, and spoke rapidly in her own language to Annaig. 'We did not intend to punish you.'

Though small, she had a bearing, a confidence, that made them trust her. Had he been able to do so without offending Rome, Sextus would have taken off his blades then and there. As it was, he now wore them more self-consciously than was his habit. Crassus' belt and blades were brought, and, on a signal from Aucissa, they were presented with reverence to him. Annaig even tried to untie the rope he wore instead of a belt, but he politely declined.

Aucissa had a quality that Quintus could not put his finger on. Her nose was bold and straight, and, when in repose, her lips dropped naturally into a slight smile. She had twinkling blue eyes that stood out in her suntanned face, and her hair fell to her waist in tumbling black curls. At its margins there were braids, held in place by clips of shining metal — bronze, probably, he thought, as it was bright but neither silver nor gold. She wore a red and white cloth around her head which pulled back her hair to reveal a forehead that was high and smooth and spoke of intelligence and wisdom. Her face was not particularly weathered, but it seemed to the legionaries that she might be older than she looked. They would not like to guess her age.

How, thought Quintus, could anyone call such a woman a barbarian? He was enchanted by her, to the extent that initially he barely heard her speak, and had to drag his attention back from the study of her features.

'I am sorry,' he interrupted quickly. 'It is not just us who were lost at sea — there were others, comrades on our ship, and many other ships besides. Do you have tidings of any of them?'

Aucissa looked towards Tincomarus, a man who had reached late middle age with less hair than when he had started on the journey. What was left was exclusively white, but this was compensated for with a moustache that was full, long and black. His face spoke of wisdom, and his Latin was at least as good as Aucissa's. 'As of yet, no,' he said. 'The wreckage that we have found would seem to be from a single ship — there is not enough for more than one — and no other bodies have washed ashore, either human or animal.'

'This at least leaves the door of hope open,' said Aucissa.

'But we have many ships still upon the waters,' Tincomarus added. 'They will have seen the storm coming and found safety in ports or coves known to them. They may also have rescued your comrades. Only two ships found safety in our own inlet — those you will have seen at anchor — but we are not yet concerned for the others. The storm has gone, and our gods are strong and protect us. Tomorrow, the men will start returning.' He turned to Commios and gave a brief explanation of what he had said, then relayed the response. 'Commios says that it is important that they do. We are now approaching the summer solstice, and the men, especially the young men, must be here.'

The legionaries now realised what had seemed odd about the village. It was populated by mothers and children, women and the old; the men in their prime were not here.

'Then it is too soon for us to be concerned?' Crassus asked. 'You think they will have survived that mighty storm?' It was the first time that the blacksmith had been on a boat on the ocean. He had not enjoyed his time under Jupiter and Neptune's cudgel. He hoped that the stretch of water they had been blown across was narrow enough at some point for a bridge. He would happily work on the building of it if it meant he never stepped on a rolling deck again.

'Too soon,' Aucissa confirmed. 'Surely your own sea gods protect you?'

'I think not,' the blacksmith said in a low voice, shaking his head. 'My family look to Vulcan, he of the hearth and the forge, not to any gods of the deeps.' He lifted his head and smiled. 'But I would happily sacrifice a bull or a ram to Neptune if I thought that he would let me return undrowned!'

Sextus nodded enthusiastically. 'Me, too,' he said, and they all laughed in agreement.

Commios interrupted, with a hint of impatience in his voice.

'He wants to know what you are doing here,' Tincomarus explained. 'Whether you come as friend or enemy. He reminds me that we have seen the colour of Rome before.'

VIII: AQUILIFER

Sextus knew his history. 'So you are old enough to have met with the army of great Caesar?'

'That is how we knew you were Roman,' Aucissa said. 'Some of us have met legionaries before.'

'Did you meet them in battle?' Quintus asked, wondering if his forefathers had been defeated by these people, friendly as they were.

Aucissa did not answer directly. 'We have many cousins across the water — it is not so terrible to cross it when the winds are fair. We are Atrebates. There is a tribe across the water called the same. We share common ancestors, we speak the same tongue, we marry each other, though the water keeps us much apart. Our cousins, and other tribes, spread down the rivers of what you — and your general — call Gaul, though we have many names for it.' She became thoughtful. 'We did fight, yes, we all did, my cousins included. They were of the Veneti and the Tencteri. Tribes that lived peacefully on either side of the great river until your general arrived.'

She lowered her head and placed a hand on her breast. Her voice filled with sorrow. 'Your general was something we had never encountered — a monster of unheard-of proportions. Our cousins of the Veneti defeated him to begin with; they had better ships — better built, better manned — and they knew the sea. But at last our gods deserted us.' She sighed. 'They let the winds fail, and the great hooks of the enemy tore into our unfilled sails. The army of Rome strode across onto our decks, and a sea battle was turned into a land battle, though it was on the water still. You are better soldiers on land. Your general destroyed our cousins, executed the elders, sold the people into slavery.'

'This is normal in war,' said Quintus unemotionally. 'Why do you call him a monster?'

'The Tencteri defied him, so he slaughtered them,' she said simply. She held her hand up as Quintus made to object. 'I do not mean the warriors. Your general could not defeat all the warriors — they sent one of his armies running — so instead he slew every other living thing he could find: women, children, grandmothers, babes in arms, all defenceless.' Her voice was close to breaking, but she mastered herself, took a deep breath. The legionaries knew of Caesar's fearsome reputation — which included a penchant for cruelty and massacre, intended to drive home his superiority, his invincibility.

In the silence Commios spoke. Tincomarus had been murmuring a translation to him, now he put his words into Latin. 'We were overfond of freedom, he says. We always have been. Our tribes elect their leaders and rule their own; we do not easily bend the knee to anyone.'

'We were thus ourselves in the time of the Republic,' said Quintus, knowing that Augustus' new empire was but a shadow of what had once been. A string of dictators and generals — Marius and Sulla, Pompey and Crassus, Caesar and Marcus Antonius — had torn the Republic from its moorings and turned its institutions and traditions to their own advantage. What they had now merely aped the glories and freedoms of the past.

Sextus did not look on the Republic with such favour. 'They shared power if they were rich and landed, with the masks of their noble ancestors in the atrium,' he sneered. He saw more opportunity for people of his ilk in the new system than in the old. 'I was never held aloft by my father, never acknowledged in public, never given a family. For my citizenship, I had to rely on a label tied to a toe and a leather pouch round my neck.' He fingered the *bulla*, the lead locket that denoted his citizenship, which hung in the bag at his throat. He had never given it up, as he had never had a father willing to fit him for a manly gown.

'Your history does not concern us here,' said Quintus softly, putting a friendly hand on Sextus' arm. 'I know it pains you but — for now, at least — let it go.' Quintus knew his comrade's background, and also that this was not the place to explain it. Sextus tensed, then relaxed with a shrug.

'We are proud,' continued Tincomarus. 'Though we worship much the same gods, each tribe has its own traditions, its own identity. If your leader — or our leader —' he looked sideways at Aucissa — 'gives us an order, we question it. We want to know the reasons behind it, the intended result; we suggest better ways of achieving the same outcome. You, however, seem to relish being organised, being told what to do.'

Aucissa smiled in agreement and continued. 'When this general of yours came to us, he came with a reputation for cruelty and violence. We thought we could never negotiate a peace, for we knew it was the habit of the Romans to destroy everything they laid their hands on.'

Quintus harrumphed. He knew what had happened in the past. He knew that if a city resisted the legions, they would break that resistance, with ballistas and battering rams if they could, with starvation and disease if not. Once broken, they would then kill every living thing in the place.

All the men, of course, as well as the women, even if they could have been enslaved. They killed children too, down to the tiniest babies. Dogs, cats, cattle, pigs, chickens and ducks were also slaughtered. They would have killed the insects if they could. None of this was done in a frenzy. No, the legions moved through methodically, killing efficiently. It was both a punishment and a warning. Cities fell more easily under the threat of annihilation.

'Such methods are only employed if people resist the civilising hand of friendship,' Quintus said, pushing the vision of the dead children from his mind. He was not sure if he truly believed what he was saying. 'That was then, this is now.'

'That was Rome,' Aucissa said simply. 'We did not, could not, trust Caesar. Each tribe along the coast drove the general from their land, harried him, sent him and his ships ever further east. Our warriors watched them from the clifftops, harassed them into moving on, one tribe sending them to the next. They struggled to do anything but fly before the wind. They even lost some of their ships, though the seas were calm. They did not seem to be a threat; there were not many ships, and our priests told us that the men on board them feared the sea.'

'How do you know this?' Sextus asked.

Aucissa raised a finger. 'I see you wish to know our methods of divination, but it is no use asking. They are as hidden from us as they are from you. Our priests, our wise men, they knew.'

Once more Commios interrupted, speaking in their native tongue. Tincomarus translated. 'He says that when they finally landed, it was more in fright than might. Even the children were unafraid.' He pointed to his own chest and to Commios as he spoke. 'I was a child of nine summers, Commios a little older. We watched and threw stones. We wanted to throw spears.' He made a face. 'But we were not allowed.'

Quintus silently wished the rule against spear-carrying children was still enforced.

'You knew of the massacre of the Tencteri, yet you allow us to live?' Quintus' hand had strayed towards the hilt of his sword.

'We keep a watch on the waves,' Aucissa said, 'lest more Romans land on our shores. You were watched, and you did not appear to be a threat. It seemed better to have you as a friend rather than a foe.'

Before any of the legionaries could respond, a messenger arrived and claimed her attention. Aucissa turned and there were brief words in their own language.

'There is news,' she said.

The messenger bowed from the neck, a nod really, and withdrew. He was young and bare-chinned, though the shadow on his upper lip showed that he was already trying to grow the moustache that was the mark of manhood in his people. He was one of the adolescents that had been observing the arrival of the Romans down the cliff path, perhaps one of the ones that had seen them first land.

As he turned and departed, a number of tribesmen and women arrived, bearing platters of food. The legionaries recognised some of the items, but chose to avoid the others, though their hosts urged them to try. There was a type of flatbread and cuts of dark meat, oysters and other produce of the sea but also, to their surprise, a grain pottage filled with honey. Although Tincomarus said that this was simple fare, Crassus explained that they were used to certain rations, designed to keep them strong, and that rich foods — by which, his hosts decided, he meant anything he had not tasted before — should be avoided.

They ate awkwardly, watching Commios and Tincomarus closely to see how they handled the food. They had shallow wooden spoons, eating knives and no other implements but their hands, and they ate squatting or sitting, as if they were on campaign. There was no wine, just a weak beer with a sour taste. Quintus thought the pottage and the bread acceptable, especially as he had not eaten properly for a long time, and the legionaries had all finished what they were willing to try long before their hosts had completed their meal.

Aucissa continued the conversation, although she explained that it was not their custom to discuss politics when eating. 'The messenger says that there are sails on the horizon; the first of our ships are back.'

Quintus' immediate thought was that they would not be able to reach the wharf, but then he realised that they would be sailing on the tide and would follow it up to the quay as the inlet filled with the sea. Since their arrival, the sun had crossed the sky and now crouched behind a bank of rolling white cloud in the west, but there was still much of the day left. There were fair winds, and no sign of further storms. The ships should arrive if not before sunset, at least well before the short night's darkness.

'When do you expect them here?' Crassus asked. He did not know how their arrival would change his fortune, whether for good or ill. Sextus, the seer, thought he knew.

'They will bring good news,' he said, as he tore at a piece of the rough barley bread, dipping the crusts in the pottage.

In time, Tincomarus clapped his hands and servants — slaves, perhaps — removed the remnants of the meal and brought bowls of fresh water. The Romans watched as the Atrebates used the water to wash their hands and lips, and, in the case of the two men, their moustaches. They followed suit.

'When will the ships arrive?' Quintus asked, realising that Crassus' question had not been answered. Really, he wanted to know what would then be done with them. For now they were being treated as friends, but the men who arrived with the ships might have different ideas.

'It depends on the wind and the tides,' said Aucissa, pushing the cloth band high up her forehead as she looked in the direction of the sea. 'What do you think, Tincomarus?'

'The wind is brisk, and will become brisker. They should beat the dark.'

Aucissa nodded. 'So they will be here soon, in a matter of hours, Roman — they might have news of your comrades.'

'This is what we hope,' said Crassus. 'Have you seen anything, Sextus?'

'Nothing clearly, my friend,' came the reply. 'We must wait.'

'Is there time for you to finish the tale you were relating?' Quintus asked. 'About what happened when your people came across legionaries of Rome?'

Aucissa looked at Tincomarus and Commios and asked something in their own tongue. The two men conferred briefly, then nodded in agreement. Aucissa opened her palm and looked at Tincomarus, who took the cue, first asking, 'Where were we?'

'We were being visited, invaded perhaps, but it is hard to be sure,' Aucissa answered wryly. 'Great Caesar has arrived. He is in a boat, which we think is unfamiliar to him, and the sea does not obey his commands.'

'So we were,' said Tincomarus. 'Are you sure you would like to hear the rest?'

Quintus responded. 'Only if it is not too distressing to tell,' he said diffidently.

'No, no. It is not painful to me. I will tell it,' Tincomarus replied with a smile. 'They could not land when they first came close to our homes. Along the coast, the cliffs stood in their way, tall and white and forbidding, with feet of fume and foam.

They tried to row inshore but capricious currents twisted and rejected them, bore them out to sea. The many jagged rocks that guard our shores stood sentinel, sharp and spume-flecked.' Tincomarus' hands did some of the talking for him, playing the parts of cliffs and waves and boats upon the ocean. 'They were not — you are not — a seafaring nation. You are not comfortable on the water; that much was obvious without any divination.'

Commios clearly understood at least some of what was being said, as he interrupted enthusiastically, forcing Tincomarus to stop and interpret again.

'He says your boats are built like wooden huts, or baskets for fruit, not like boats at all, and that you cannot be sailors if you have no sails. He says it is no wonder that you struggled.'

They all laughed, the Romans more out of courtesy than amusement. They were not used to having their deficiencies pointed out to them. They were proud of great Caesar's achievements. The Dictator had been assassinated, but to the legionaries he was still a conquering general and a hero, and he now sat amongst the gods — something of which these natives were clearly unaware. Emperor Augustus had been *divi filius* — son of the god — for twenty-five years now.

'We are an island,' Aucissa explained, 'with many bays and inlets, many lakes and wide rivers. We know boats; we know them of necessity. In many cases, the waters are our roads.'

Tincomarus continued, although the listeners detected a note of bitterness in his voice. 'He did not give up, this general of yours, this killer of cities and babies.' Sextus' hand went to his sword hilt at this, but the older man put a palm up to stop him. 'It is true,' he said. 'There is no point in denial.'

Sextus' ire subsided. 'It is true,' he said quietly, 'though it is not often said. Go on.'

Tincomarus took the cue, as the other legionaries, not quite as eager to defend the general, also relaxed. 'He did not leave. Instead he sailed on, seeking a beach, some landing place with no rock or cliff or current, where no enemy could harry him with spears and slingshots. In the end he found one, but still his men were reluctant to dare the sea. We watched and thought they would give up, but at last one soldier jumped from a ship with a device — a great golden eagle on a pole, wings spread, tassels and roundels hanging from it. He was clad in the skin of an animal, its head framing his head. Our people thought him to be either a god himself, or at least representing a god. The men on the boats did not hesitate; they followed him, though their shields and armour dragged them down in the waves and made them stumble and fall.'

'Not a god,' Crassus said, shaking his head, 'an aquilifer, one who carries the eagle, the symbol of Rome. Not a god, but an idea — as such perhaps stronger than many gods.'

IX: OCEANUS

Crassus was full of pride. 'We met the aquilifer's son, a brave and noble man who stood with us against greed and hatred. He, too, bears the standard; he sailed with us.' He turned wistful. 'Unlike his father, he is probably lost to the sea.'

'Your comrade may yet survive,' Aucissa said, recognising the tone of loss in the Roman's voice.

'And so great Caesar landed?' Quintus asked.

'He did, though we never really knew why. He was confused — afterwards it was said that on the one hand he was punishing us for helping our cousins across the water, but on the other that he wanted us as friends.' Her voice turned dismissive. 'We could see that it was all a show. Men died so that your great Caesar could say he had set foot on our shore. So that they could witness that he had crossed what we call the Narrow Sea, what you Romans called Oceanus, thinking it a great river that encircles the world. It was political.'

Quintus was indignant. 'You think this is true? Political?'

Crassus was unequivocal. 'Which of our wars were not?'

Sextus was slower to make a judgement. 'Perhaps it was about sending a message.'

'But to who?' Aucissa asked. 'Who was the message for? Not for the people of this island, for he never saw most of them. Most of them, I would wager, never even knew that he had stepped upon our shore.'

'For Rome, I suppose,' admitted Crassus reluctantly, then he asked Aucissa, 'What happened?'

'All I can tell you is that before Samhain eve, they were gone. All of them. Our own gods finally remembered who we were

71

and came to our aid. The heavens darkened as they raised cloud, wind and rain and, with the first storm of autumn, they filled the Roman ships with water and fear and drove them out to sea, dancing on the waves. The legionaries ran and splashed their way on board. It was not dignified.'

'That is why they were back within a year,' Quintus said with pride. 'Roman dignity is not a thing to be offended.'

'They came back, yes,' said Tincomarus, 'but even then we never really knew what for. They brought many, many ships. They had adapted them; they were lower in the water and had flat keels for beach landings. They even had sails. By the gods, they learn quickly. This time there were horses. Again, they had learned: our war chariots had outmanoeuvred them and confused their infantry, so they needed something with which to oppose them. And they brought many men — three or four times more than they had landed before.'

'The landing was better, but still we are not sure why they came,' Aucissa said. 'They claimed to have put certain chieftains at the head of certain tribes, to have made kings — but no-one really took any notice. There was nothing that might be called a battle. There were skirmishes, raids, that was all. The soldiers marched in a column, paced out measurements, and threw up temporary camps, but they did not fight. They dug up fields and made roads, to and from nowhere. They did not even stay long enough to learn about the weather.'

'The weather?' Sextus asked, looking suspiciously at the unthreatening skies.

'The weather,' Aucissa said, 'turns on a whim, a breath. One day it is hotter than a summer bonfire, the sky deep blue and clear; the next it is cold, flakes of snow swirling in the air, frost on the grass. One day the winds are light and favourable and it is dry; the next there are purple and black clouds and great storms roll in. Caesar's fleet — that he thought safe — was again caught in a storm, and his ships were driven into each other. Horses panicked, masts cracked, siege engines toppled into the sea. They were built to transport troops, animals, and equipment, not to withstand storms. They left our shores, their ships, men and banners all fleeing across the ocean, followed by a great storm. You are the first Romans we have seen since.'

Quintus knew that the cohort's mission — disrupted by the storm — was to provide a bridgehead for Emperor Augustus. He stayed silent.

'Our friends across the water brought us news,' Tincomarus said. 'Caesar, it seems, claimed victory and dominion over the tiny corner of the land he had seen. He demanded tribute and slaves but received nothing other than what the people carried with them. He sowed confusion and dissent, claiming to make chieftains of those who were not chieftains, deposing legitimate leaders, brokering alliances between tribes that had been at war for generations, and saying that this river, or this hill, this bay, or this lake belonged to such-and-such a tribe when it did not. And when the Romans left, no force was left to hold the land they said was theirs.'

Tincomarus was suddenly interrupted by a cry of alarm from the huts to the east of the village and the sound of running footsteps. A stream of people — women and children mostly, with a smattering of old men amongst them — hurried past towards the large round building in the centre of the huts.

Aucissa shouted out in her own language, as did both Commios and Tincomarus. A few words passed between them, and then she turned to the legionaries, who were also now standing, hands on weapons.

'It seems we are under attack,' she said.

'Romans?' Quintus asked, gripping his sword hilt, not wanting to fight his own people, but feeling a duty to protect his hosts.

'Let's hope it's our people!' cried Crassus joyfully, slapping him on the back.

Quintus was jolted back to reality. Of course he could not fight with these natives; it would be unthinkable. He shook the nonsense from his head and began to assess the situation. Survival first; the glory of Rome second.

Commios had already gone to find out what was happening, whilst Tincomarus, with surprising nimbleness for one of his years, ducked into one of the nearest huts. There was already a cacophony of voices, shouting and crying, including children demanding their mothers, and the sound of running feet throughout the settlement.

Quintus climbed up on to the bench on which he had been sitting. Over the roofs of the huts he could see a group of native tribesmen — definitely not Romans — making their way down the same cliff path that they had used earlier that day. The track was rough and steep, he knew from his own experience that it was not an easy descent, yet these natives moved quickly. They were, he surmised, a different tribe to his hosts. They were armed with spears, although they might also have swords hidden at their belts, and some carried lit torches. They wore tunics, but no armour or helmets. Many of them had fair hair, some almost white, though the lithe movement of their bodies down the track suggested that they were not old. Some had hair that stood up in unnatural spikes.

Sextus stood on the bench beside Quintus. 'They seem to have adopted a Roman quirk,' he said, 'but late.'

'A quirk?'

'It was a brief fashion amongst the harlots with whom I worked; they made their hair stand on end with a wash of some sort, a glue, I think. It ended — as many of these things do — almost before it began.'

'And the whiteness?'

'Women have always coloured their hair — though few would choose white!'

As they watched, the first of the invading force vanished behind the promontory that hid the majority of the settlement from the path. When they emerged from its shadow it would be on level ground, and they would not be any distance away. For now, there was a little time to plan.

'We need a strategy,' said Quintus, looking at his comrade, 'a defence.'

Sextus nodded. Already, the legionaries could see a steady stream of people — mothers with children, elderly men and women — making their way towards a larger building in the centre of the huts.

'Where are they going?' Quintus asked Aucissa.

'The caves or the roundhouse — the big building there, in the middle,' she said as she pointed. 'That is where we would traditionally seek shelter. The caves are safer, but further away.' There was a quiver in her voice. 'We only ever expect attacks from the sea; the caves give us protection. The enemy might burn huts and steal grain, but at least the people are saved if the men are away. Raiders will sail away rather than face the unknown — they have no idea who is defending the caves. We can rebuild huts, sow more seed, raid and take grain for ourselves. But a land attack… These are our neighbours.' She pointed again. 'They are making for the roundhouse…'

'Who are they?' Crassus asked.

'Not Romans,' said Quintus, shaking his head as Sextus jumped down from the bench. 'A neighbouring tribe of some sort. A local dispute, I would guess.'

As he hopped down himself, it struck him that he could be the cause of this raid, that the boys on the beach could be the sons or grandsons of these warriors. If that was the case, he had put his hosts in harm's way. He had a duty to protect them.

Crassus was disappointed. 'I had hoped for more of our own people. I wanted a rescue, not a fight. Sextus, I thought we were in for some better luck?'

Sextus shrugged but gave no answer, his handsome face showing no emotion. There was always a chance he could be wrong; it was dangerous to predict the will of the gods.

Tincomarus reappeared, armed, a long sword in his hand and a knife at his belt, urging Aucissa to safety. 'You too,' he told the legionaries breathlessly. 'Make for the roundhouse. You will be safe there.'

'We do not run and hide with women and children,' Crassus said, half drawing his gladius. 'We are Roman. We are armed. We fight.'

'It is not a Roman fight,' said the elder, adding an elaborate — and sarcastic — bow, 'but you are welcome. It is your choice.'

He turned to leave, but the passage between the huts was suddenly blocked and the little space where they had eaten was filled as Jovan and Maxim rushed into it, laden with the gear that Quintus had left stashed at the top of the cliff path.

'We were on our way down when we saw them coming,' Jovan said. 'Even better, we were able to raise the alarm. Here.' He put Quintus' shield, helmet and spear on the ground, along with spare daggers, cooking gear, and an assortment of ropes and other material they had thought might be useful.

'Well done,' said Quintus. He picked up the helmet, tucking it beneath his arm. 'And I have my dagger and my own sword, though not my own spear.' The spear they had rescued was not one of the lighter *pilum*, the throwing spear, but the heavier kind of spear used by the infantry to bring down cavalry. Quintus hefted it and liked its weight. 'Do they have cavalry?' he asked Aucissa.

'They will have chariots, but even a skilled charioteer could not manage the slope that the men are descending. The chariots will be coming down the valley.' She pointed north and Quintus looked where she indicated, expecting to see a cloud of dust.

'They are not here yet,' she said, 'but they will come. You cannot protect us. Roman you may be, but there are too many of them. We will be safe. Our boats have been sighted, so the men will be here before night closes in. We can hide until then.'

'Aucissa, the roundhouse is no protection.' Quintus could see that, like all the buildings, it had walls of interwoven hazel and mud, with a thatch roof held up by poles. 'It will burn. Those warriors will be here long before your men arrive — and I can see that they carry fire. They will burn your people out. There must be another way. I have not survived Jupiter's thunder to be spitted on a Briton's spear or roasted in an enemy's fire. I think I know a way that we can protect you. You two —' he turned to Crassus and Sextus, a note of command back in his voice — 'where is your gear? Do you have armour still?'

Aucissa answered for them. 'Their armour, spears and shields, along with other items rescued from the sea, are stacked there.' She pointed to a long low hut set apart from the rest on rising land.

'Go and fetch them and arm yourselves. Jovan, Maxim, help them. Quickly, I have an idea.'

X: ADOLESCENTI

Crassus and Sextus ran for the hut that Aucissa had said held their weapons. Jovan and Maxim followed, keen to help tie their masters into their fighting gear, to sort shield and spear from the cache. Inside they found a jumble of metal and material, stuff that had been stored in the holds of their ships. Once it had been boxed and carefully labelled, but as the boat broke up the boxes had smashed and were now nothing but firewood. This pile was amongst that which had been left on the beach. Crassus picked up a bundle and shook it in frustration, hoping that something useful would drop out.

'We cannot sort this,' said Sextus. 'There is no time.'

'Sirs!' Jovan exclaimed. 'Look, we do not have to sort it — not yet, anyway.' He had pulled aside a thin leather curtain and there, in an alcove, hung on trestles turned on their sides, was the legionaries' own armour, their own tunics beneath it. Their helmets, shields and spears were stacked at the side.

'Is this ours?' Crassus asked in amazement.

'It would seem so,' said Sextus. 'They have cleaned it and polished it.'

He picked up a helmet, impressed by its undented and shiny surface, and looked inside. There, where he expected them to be, were the initials of its previous owner and the letters DVF. These stood for *deducere velatos fortuna* — 'bring the wearer luck'.

'DVF,' said Sextus with pleasure, 'and look, next to it, PSE — this is mine!' Next to the deeply engraved DVF, he had had carved his own initials, PSE — Pupillus Sextilius Esquilina, the name given to him by the priestesses who had taken him in as a child, though he called himself Sextus.

'Do you think they were keeping it from us?' Crassus asked, as he undid his belt and pulled off the ill-fitting tunic he had been given before picking up his own. 'Or were they keeping it for some other purpose?'

The tunic was clean, dry, and mended where it had been torn. He pulled it on and began to don his body armour over the top of it.

'I do not know,' answered Sextus. 'Maybe they thought that if we had it, we would attack them.' He dropped his voice. 'But I suspect differently. I think they may have been venerating it, judging by the way it was displayed and hidden behind a curtain.' Then a more mundane thought struck him. 'Or preparing it for sale.' His voice was muffled briefly as he slipped his tunic over his head.

'Perhaps we will find out later — if there is a later,' said the blacksmith, always happy to be heading for a fight. He tried on three helmets that Jovan presented to him, until he found one that was a snug fit. 'Now I feel like a legionary again,' he said, as he fastened the laces beneath his chin.

Maxim and Jovan took a legionary each and tied their lorica laminata for them. The new armour, favoured by the emperor, covered their shoulders, the tops of their arms and their torsos, protecting all the vital organs. Once they had retied their belts and aprons and settled their weapons, they turned to see what else was here. The legionaries had both kept their own sword and dagger, but there were also spears and, most importantly, shields.

'Even your cloaks are here,' Maxim exclaimed, lifting up one of them. 'They are dry.'

'And they have been mended where they were torn,' added Jovan, holding up another, 'though I would have done a better job.' With a grimace, he pointed out the ugly — but serviceable — stitching.

'We do not need them,' said Crassus. 'For now, leave them here.' The slaves would happily have worn the warm woollen cloaks, and even the discarded tunics, thicker than theirs, that had been provided by the Atrebates, but Sextus and Crassus took no notice. Crassus grunted as he adjusted his armour over his battle wound — which restricted the movement in his back. Satisfied with the adjustments, he gave the order.

'Let us take ourselves back to Quintus,' he said.

They left the hut and strode the dozen or so paces back to where Quintus still talked with Aucissa, feeling that all eyes were on them, that the splendour of Rome and its soldiers had arrived in this place. Quintus was speaking earnestly and urgently.

'You must listen to me,' he said. 'We can do better than hide in a firetrap. Even our own Temple of Jupiter on the Capitoline, though built with stone, was not safe from fire.'

He had, of course, seen strategy in battle, and had been taught tactics during his training on the Campus Martius. He had seen the devastation caused to a marching column if they were caught in a narrow defile; he had been forced to march past the remnants of a cavalry troop that had been gutted by an enemy that knew the ground and had employed a better strategy. This is what had given him his idea. The narrow valley in which the cavalry had been slaughtered was a trap, admittedly, but it was a trap because it had prevented the soldiers from manoeuvring, from attacking in any number.

With this in mind, Quintus continued. 'The bridge over the river is narrow,' he said to Aucissa. 'We can defend it. There are three of us fully armed. With support from some of the men here, we can defend the bridge.'

The narrow bridge led from the wharf, the area where ships would be loaded and unloaded, to the opposite bank, beyond which the field and hill held ripening summer grain, much of it still green. There were no buildings there, no fence or hedge and only a few trees, which bent north in the winds that blew from the sea. To the back of it, on a small rise, were a circle of large stones, some standing tall, some crossing others to form square arches.

'There is nothing to defend,' she said, 'no fort or ramparts, hardly even a tree to hide behind, and the people here carry few arms. We need to hide. It would be suicide to do anything else.'

'What about the stones?' Quintus asked. 'Surely your people could hide behind them. It looks like the remnant of a building of some sort — is it not defendable?'

Aucissa's refusal was absolute. 'It is holy; it is not a place for war.'

Quintus' voice was pleading now. 'Aucissa, Horatio saved the whole of Rome by defending a bridge on his own — if the three of us stand shoulder to shoulder, they can only pit three of them against us at a time. And your ships are on their way — we would not have to hold it for long.' He looked directly at her. 'Quickly, order the people to cross the bridge. The tide will be high enough to protect them from any that would ford. Your boys and men can fling spears and stones against any attacker that would swim; no chariot could come against us. No fire will threaten us. Send your people to the other bank. We will defend the bridge until your menfolk arrive.'

'You cannot reach the caves, and the roundhouse will burn,' urged Crassus as he approached. 'Listen to me. We are fighters; it is what we are trained to do. We can hold the bridge; it is narrow enough.'

'I think he is right,' said Tincomarus. 'We can hold it until the boats arrive.'

'Head them off, then,' commanded Aucissa, making a decision at last.

'It must be you,' said Tincomarus. 'They will obey none other.'

'Very well,' she assented and stepped out of the shadow of the huts.

'Take Crassus with you,' said Quintus. 'He can help and his armour will impress. Tincomarus, come with me; we will need your voice. Sextus,' he went on, looking at his comrade, fully armed and armoured, 'come with us. You too will dazzle.'

The three of them, two legionaries and one tribesman barely armed, headed straight for the narrow stone bridge. Their job would be to shepherd people across as they arrived, with Tincomarus to reassure them, and to find boys and men that could throw a stone or a spear. Quintus took up position at one end of the narrow bridge, Sextus in the middle and Tincomarus on the far bank. Behind them, Aucissa, helped by Commios and Crassus, shouted at the retreating backs of the Atrebates, telling them that the roundhouse was not safe and urging them to follow where the Roman legionary pointed. It took what seemed an age, but gradually, her voice was heard, and her instructions heeded.

The stream of people gradually changed direction as Quintus anxiously looked for the appearance of the enemy at the base of the promontory. At first many came, so that there was a crowd that moved slowly, forming a queue, then there were fewer, until finally most were on the far bank, crouching down amongst the unripened corn.

Aucissa and Commios stood with Quintus now, urging haste, whilst he nervously scanned for the enemy. A final tribesman, elderly, stooped, white-haired and white-moustached, limped across the bridge.

'Is that the last?' Quintus asked sharply. The old man came slowly, Crassus behind him, trying to hurry him along. 'Help him!' Quintus shouted at his comrade.

'He refuses!' Crassus called. 'He wants no aid. He did not want to leave his fireside, even though there was no fire lit within it.' He opened his arms in a gesture of helplessness.

'He is old and confused,' said Aucissa. 'The gods will take him soon enough.'

'But not this day,' insisted Quintus. 'This day we stand. This day we live.' He called across the bridge. 'Crassus, carry him if you must, but make haste!'

The old man, though he did not understand the words, caught the tone and turned his shuffle into a trot, Crassus at his heels.

A youth ran forward from behind Quintus, ducking under his flailing hand, first shouting at the old man, then taking him by the arm in support. Crassus would have taken the other arm, but the boy waved him away imperiously, muttering loudly, the tone of admonition unmistakeable, even though speaking in his own tongue. He was tall, on the cusp of manhood, with the same cast to his face as the old man. He turned and spoke softly to him, and the man moved a little faster.

'A son?' Quintus asked Aucissa, as he watched them.

'A grandson,' she answered. 'His son is helmsman of one of our ships.'

As the two of them reached the bank, Quintus congratulated the youth, praising him for the help he had given. Of course, the boy did not understand and waved away the strange words of the peculiarly dressed man. The old man just glowered.

Quintus shrugged — Aucissa or Tincomarus could pass the message on.

The bridge was no more than fifty paces long. It was made of great slabs of grey rock, set on piers buried deep in the earth, and it looked like it continued further, sunken deep into some ancient track. As it approached the river valley on either side, the ground began to dip, so that some of the bridge would cross over shallow water and salt marsh land, the rising tide lapping at the pier stones. Then the bank became steeper still, dropping suddenly to the river bed, several paces below. In the centre, the defendable position that Quintus had marked out was crossed by a monumental flat grey stone, stretching from pier to pier across the deep channel sculpted by the river and the tide. It was three to four paces wide, with no parapet and a long drop to either side. It would even the odds.

Quintus had made a number of swift judgements. The width of the river here was too wide for an attacker to leap, although not so wide that a spear could not find its mark cast from one side to the other. The banks were steep; no trees or plants grew there, for the salt of the tides made the land barren. The ground fell precipitously to the river below and, Quintus judged, whilst a determined man might scramble down the bank into the bottom, he would then have deep and swirling water to negotiate. It was already at a depth that could not be waded, so it would have to be swum. Even at its height — or so he gauged from the tide marks — an attacker would need to climb the crumbly far bank without a handhold or foothold. He would also have to carry a spear, sword or axe if he wished to be armed, and he would be facing spears and stones flung by the defenders above. No, they could not come this way.

The deep cleft of the river snaked away to the north, fast flowing in its steep banks as far as he could see: there was no easy crossing there, the very reason for the bridge. As long as the tide was coming in, and the water was deep, it was a defendable position.

Tincomarus had detailed the boys to collect stones, ready to hurl at the enemy should they try to cross, and to pile smaller rocks for their slingshots. The group was led by the adolescent messenger they had seen earlier. His hair was long, his chest was broad and he was tall, but his skin was still smooth and unblemished, and his face — even with its sparse excuse for a moustache — betrayed that he was caught in that no-man's land between child and adult. He was too old for childish games, yet too young to be taken seriously by fighters and fishermen.

The Romans were impressed by his air of command as he organised his companions. In Rome he would be called *adolescenti*, not yet old enough to fight in the legions but old enough to take instruction and be given some of the responsibility that he craved. As Quintus watched him in his chosen role of leader, he mused that legend claimed that Gnaeus Pompeius was only this age when he had been precocious enough to lead legionary troops in support of Sulla the Dictator. *Carnifex adolescenti* they called him, the 'teenage butcher', named for his savagery, yet he became Pompeius Magnus thanks to his victories and the loyalty of the legions he had led. Quintus hoped that this boy had the same instinct for command, but, for his own sake, not the same lust for blood. He narrowed his eyes and looked more closely at him as he moved to and fro, issuing commands and wearing authority as if it were a well-fitted tunic.

'He looks like one I have seen before,' observed Quintus. He noticed a resemblance to the youth who had supported his grandfather across the bridge. 'Is he a brother…?'

'Another grandson,' said Aucissa. 'There are many of them, though some will have different mothers and different grandmothers. It is our way.'

Quintus made no comment on this. He had never tried to understand how other cultures, other peoples, were different to those in Rome. Clearly, the Roman system was better than anything else so should be universally adopted. However, seeing the contribution made by this lad did make him think that perhaps it was easy to overlook the potential of the young.

He had been a young man before he was tempered in Hispania, in battle and through witnessing, suffering and even inflicting harsh punishments. He might still look like a young man due to his fair skin and complexion, but he felt much older.

XI: VIA APPIA

Commios had taken charge of the evacuation, and was now organising the people into groups to support each other. His calm demeanour washed over the panicked populace and gentled them; his voice, though the Romans could not understand the language, was smooth and conciliatory, yet had authority in it.

Tincomarus stood with a group of older men, armed with an axe, a spear and a sword, ready to defend the defenceless should the enemy force the bridge. He, too, was calm and the men talked quietly amongst themselves. There were women there, too, Quintus noted with surprise, carrying axes or spears and small round shields. None of them wore armour.

Aucissa was standing with the Romans at the edge of the bridge, waiting for the inevitable charge. They had expected to be chased to their refuge, but were not, and a strange silence had descended over the scene. The people behind them had formed circles and groups and were mostly sitting on their haunches, though a few still stood. Mothers fed and calmed babies and children, and voices were low. The populace had clearly managed to draw breath, and the braver of the inhabitants began to edge towards the bank to see what was happening. On the far bank, where their homes lay, there was a space between the end of the bridge and the first of the huts, far enough that little sound travelled from the settlement. The legionaries and the leaders of the Atrebates were puzzled as to what the attackers were doing.

'What is happening? Can you see?' Aucissa asked Quintus, hoping that his height would give him a better view. She whispered the question as if her voice might somehow carry across to the huts, where shadowy figures could be seen moving between the buildings.

'I can see no order in what they are doing,' Quintus replied, craning his neck and shading his eyes to see further. 'I would say that they are probably searching the huts or the caves — I am not sure where they are.'

'Nearer the sea?'

Quintus turned his gaze that way. 'I do not see them there.' He turned back to Aucissa. 'At least they do not seem to have set fire to anything yet.'

As he spoke, a spiral of black and white smoke rose from the buildings, quickly followed by another.

'They have found no-one to rob or kill, so they are annoyed,' offered Crassus. 'They had hoped to find easy pickings, for they can see that the boats are not here. But there is no-one else there. They are burning buildings out of frustration.'

'They must have seen us cross the bridge?' said Quintus, the slight rise in his voice betraying a doubt, a question.

Aucissa was thoughtful. 'They may not have done. The bluff that they came around blocks the view from the cliff path to the settlement. Until they emerged, they would see only one or two huts and, as they descended behind it, they would not see the bridge. They will only see it when they come to this side of the roundhouse.'

'It is true,' said Quintus. 'We did not see it either until we had rounded that rock. But they must have seen us now. Perhaps they are waiting for reinforcements, for the chariots that will come down the valley,' he added, looking in that direction. A sudden thought struck him. 'What if they come from this side?'

'Then this was all for nothing, and we die,' she said simply.

Sextus nodded in agreement. 'If the fates have decided that this is what the outcome should be, then that is what it will be. We are in the hands of the gods.'

Crassus was shocked. 'But our actions can prevent such an outcome,' he insisted.

'It does not matter what we do if it is already decided,' said Aucissa. She and Sextus looked at each other with an understanding not shared by the others.

'Will they come down this side of the valley?' Quintus asked.

'Only if they know that this is where we are. The eastern bank is a more difficult and treacherous road. It is hilly and broken, crossed by the streams that feed our river. Trust in your gods,' said Aucissa, 'and I will trust in mine.'

'Look!' Crassus exclaimed. 'It is time we took our places!'

Clearly, they had now been seen. Where he pointed, a stream of warriors was coming from the settlement, the two columns of smoke rising and swirling behind them, the noise of their approach growing as they shouted at each other. A group of them ran to where the two boats were beached, and Quintus realised that he had foolishly overlooked these. Of course they would cross the river in them.

'They will not get them into the water,' Aucissa said with confidence, reading his thoughts. 'The tide is yet too low.'

On the far bank the men struggled, pushing and grunting at the boats, but Aucissa was right; they were too far up the bank. They had been beached when the tide was high; only the sea would move them. It took only a moment or two for the attackers to realise that the boats were not an option, and their curses were carried on the air.

The three legionaries stood on the bridge, not yet in a position to defend, with Aucissa now a pace or two behind them. She had stayed to translate what the attackers said, but

Quintus sent her back, saying that he was sure he would understand. 'In battle,' he told her, 'it's all about our mothers and fathers and gods, and the size of our manhoods. Few are any more inventive.'

Crassus and Sextus both smiled, knowing this to be true. Maxim and Jovan also stood on the bridge.

'You can go, too,' Crassus told them.

'They stay.' Quintus raised his hand to stop them. 'They are armed.'

The slaves did not quite know who to obey, but they decided that Quintus was the most commanding voice — after all, he was the one who had made sure that each of them had a dagger, and specific instructions to go with it.

'Armed?' Sextus was alarmed. 'I do not hold with the arming of slaves. It is unnatural. Look what happened when the Thracians were armed.'

The Servile War had taken place more than fifty years before, but the memory of the slaves — Spartacus and Crixus, Oenomaus and Castus — and of the Via Appia lined with six thousand crucified rebels had been passed down from father to son, along with the command that such a revolt should never be allowed to happen again.

'Macedonian slaves who still look for a new Alexander should definitely not be armed,' added Crassus.

'I cannot make room for your politics, your likes and dislikes.' Quintus was emphatic. 'Maxim and Jovan will stand behind us, armed with a dagger each.' He cut off their protests with a sharp gesture. 'There is a reason for this. Should any of us, or all of us, fall, it is they who will end our life. Their job is to make sure that no Roman is taken captive by these tribesmen, these barbarians, and that no shame falls on the mother of cities from this escapade.' The other two legionaries were immediately silent. 'Nor will they be taken captive themselves.' Quintus looked sternly at the two men, both of whom had once been warriors. They did not look afraid. Jovan, if anything, looked haughty. Maxim, seemingly healed after his ordeal on the beach, appeared equally determined. 'Should we fall, they will end our existence; then they will take their own lives. I have promised them entry into the Elysian Fields.'

Sextus began to protest. 'You do not have the power...' He stopped himself. What men believed was up to them. If these men believed that they were sailing to Elysium, then maybe that was where they would go. 'What about us? Have you made any promises to the gods about us?'

'They will send you onwards, Sextus, and if they do, it will be because you fought with honour, took injuries, and died as a legionary. You will not have Charon's obol on your tongue; although, if what you tell us is true, the Vestals will already have paid your passage, will they not?'

'They will.' Sextus had assured them all as they had prepared to fight in the mountains of Hispania that the Vestal Virgins now paid the boatman's fee for any that died honourably in battle, and that for them the Elysian Fields awaited.

Quintus placed his helmet on his head and tugged his armour down at the back. Crassus rubbed at his wound, but then straightened himself up; Sextus, incongruously, pushed his hair from his forehead and under his helmet — the better to show his handsome face to the enemy.

The attackers had seen them now and ran towards the bridge, teeth bared, curses flying, weapons raised. The legionaries prayed, each of them to his own guiding deity — Crassus to Vulcan of the forge, Sextus to mighty Jupiter, Quintus to Ceres and to the gods of the field and farm, and all of them to the red god of war, to Mars the slayer, the patron of Rome's military might.

'Set,' ordered Quintus, as they took up position.

Quintus stood in the centre, half a head taller than the other two, Sextus to his left, Crassus to his right. They stood with their feet planted hip width apart, one leg a little back from the other, knees slightly bent ready to absorb the power of the charge. On his command their spears were hoisted, ready to throw, their swords were drawn, and their shields formed a wall across the narrow width of the bridge.

'Hold,' ordered Quintus. 'Stand — for Rome, for the legion and —' he hesitated, but decided it was fair — 'for Aucissa and the Atrebates of Britannia.' The three legionaries stood side by side, shield to shield, gazes grim. Immobile.

There were no supporting officers with great plumed helms and even greater voices; no general, not even a centurion…

They had no signifer, no eagle, no cornicen, no banners, no pennants…

Still their helmets were bright and golden and reflected the glow of the afternoon light, their cheekpieces were neatly tied beneath their chins, and their hair was tucked out of sight. Their faces, calm and grim, were framed in bronze.

They had found material to make scarves, *focalia*, to protect their necks from the harsh metal of the armour. On the parade ground, they would all have been the same colour — a regulation red or white. Here only Quintus wore red, whilst Sextus and Crassus had made their scarves from the same blue cloth. But they did not look out of place.

Lorica laminata covered their upper arms and was tied tight around their chests and bellies. The long curved plates were not as polished and shining as they should have been. Instead, there were spoiled patches where salt had gnawed away at them, or where they had been dented in their uncertain journey via storm-driven waves from the sinking boat to the solid shore. Some plates were even missing. But it was better than no armour at all.

Each man wore a leather belt, which held the pugio, and from which swung the weighted leather strips of the baltea that protected their upper legs and soft parts. Over their shoulders hung a baldric carrying scabbard and gladius. They carried weaponry enough and more for the work of butchery for which they were trained.

Perhaps most importantly, each legionary had a tall shield, more than half a man's height, rectangular in shape and slightly curved to ensure that arrows, missiles and sword strokes bounced off. The heavy boss in the centre was a fearsome weapon in itself.

They stood motionless and silent. At this moment, they were Rome.

On the sloping ground between the huts and the bridge, a mass of men, disappointed at the lack of enemy or bounty to be found in the settlement, now gathered in a swirling horde, running towards the river, shouting insults and challenges.

The hours had drawn on apace and the sun was well on its way to the horizon. It had dipped behind a bank of clouds to the west, and already the cliffs had gained a red and orange hue, backlighting the attackers in Mars' fiery tinge. Quintus knew that no Roman general would have attacked at this point in the day, unless in desperation. Nor would he have attacked with no strategy. The approaching tribesmen appeared to have no leader, no order, and no discipline. Perhaps they were desperate, he thought. Perhaps they had also spied the sails on the horizon and knew that the men were returning; maybe this was their only chance.

The legionaries' instinct was to attack, to throw spears and thrust with their swords and daggers. But Quintus knew that, if they were going to succeed, they had to defend. It went against the grain, but he had to command it.

'Hold; do not strike, not yet. Brace and hold. If one of us falls, we all fall.'

This was not strictly true, as a group of Atrebates crowded onto the bridge behind them with a fully armed Aucissa at their head. Any one of them could have stepped into the line in place of a legionary, though without a shield or armour, they would not last long. Quintus did not want this to happen. He wanted this to be a Roman rescue, a Roman victory. After all, he alone suspected that it had a Roman cause.

The attackers had no tactics, no patience — they rushed on, gathering pace, young and old, big and small, stout and thin, crashing and careening into one another. They suffered for their indiscipline and eagerness almost at once, as too many tried to gain the bridge. Men fell to either side of the smooth stone, pushed aside by their fellows, shouting and yelling in anger and frustration, then causing more confusion as they tried to regain their feet, grabbing at clothes, legs, hair and anything else they could reach. Some managed to find their feet again, to rejoin the advance, elbowing their way back into the crowd. Some stumbled and fell down the bank and into the waiting water, then tried to scramble back up the steep side, the soft earth crumbling away between their fingers. Some, having fallen, sought to wade across, to attack from the river, but they soon realised that the water was too deep and flowed too quickly.

Only those that stayed towards the centre of the stone path found themselves on the bridge itself, and they advanced at breakneck pace, all the while yelling threats and insults. The legionaries could see the fire in their eyes.

'Ready spears,' Quintus repeated. Behind them, some of the Atrebates copied the move, raising their own spears. 'Loose!' Quintus shouted, and the spears flew from the right hands of the Romans, three attackers falling — and not just falling, but taking comrades with them as they grabbed at whatever they could to steady themselves.

The Romans wished they had more spears, a second or third row of comrades.

Instead, as one they drew their blades.

XII: H'WYLIO!

There was help from the Atrebates. Spears whistled over the legionaries' heads from behind them, some barely missing their helms as they flew into the enemy. The attackers answered with a volley of missiles, some landing low enough to clatter from the face of their shields or to be turned by its curved edges.

Despite the spears and slingshots and their own comrades falling and blocking their path, the horde continued moving forward, now too close for anything to be thrown, the waiting Romans able to see deep into their eyes, feel their very breath.

The first impact of their full weight made the legionaries strain their knees to hold the line as axe and sword smashed into their shields, the enemy striking down hard. The noise rang from the edges of their shields and from their blades, as each man parried using their gladius or shield boss. One attacker, yelling incomprehensibly, grabbed the top edge of Sextus' shield and tried to pull it down or twist it from his grasp. A short stroke, and the man's fingers fell at Sextus' feet, the pain causing the attacker to step back, lose his balance and with a splash fall into the river.

Crassus' eyes had glazed over and his mind was clear of all other thoughts. He no longer felt anything as he struck and thrust, using the shield for both attack and defence, the boss held high and working like a battering ram, the gladius darting out from behind it to puncture and cut and sting before withdrawing again. The bloodlust was upon him, yet his training still did not allow him to take risks — his shield was gripped firmly, his sword arm dashing out from its protective shadow and ducking back in again, the blade running with blood, hot and sticky on his hand and arm.

Sextus was less brutal and more clinical. He struck in a slower rhythm and with less force, but he made every strike count. Not for him a two-inch gash or a minor wound to an arm. He sought necks and eyes and, if sorely pressed, chests — he would rather have a dead opponent than a half dead one who could yet rise in agony. The point of the sword into the yielding flesh of the eye, or its edge across the soft flesh of a neck, ensured that most of his opponents did not rise again, many falling from the bridge, whilst others blocked the passage of their furious comrades

Quintus used his height to good effect, striking downwards, his place in the centre bringing both peril and reward. Peril in that he was perceived as the leader, and so the most dangerous of the attackers sought to bring him down and claim the honour of defeating the captain. Reward in that as soon as he had despatched the first of these, not without difficulty, the attacker needing three blows before he joined his gods, the man's carcass had nowhere to go. Until he was hauled out of the way, no further attacker could face him. The next one, standing astride his fallen compatriot, swung a short-handled battle axe at Quintus' shield. Had it hit in the right place, it might have bitten into the timber; instead, it bounced with a clatter from the metal boss, which Quintus then thrust into the man's face. The slash with which the Roman caught him as he fell backwards was not a killing blow, but blood still spurted and his comrades barged him out of the way, intent on their own glory.

To either side, Quintus could see the bloodied blades of the others darting again and again, Crassus sometimes finding flesh, sometimes air, Sextus seemingly blessed by Mars, finding a target every time. Though they struck and struck, the press against them did not seem to slacken, and gradually they were forced backwards. The blood and guts at their feet made the bridge slippery, and the hobnails of their caligae, designed for grass or plain, scraped against the stone. Behind them, however, Aucissa and the tribesmen could not or would not fall back, leaving the legionaries with no room for retreat. Boys and old men threw rocks or sling-shotted stones at the increasing numbers of injured enemy warriors, and tipped off balance those that tried to scale the steep bank of the river.

'Hold!' Quintus shouted, his voice hoarse. 'Hold, stand!'

Sextus stumbled as he took a glancing blow to his arm, almost making him drop his sword. Quintus knew he was not seriously hurt, as he smiled, revealing teeth that were framed with blood, each white rectangle with its own red scaffold. He clearly had an injury somewhere. Quintus glanced at his amicus, but there were no worries there. Had Crassus taken a wound, a thrust to the heart or a blade across the neck, Quintus truly believed that he would not have noticed. Vulcan would make sure that he stood until the end. The blacksmith looked straight ahead as he thrust his blade into yet another neck, turning his head to avoid the spurt of bright blood.

Quintus raised his own blade again. This time, the stroke found the arm of a man who was holding an axe. As the gladius bit, he dropped it with a scream of pain, his hand and lower arm hanging uselessly. He fell, but this time no-one at once took his place. The number of attackers who had fallen was clearly giving the others pause. Quintus could see that, at the back of the melee, men were no longer joining the fight. Instead, they were helping comrades up the bank, an easier task now, as the waters had risen with the tide. They had seen that it was hopeless — that there was no way that any more men could be brought to bear against these shields and helms. But they had also seen the tide rising, lapping at the hulls of the two beached boats: they still had hopes of using these to outflank the strangely dressed warriors on the bridge who were clearly blessed by the gods.

They did not know that the legionaries were close to exhaustion. Limbs aching, cuts bleeding, sweat dripping from inside their helmets. They had been forced to take some steps back, but they had moved in formation and no gap appeared in the shields. Another few steps and they would no longer be defending the bridge; instead they would be defending the wide stretch of riverbank, the fields of unripe corn — an impossible task. From the corner of his eye, he could see that Jovan and Maxim were still close, that they had their blades unsheathed. Now was the time to abandon defence; now was the time to attack.

'They are tiring!' Quintus yelled. 'There are no more joining them. It is time we pushed them back.'

Sextus yelled something in response, which Quintus took to be agreement. Crassus nodded his head and began to bang his sword against the edge of his shield.

'Good, good,' said Quintus, beginning to strike his own shield in time with Crassus. 'Sextus?'

'With you!'

Sextus understood at once and joined them, the three of them striking their shield edges with their swords, making a sound that at once spelled order and discipline and danger. Behind them the Atrebates, realising what they were doing, joined in with the stamping of feet, the clapping of hands or the banging of weapons. The noise, the regularity, was terrifying, making the enemy pause.

'By the right. Step,' Quintus commanded. The three legionaries pushed forward, moving forward on their right legs in unison. Their left legs then closed up behind them, their opponents now seemingly more interested in moving out of their way than in killing them. The legionaries could not advance far — the dead and injured were piled in front of them.

'Do not break the line,' Quintus shouted. 'Ready...' He was about to order another step when he felt space in front of their faces. Suddenly they could see doubt and fear in the faces of the tribesmen; a shout had gone up that made them pause.

To the back of what enemy remained, men were shouting and pointing. The legionaries did not understand what was being said, but Quintus' heart was in his mouth, fearing the worst. He looked up the valley, expecting to see the tell-tale dust cloud thrown up by the hooves of horses and a hundred spinning wheels, expecting the end of their defence to come as chariots moved swiftly down the combe.

But there was nothing — only the almost cloudless sky, losing its colour as it readied itself for the night. He turned and realised that the attackers were not pointing down the valley, but out towards the sea.

H'wylio! H'wylio!' The attackers' call echoed from the far bank. As they heard it men fell back from the bridge, and began to retreat the way they had come, running for the cliff path. Those who had gone down to the beached boats were unsure what to do, pulling at ropes half-heartedly, yelling instructions to each other, even as some of their party broke off to join the other retreating men.

On the bridge, the legionaries could finally breathe, but still kept formation. 'Stay where you are,' Quintus ordered. 'It could be a ruse.'

'H'wylio! H'wylio!' The call went up from the Britons behind them. Though the words were the same as before, this was a call of triumph. Men and boys were clapping each other on the back; women were holding their children up to see.

'Aucissa?' Quintus yelled. The three legionaries were still frozen in place, with Aucissa and her compatriots close behind them. 'What are they shouting? What is it?'

'*Sails*, they shout, *sails*,' she answered happily. 'It is our ships. We have spotted them on their way in, as have they. They have rounded the point and can now be seen clearly. And they are close. You can stand down. The enemy are fleeing, and our menfolk have returned.'

Quintus looked in the direction Aucissa was pointing. He saw a set of brightly striped sails — not on the horizon but now much closer, having been hidden by the edge of the cliffs, the tall crag that marked the start of the channel. As they watched, the sails were being taken down, dropping out of sight as oars took over. The lead ship was already in the inlet.

'It is our husbands and sons,' said the woman happily. 'Our attackers have seen them too; that is why they run.'

Quintus was about to sigh with relief, but his attention was grabbed by Tincomarus. 'Barely in time,' the older man said, pointing down the valley. Commios, too, was gesticulating. Whatever it was in his voice, it was not joy. Quintus narrowed his eyes in the direction indicated, trying to peer through the gathering dusk.

In the gloom of the coming night, there was a cloud of dust, and beneath it the churning wheels and shadowed outlines of a dozen or more chariots. Their drivers stood tall, silhouetted in charcoal grey against the black of the hills. At first they slowed, then came to a halt as they reached the scattered band of their own comrades.

Quintus could not hear their conversation, but it was fairly easy to work out what was happening. The chariots had arrived too late, as far as the fighters were concerned. Had they arrived before the ships, then they might have been a factor in the action.

'Will they attack?' Quintus asked.

'They will not,' Aucissa said confidently. 'Stand your comrades down.'

'You are sure?'

'Certain. They have lost the light, and the advantage of numbers.'

'Sextus, Crassus, our job is done. Rest.'

Each man laid down his shield and looked at the other, the smiles they exchanged more of relief than anything. Sextus was pensive, stroking his chin as he surveyed the carnage. He wrinkled his nose at the smell that rose from the shattered corpses and closed his ears to the groans that emanated from the crush of bodies on the bridge. Parts of it were still moving, like some great tentacled sea monster writhing in the deep. There were not as many as Quintus had thought, but enough that on wider ground they would have been overwhelmed. The two boats that they had tried to manhandle into the water now floated free, swinging on their hawsers.

Sextus was immediately joined by Annaig, the young woman who had been teaching him some of her own language. Her round, innocent face looked concerned as she helped to unlace and pull off his helmet, taking a wet cloth to his brow. For his part, he subsided to the ground with exhaustion, only now beginning to feel the many cuts, bruises and blows that he had taken. She spoke to him softly, and though he did not understand the words, he felt the warmth in her voice.

Crassus also pulled off his helmet, groaning a little as he did so. The old injury to his back was complaining bitterly at the treatment it had just received. He took a cloth handed to him by a grinning youth — the one who had escorted his grandfather across the bridge — who spoke to him excitedly in his own tongue, reaching for his gladius, wanting to hold it in his own hand. Crassus at first resisted, then allowed the boy to handle it. The youth hefted the sword, felt the balance of the weapon and swung it around dangerously, making the blacksmith duck. Then, with an evil grin, he ran his tongue down the full length of the bloodied blade. Crassus was too exhausted to be shocked, and anyway, he had seen such rituals before. Essentially, you were taking in your enemy's strength. 'Still,' he said, as he took the sword back, 'it is not the way that I would have chosen to clean it.'

The youth smiled a little, not sure whether or not he was being told off. Realising that he wasn't, he broke into a wide smile and slapped Crassus on the back like an old friend. His skin was still smooth, his voice newly broken, and his long hair was tied neatly at the nape of his neck. He would have been frustrated at not being old enough to sail with the men, but he was finding his place, and this fight would have helped. He would definitely sail with the men next time.

Quintus leant on his shield, breathing hard, Aucissa honouring him by helping to remove his helmet. He, too, was spent, his heart still racing, sweat running into his eyes and down his back despite the *focale*, which he unwound to allow air to his neck.

He looked at his comrades, at the Atrebates, at the retreating enemy and decided that, at least this time, he had honoured the memory of Ursus. He tugged at the bottom edge of his armour, as if to straighten it, a tic that betrayed his quiet pride in what they had done.

Jovan and Maxim were keen to return the weapons that they held, thankfully unused. Had they been forced to kill one of the legionaries, they were certain that the others would have cried murder and killed them in turn, or told them that death was the only honourable course. They had not wanted to be the ones to execute their masters. They were relieved.

XIII: SIC VITA

By this time, a crowd had gathered around the legionaries. They were all speaking together and, like the youth, slapping them on the back.

'Aucissa,' Quintus said, raising his voice above what he took to be general congratulations, 'is it over?'

She nodded. Water was brought and, to Quintus' delight, watered wine. He realised that he should not be surprised — they had boats, and so they would trade.

Quintus glanced sideways at Aucissa, a feeling of warmth betrayed in his look. Though he turned his head away quickly, she still caught his glance and smiled. The emotion that had softened her features vanished swiftly as she issued a series of commands. A group of boys immediately began to clear the dead from the bridge, either heaving them into the waters below, or dragging them onto the bank. Another group set off at a run towards the huts.

'I have sent them for torches,' she said, in answer to the question that Quintus was about to ask. 'It is too dark for this work.'

There were many women, many children, many old men and boys. But they all considered themselves to be warriors, to have a part to play. Commios was also issuing orders and, as soon as he had finished, they went about their grisly work. Several of the women collected weapons from the fallen, as well as anything that looked like it might have had value: torcs, armbands, hair ornaments, rings — even if it meant cutting off a finger.

The old men had taken on the task of dividing the dead from the hopelessly injured, and the hopelessly injured from those who would survive. The boys rolled the first to one side, and, if they had access to a knife or spear, they sent the injured onwards to their gods. Crassus' friend, the youth who had licked the gladius, came to plead in sign language for the two long daggers that the slaves had returned. On being given them by the blacksmith, he grinned with pleasure, kept one and gave one to an older boy who looked to be his brother or cousin — certainly they were of an age. They set off together, enthusiastic in their butchery.

'*Sic vita*,' said Crassus to himself — such is life.

Though it was a grim task, and hard work, the boys chattered and laughed merrily as they cleared a way across the bridge. As a path opened up, those not involved in the capture, clearance or killing began to cross the river, mothers carrying or leading small children, old men leaning on boys or women for support. The old man who had been last to cross refused to leave until his grandsons could accompany him, but the grandsons were keen to play a role in the sorting of the fallen. Eventually, the grandfather accepted that they had a duty to perform, and sat on a rock, waiting until the work was done.

The dead were put at either side of the bridge — wherever had seemed most convenient, although the greater number was on the side where the settlement lay. In addition, there were bodies in the water — some of which would be washed out when the tide turned, others which, Quintus was sure, would need to be pulled out with hooks as the sea refused to take them.

The living were judged quickly. Aucissa, with one of two clear signals, briskly decided the fate of those whose chances of survival the boys could not determine. In the flickering torchlight, a number of walking wounded had already been led away, but on the bridge there were still those whose life hung in the balance. Belly wounds, although in some cases perhaps not seeming too severe, were all considered to be fatal — few recovered from such injuries, and many died a long and agonising death. Other wounds would seal a man's fate also — a severed hamstring, for instance, that would prevent him from ever walking again, or a blow that had blinded him.

For their part, the three comrades had stayed to help sort out the injured and the dead, and in turn were helped to clean some of the blood from themselves. Crassus wanted to tell the youth — who seemed to have adopted him as a friend — about the defence of Rome by Horatius, but did not have the language for it. The pair of them fell into gales of laughter as the combination of single words and short phrases in both languages failed to get any message across other than that one was trying to tell the other a story. Though he feigned disapproval at some of what he took to be the cruder expressions of the youth, Crassus smiled with his eyes, a spark that few had ever seen.

Quintus was exhausted, but did not wish to show it, so helped where he could, emotionlessly deciding on a fate and then making it so. He had given Jovan and Maxim the task of taking the shields and helmets — and any other equipment — back to the settlement, but he had, of course, kept both gladius and pugio, putting them to good use. Sextus would have had the slaves pick through the dead to find the spears that they had cast, but all the weapons that could be used again were already being collected, so Quintus said the shields and helms were enough.

As the way was cleared, many voices were soon raised, questioning Aucissa, Tincomarus, Commios and the legionaries. Though neither loud nor ill-mannered, they were insistent in their tone.

'They want to know if they can go back to their homes,' said Tincomarus. 'I say they should.'

'Though they should beware of what they might find,' Quintus added. 'There was fire.'

'I think they are aware of what happened,' said Aucissa gently. 'They still want to put their children to sleep in their own beds if they possibly can. They also want to be home to greet the men as they return.'

'Is it safe? What are the attackers doing?'

'They are waiting out the night,' she said.

'To attack in the morning?'

'No, I think to strike a bargain.'

'They may want the bodies of those who have fallen,' explained Tincomarus. 'There may be injured men or captives of high status that they wish to ransom.'

Commios spoke and Aucissa translated. 'He hopes that they may be able to share the reason for the attack.'

Quintus, suddenly full of guilt, turned away, but still did not confess, in the faint hope that he was not the reason. 'Of course they should go,' he said.

As they left the battle scene, they all looked up the valley to see what was happening now it was dark. Many of the defeated men had continued round the base of the outcrop, presumably heading for the cliff path, but a number had joined the charioteers on the plain. The charioteers had not retreated; instead they had gathered into a more tightly knit group, ready to camp. There was no risen moon, but the shapes could still be made out, and campfires were soon ignited.

As the groups of people returned to the settlement, the first of the ships were tied up alongside the two boats — now fully afloat — that the enemy had tried to use to their advantage. The men aboard leapt down, fully armed and ready to fight, running towards the bridge carrying torches, meeting their triumphant sons on the way. The boys were walking back proudly, marked by torchlight, a string of captives with them. All were to be incarcerated at least until the morning. The two groups met and there was a conversation. The men then approached the bridge at a brisk pace, their torches lighting the way.

Commios had already crossed the bridge and approached the men, stopping them so that they could hear his explanation, shouting to the boys to take their captives and secure them. He did not want a stray spear or a spark of anger to be directed at the unfamiliar sight of the Roman legionaries. If he had expected a simple explanation to suffice, he was disappointed, as many questions were asked of him. The men wanted to come to the bridge, to inspect the battle site for themselves. Commios was clear that this was not necessary, that they would be better employed greeting their wives and children. Quintus only knew this because Tincomarus heard and interpreted, all the time predicting that the men would not listen to Commios, that they would insist on their right to gaze on both the remnants of the battle and the legionaries who, it appeared, had saved their people.

But Tincomarus had failed to factor in the pull of the mothers and wives returning after their terrifying ordeal. They were calling for their men, scolding them for not being there during the battle, whilst hugging them with relief now they had returned.

'*Sic vita*, indeed,' laughed Quintus when Tincomarus explained. His own history had made him overlook the power of the strong familial bonds demonstrated here.

The noise, smell and sight of the dead had been softened by a blanket of darkness. Only the lapping of the water could be heard, and the outline of the piles of corpses seen. Night animals, they knew, would soon come to disturb the peace.

It was full dark by the time the party made their own way across the bridge, noting wryly as they did so that their defence would have been doomed had it been a different time, as the tidal river now lapped at the base of the stone bridge, and bumped the dead against it. Had the tide been this high, a few hours earlier, then the enemy could have swum across easily.

'It is time we left,' said Aucissa. 'A few of our men are coming — either to see for themselves or to question us. We need to rest. It will be a short night; we are close to midsummer's eve. The Regni — the tribe that attacked — will no doubt arrive at first light.'

There were only a few of them left. Tincomarus and one of the old men were talking together, seemingly composing a song or saga of the battle on the bridge whilst directing the last few boys.

Sextus had been enjoying the ministrations of Annaig, who had not only wiped down his face and hair, but had also unwrapped his focale and eased his armour by loosening the laces. She then brought him watered wine, and as he drank gratefully, she gently lifted the lorica laminata from his shoulders and handed it to one of her brethren. After that, she continued to teach him words in her own language, pointing to objects or parts of the body and giving him the name for it, both of them laughing as the parts pointed out became more intimate. In turn he had pointed out to her some of the stars with which he was familiar, though she shook her head at his names for them.

Crassus was still laughing with the youth who had helped his grandfather across the bridge — although the old man still managed to look disapprovingly at him. The other boy had already run to greet his father, who had arrived on one of the returning ships.

Quintus and Aucissa walked together, not speaking, at the head of the little group. They met with Commios and three men who had decided to ignore the ministrations of their wives and the advice of the elder and see the battle site for themselves. Each was captain or helmsman of the first ships that had arrived. At least one, Quintus guessed by his reaction, and by the proud youth who walked with him, was the son of the grandfather, and the father of one or both of the two boys. Annaig ran to one of the other men, who enfolded her in his arms.

The man who seemed to be leader spoke, and Tincomarus translated.

'He says that he has seen men like you before, that there are some on the ships that follow. He is not sure how many, but the metal coats and strange shoes are familiar to him. The idiots that were plucked from the belly of the sea had not the wit to realise that the metal they wore would drag them to the bottom of the sea.'

'Idiots?' Quintus asked, bridling.

'I am just translating,' said Tincomarus. 'These are not my words. Though you must admit that jumping into the water clothed in metal is not a wise move. He says there are two or three of them. See the ships that are coming up the inlet now? They are on one of those.'

The three legionaries stared at the dark shapes that approached in the distance, and hope rose in their hearts. The man speaking with Tincomarus was not shouting, but he had definitely raised his voice, and his hands were not still. He was tall and well built, wearing the short tunic favoured by the sailors so that they could move around with agility, belted at his narrow waist. His face was florid behind his magnificent black moustache, and the pulse in his neck jumped visibly. He was clearly holding back his ire.

'The captives say that these — invaders — these Romans — killed some of their children. Not only killed them but sacrificed them to their gods. They say that they burned them in a sacrificial fire.'

'These men?' Aucissa asked incredulously, pointing at the legionaries,

'Men in similar garb. If not these men, then others of their stamp. Romans.'

'But perhaps not these actual men?'

'Whoever they were, they made a fire and burned the children.'

'Along with some monstrous thing that they pulled from the sea,' added another, equally agitated.

'How are we to believe them?' asked Aucissa, at whom the tirade was directed. 'Those men were captured whilst trying to raid our unguarded settlement. They were captured in the act of trying to kill us all. They would say anything to save themselves.' Though her own anger was also controlled, it was still apparent from the strain in her voice.

'And how can you believe these men?' He pointed dramatically at Quintus and his companions. 'I know your ancestry, Aucissa, but they are not our friends. You should know that.'

'And yet they saved us. They held the bridge until your return.' She narrowed her eyes. 'They could have cowered in a hut. They could have hidden with us in the caves. They could have run. But instead they saved us.'

'Why did you not go to the caves? Did they persuade you not to?' Again the man pointed at the legionaries. 'The caves are our traditional hold. Why would you listen to them instead of our forefathers?'

'Had we not, we would have died, or been sold into slavery. They saved us.' Aucissa was tired, battle-weary, and did not want to discuss the motives of the attackers. It was late and she wanted to rest.

Tincomarus was doing his best to keep up with the translation, although Quintus suspected that he had cut out a great deal of the detail. The heat of the exchange, he could guarantee, was fuelled by curses and appeals to gods and ancestors.

The Romans, too, were bone-tired and seemed to have become unwelcome guests.

XIV: IN VERITAS

They congregated in the roundhouse, the largest building of the settlement, its low roof smoking with the remnants of the fire that had been allowed to burn low, the door open, the night warm and sticky. The breeze that had helped speed the ships into the inlet had dropped, and the bright stars had gradually dimmed as cloud had spread across the sky. The sailors would have read these signs, would have known that another thunderstorm could be on the way. Inside, the air was even heavier, the heat suffocating. There were too many people in the building and not enough ventilation. The smell of unwashed flesh was ripe.

The Romans were very uncomfortable. Two of them were still armoured, though not helmed, and they were all clothed in tunics that had been soaked in sweat and stained with blood. Their skin prickled with both the heat and the need to be washed; even the most meagre of Roman baths would seem like Elysium right now.

The Atrebates had created distance between themselves and the Romans. Quintus thought that this was not because they no longer had any amity towards them, but because it was politic to do so.

Annaig had gone from Sextus' side to that of one of the captains of the fleet. Although she had brought them a bowl of water with which to wash away the worst of the grime, she had quickly retreated back to her place on one of the benches that lined the inside of the building. Her man — if such he was — was part of the deputation speaking with Aucissa.

The grandfather and his sword-licking grandson had been more reluctant to leave Crassus, but one of the other captains appeared to be father to one and son to the other, and he gently persuaded them to leave the Roman be.

Aucissa now sat on a carven chair, raised up on a podium in the centre of the roundhouse, the only seat other than those around the walls. She was listening to the complaints of the returning men. Commios stood at her right shoulder, whispering into her ear.

The sailors were rightly angry and confused. Strewn abroad by the storm before they could make port — the same storm that had scattered and sunk the Roman fleet — they had rushed back home to see the tell-tale signs of smoke rising from the settlement, motivating them to raise sail and ready the oars. They had expected to discover huts burning, their families killed or taken, the settlement destroyed in their absence. They had not expected to find their grandfathers, womenfolk and children in a field of unripe corn on the unprotected side of the river, with three Roman soldiers, in full panoply of war, holding off a horde of tribesmen whom they considered neighbours and allies.

Aucissa was trying her best to mollify them, with some success, as Quintus observed. One or two of the men were quietened down, and others seemed to be trying to persuade their comrades to let the matter drop. Their leader, though, the big man who had spoken first, was the one who needed persuading.

The heat in the building, the smoke from the fire, and the smell of unwashed bodies was not conducive to sensible, ordered, debate. It did, however, make the men more motivated to accept a judgement so that they could leave. The captain recognised this. 'Judge,' he said, 'I will argue no more.'

The men kept a distance from her — a ceremonial distance, Quintus surmised, as for the moment at least, she was the official interpreter of events and arbiter of their fate. Commios obviously had a part to play, but the final judgement would be hers. She looked at the legionaries and shook her head gently, lips pursed. They took this to mean that they should say nothing. The tribesmen took it as a sign of her disappointment in the Romans, and the clamour of their voices and their demand for instant justice increased.

She had heard enough and raised her right hand. Gradually, the complaints ceased, as did the chattering around the benches. She did not speak until the peace was absolute, with only the spitting of the torches breaking the silence.

As Aucissa spoke, Tincomarus translated in whispers, so that the legionaries had to strain to hear him.

'Aucissa judges. She says we will find the truth in the morning and test the stories of the Romans. But against whatever we are told, she will hold the fact that you saved us all. Otherwise, she thinks the men would have arrived too late, and we would even now be riding in the back of the enemy's chariots or lying dead in a burning village.'

As she finished speaking, Commios bent down and hissed urgently into her ear. Some still heard what he said, despite his attempts to keep it private. Tincomarus was one of them.

'Commios is stating a precedent. He is saying that we cannot wait. That any judgement must be tonight. Tomorrow — in a few hours' time — it will be Midsummer's Eve, and, storm or no storm, all such business must be suspended until the closing of Midsummer's Day. It is our custom.'

Aucissa looked across at the three Romans — dirty, dishevelled, but still standing tall. She asked them a question in her own tongue. As Tincomarus made to translate, she waved away his efforts, and repeated the question in Latin.

'Are you friend or enemy?'

Before Quintus could answer, she silenced him with a downturned mouth and the slightest shake of her head.

Quintus guessed that this was some sort of ritual question, that to answer it now would be dangerous. She spoke to the assembled company again, in her own language, and many faces turned to look at the legionaries.

'Tradition says you must be given time to consider your answer,' Tincomarus whispered, 'either tonight or in two days' time, after midsummer. She judges that our obligation to our guests overrides giving judgement tonight, that we have failed to honour you as guests. She scolds us for the condition you find yourselves in. The answer will be given after the fires of the midsummer festival are quenched.'

'The prisoners?' Commios asked.

'Remain prisoners, for now,' Aucissa replied.

As soon as the judgement was given, the atmosphere seemed to change. It was as if people had been holding their breath, and could now let it out. Many made straight for the door.

Annaig ran across to Sextus and helped him to sit on a bench, which he did thankfully. Once he was settled, she called for food and water. Her man came across and spoke harsh words to her, but she stayed at the legionary's side, dipping a cloth in the water that was brought to wipe his face and forehead. She hissed one word at the man, who shrugged his shoulders and turned away. Whoever he was, relative or lover, she still had the power to refuse him.

The grandson, the youth who had tasted the blood of his enemies, approached Crassus with more diffidence, taking him by the arm and leading him away. One of the older men, neither his father nor grandfather, spoke sharply to him, but the boy shook his head violently and continued to walk with the legionary. He took him to a bench near the door, where Crassus lowered himself somewhat slowly, sighing as the muscles in his back creaked and his old injury complained.

The youth sat beside Crassus, pointed to himself and said, 'Tan.' He then pointed at Crassus, a query in his face.

Crassus looked puzzled, then realised that the boy was asking his name. 'I am Gnaeus Crassus Malleolus,' he announced importantly, 'tribe of Collina, son of Vulcan, once blacksmith, now legionary soldier and citizen of Rome.' He smiled and added, 'Truly, just Crassus. The rest is but wind-blown leaves.'

'Crassus,' the youth repeated, then pointed again to himself. 'Tan.'

'Tan,' Crassus repeated dutifully.

Crassus guessed that Tan was bending the rules by even being here. His dark hair, instead of being tied at the nape of his neck, had been allowed to come loose, which meant that his face was hidden and he was not instantly recognisable as one so youthful. His clothes were bloodstained and crumpled, and he held a flask of wine, purloined from somewhere, so he was welcome. He smiled and reached into his tunic, pulling out several heels of bread. Clearly he had been busy whilst judgement was being awaited.

With sign language and gestures, he offered to divest Crassus of his armour, which help he accepted gladly. When Tan signalled for a man to remove it from the hut and Crassus looked concerned, he was able to indicate that it would be unharmed.

Quintus and Tincomarus sat on either side of Crassus and his companion. Leaning across the two of them, Quintus asked the older man, 'What of our comrades? The men who came to meet us said that they were carrying some of our own people.'

'They may be,' said Tincomarus mysteriously, 'and then again, they may not.'

'They said they were,' said Crassus, through a mouthful of the rough bread. He swallowed quickly, turning to Tincomarus. 'We had comrades, members of our own contubernium — close comrades with whom we shared a tent. They were on board the ship with us. I did not see any of them die.' He looked across at Quintus. 'Did you?'

'I did not.' Quintus shook his head.

'If we survived the storm,' Crassus continued, 'then others may also have done so. From what your men say, it sounds like some did. Yet we do not see them here. What is the truth of it, Tincomarus? What should we know?' He looked questioningly at Tincomarus and asked sincerely, for he was weary and did not want to play games.

'*In veritas*,' began Tan, both unexpected and unexpectedly confident, 'the truth is they have some of your people, maybe your comrades, on board one of their ships, but like sensible barbarians,' at which he opened his arms and smiled diffidently, 'they are not about to compound their troubles by adding more soldiers to those already here. As you have heard, they did not know what was happening. They just saw smoke and maybe heard the noise of battle from across the water. Would you have released one who might be an enemy?'

The two legionaries stared open-mouthed and speechless at the youth, who had spoken in near perfect Latin, marred only by an unusual accent.

'My nephew,' Tincomarus explained modestly. 'He has a facility for language. He speaks others besides mine and yours.' His tone was disapproving. 'It is supposed to be his secret.'

Tan shrugged.

Crassus recovered his equilibrium first. 'You did not say,' he said, half accusingly, half approvingly. 'But I would have done the same. Such skills are sometimes more useful if kept confidential.' He patted Tan on the shoulder. 'In answer to your question, I would hold the men until I had at least determined what was happening.'

Quintus allowed his surprise to pass and turned to Tan. 'I am impressed, though I am not sure if I would have yet revealed the skill — at least not until I had determined whether the enemy, with or without these Romans, posed a threat to our existence. If they have ever come across Rome before, I doubt they will be expecting us to bring them good.'

'They have come across Rome before,' said Tincomarus with regret, the youth nodding in agreement.

'Their experience was not — positive?' asked Crassus. 'Am I right?'

'I think perhaps you are,' said Tincomarus, with a wry smile.

'But there is more our men did not know,' said Tan. 'They did not know that you proved to be our friends, that you saved us today.' His uncle gave him a withering look, but he continued defiantly. 'They know that now. It should be enough.' There was a pause. 'There is more you should know,' Tan went on, 'about your fleet and your friends.'

'Good or bad tidings?' Crassus asked softly.

'It could be either,' said Tan, gesturing at the many men departing. 'These men sought shelter from the storm by speeding to the nearest coast. This meant that many ships found harbour in Gaul and Frisia. Many ships rescued legionaries — Romans like yourselves, along with animals and goods, and left them on the further shore of the narrow sea.' He held his hand up before Quintus could interrupt. 'This was not cruelty, not abandonment; many Roman ships were steered into the same harbours or blown ashore, and others were beached or run aground. There were many, many legionaries disembarked in Frisia; our people just added to them. The ones they plucked from the sea after the storm, the ones who are on board the ship in the inlet, may not be your friends. Your friends may have been taken to the far shore.' He then added, rather proudly, 'I am sure that if any of your comrades are still aboard our ships, they are being well looked after.'

Tincomarus clearly disapproved. 'It was not for you to tell them,' he scolded, then suddenly changed his tone, 'but you have, and so be it. Maybe it is for the best.'

'*Sic vita*,' said Tan, soft amusement in his eyes.

'Will the men in the boats be brought ashore tomorrow?' asked Crassus.

'That is up to Aucissa. She may wait until after the midsummer festival. She has a role to play.'

At this moment Aucissa, her duties completed, was leaving the roundhouse, flanked by Commios and two tall men who looked like they were guarding her. She was surrounded by people trying to get her attention, including some of the captains, buzzing like bees around a flower head.

'What is she?' Crassus hissed at Tan. 'I thought she was your chieftain, but is she more?'

'She is more,' Tan whispered. 'She is both chieftain and chief priestess, judge of men and reader of the stars, honoured and venerated. She is our queen and spiritual guide.'

As Aucissa stood in a pool of flickering torchlight, answering some people and dismissing others, Quintus studied her profile. Her jaw was strong, her nose straight, her forehead high. Her hair was raven's wing black, long and thick. Her skin was dark, though he guessed this was a deep tan from a life spent out of doors. Paler lines of skin could be seen at the ends of her sleeves and at the hem of her tunic. In Rome, the trend for having a complexion like the Egyptian queen had faded with her memory; ladies of fashion had ceased to colour their skin with walnut juice or other such concoctions. They instead favoured the shade, slaves following them around with parasols to keep the sun from their brows.

As Aucissa approached him, Quintus made to stand out of respect for her position and to thank her for their temporary reprieve, but with a gesture she told him to stay seated. She passed by him imperiously, affording him a gentle smile — one that reached her eyes and was just for him — and she brushed her hand over his shoulder and let it rest on his shoulder straps, just a little longer than was necessary. She then swept out of the door.

Quintus was no fool. He knew what the smile and the lingering touch meant. He also knew the danger that he would be putting himself in if he accepted this summons, but he was determined to follow anyway. *Sic vita.*

XV: CIVIS ROMANUS SUM

Quintus did not find it as difficult as he thought it would be to extricate himself from his friends. He had taken some of the wine from the flask, and it had immediately had an effect. He had fallen into a reverie, his eyes half closed and his attention elsewhere, his tiredness washing over him like a warm breeze. His head lolled then dropped sharply to his chest, jerking him awake.

Tan, Tincomarus and Crassus were deep in conversation, Crassus apparently teaching the two of them how to curse in Latin. They were teaching him similar skills in return, all of them breaking into hearty laughter from time to time. Sextus and Annaig were nowhere to be seen, nor the sea captain who had been so keen to bring a charge against them. Of those that remained in the roundhouse, some murmured amongst themselves and many lay by the walls, sleeping.

Quintus rose quietly and made his way outside unchallenged. The heavy threat of thunder had lifted as quickly as it had descended, and a breeze blew from the west, pleasant on his face and skin. The sky had moved from the swirling charcoal greys of a threatened storm to the inky black of full night. There was no moon yet and few stars.

He knew where he wanted to go, but he did not want to ask directions of anyone, for he was not sure that what he intended was permitted — in fact, he was fairly certain that it was not. But he was confident that he had not misread Aucissa's signals.

Many of the huts were in darkness, some with just a little light showing at the edges of the door coverings, but many of the people were still wandering about quietly in the dark. The sound of the water, the sea, was comfortingly rhythmic, but seemed far away. One building, no larger than the others, but in a prominent position, had more light spilling from its doorway. Quintus took a chance.

'It is I,' he said diffidently, pulling the leather door hanging back and peering into the hut, the flickering glow of the torches reflecting off his armour. Inside, with the light from the fire and torches, it looked inviting. He could see the outline of the meagre furniture, with Aucissa propped up on one elbow on the cot that was placed against the far wall. As his eyes adjusted, he saw that she now wore white, and had placed a ring of flowers in her hair.

'Then come in,' she invited him. 'At least you are a man and no wight or faerie come to visit on this most magic of evenings.'

'*Hic ego sum*. I am real,' he responded, pulling the door hanging closed behind him and taking the two steps to her side. He sat gently at her head and stroked her hair, trying not to disturb the garland that she wore. She responded by snuggling up to him, like an affectionate cat.

'I am glad you came,' she said, tipping her chin to look up at him. 'I thought that perhaps you would not.'

'So did I,' he admitted, 'but your message seemed clear.'

Quintus was nervous. He did not quite understand why — he was no virgin; he had been with women before, many of them. His father had gifted him a slave girl when he had first put on his manly gown. Perhaps it was because this was the first time he had been with a woman as seemingly powerful as Aucissa. Perhaps that was the problem — he had had women, but never a lover.

With this woman he was suddenly afraid, afraid that she would be honest with him, that there would be no gasp of surprise or appreciation, that his performance would be inadequate. The doubt was enough to give him pause.

'I should not be here…' he began.

'It is Midsummer's Eve,' she said. 'Where else would you be?'

It was clear that she understood the reason for his hesitation. She smiled warmly, drew him close to her and whispered kind words in his ear, soft words. She used gentle hands to bring back his confidence, tenderly turning him by the shoulder, so that he sat with his back to her, and unlacing his armour. He undid his own belt and laid it aside with his weapons, then bent over for her to pull the tunic over his head.

'On this night of all nights, there is not much time,' she said, 'but there is still no need to rush. The night will be short and dawn in a hurry, and I must be there for sunrise.'

'The state of me,' Quintus said despondently as he straightened up and stood in just his undershorts, looking at the half healed cuts, the bruises, and the dirt marks. 'I am in dire need of a bath.'

'I am looking,' said Aucissa, unfastening her own tunic, but taking in the sight of the Roman, tall and muscular, broad of chest and flat of belly, the hairs on his arms and legs like down, that on his chest sparse and fair, his whole body criss-crossed with bruises and scars. 'I do not mind a little wear and tear,' she went on, placing her hand flat on his chest. 'Let's think about cleanliness later.'

She kissed him softly and sweetly, though later it would turn into something more demanding; she stroked his thick hair, and later twined her hands in it more vigorously. She nibbled at his ear, standing on tiptoe to reach it, and later almost bit it off. He pulled her shift over her head, the flower garland going with it, and drank in the sight of her hard, muscled body. She had been naked beneath the shift and now stood before him, hands on hips, breasts pert, belly flat, her sex all but clean shaven, the tanned skin of her arms and legs contrasting with the white of her torso where it was usually covered. With a grunt more related to recent bruises than anything else, Quintus stepped out of the undershorts that were now barely containing his swollen manhood.

Their first coupling was fiery, burning brightly and briefly like the flare of a pitch-loaded torch, made clumsy by his caligae still being on his feet, and by their eagerness to explore each other's bodies. The second coupling, after she had cursed and untied the caligae, was slow, as warm and tender as the first had been bold and hot.

The third, they decided, could wait whilst they drank water and wine and enjoyed the intimate touch, the enfolding presence of each other's flesh. As they lay in the rumpled sheets of the cot, Quintus spoke quietly of his past, and Aucissa of hers. They did not know why they were sharing their stories; it just seemed like the right thing to do. Their lovemaking had been intensely deep, and it needed a background, a foundation.

'You heard Elrik in the roundhouse,' Aucissa said. 'He alluded to my ancestry.'

'I heard. I thought nothing of it.'

'My father,' she said as she cuddled up to him, 'was no Briton, nor was he of any of our tribes. It has always weakened my position.'

'You do not seem weakened,' Quintus said, kissing her neck.

'Yet I am,' she responded simply. 'Elrik would like to be chieftain one day. Commios or Tincomarus could be chieftain now, if they wished it. I am younger than either of them, and not as wise.' Her hand stopped Quintus' protestations. 'It is true,' she went on. 'Commios at least has greater knowledge. Fortunately for me, he has less ambition.'

She sat up, letting Quintus' head fall into her lap. The torches had burned low, and the door hangings kept the last of the night at bay. It was a comfortable light. With her palm softly on his hair, she continued, 'My father was a Roman.' Quintus started, but she pushed his head down firmly and carried on stroking his hair. 'Don't be surprised. He came over with the army of your great general, with eagles, trumpets and horses bigger than any I had ever seen.'

She looked down at him as he turned his head to face her. 'It was the second time the general visited our shores. The first time he was lucky to escape with his life, as you have been told — first wrecked on the shore, then with few soldiers, then sent away in the midst of a gathering storm.' She laughed, her eyes sparkling as Quintus made to argue. 'So it passes in our history. No doubt your history tells a different story of victory, certainty and tribute given.'

'Perhaps,' said Quintus doubtfully, but subsided anyway.

She carried on. 'The general did not like to be chased home, so the second time he brought many more soldiers, ships with sails and much cavalry. I am told that he even brought a bull to sacrifice. He was determined to make his mark. I was not born when your Caesar first landed and we sent him home. Nor was I born when he came again, this time in force.' She paused, speaking with just a little sadness. 'But I was born soon after, and I knew my father for a brief time — before he returned to Rome.'

'Then you are Roman,' exclaimed Quintus, this time managing to raise his head. 'You were acknowledged by your father — you are a citizen.'

'He was less than interested — I was a girl.'

'But he acknowledged you.'

'So my mother tells me. Though I think he never loved me. Nor her. He thought we shared wives in common, when in fact we share the upbringing of children.'

Quintus sat up and faced her. 'But you are a Roman citizen, with the same rights as I. You can claim *civis Romanus sum* anywhere in the world.'

'Doesn't mean much to the Atrebates,' she said. 'Rome was not here for long and learned little. My father, as I believe it, was a Roman nobleman. From what we have been told, he would have had nothing to do with bringing up children. He will never have had a childhood himself.'

'True,' mused Quintus. 'It is all about service, name and *gravitas*. The young of our leaders are not encouraged to be children; they must grow up quickly, to serve.' He paused. 'What do you mean when you say that they learned little?'

Aucissa smiled. 'They claimed to know so much, but in truth knew hardly anything. They sowed confusion, and in turn were fed confusion, often accepting what they were told even though its sole purpose was to mislead. They misnamed tribes and displaced peoples, even whole areas of our country. Our land is much bigger than General Caesar ever imagined; he marched in a little circle around a corner of it. He named people what they were not; for example, the people he called Agravantes, this is not what they call themselves. He called some Celts, though they did not call themselves Celts; he called some Britons, when they were not Britons.'

Quintus nodded, but warned, 'General Caesar, as you call him, is now a god; he did not make mistakes.' She looked sideways at him to see if he was being serious, and he just shrugged. 'I suppose it is like calling a Macedonian a Greek or an Italian a Spaniard. There is no doubting that they are cousins, but they know the borders of their own lands, and they are not the same.'

'True,' said Aucissa. 'You would not conclude that all of a race were tall, fair and bearded just from seeing one individual, would you? Both Caesar and my father misunderstood many of our customs, though neither had ever met a priest or a druid. They had never come close to knowing the magic that is hidden in the stones; they had never bothered looking.'

'But you are still a Roman citizen,' insisted Quintus. 'That must count for something.'

'Not here,' she said. 'Rome was here for plunder, not conquest — the army was gone before Samhain. I was but a child left behind.'

'Yet you are queen of this tribe?'

'I work hard, I listen to advice, and I carry a weapon.'

'How…'

'Enough of me. Tell me something of you,' Aucissa commanded. 'Why were you afraid to lie with me? It was not a slight, I could tell. Yet I am not your first — that I could also tell.' This time, she pulled the sheet across her bare shoulder and placed her head in his lap, looking limpidly at him and whispering. 'Tell me.'

'You are not the first, no.' He stroked her hair. 'My first was a slave girl, a gift from my father.'

'Not a gift you wanted?'

'I was never sure. It was what was done. Certainly my father did not love me either.'

'That much we share.'

'My father never forgave me for being supposedly weak, but he did not wish to deprive me of my entrance to manhood. In truth, I reminded him too much of his dead wife, my mother. I had her looks, her light hair and long limbs. He accused me of being long of limb and short of brain, but he would not want me to shame him in front of his friends. So he arranged for the slave girl to be made available. She was petite and Greek, plain but serviceable, olive skinned — he intended to have her for his own use once his son had finished with her.' He grunted. 'At least I did not fail my father on that occasion, though I did not know — until he revealed himself with applause — that he and his friends had watched from behind a curtain whilst I performed. They did not have long to watch.'

'Then why fear me?'

'You should know that I have lain with many slaves and harlots, who knew ruses and artifices, and who would treat me as Mars or Hercules — even as the little Greek slave girl had done all those years ago. I have no idea what was feigned and what was genuine. I was afraid that tonight would not be … real.'

'It was real enough,' she said, drawing his face close and kissing him, a kiss he returned lovingly.

The moment between them was tender, but it did not last long. There was a hissed summons from the other side of the door hanging.

'Aucissa?'

'It is time,' she said. 'Our night is over. Midsummer's Eve may be magical, but it is brief. Give me a midwinter's night anytime.' She answered the caller, then turned again to Quintus, stroking his cheek, pushing the hair from his eyes. 'I have duties. I must dress, and so must you.' She touched the metal plates with her toe. 'I will have your armour delivered to your slaves. You will not need it today.'

'Should I be found here?' Quintus asked as he reluctantly began to pull on his grubby tunic.

'It is of no matter. A queen and priestess does what she will, especially at midsummer,' she told him, 'but you should wait a while once I am gone.' She laughed. 'You will have to tie your own shoes. I must go — an embassy of our attackers craves an audience. He has come on foot, unarmed, and with just two attendants. I must speak with him.'

XVI: SOL INVICTUS

Quintus sat on the cot, not quite knowing what to do. The leather that had shut out the night twitched again and a voice spoke in passable Latin. 'You had better dress yourself. Come barefoot if those things are a trouble to tie.' It was Tan, smiling broadly. He clearly knew what had happened here. He eyed the tumbled metal. 'I will make sure your armour reaches your slaves,' he added.

Quintus gave up the attempt to put on his caligae and stood. He fastened his belt, ensured that his weapons were in place, pulled his tunic as straight as he could, pushed his hair back off his forehead and faced the youth. 'I am ready,' he said.

'Really?' Tan said, amused. 'I think my moustache, pale as it is, is better than yours. Your chin needs scraping, and your hair would benefit from the attentions of a comb. Oh,' he added, failing to hide his laughter, 'and your belt is twisted and your shoes are missing.'

At another time, Quintus would have laughed along with the youth, but the presence of the Regni ambassador troubled him. He did at least manage a weak smile before straightening his belt and asking, 'What is happening? Why the rush?'

'Morning comes; it will not wait,' said the youth. 'Here, this will make you more presentable.' He held out a bowl of water and a cloth. The water had rose petals floating in it — a nice touch and not Tan's doing, Quintus guessed.

Whilst he washed his face and hands and used the water to flatten down his hair, Tan continued chattering. 'One of the leaders of the Regni, the tribe who attacked us, has come to speak with Aucissa. It must be brief; there are more important things to concern us this morning. Come, I know you have had a tiring night, but it is Midsummer's morning; your step should be light and your heart glad. Do not worry that you look like a poor wanderer; it will be all right. Come barefoot if you will; we only walk on the grass.'

Quintus gave up any attempt to tie his footwear. Tan himself was clothed in a spotless white tunic, tied with a girdle plaited with summer flowers, his thick black hair once more secured at the nape of his neck. He took Quintus' arm. 'Come,' he insisted, 'we cannot miss the sunrise.'

As he was pulled out of the door, Quintus could see that the people of the settlement were already gathered, crossing the bridge in family groups. There was no sign of enemy dead, though the waters had once more receded and there could be corpses floating out of sight.

The women and girls were all wearing white or green, and all had flower crowns in their hair or blooms behind their ears. The men, in spite of the travails of the day before, in spite of only just arriving after a sea voyage, were also all dressed in clean linen, with their moustaches trimmed, their chins scraped and their hair tied back. Here and there were glints of gold or silver — torcs or earrings or brooches, signs of wealth and status. Quintus felt dirty and disrespectful amongst them. Many looked his way with their disapproval barely disguised, though none seemed interested in whose hut he came from in the half-light before the sunrise. The morning star was still visible, the sun yet to appear. Perhaps he should not be here at all — these were, after all, someone else's gods.

'These are your gods,' said Quintus haltingly.

'Do you not have the sun in your country?' Tan teased him. 'Surely you worship light and warmth. It is all about the cycle of the seasons, the high days that mark the changes of direction. It's about the time to harvest, or feast, or to sow grain. Do you not have such ceremonies?'

Quintus thought of the ancient rites of Sol, older than any others in Rome, of the festival and celebration of Sol Invictus, their own sun festival, held in the winter when the sun dipped to its lowest point. It was a celebration of light undimmed, unconquered and reborn on the day that the sun stood still. He remembered the legends of Proserpine and Pluto, of Ceres, his own household goddess of plenty, of the Roman midsummer festival of Vestalia — the celebration of the hearth and the continued light of the flame of Rome, kept by the Vestals. He also remembered the mysteries of the Mithraic cult — saluting fire, light and the sun — which had swept through the army whilst he had been in Hispania. 'We have such markers,' he said. 'We celebrate them with games and sacrifices.'

'We have sacrifices,' said Tan. 'We also have games. Perhaps we will see if you can leap the great fire later. I think that would bring our village much good fortune.' He looked up from beneath his brows, conspiratorially. 'I think you played some of the games with Aucissa last night?' He did not wait for an answer, as he was bubbling over with pride, dancing at the side of the legionary. 'As did I, Quintus, for the first time — as did I!' He waved gaily at the crowd crossing the bridge, and a young woman's hand waved in reply. 'Last night was my first time. I was at first nervous, but then I was so strong, so — manly. You would not believe it.' He waved enthusiastically to her again.

'I think I would,' said Quintus, clapping the youth on the back. 'But what is happening now, Tan?'

'Now it is almost time. All you have to do is follow.'

Most of the settlement were already on the eastern bank and continuing across the field, following a well-trodden path. In the middle distance, Quintus could see the crowd facing the stone circle about which Quintus had speculated earlier, itself black on grey in the uncertain light. As he and Tan hurried to catch the tail of the throng, Quintus asked, 'Did your people build that?'

'Perhaps our ancestors, perhaps a race of giants that once lived here. There are many such circles in this land, and we do not have the skill to build them anew. Not even to repair those that have fallen.' He pointed to the broken lintel nearest to them. 'Our grandfathers tell us that their grandfathers remembered them, and that this broken stone to the west has always been broken, but I spy the marks of lightning on it. I think they were made by giants, but subject to the will and anger of the gods.'

'And their part today?'

'Watch the central window, and you will see.'

The sky was no longer the vibrant blue that it had been during the long day of the battle, nor was it the inky black it had become as the storm threatened. Now it was a deep shade of red, the colour of blood, the few small clouds dark against it. A band of broken mackerel scales in pink and white marked the horizon, lit from beneath.

The growing light of the new morning was brightest where the eyes of the people were focused —Tan pointed out the square arch of stone, with brother and sister arches on either side, behind which the red and gold of the dawn could be seen appearing. In minutes it was as if a fire burned behind the stones, silhouetted against the brightening sky.

He and Tan were amongst the last to cross the stone bridge. Not only had it been cleared of bodies, but also scrubbed until it was clean. Though he sought them, Quintus could not see his comrades anywhere, nor anyone he might count as an ally.

There was no sign of Commios or Tincomarus, nor of Aucissa. There was nothing he could do but behave as his young friend instructed him.

Everyone faced the stones, their backs to the bridge and to the settlement. The crowd gradually became quiet, just the piping query of a young voice, or a baby's cry soon stifled, breaking the silence. Colour came to the stones first. They were revealed as grey and pale blue, full of shadows and legend, old beyond counting and sunk deep into the earth. The cross stones sat firmly on their two supports for the most part, though in some cases they had fallen or split, like the one pointed out by Tan. *Weather, lightning, age?* mused Quintus. *Or the wrath of the gods?*

After the first fingers of light had reached out and touched them, the clouds began to take on the glints of morning, the burnished gold of the sun spreading rapidly, chasing away dark and shadow as it rose directly between the two upright stones of the central arch.

As it mounted the sky, the people standing within the stone circle were bathed in the clear light of the morning. Mothers held up their babies; fathers held up sons. Young men and maidens — paired at least for today — turned their faces to the light together.

As the bright rays stretched out to the bridge, the watchers turned their backs to the rising sun and focused on the crossing, where a small party now approached to the sound of drums, bells and cymbals.

As Sol shook himself and broke free of the horizon, the group reached the far bank and stopped. The watchers had now joined in, clapping, stomping their feet and singing words that Quintus did not understand. The noise rose high into the morning sky.

Aucissa stepped out from the centre of the group, her bright garments catching the sun's rays, her flower coronet in place. She was leading a great black horse, a stallion with a coat as smooth and shiny as the surface of a holly leaf, a clipped mane and flared nostrils. He had a high step and looked spirited, but the priestess — for thus was her role this morning — had a firm hold of his bridle. To his left-hand side stood another, one that Quintus had not seen before — a tall and broad-chested man with dark hair waxed into spikes. His great moustache stretched to his chest and was finished with knots, braids and shining clasps. Torcs on his upper arm and silver wristbands completed his jewellery, whilst the belt that cinched in his tunic — which was open to the waist — was made of interlinked circles of bronze.

'Who is that?' Quintus asked Tan. 'Who is the man with Aucissa? Is he her husband?'

Tan laughed, then apologised as he saw the anger briefly cross Quintus' face. 'Our chieftain, our priestess, has no husband but the gods, although she may take one whenever she wishes, as I think you know.' He could not stop his face from breaking into a wicked grin. 'No, that is the leader of the Regni — their king and chieftain Coginus, charioteer of our erstwhile friends and recent enemies. He must have come to negotiate this morning, to free the prisoners at least, but he will also have wanted to take part in our festivities, not having time to return to his own.'

His presence once more plunged Quintus into presentiments of doom and thoughts of escape. He looked around; he was as trapped as he would have been in the Carcer Tullianum in Rome, though his wardens were a crowd of strangers celebrating a holy day.

As the horse was led slowly onto the bridge by the priestess and chieftain, Quintus recognised Commios and Tincomarus amongst the party, both in plain tunics, but with their moustaches plaited and braided, and the glint of silver on their hands and arms. In addition, Commios wore a necklet of intertwined beads of many colours run through with silver, the image of a hammer hanging from it. Following behind came the senior men of the tribe, the captains and other counsellors; close to the front was Elrik, the angry captain of the night before.

'What happened to the bodies?' Quintus asked Tan, as the noise of clapping, drums and cymbals rose to a deafening pitch.

'They came last night to ask for them,' Tan hissed. 'Many have claimed fathers, brothers and cousins in the scant hours of darkness. The Regni are no longer camped afar, but here amongst us, and we are now at peace.'

'Is this the end of the matter?' Quintus asked.

'They will accept Aucissa's judgement. There is no need for further fighting.'

Quintus did not know whether to be worried or relieved, but at that moment he did not have the chance to be either. The cacophony reached a climax, then, at a signal unseen to him, it suddenly stopped. Aucissa leant across the long neck of the horse, seemingly to stroke it, but her hand came away clutching the hilt of a bronze knife, and the blade of the weapon glistened with the beast's blood. Its nostrils bubbled pink and white, its head dropped and its front legs buckled as its great heart stopped.

Aucissa held the bloody knife aloft and uttered a single short phrase, which all the company on the bridge and all the watchers called out with her and repeated. Tan mouthed a translation to Quintus in the din, but the legionary could not interpret what he said.

The white tunic of the priestess was splashed with the beast's blood. As the horse was lowered to the ground by the hands of many men, the Regni chieftain drew an axe from his belt and, with a single sharp blow, severed the neck bones at the centre of the mane. By the time the animal lay flat, its head was separate from its body, the body manhandled onto a kind of litter, ready to be dragged away. The Regni chieftain then smeared blood onto his chest where his tunic lay open.

Quintus only now noticed that a pit had been dug on the eastern bank, into which the horse's head was placed, with reverence, its once bright eyes now glazed and dull. It was done efficiently — Quintus guessed that this was not the first time these men had buried such a trophy. Some were mere boys, perhaps it was a rite of passage.

Tan saw him looking. 'I helped last year,' he said. 'It is the turn of others to have the honour.' The young woman hanging on his arm pulled at him and whispered something, to which he replied in kind.

'You can go,' said Quintus, reading the signs.

'I cannot. It is my appointed task to fetch you from wherever you slept, bring you to our celebrations of midsummer morn, make sure you are fed and watered, then bring you to the roundhouse at the appointed time — which I think will not be until after sunset.'

So he was, Quintus thought dejectedly, a prisoner in all but name.

XVII: RUFUS, TULLIUS, CATO

Tan's companion looked shyly at Quintus from beneath her thick fringe. Her skin was smooth and clear, her hair long and fair — usually light brown, he guessed, but touched now by the summer's sun. He thought her smile was forced, and he could not read her eyes. Her body was lithe and limber, and she clung to Tan tightly, as if they might be somehow stuck together.

Quintus bowed his head. 'Today, then, you shall be my companions, and I yours,' he said. 'What is next?'

'Bonfires, then breakfast,' said Tan. 'We are invited to the great fire. Perhaps I will leap over it.' He repeated his boast to the young woman, whose face at first looked mock horrified then broke into a warm grin. He smiled and kissed her softly on the forehead, whilst Quintus felt more and more like an unwanted guest at another's party.

In front of the roundhouse, a huge bonfire had been built but not yet lit. In the fields and margins of the settlement, there were lesser fires already burning, some large, some small. Around them were family groups or groups of friends, none smaller in size than eight or ten by Quintus' reckoning, some a great deal larger.

Youths of a certain age — like Tan and his companion — were paired up, sitting coiled around each other like ivy on a tree, or in each other's laps, or were shyly holding hands and peering longingly into each other's eyes.

As they approached, the fire sprang to life, flames licking hungrily at the dry kindling, a column of smoke rising in the still air, and a great shout, a cheer, went up from all around, Tan joining in and urging Quintus to do the same.

As the cheering died down, in front of the flames he saw gathered a sort of deputation. Here was his paramour of the night before, the Queen of the Atrebates, along with Commios, Tincomarus and the sea captain Elrik.

To his joy, here also were the tall figures of Sextus and Crassus.

To his dismay, present too was the spiky-haired Coginus, king of the Regni, bloodied axe still in his hand.

Quintus instinctively went for his gladius. The move was not as obvious as it might have been, as the sword was drawn from his right hip by his right hand, rather than across his body. Nevertheless, the swift movement was noted by the youth accompanying him.

'No need,' said Tan firmly, placing a restraining hand on Quintus' sword arm. 'We are all friends here, and this day is blessed.'

Quintus looked hard at the young man, surprised at his intervention, but his eyes were unreadable. Clearly, though, he was no longer a silly youth lost in new love. The young woman had vanished from his side.

He spoke slowly and seriously. 'This task I do for my queen. I do not take the responsibility lightly, however much I enjoy your company. Do not test my commitment with your sword; do not impugn my honour by belittling me or trying to oppose me.'

The action and the exchange of words had taken but a moment, and had been witnessed by the king of the Regni with a mixture of surprise and disapproval.

He muttered something briefly and harshly to Tincomarus who, in turn, spoke to Quintus. 'Our honoured visitor asks why you wish to draw your weapon on him. Is he not a stranger and a guest?' The man added something guttural, and the translator finished, 'He asks do all your people strike before they speak, or is it just you?'

Quintus read the situation rapidly and let his arm fall, a sharp glance at Tan being enough for him to remove the hand that sat lightly but deliberately on his wrist. The other two legionaries, whose hands had gripped the hilts of their weapons, also relaxed. 'My pardon,' Quintus said, dipping his head. 'I was taken by surprise.'

Tan, his secret skill no longer hidden, translated and the king answered with hard laughter and harsh words. 'He asks, "As you took our sons and grandsons by surprise?"' Tan said.

Quintus was dumbstruck, taking a moment to master himself. 'Tell him that we defend ourselves when attacked, as I think he would.' He nodded in the direction of the Regni king's axe, which the man quickly and angrily stuffed into his belt, all the while glaring. Elrik also spoke, a long and complicated speech full of anger and sharp hand gestures. Tan held up a palm to make him pause, then began to interpret as best he could.

'He speaks of a group of boys who were innocently scavenging some wreckage being murdered. He says that both his friend —' he indicated Coginus — 'and himself, seek those responsible, for the incident has caused many deaths. Some of his captains have told him of a man, very tall and very pale, coming ashore with attendants, another who came riding a great sea creature, and a sacrifice made.'

The hard-faced king interrupted, speaking rapidly, and this time Tan looked to Tincomarus for help. Before the older man could begin, Aucissa spoke sharply.

'Enough,' she said to each man, adding words in their own tongue. 'I said that this matter is not to be spoken of today. When the sun has set and risen once more, then we will speak of it.'

The Regni warrior grunted and threw a glowering look at Quintus. Elrik also looked daggers at him but, for now at least, remained silent. Men of both tribes who had been standing close to Sextus and Crassus stepped back, the two legionaries realising with shock that they had been within inches of a swift and lethal blade. Quintus looked in their direction, but men were still placed strategically between he and they. He cast around for a friendly face amongst the Atrebates, but only Aucissa seemed anything other than hostile. Commios and Tincomarus would not meet his eye, and even Tan had turned his face away.

'Quintus,' said the queen gently, 'you are no caged animal, but a guest — one who has found great honour amongst our people — but your weapons, if you are to keep them, must stay sheathed. Your armour is with your servants. It will stay there until I order otherwise.' She mollified him just a little with a wan smile. 'Your shoes I have had brought.'

She signalled and a servant, dressed like all the others in white, with flowers woven into her long hair, came forward and placed his caligae on the ground in front of him. He nodded his thanks to her and she withdrew — clearly he would be lacing his own footwear.

'It is my wish,' Aucissa continued, 'that Elrik sends to the ships for your compatriots, to see if they are those close to you. But before he does, you must all promise — swear on whatever gods or tokens you hold dear — that you will accept my judgement.' Sextus and Crassus looked to Quintus, who nodded.

He drew his gladius, to him the epitome of all things Rome, and turned its blade so that it reflected the rays of the risen sun. 'We swear by Mars, god of war and of soldiers, and by mighty Jupiter, best and greatest, to honour your wishes.'

'I swear by my own patron, the lame smith Vulcan,' said Crassus, placing his palm on the flat blade of the sword.

'I swear by this,' said Sextus. He did not touch the blade, but instead patted the leather pouch containing his bulla at his throat.

'And I also swear by a token I will not reveal, but in memory of a friend, Ursus.' Quintus put his hand on the hidden package.

'I will demand the same solemn oaths of Elrik and Coginus,' Aucissa said, so all could hear. 'I will not be responsible for the tribe's ill fortune if this day is marred. Tomorrow, once this holy midsummer day and its festivities have ended, I will give judgement on the complaint.' She smiled then and spoke softly to Quintus. 'Perhaps you will be shod by then.'

Whilst he sat and tied his caligae, Aucissa spoke to Elrik and to the men of the Regni who, Quintus surmised, also acquiesced to her terms. Bizarrely, at least to him, that seemed to be the end of the animosity. The Regni king clapped him on the back and laughed, a harsh and guttural sound, but there was no sign of malice in his face. Commios and Tincomarus seemed friendly again and Tan, with his friend once more on his arm, was happy and helpful.

'They are like children,' Quintus said as the two other legionaries joined him. 'They live for the moment, fury replaced by light and laughter in a trice.'

'Except that one seems capable of holding a grudge,' Sextus observed, nodding in the direction of the man with the magnificent moustache who had led their enemies less than a day since.

'And that one is less than happy.' Crassus pointed to Elrik, who was giving orders to some of his men. The legionaries hoped he was telling them to fetch whoever they had on board. Though the three of them had held the bridge, they now felt vulnerable and would be happy for some companions.

'I no longer feel welcome here,' said Sextus.

'We are avoiding portents of bad luck,' Quintus said sarcastically. 'You at least should be familiar with that.'

'I have seen no two-headed calves, no withered trees out of season, no falcons falling from the sky, not even a diseased liver. They did not even read the entrails.'

'They did,' said Crassus. 'The burning flesh that you smell is the guts going up on the fire. It would seem that they do not waste the heart; they eat it.'

'Come, eat,' said Tan gaily, all trace of the determined young man gone and the carefree youth returned. 'The heart is shared by our leaders. The rest of the sacrificial flesh will not be cooked yet, for it needs butchering, but there are many other delicacies. And, my friend —' he patted Quintus on the back like an old comrade — 'we shall have to see who can leap the greatest fire! Crassus, you must try too — and the pretty one!' The sweep of his hand included a nonplussed Sextus.

Benches and trestle tables were set up outside, where many people were already sitting and eating flat cakes, dipping them into a tart sauce, and drinking. Some, the legionaries noted with a professional eye, were seated too close to the fire, and would have to move as the heat grew stronger. Already, the thick black and grey smoke had diminished and turned white as the fire grew hotter. It had been lit at the four cardinal points simultaneously, and now red and orange flames danced from bough to bough. At its centre was a chariot, whose spoked wheels could be seen black against the glowing heat of the fire. Quintus assumed it was part of the offering, whilst secretly decrying the waste. It had been loaded with and surrounded by dry boughs in addition to the detritus of the roundhouse and many other buildings. In its driving seat, a straw and wooden driver was soon no more than a skeleton of black sticks. Quintus noted with surprise that it had all been treated with some sort of grease or tar that encouraged flame. Boys, younger than Tan, were feeding the fire, daring each other to get closer; the entrails of the horse sizzled and spat where they had been flung. He was not near it, and already too hot.

The leaders of the two tribes sat on a sort of platform, slightly raised and back from the intense heat — Aucissa and the Regni chieftain in the centre, Commios and Tincomarus there also, as was Elrik, though he sat at the side occupied by the Regni leader. This puzzled the legionaries, who did not know if this was a mark of friendship or of defiance. Their only friends seemed to be Aucissa and Tan.

Tan showed them to a bench near the raised one, but at a lower level, and they were given food and drink, following Tan's lead as he made some sort of silent blessing or gesture of thanks over the fare. Their army training had drilled into them that whilst Rome was always right, it was usually a good idea to follow local customs as long as they did not interfere with discipline and order.

Following Quintus' lead, each legionary spilled a drop of the sweet drink on the ground and accompanied it with a whispered prayer to their gods. They invoked Jupiter; Ceres of the golden fields; Father Dis and the gods below, and Mars, god of the legions — as well as their own household deities. Tan watched curiously and then did the same.

'We always offer the heart and liver of the sacrifice to our gods, to honour them,' said Quintus.

Tan laughed. 'Our leaders eat it! The gods get the entrails once they have been read for omens.'

Quintus found this disrespect shocking, but said nothing. These people seemed to have a much more equal and friendly relationship with their gods, and were not in fear of them at all.

They ate. It was noisy — pipes and drums and some sort of droning instrument were being played, and songs were being sung. There were different songs at different times at different fires, which — combined with the crackling of the flames and the shouts of the younger boys as they competed in the fire-jumping — made a din over which the legionaries had to shout to be heard.

The lads were daring each other to leap ever further and higher across the flames. Successful leaps were met with cries of encouragement and applause, failures with cries of pain as bare feet met coals. Even the smallest boys, tiny versions of their brothers and cousins, made brave attempts to cross at least some fire, controlled by mothers and helped by fathers who swung them high.

'It keeps the gods happy,' explained Tan. 'It brings us good harvests and good fortune.'

'Belief is a potent drug,' Sextus said into Quintus' ear, cupping his hand to make himself heard, 'especially for those who wield it.' He indicated the party on the raised platform, whose jumping days appeared to be behind them.

Quintus' attention was taken by these leaders; they had all risen as one and were now looking towards the shore and pointing. Tan picked up what they were saying. 'Your people are coming,' he said. 'Look, they are here.'

The tribesmen who had been sent to the ships to fetch the Romans whom they had plucked from the deep were walking rapidly along the side of the inlet. The legionaries strained to see if there were faces amongst them that they might recognise.

'Rufus!' Crassus was the first to spot the unmistakable flash of Rufus' red hair.

'Is it truly he?' Sextus asked.

'I think it is,' said Quintus, delighted that another of his contubernium had been found. 'He even has a moustache fashioned like a British chieftain.' He glanced up at the Regni king, still standing and talking with Elrik. 'In time it will be as long as theirs. But is that the bald head of Tullius, shining in the morning light?'

'And beside him Cato,' added Crassus. Quintus recognised Nox — his dark skin and the tight curls of his hair singled him out.

'Are there more?'

'Is Marcus there?'

'What of the centurion? I hope that bastard drowned!'

'Is Publius there?'

'Are there others from the other ships?'

Quintus could answer none of these questions. For now, he didn't try, but opened his arms in welcome as he thanked the gods — Jupiter, Mars, Neptune and the greedy gods of the underworld — for the return of his companions. All of them jumped up and down, waving and shouting names and nicknames.

XVIII: MACILENTUS

At first the new arrivals were hesitant, uncertain of what greeted them, having been given no prior information by the sailors or their captains. Then suddenly Rufus recognised the unmistakably lanky figure of his decanus, his contubernium leader, and shouted his nickname to the heavens.

'Macilentus, you long streak of piss, how did you manage this? And who is that with you? Crassus, you dour bastard, and, by all the gods, Sextus! You are a sight for my lonely eyes, you pretty boy! I have a place for you in my cot tonight!'

Macilentus — Quintus — laughed merrily; Crassus, not one for showing emotion, was more enthusiastic than usual, waving and smiling. Sextus, who had quietly suffered the indignity of being referred to as his amicus' catamite ever since they were first paired, made a filthy hand sign that matched the lewd gesture with which Rufus had greeted him. Cato and Tullius had by now also joined in the waving and shouting. On a signal from Elrik, the tribesmen guarding them parted and allowed the three men to run towards their companions, greeting them, hugging them, and clapping them on the shoulders. Sextus allowed Rufus to ruffle his perfect hair, before greeting the other two almost as cordially.

Tullius smiled, but only just, the glint of his earring and the sun's reflection on his bald head being the brightest things about him. He sought his own amicus, Marcus. 'Is he here?' he asked. 'Is there anyone else?'

Cato was the same, seeking Publius amongst the tribesmen — the fair-headed Lux, day to his night, who teased and annoyed him incessantly, but whom he loved beyond telling and whom he would protect to death. The two of them were like the two halves of a walnut, or the two sides of a coin.

'Publius. Is he here? Does he live? Do you have news of him? Please don't tell me he is drowned.'

Quintus wanted to explain their situation, apprise them of the peril they were in, but right now he needed to give them news of their comrades.

'Our slaves are here somewhere.' Why he started here, he did not know — none had asked after Jovan and Maxim. 'They are safe, and looking after our armour, helms and shields, all of which were rescued.'

'Lux?' Cato asked again.

'Marcus?' Tullius demanded.

'They are absent. I have no news of either man, good or bad,' Quintus admitted, opening his arms in a gesture of futility. 'I was thrown up on the beach with the slaves. Crassus and Sextus were rescued by these tribesmen. It was fortune that threw us together...'

'Good or bad?' Tullius had given himself the nickname of *Mal Fortuna* — ill fortune — after losing previous comrades.

'It led us to a battle — a small one, but a proper fight nonetheless,' Crassus said, eager to tell the tale.

'It was fun, Rufus — pity you missed it.' Sextus affectionately punched his friend on the arm.

'But our coming has also led to jeopardy,' said Quintus. Before he could explain further, Tan called across to them, his accented Latin causing the newcomers to raise their eyebrows.

'We are used to it,' Sextus explained. 'Be careful what you say; there are others who have learned.'

They walked back towards the fire. Tan and Aucissa, along with Elrik and the Regni chieftain, met them halfway.

'Your compatriots?' asked Aucissa.

'Our friends,' answered Quintus. 'Our companions in arms.'

'They must swear also.'

'They cannot,' Sextus interjected.

'Why?' Tan asked harshly. He was immediately shocked that he had spoken before his queen and bowed his head to her.

Aucissa forgave him with a wave of her hand, but repeated his question in softer tones. 'Why?'

'They have nothing on which to swear a sacred oath,' Sextus explained. 'They have no sword, not even a knife, and I wager that none of them still has the bulla given to him in his infancy. They cannot swear an *ius iurandum* on empty air. They need a blade.'

It was true. Rufus, Tullius and Cato appeared to be wearing their own regulation tunics, much darned and gathered at the waist with their belts, so that at least they were not shamed by having to wear a tunic as a woman would — a punishment that still burned from their shared past. They wore no armour, save the baltea, the heavy straps that hung from their belts. They also wore their own caligae but, startling for a legionary, no gladius or pugio.

Aucissa spoke at length with Elrik and Coginus, and they argued, their arms and hands as voluble as their voices. Tan attempted a translation as the heated discussion continued, struggling to keep up.

'She orders that your friends be given their weapons, so that they may swear a solemn oath on them. Elrik argues that they could swear such an oath on the fire, the Regni that six of them armed would be too much of a threat. Aucissa says that she will not have the day spoiled with mistrust. There, she has sent for your blades; the discussion is ended, though the men are not happy.'

Tan was right. A runner loped off and returned quickly with six blades, three short, three longer, bound in a soft leather wrap that he unrolled. He asked something diffidently, looking at both his queen and his captain. Tan translated.

'He asked if they should have both blades. Elrik said no, just daggers. Aucissa overruled him.'

'Take them all,' directed Quintus, 'quickly.'

'What are we swearing to do?' Tullius asked suspiciously, as he took his own weapons.

'To respect her judgement,' said Quintus. 'Trust me.'

As the sun sat high in the pale blue sky, with just a line of fair-weather cloud above the horizon, the men swore the solemn oath that they would be ruled by a woman they had barely met. They were not happy about it.

In and around the settlement, smoke rose from the many fires and the noise of merriment mingled with it. Groups of men and women of all ages stood or sat around fires of their own, others in between the blazes, drawn together by sons wooing daughters from other families. The accepted couples paired off and vanished from the parental gaze whilst families negotiated dowries in case the match should stick. That was what this festival was all about — new life, new love. Even the toddlers played at it, chubby six year old girls holding hands with chubby six year old boys and skipping about.

The other major addition to the festivities was the arrival of horses and chariots. The chariots of the Regni were no longer camped in the valley, but instead now raced up and down the banks of the inlet, coming dangerously close to knocking each other into the water, but managing to turn at the last minute, sometimes spinning on a single wheel whilst the horse in the traces seemed to fly through the air. A crowd had gathered to watch them — half hoping that someone would misjudge and end up in the sea. The legionaries could not help but be impressed and applauded at each more difficult and dangerous feat.

In addition to food, drink had been taken. There was wine, of course, traded across the sea and drunk unwatered, so that intoxication — and the foolishness that went with it — came quickly. Quintus avoided it, instead sipping a bitter drink seemingly favoured by the older people, as well as trying and rejecting the sweet liquid that seemed to go straight to the heads of the younger, causing gales of laughter.

The six legionaries sat at a long trestle table, with Tan and his young paramour. Annaig had attached herself once more to Sextus, and seemed to have brought a sister or cousin, one who looked remarkably like her, who toyed with Rufus' red locks. Rufus enjoyed the attention; he had always taken his pleasure as it came to him — consequences came later — and food, drink and a young woman amidst music and games were distraction enough for him.

Crassus sat on the edge of this group. He and Tan were once more exchanging obscenities in their respective languages, now with an audience of the three giggling women. Clearly they were trying to see what would turn them the most red, or cause them to gasp with shock.

The other legionaries were not so insensitive to their situation. Tullius sulked, sitting apart from his companions. He had been admonished by Quintus, an admonishment he did not accept, although he backed down with bad grace. He had demanded that Quintus tell them at once what it was to which they had sworn, and why the woman should feel the need to sit in judgement on any of them. Quintus had advised him to wait. After all, though seemingly engaged elsewhere, Tan was still with them, and could be listening. He tried to explain this to

Tullius, but the dour legionary did not wish to wait. A holy oath was a holy oath — he had sworn it reluctantly and did not like to be kept in the dark.

Cato did not sulk, but instead sat in a fug of depression. He was devastated that Publius was not with them, and felt guilty for surviving himself when his amicus appeared not to have done so. Quintus tried to reason with him — perhaps Publius was alive and had just landed somewhere else, maybe in Frisia or Gaul. He could even be with Marcus, and what better person could there be to protect him? But Cato, though he gave the appearance of listening, did not really hear and continued to rehearse in his head the worst possible fates for his friend.

'How can I be Night, if there is no Day?' he moaned. 'One is necessary to the other; they cannot be separated.'

'You survived; so might he have done.'

'Sextus cannot see him.' Cato looked along the table at the stargazer and prophet, who was laughing with Annaig. 'I have asked him to look, but he says all he can see is a mist, no clear picture.'

'But he does not see Publius' death.'

'That's hardly a guarantee that he lives,' snapped Cato, and turned his face away.

Quintus shrugged, he had done his best to uplift Cato's spirits. He had always played this role, ever since he was a boy. His outlook was always positive, despite the disappointment that emanated from his father. He saw the good in people, took his father's jests in good part, smiled as he rode the cart to market, chuckled with his father's coarse friends as they made fun of his height and breadth, sniggered at their crude and vulgar jokes (though he did not understand them all).

He sympathised now with the curly headed legionary, tried to convince him that there was no need to worry, whilst knowing himself that the miracle which had brought the six of them together was unlikely to be repeated.

Eventually, he left Cato to his sombre thoughts and black mood — though he seemed not to notice his going — and joined the group at the far end of the table.

'There is no need for you to remain,' he told Tan, 'nor the girls. They are missing the merriment.' He was right; there were groups of young women chattering, some engaged in dancing or breathlessly sharing stories of the night just passed. 'How will others know of your prowess unless she tells them?' he added.

'She has cousins and sisters,' said Tan with a smile. 'They know already.' He said something in his own tongue and the three women nodded with mock-seriousness, trying to suppress their laughter.

'Yet still they are missing the festivities,' Quintus insisted.

'They choose to stay,' Tan replied, 'and I have my orders and will stay also. I will not report any of your utterances, should you wish to speak to your men. You have my oath. You know that you can trust me.'

Quintus decided that he knew no such thing. 'You kept your skill from us,' he said. 'Perhaps I should not trust you.'

'What do you think of our cavalry?' Tan changed the subject suddenly, although it was hardly possible not to be drawn to the noise and dust of the chariots racing up and down.

'They are lightweight,' said Quintus, with a touch of admiration, 'and this makes them fast and manoeuvrable. It looks as if they are capable of turning almost as quickly as a horse.'

Unlike Roman chariots, these were two-wheeled, the wooden wheels brightly painted, and drawn by two horses. The horses were linked by a pole and crosspiece on which, at times, the charioteer would stand, the most daring putting one foot on the back of each horse to prove his skill.

'A good charioteer can control them with his feet,' said Tan, 'and I am a good charioteer.'

'You can do that?' Quintus asked with amazement.

'Of course, though I would have to change first.' Instead of tunics, the charioteers wore a kind of leg covering, gathered at the waist, like a pair of undershorts, only longer and gaily patterned. Above the waistband they were bare-chested, though their moustaches and long hair made a fine display. 'A tunic does not allow enough movement,' he added.

A double trace led from the charioteers' hands to each horse, and with these he had absolute control — except when he didn't, when a manoeuvre pushed the laws of land and air, and the patience of the gods, a little too far. A number of the chariots tipped over and a number of the drivers, Quintus guessed the less experienced ones, ended up in the dirt, though their passengers — the men standing behind them on the chariot, holding a shield and javelin — tended to jump free first.

'In war, he would be better armed,' said Tan, 'but here it is all for show. There will be races soon.'

'Will you compete?' Quintus asked, hoping to release them from the listener in their midst.

'Not whilst I have this charge from my queen,' said Tan, smiling knowingly.

Before Quintus could reply — he had something to say about trust — Elrik appeared at the end of the table where Cato and Tullius sat sullenly. He was flanked by his own men and, thumping the board, said something that sounded like a challenge. Whilst Tullius half greeted the man — he had been their saviour, after all — Cato ignored him, lost in his own world. Quintus' hand once more moved to his weapon.

'He asks if your men are up for a contest,' said Tan quickly, putting a hand on Quintus' arm. 'There is no need to draw.'

'A chariot race?' Quintus asked, thinking that they were likely to be killed trying to control one of those things.

'No,' Tan laughed, and repeated the comment to Elrik, who also laughed heartily. 'Of course not. He would rather have you compete at something that he thinks is within your capabilities. He challenges the six of you to pull his six into the fire.'

This was a game of strength that Quintus knew. For a moment he was back on the Campus Martius, where he had fought and trained so hard in order to join the army. He had played this game with other boys and, later, in his probationary training, with other legionaries. It had helped develop strength and teamwork as they sweated in the shadow of Gnaeus Pompeius' great stone theatre.

For this sport Quintus was often first to be picked, as his height at the front of a pull had been an advantage. It was a game that he thought they could win.

XIX: DUM VIVIMUS VIVAMUS

'Tell Elrik we accept,' said Quintus unhesitatingly.

Tan relayed the acceptance, and its reply, asking, 'Will you take a wager?'

'We have nothing to stake but our honour.'

'He would compete for the women — not mine,' he added quickly, 'but Annaig and the other.'

Their Roman training would bring them victory. The women were nothing to Quintus. Without thinking or consulting, he agreed.

Quintus decided, out of deference to both Pompeius Magnus and the Caesars, to dedicate his team to Venus, rather than Mars, though he had nothing to sacrifice to either. Though Jupiter guarded Rome, the dictator Sulla's personal goddess had been Venus, as mighty as Jupiter and more wily, able to use charm as well as raw power. Sulla had relied on her to gift him the rule of the city — and had succeeded. The god Julius Caesar — and Augustus Caesar, the emperor, his son — also venerated the goddess, claiming her as an ancestor of the Julian house. She was also Pompeius' patron: it would be a fitting tribute.

Quintus had agreed to the contest before involving his men. Technically, of course, as their decanus, he was not obliged to ask them, but they were hardly on a parade ground or battlefield. As he looked them up and down, he realised to what a parlous state they had sunk. All, except Cato, who seemed incapable of growing one, had scraggy beards or at least rough shadows. Rufus' ginger hair, streaked with white from the sun and sea salt, stuck out at all angles. Sextus, so often immaculate, had controlled his curly brown hair in the tribesmen's way with a tie — probably provided by Annaig. This served, he knew, to better highlight his noble features, but could not hide the lack of a razor. Tullius always looked unkempt, but now could easily have been taken for a brigand. His balding head, ragged right ear and the shiny earring that hung from it gave him the air of a pirate. Quintus had not shaved since the wreck, and his stubble had grown into a scrubby beard. All of them were in tunics that had seen better days, especially when compared with the stark white attire of the tribesmen. None of them wore the bronze and red, the cloak and clasp, that spoke of the might of the mother city.

Yet they were legionaries still, whatever their feelings. Cato was bereft; Tullius depressed and dangerous; Sextus and Rufus happy with their full bellies, one unable to see into the future for now, the other not wishing to, happy to live in the present. Crassus seemed torn between befriending the Atrebates and mistrusting them. He liked Tan, but could not set aside the fact that the youth had hidden his language skill from them. Quintus thought that a game — preferably a contest won — would lift all their spirits, and he said so.

'Marcus would not have me play a stupid game.' Tullius was forthright, spitting on the floor in disgust.

'Nor will I without Publius,' added Cato.

'Then you will forfeit the wager,' Quintus said angrily.

'Wager?' demanded Tullius. 'Who said anything about a wager? What have you tied us to now?'

Sextus was the unlikely saviour who came to Quintus' rescue. 'Would you turn down an enemy's challenge, Tullius? It is not like you,' he said mildly, 'and Cato, would you not defend your absent friend's honour?'

'I understand the contest,' said Rufus. 'What is the wager?'

'The young woman you are with and her cousin,' said Quintus, expecting an explosion of opposition.

Instead, Rufus laughed heartily. '*Dum vivimus vivamus,*' he exclaimed. 'While we live, let us live. What is life without risk? Crassus, you are with us?'

'I am.'

'So that is four — do we have to recruit Tan to our cause?' He stopped mid-sentence and yelled at the youth. 'Stop!' Tan was relaying the discussion to Elrik. 'These matters are ours, not yours to share,' he admonished sharply. Tan at least had the good grace to look sheepish. 'Well?' Rufus demanded of Cato and Tullius.

'If you agree,' said Cato, looking at Tullius.

'So be it,' said Tullius, rising from his seat and growling. 'Let me not be the one to let down Rome.'

The two sides faced off across the crackling and glowing embers of a fire, pulsing red as the breeze caught them, the air above shimmering with the heat. It had been raked to provide a circle around three paces across. There was no rope; instead, the leather traces that had seen service on the chariots had been plaited together, soaked with water in the middle so that they should not catch fire. Crassus took up station as anchor, the traces passed around his waist. Quintus took up position at the front, at risk of being pulled into the embers. He dug in his heels and sat on them, bending at the knees. He would be difficult to unwind.

A crowd gathered to cheer for the Atrebates and jeer at the Romans, although Tan and the three young women were brave enough to support them. Nothing was at stake except honour, but to both groups honour was paramount.

The Roman squad took first blood, surprising their opponents with their training and organisation. Immediately after taking the strain, the two teams leaning back on the rope, Quintus called out a march time — left, right, left. In unison the six legionaries moved relentlessly backwards, the first of their opponents letting go within seconds as his feet touched the fire, the rest of the team pitching forward and letting the twisted leather rope fall as the Roman momentum easily pulled them forward.

Elrik, who was anchoring his fellows, at once cried foul. He would have been forced to back down had he not suddenly hit on a key difference between the two teams.

'It is those things on your feet, those shoes. They have studs or grips of some sort.'

Any unbiased observer would have seen that the footwear played little or no role in the defeat, but there were none without bias present. Quintus knew that it was discipline that had won, not caligae. Nevertheless, he was forced to agree, via Tan, that they would remove their shoes.

'No excuses,' said Elrik. 'We will also go barefoot.' He smiled as he said so, for many of the charioteers went barefoot anyway, the better to feel the timber of their chariots beneath them.

This time it was not so easy. Elrik had, during the time it took the Romans to unlace their caligae, instructed his men on the simple discipline required to counter that of Quintus' men. When he gave the order, Quintus found that unshod heels did not grip as well, and ordered his men to lean on the rope — but the leather slipped and cut their hands and, this time, it was Quintus who was forced to let go and leap the flames before he was pulled headlong into them.

The third pull — the deciding contest — did not take place until both Elrik and Quintus had taken time to brief their men on tactics. The teams were evenly matched; brute force would not do, so it would have to be strategy.

Elrik, confident, came to pull at the front, opposite Quintus. He grinned at the Roman and waved at the young women, who just seemed thrilled to be involved, and did not really care whose company they ended up keeping.

He called to the legionaries and laughed. Tan translated, 'He wants a good view when you Romans dance across the embers, and he will be able to claim his prize.'

Both teams rubbed their hands together, trying to remove any grease or sweat, then, with determined expressions, they took the strain, leaning on the rope.

Tan raised his hand to give the signal to pull. As they took the strain, a shadow passed across Elrik's face when he saw what the Romans had done. Instead of the plaited traces all being to one side, Quintus had threaded the rope, like a stitch made with a needle, between the men, hoping that this would provide a better bond. Elrik could not recall any rule that forbade this, but thought it unfair nevertheless. In his determination to win, he called on his men to pull too soon, hoping to catch the legionaries off guard. But Crassus — the solid figure of the blacksmith — had passed the rope around himself several times and was not of a mind to be moved. Not this time.

For a while, it looked as if no-one would win, as if the two teams would pull equally, but Quintus knew that his team, by taking tiny steps and then digging in again, was gradually and inexorably moving backwards.

Elrik only realised when his front foot touched the embers, but he was stubborn and pulled back, grunting. Then his other foot reached the fire. Though it began to sizzle and burn, still he pulled, his teeth gritted against the pain.

'Stop,' called Quintus. 'Tell him to stop, Tan. He has lost. I would not have him burned.'

The reaction when Tan relayed this was one of anger and insult. His feet by now were scorching, but he held his ground, hoping to pull the soft-hearted Roman from his pedestal.

But it was not to be. He let go of the rope with a shout and a call to the rest of his men to let go, and the legionaries, suddenly pulling against nothing, tumbled backwards into each other, falling to the ground. Elrik strode, barefoot, across the middle of the embers, the hottest part, and looked down with rage at the fallen Quintus. He spat a word in his face, then strode off quickly, the crowd parting for him.

'He says, "you win",' said Tan, 'but he did not stop to congratulate you.'

Despite the victory, the six legionaries returned to their places in glum silence. The hot anger of Elrik and the rest of his team — convinced that they had been beaten by trickery, or even witchcraft — was a solid wall of hatred, crushing any joy they might have taken from the victory. Even now, the captain was with a group of his comrades, all pointing at the Romans and jeering, making lewd gestures with their hands.

As they tied their caligae back on, Annaig and her cousin decided that, on this day of all days, they did not wish to be in the company of such melancholy. They slunk away quietly, but could soon be seen giggling with Elrik and his men. Rufus seemed the most despondent of all of them — he had thought that he might spend the night with the woman who had been toying with his hair, and had mentally prepared for a long evening of pleasure.

'You, boy,' he told Tan, 'find me some wine. If I am not going to get laid, I am going to get drunk.'

Tan could have refused the order, especially given the way it was said, but he did not. He did not want to offend — not yet, anyway. He sent his girl off in search of wine, and she soon returned with a full skin.

'Water it,' ordered Quintus, concerned.

'Or what?' Rufus demanded, and took a long swig in defiance.

Crassus had been the anchor, and his sturdy bulk had helped them win the contest. Now he was suffering, with the injury to his back inflamed by his efforts. He found it painful to stand, even more painful to sit. He longed for a couch on which to lie, or a rub from a slave, or a hot bath.

Tullius once more descended into that place from which no-one could bring him back. Once again, he had decided that it was he that was the carrier of their ill fortune, that even when they won, they lost, and that it was all his fault. In truth, Quintus recognised, he had become increasingly unstable. He had always been prone to swinging precariously from deep depression — a quiet but dangerous mood that should not be disturbed — to flashes of violent temper and destruction. Now, he seemed on the edge of a permanent melancholy. Quintus tried to shake him from it.

'It was not your fault, Tullius. Do not own the blame.'

'I own nothing,' Tullius mumbled in response, putting his head on his arms on the table.

Cato also sat in silent contemplation, maintaining his sadness at the loss of his friend. Sextus provided comfort, but was still unable to see in the mists of vision and prophecy whether or not Publius survived.

Surveying the scene, Quintus' mind wandered back to the beach. He wondered if they had indeed offended the gods, and thought about what they might have to offer in sacrifice to appease them.

He was seized by sudden visions of his own. The first was the sight of the legless ship's boy still tied to the mast, his skin white and shining in the morning sun. He remembered the lad's bright eyes, his merry laugh, the echo of his final advice to Quintus, advice that had surely saved his life.

Second, as clear as if it was before him now, he saw the bodies of the young native boys he and Jovan had killed, lying next to the ship's boy on a damp pyre, their flesh beginning to smoke and curl and smell. He saw the fire at last failing, and their ghosts, all three of them, fated to wander the earth half-burned, in blindness and pain.

Together these visions conspired to bring a sudden wave of loss and despair.

So the legionaries drank, the veterans foolishly deciding on unwatered wine. Rufus was depressed that the young woman was gone, Crassus bemoaned his injury, and Cato refused any solace, though Sextus tried to comfort him. Quintus took small sips in self-pity. Each man poured a drop of whatever he had chosen onto the earth with a brief prayer, but this was more out of habit than anything. A bigger sacrifice was needed to appease great Jupiter and Mars. Jupiter required a white ox, and Crassus would have been honoured to swing the hammer.

So they drank. And each descended deeper into his own particular pain.

The festival of the sun continued rowdily around the morose group, still full of songs, dances and competitions. Quintus was the only one of the group to look outwards, to take note of what was happening as he absentmindedly retied his caligae. Midday came, and the sun stood high above them. When the shadows had shortened to nothing, a course was marked out next to the inlet and a series of chariot races began to take place, the participants performing screeching turns around a marker in the field and then racing back. Tan noticed his interest.

'These are trials only. See, boys try their strength and skill. The real charioteers keep their horses fresh.'

'Women, too,' noted Quintus, surprised to see bare-chested female riders holding traces.

'Of course. Why not?' said Tan. 'Commios is down there, and Elrik, and others of our captains and leaders. They will organise proper contests for this afternoon.'

XX: CIRCUS MAXIMUS

Unlike the races in the Circus Maximus, there were only ever two contestants matched at one time — but like the races in Rome, there seemed to be few, if any, rules.

Quintus had been taken as a boy to see the re-dedication of the Circus, its vast banks of seating having been consumed by fire not long after his birth. He had watched from high in the stands on the Aventine as the greens and the whites, the blues and the reds, hurtled around the track. Mistakes or treachery often caused injury, sometimes even bringing fatal consequences to their drivers. In between the races were beast hunts and gladiatorial combat; it was here he had seen his first lions, elephants, lynxes, wolves and bears. It was here he had seen his first executions, which his father made him watch — no room for squeamishness — strangulations followed by beheadings. He had no idea what crimes had brought such a destiny on the men's heads.

The spectacle he was watching now was a mere shadow, without even any teams or team colours. Only one charioteer would be crowned supreme. The winner soon raced again, against the winner of another bout; the loser remained defeated, with no chance to redeem his honour, which to Quintus seemed harsh, but those who had been beaten did not seem to mind.

It was clear from Tan's knowledge that he could have been one of the contestants, but his duty was preventing him from taking part.

'I would have beaten him,' Tan muttered, watching a triumphant bare-chested youth of his own age take a round.

'He was poor on the turn; he took it too wide and kept his wheels on the floor.'

Hour after hour the spectacle continued. The crowd grew as the number of remaining contestants shrank. Other activities diminished — although many fires were still being fed, especially the big one. In the late afternoon, there was a pause as senior people from both tribes moved down and were seated, Aucissa and Tincomarus amongst them, Commios already there. Quintus and the legionaries were not invited. The Regni chieftain, along with Elrik and some of the other captains, were amongst the final charioteers, stripped to their trews, hair tied back, moustaches flying as they competed.

Each charioteer that remained had been given the name of an animal — raven, wolf, squirrel, even dolphin — and then Commios pulled marked sticks from a bag in pairs. These decided who would compete against who; some were lucky in the draw, in that a charioteer's horses were known to be tired, or a fall had been taken, or a man was known to be not as skilled or experienced as his opponent. Some were unlucky, in that they were matched against one thought likely to win — Elrik, Tan told Quintus, was considered the best of the Atrebates. The Regni charioteers were mostly unknown quantities, though their chieftain, Coginus, had driven well in the trials. Many wagers were laid, Tincomarus keeping the stakes — a torc or ring or wristband — or holding a man's honour in his hands if what was wagered was slaves, chariots, weapons or promises for the future. Elrik and Coginus were in separate halves of the draw, possibly by design, although it was meant to be random. Inevitably, as round after round was complete, they became closer and closer to being the last two to race.

At last, they were the only charioteers left. In earlier rounds they had been allowed to change horses; now each reverted to their favourite pair, their best pair, ready to throw everything at winning.

Elrik had a pair of matched dark grey ponies, sturdy and strong and, from the way they tossed and fretted, born to run. His opponent's beasts were a reddish black, which could have been sired by the stallion that was sacrificed. They also stamped in agitation, eager to be let loose. The chariots were of similar design to all the rest. Tan told Quintus that they had been stripped down for speed, but the legionary did not have sufficient knowledge to appreciate how they had been streamlined.

'Are there rules?' Quintus asked.

'For the purpose of the race, the charioteers must stay in the chariot, rather than mount the horses. That is the only rule. There will be a draw for who gets the bank and who the hillside. For this contest, the hillside is favourite; it is the shorter, inside track, but the turn is harder, so there is more chance of a spill.'

Coginus' hair was still waxed, and his moustache still braided, but now he was bare-chested, having discarded the bloodstained tunic, although the blood he had smeared on his chest remained. Tan claimed that it was meant to bring him good fortune. The torcs and ringed belt had gone, but the silver wristbands remained, glinting in the westering sun as he mounted his chariot. Elrik's long moustache was also decorated with braids and he was stripped to his trews, as tall as his opponent, but narrow-waisted and lithe where Coginus was stocky.

The draw gave Coginus the inside track, to the disappointment of the watching Atrebates, who roared their disapproval. A start was marked across the course; a boy — Tan's cousin, it seemed — stood bare-chested in the middle of the racetrack, a rope end in each hand, his arms stretched wide. Other boys held the ends of the rope so that it was taut. Its release would ensure they both started at the same time, and the two chariots jostled for position behind it. Elrik took a long swig of whatever was in the skin he was offered. Tan called it the water of life, or the touch of fire; Quintus had no doubt that it was something stronger than wine. Coginus shared it, then held the skin up to the sky in blessing.

Encouraged by their leaders, the crowd began a countdown. At its end Aucissa dropped her arm and Tan's cousin let go of the two ropes and dropped to one knee, covering his head as the charioteers flicked the traces, yelled at their horses and galloped away in a cloud of dust. The boy ran to the side as the dust swirled and settled.

The two chariots were wheel to wheel, the horses pulling them baring their teeth and snapping at the opposing animals. Elrik had the inlet on his right, the tide already rising in it. The bridge was the first point at which the crowd could judge who was in the lead. A great roar went up as Elrik's matched pair reached the marker a good head clear of the Regni chieftain.

'He seeks to steal the inside,' panted Tan excitedly. 'If he can make the turn before the Regni, he can cut across him and come back the way he went out. It is inspired, inspired!'

He was ecstatic at the prospect of his captain's victory and screamed his support, as did the crowd, a scream that died as they realised that Coginus had a counter move. He had seen the tactic and urged his chariot on to close the gap.

It was not just the speed of the horses that was necessary to win, but the skill of the charioteer, and the Regni chieftain was certainly skilled. He pulled across to block the other's chosen line and urged the horses to greater speed; if he could turn first, he would deny Elrik his plan. But by the next marker, Elrik had extended his lead. He was now almost a full chariot length ahead, making Coginus blind, eating dust. Only at the last minute did he avert disaster, pulling up sharply before he crashed into the back of Elrik. Had he made contact, he would have destroyed them both.

Lifted by a great roar from the crowd, Elrik reached the turn first and, cutting across Coginus' line, rounded the stone pillar set deep into the ground. He aimed to claim the inside track, his horses rearing onto their back legs, front hooves raking the air, his chariot spinning on one wheel. It was the most dangerous and daring of manoeuvres, and surely enough for victory if it succeeded. Behind him Coginus cursed as he himself took the turn — not with quite the same bravado, but with flair nevertheless.

Now it was Elrik's race — all he had to do was keep his head, keep straight, and gallop for the finish, a line stretched across in front of his own people. He raised both arms in triumph in a perilous show of skill, shouting his thanks to the gods. Today would be a good day.

But it was too soon. Elrik had allowed his concentration to waver, taken the turn too wide, found himself on the side of the hill, scattering the spectators that stood there to watch the turn. Coginus, seeing his chance, made to cut inside him. Hubris could yet be his downfall. With a yell, he grabbed at the traces he had so recently let go of and yanked at them to bring the beasts back on course, back down the slope and ahead of Coginus, who threw curses at him at he careered across his path.

Now Elrik had once more pulled ahead of Coginus and was again by the inlet — but the Regni chieftain did not slow. He instead renewed his efforts, urging the beasts to greater and greater speed, though their hearts might burst. He gradually drew level with his opponent, so that as they approached the bridge, they were wheel to wheel, both standing high on the crossbars of their chariots, their horses' hooves flying in tandem, Elrik still holding the lead, but now barely.

As they passed the bridge, the noise of the crowd changed, there were groans and hands put on heads in growing horror as they realised what Coginus was going to do. He had stayed on Elrik's shoulder deliberately, unable to catch him, and now veered towards him, turning his horses so gradually that Elrik did not notice until warned by the shouts from the watchers. He dared to glance back to see his left wheel dangerously close to the bank, and he looked across to see Coginus closing the space. At the final moment, before disaster hit, he had to brake, pull on the traces and straighten up, but it was too late. Coginus had, at the last, outwitted him, and now raced towards the finish line, half a head clear.

Elrik screamed with anger, cursed every god he could think of, and tried his best to catch the Regni chieftain. But the move had been timed to perfection. There was not enough course left to remedy the mistake and, in triumph, Coginus crossed the line first. The crowd drew its breath in as one — a mark of respect for Elrik, perhaps, or just a sign of partisanship. It then roared its approval, clapping and stamping — it had been a good race, after all and, apart from the wagers won and lost, only honour had been at stake.

The Regni chieftain pulled up, jumped down and rushed to the heads of his panting beasts to congratulate and stroke them. He then raised an arm to the crowd in triumph and called his men across to wipe the beasts down, then water and reward them.

Elrik jumped down and angrily passed his horses to one of his men that stood by. He kicked a chariot wheel in frustration and stomped up the slope from the inlet.

Whilst the victor called to him, presumably in congratulation or commiseration, Elrik waved his hand dismissively and continued towards the little group of legionaries, isolated from the rest of the celebrations. He looked like he would visit violence on them, though they had no part in his loss. Quintus, who was returning up the slope with Tan, once more itched to draw his blade. Elrik swerved as he spotted the two of them making for the others, and strode purposefully towards them, shouting as he came.

'He issues a challenge,' said Tan. 'He blames his loss on his burnt feet; he blames his burnt feet on you. He is determined to win something this day and challenges you to leap the fires in honour of the day. He vows to leap further and higher.'

He stood directly in Quintus' path, issuing the challenge in his own language and then, in passable Latin, he added, '*Iustus tu, Romanus.*' He then gave up with the strange tongue and instead turned to Tan, who translated.

'He says he will compete with just you. Leave your men to their drink; they do not look fit to enter into competition.'

Quintus nodded a mute agreement and the three of them set off for the main fire, a blaze that had been continually fed with fresh wood and still burnt fiercely, its red and orange tongues reaching for the sky, its heart white and pulsing, the very air above it shimmering like a reflection, flowing like water, twisted out of shape. A fall into it could be fatal.

Elrik drew a line in the earth with his foot — not, Quintus thanked the gods, next to the main part of the conflagration, but by coals that had been raked out of the fire. The length furthest from the fire did not seem too daunting, though the coals were still glowing red and white; the length nearest to the flames was both hotter and further to jump. Quintus guessed that this was the nature of the competition — the easier distances first, over the less dangerous paths, until one of them either could not make this distance or could not bear the heat.

Elrik had drunk more of the 'fire of life' and now offered it to his opponent, who took a long swig and then wished that he hadn't. Unlike the other drinks that he had tried, this burned his throat on the way down and then set up a blaze in his belly. He stopped himself from crying out, but could not prevent a twisted grimace from overtaking his features. Elrik and his supporters laughed at the Roman's discomfort.

Tan stood close by. 'He tells you to take off your tunic,' he said. 'It will be safer — it is more likely to catch fire than you.'

Quintus drew both gladius and pugio and carefully laid them down before he undid his belt and pulled the tunic over his head. Where the tunic usually sat, his skin was white, covered in scars and bruises. Elsewhere his legs and arms and neck were tanned and bronzed, making it look as if he wore the tunic still. He did not like being unarmed. Ursus' package, that he had sworn to keep safe, was taped within his undershorts. If he died, then he could not fulfil his promise, and it would burn with him.

Elrik had drunk a lot, enough to make him oblivious to the harm. He had also gained a following, cheering for him whilst jeering Quintus. He took a run, launched himself from behind the line and easily reached safety, then turned to encourage Quintus to do the same. But Quintus was long-legged and taller than his opponent; he needed less of a run-up but could still easily outjump him. As he landed, a jeer went up and many fingers pointed at him. He looked at Tan.

'Your foot coverings; they protect you,' he said. 'They accuse you of cheating.'

Quintus angrily sat down and once more removed his caligae. He then crossed the fire again in the opposite direction, turning in defiance to the crowd. Elrik shouldered past him and jumped again, a longer jump, nearer to the intense heat, to a roar of approval. Needled, Quintus followed, again easily making the distance. Elrik raised the stakes again, this time a jump that was barely within his capability, his back heel crunching on the coals, sparks flying, the unmistakeable smell of burnt flesh in the air. He grimaced, but otherwise made as if not to notice the hurt, saying something that again had the crowd shouting. This time Quintus bothered with the run-up and landed well clear of Elrik's footsteps. Incensed, Elrik ran and jumped again, once more catching the coals with his heel. Quintus prepared to follow, then in a moment of sense amidst the madness, he thought better of it and spoke breathlessly to Tan.

'Tell him I cannot beat him. Tell him he has bested me. Tell him that I will not risk further danger.'

Tan spoke quickly to Elrik, who shook his head emphatically, then barked a question.

'Do you yield?' Tan asked.

'If that is what it takes,' Quintus replied swiftly.

After a brief exchange, Elrik turned to the crowd, arms raised. Some cheered, but most had already turned to other entertainment — drink, food, songs, or other contests of strength and skill. It was an empty victory.

XXI: NON DUCOR DUCO

Quintus picked up his clothes, weapons and caligae. He would not dress here, but up by his own men, who had missed the excitement. What was left of the crowd ignored him. At the table two of his comrades were seemingly asleep, heads on their arms. Two were seemingly arguing over some trifle or other, and one, Tullius, was pacing up and down and muttering darkly to himself. Tan had followed him, as was his duty this day. Quintus sighed as he pulled on his tunic and fastened his belt; he did not think the day — that had seemed to start so well — could be less auspicious. As he yet again bent to tie his caligae, Commios approached them.

'Aucissa summons him,' the older man told Tan. 'I will take him; your work is done.'

The youth immediately brightened up and moved towards the main fire, no doubt to find his girl. Quintus thought the day might have finally turned, that Aucissa wanted to make love to him once more. Perhaps the day would not turn out so badly after all.

He was shown to the same place as the previous night, but this time the atmosphere was very different. Commios left him within sight of the hut. The door hanging was open, and Aucissa hurriedly beckoned him inside. This was no seduction; this was business.

There were no torches lit as the long day continued. Darkness would be a long time coming. Still, the space felt gloomy, whereas the night before it had felt warm and welcoming. The bed had been rolled away and Aucissa, standing, indicated where he should sit — on one of two stools facing each other, deliberately separated by a small table. A jug of wine and a flagon of water stood on it, though neither of them touched them.

Aucissa paced, and Quintus could feel her wrath. 'What did you do?' she hissed, quietly incandescent with anger. 'What did your arrogant Roman heart do? Men have died, alliances have become brittle, the day is marred. What in the name of all the gods did you do?'

Quintus did not even think to dissemble; it would not have been possible. 'We defended ourselves,' he said, as if it was enough. 'That is all; we defended ourselves.'

Her voice rose. 'Then if so innocent, why not tell us? Why not admit what you did? Why let the Regni tribe descend on our people in war? Why cause so much death, such horror?'

'We are Roman. We were attacked and we defended ourselves.' That was all that the legionary could say — yet he managed to say it with pride.

'You egotistic piece of horse shit,' she said, raising both her voice and her hand, as if to strike him. Ill advisedly, he grasped his sword hilt.

'And now you would murder me also,' she spat through clenched teeth, 'in my own home. Amongst my own people. There is no name for you.' She pointed to the door, long shadows of men falling across it. 'Know that with one word you are dead — you are all dead.'

Her fury was such that her breath was coming in short bursts, her face was reddened, her hand clutching the edges of the table that stood between them, the flagons on it wobbling, in danger of tipping over.

'I did not think it — wise — to tell you,' Quintus insisted. 'They could have been relatives of yours, cousins or children from this very village.'

'And that would have made the slaughter more justified? Or less? I do not follow your Roman logic, legionary.' The venom and disbelief in her voice was palpable. 'Your silence cost the lives of many of the Regni tribe — you and your comrades killed them. Those were unnecessary deaths. Of course you should have spoken. Had you spoken, the need to "protect" my people would never have arisen. Your blades were not needed. Silence was the act of a coward.'

Quintus bristled. 'I am no coward...' he began, rising from his stool.

She cut him off, shouting, 'But you are a murderer!'

They were both standing now, facing each other in threat.

The door hanging jerked open and two men, with their weapons drawn, stood at the entrance, alerted by the raised voices. She dismissed them with a wave. Reluctantly, the men withdrew.

The interruption was enough to cool a little of the heat, although her darkly shadowed eyes still bored into him, his stiff Roman pride reflected back in them. Slowly she sat, indicating that he should do the same.

'What happened? Tell me,' she said, controlling herself with an effort. 'Though you and your men kept your oaths today, the day is still spoiled, cursed.' She held up a hand as he made to speak. 'Competitions won and lost do not matter; they are only games, and in honour of the gods. Thank the gods that no blood was spilt. But your lies and pride have marred the day. Our harvest will not be a good one.' She breathed out and looked him in the eye. 'But, Roman, I still have to judge. If the Regni tribe get hold of you, you will burn. And I could not stop them. I may not even want to. It may not help, but tell me anyway.'

Quintus understood. It would at least give her time to think. He poured a half cup of wine and carefully watered it. He made to offer her the jug but, with a vigorous wave of her hand, she refused. He could do no more than repeat, quietly but firmly, what he had already said. 'We were attacked, and we defended ourselves.'

'At least you no longer cite your Roman pride,' she said acerbically.

He was wounded, but managed to hold back his retort. He could still see nothing wrong in being proud to be Roman; Rome was the only truly civilised city in the world — better than Athens or Alexandria, even — though clearly she could see only arrogance. He took a deep breath and began to describe the incident as accurately as he could.

'The worst of the storm was over, but still it blew hard and still the waves were as mountains. Great Neptune relented at last and threw us onto the beach, exhausted and injured. We had barely survived — we were barely capable of thanking the gods for sparing us.'

'What happened? How did the innocents die?'

Quintus held up a hand to ward off the fever of her rage, then continued. 'We made a sort of camp; we even found something to eat and a means to make fire. We fell into a trance of exhaustion — I would not call it sleep.' He took another sip of the wine, knowing that now he was building excuses for his actions. He sighed, determined to try and stick to the events. 'The group of young men, boys really, arrived at first with stealth and then, seeing no people to disturb them, noisily. They examined the wreckage that had come ashore in the night. I understand that being boys, they were naturally curious. We did not want them to take anything that might have been of use to us — weapons, armour, or even food and drink.'

'And did they?'

'No. It seemed that they found nothing of interest. They might have stayed longer and looked further, had they not been scared off by a spectre.'

'A spectre?'

'The ship's boy, a pale youth, had been cut in two by the storm, and his mangled body rose from the water, fastened to a spar. It frightened them. We saw them run.'

'And that was the end of it?'

'It was not. A few came back and decided to investigate further — but not the beach, not where the spectre haunted. Instead they sought out our hiding place. They came furtively. Now I think on it, perhaps they did not even know that we were hiding there — they could just sense … difference. We had an injured man who made a noise as he slept — that is what gave us away and led them to us. We were barely awake and surprised.'

'So you killed them?' she asked with disgust.

'No, it was not like that. We heard voices — there seemed to be many of them. We had to defend our injured man. I went so far as to arm a slave, which is unheard of.' Quintus gulped. 'We had struck long before we realised the age of the attackers; we struck instinctively, to protect ourselves. Most fled. Only two remained: one dead, one dying.' He did not dare to share the truth of the second one's death — that he had put an end to the boy to cut short his suffering. Once more, he repeated his mantra: 'We defended ourselves.' He knew now that this was a weak excuse — they had not been attacked by anyone who was a real threat.

When Aucissa asked her next question, he realised that she knew the details already. She was just seeing if he would lie. 'Why the sacrifice? Why dishonour them? Why the fire?'

'It was no sacrifice,' Quintus said sorrowfully, shaking his head. 'We are Romans, not animals, not…' He was about to say 'barbarians' but stopped himself just in time.

'I know what you call us, you sons of arrogance,' Aucissa rasped.

Quintus let his head drop in acknowledgement and closed his eyes, hoping it would be enough to ward off her righteous fury. Slowly, he lifted his wine cup and looked into it, but it was empty. He did not dare refill it. 'I swear by all the gods that it was an attempt to honour them — a pyre, not a sacrifice. We did not know their customs, so we drew on our own. We placed the ship's boy with them — what was left of him. We tried to send off their ghosts in peace. We even found coins to put into their mouths, to pay the ferryman. It is our custom.' He put the cup down and wrung his hands. 'But the wood was green and wet; there was rain and salt spray. It would not burn properly; it just smoked and spat.'

'So you left it?'

'Only when we could see that it would never burn, that the tide would claim the bodies. We tried … we tried to honour and respect them.' He knew that there was nothing more he could say; surely she knew that placing Charon's obol was a sign of respect.

As his voice trailed off, his excuses spent, the queen was quiet for a while, a deep lake of silence filling the air between them. Quintus still dared not pour either wine or water. Eventually, Aucissa steepled her fingers, closed her eyes in thought, and asked, 'Did you think them less because they were children?'

Quintus knew then that she had not understood, not truly — or she did not accept his account, his reasoning. He shook his head gently as he explained, almost pleading with her. 'We did not know how young they were, not until we looked on the bodies of the ones who fell. And there were many of them...' he added weakly.

'Children.' Aucissa was dismissive.

'But children follow what their fathers do. They would have killed us. These were armed.'

'Armed?' She was witheringly sarcastic. 'With sticks, pebbles, stones maybe? And you had swords, spears, daggers?'

'We did not know...' Quintus' voice was a whisper, but still defensive. 'Some on the beach were more than children...'

'But less than men,' Aucissa replied with derision.

'Maybe... Inevitably they grow into adults, and they do it quickly.'

'In Rome, maybe. Here, less so. I know.' She tapped herself on the chest with a forefinger. 'I know.' Her tone grew bitter. 'I know that you Romans have no time for babies or children, or anyone who is not full of pride and gravity and ideas of "service". I know that as Romans you have no idea of the concept of childhood. I know this from my own brief acquaintance with my father. He knew that my mother carried his child when he went to board the boat to return to Gaul. He said he could not stay, as that would be desertion, and he would forfeit his life.' She smiled weakly. 'Honour came first, before his woman, before his child. Honour and duty and service to Rome. But my mother prayed. She sacrificed a dozen white doves to Taranis, and the thunder god stood in his way. A great storm prevented him from leaving. In the end, he was here when I was born. I was a girl. A disappointment. He might have had a slight interest in a boy, but in truth he was not interested in children at all. You are no different.'

A great silence enveloped them both, spreading to all corners of the hut, dulling even the noises of festivities and fires from outside. Quintus feared to break it, but he could not help himself. 'I tried to honour them,' he insisted quietly.

'You could have tried not to kill them,' she said archly. She had calmed now, though she was still clearly full of ire. 'I cannot unhear what you have said. The circumstances do not matter. You were not at war with this tribe. It is murder. You did not speak when you knew why we were attacked. That was foolish. Had you told me, I could have stopped them, talked with them. You knew by then that I am not led, I lead. *Non ducor duco*. I could have brokered an agreement. You could have paid for the lives of the boys, with silver or gold, horses or slaves, even with your own service.'

'The slaves do not belong to us,' mumbled Quintus. 'They belong to Rome.'

'No matter,' she said. 'They stand accused with you, so they could hardly be part of the *weregild*.'

'I had gold once…' Quintus mused, thinking of the final nugget from the goldmine in Hispania that he had flung into the maelstrom.

'But not now?'

'No longer. It was cursed.'

'Then you would have nothing to offer but yourselves.'

'No Roman would ever willingly owe his life to another. It diminishes them, takes away their pride. Caesar himself destroyed the power of many of his enemies by granting them clemency — even when their own officers delivered them up for death. A true Roman would rather die; he would fall on his sword.'

'Then do so,' she said. 'Save us the trouble. If you cannot pay with silver or service, our only other justice is death. You will be sentenced to death — although the gods may choose whether you live or die.'

XXII: OMNES

There was another palpable silence, spreading like smoke from a wet wood fire in a shuttered room, filling the space between them. It was oppressive and both knew that if they left it, it would choke them. Finally, Quintus said, 'Your gods or mine?'

'Why not both?'

'Mine are fickle and, at times, vicious. Sometimes they respond to prayer. Sometimes they strike down pride. Sometimes they save a body out of spite for another of their kind. Perhaps I might hope.'

'Mine might spare you, but I doubt it.'

'How might I live?' Quintus dared to ask.

'If it is my judgement you suffer, you will be tied to a stake at low tide. If the gods want you to live when the tide rises, you live. If they want you to die, you drown. It is uncomplicated.'

Quintus nodded. 'Have any ever survived?'

'Not in my memory. It just shows that we are excellent judges; the gods tend to agree with us. It is a custom peculiar to us, because of where we live, and the gods to whom we pay homage — gods of the river and sea as well as the earth and sky. Other tribes put their criminals through an ordeal of fire. If it is the Regni tribe that judges you, you will burn — all of you at the same time in a great straw man dedicated to their gods, or bound together on a wheel of fire.'

'All together? Only I am guilty.' The admission passed unmarked; both knew it already.

'Not in the eyes of the gods. It is Roman pride that is guilty, Roman conceit, Roman hubris. You will all burn.'

'Even the slaves, Jovan and Maxim? They are not Roman, they are Macedonian.'

'Afforded the same chance that the gods will hold back the tides on their behalf,' Aucissa said dismissively. 'At least one of them is as guilty as you. The other may yet be given in part payment to the families. The matter is closed; your arrogance is what has sentenced you. You are guilty of murder. You compounded this by allowing our allies to attack us, when it could have been prevented. I can make no case for you.'

Quintus dared to be nettled. 'I did not think I needed a case to be made,' he said, once more stupidly filled with Roman pride. 'We were attacked, and we defended ourselves. Afterwards, we treated them with honour and respect. We did not know their funeral rites, so we improvised; we used what we had. No murder was intended. No disrespect was meant.'

'Maybe. But you were hasty. These were not attackers. The boys were scavenging — and even the ones that startled you were no threat. You could probably have shouted at them, waved your arms about, and like birds in the fields they would have flapped away noisily.'

Quintus drew himself up to his full height, vanity now overwhelming him. 'Roman soldiers do not flail their arms at enemies,' he said contemptuously. 'They kill them.'

Aucissa exploded with fury. 'Rome, Rome, god-cursed Rome — I am sick of hearing of it. It angers me beyond anything. Your Roman ego brought our friends, our allies, to our doors in violence.'

'Whatever I said would not have stopped them; they would not have listened to reason. They had bloodlust in their eyes and vengeance in their hearts.'

'Because of you!' she shouted. 'Only because of you!' She paused and caught her breath. 'You saved us from them, I admit, but it was you who brought them here. There were many deaths that should not have happened. They can be laid on your conscience.' Once more she paused, controlled her anger, and spoke in measured tones. 'But you are right. I cannot judge on those deaths; only the gods can say why they let them happen. I can judge only on the deaths of the boys. You should die.'

'And yet you do not condemn me?' he asked, seeing a glimmer of hope. 'You do not call your guards. What prevents you?'

She let out a deep sigh filled with sadness rather than anger. She spoke slowly and clearly, hands now folded on her lap. 'What prevents me is what angers me most. The only way I keep our friends as allies — as they have always been — is to let you go. Not to let you fall on your sword in the misplaced name of honour. Not to face my judgement. Not to be judged by our gods, or yet theirs. Not to be burned alive. It pains me, but it is what I must do.'

'You intend to let me live?' Quintus asked incredulously. 'You mean you recognise the rights of a Roman citizen?'

She stood up suddenly. This time the flagons did not survive — they tipped onto the floor and smashed. The door curtain twitched, but a glance from Aucissa seemed to still it. 'You are stupid, man of Rome. I do not care about your rights, citizen or not. Your country brings no fear to me. You are blind and foolish.' She moved her face closer to his, the spittle from her hissed command speckling his cheeks. 'Be gone, Roman. Take all your gear, your slaves and weapons, your cloaks and helms — any evidence that you were ever here. Get from this place.'

He flinched as if she had slapped him. But she was not finished.

'I cannot stop the Regni tribesmen from following you, from hunting you. I cannot stop my people from doing the same, should they learn the truth of you. They are within their rights.' She paused, spoke as if pulling the words with difficulty from a deep well. 'But if you stay here, I will have to judge you, and you will have leave to defend yourself. Your story will be told, including my part in it. That cannot happen.' She wrung her hands as she paced. 'I should have questioned you when you arrived. I should never have let you stay free; I should not have let you defend us. Such pride and arrogance on your part cannot be excused, nor such stupidity on mine. It would mean certain war. More deaths. At least if you run, we remain allied with the Regni.'

He tried to say something, anything that might be said in vindication, but nothing came out. His mouth just gaped open.

'Go,' she repeated. 'Now. Take everything. I want no memory of you here.' She clapped her hands and two men now entered, blades drawn. 'No,' she said firmly to them. 'He lives, but he was never here. And you heard nothing. Saw nothing. Do you understand me?'

They nodded.

Quintus stood and reached out to her with both hands. She turned her back on him, spat out one word.

'Go.'

Quintus stumbled out of the door, the two armed men escorting him. He blinked, surprised that it was still light. Fires still burned, music still played, sporting contests of various sorts were continuing to take place. There was noise and merriment. The sun was sitting higher above the horizon than it had any right to.

He mulled over the chain of events. The deaths were accidental, the funerary rites the best that they could manage.

He refused to consciously make the link between the deaths and the attack of the Regni. The first was one incident — unfortunate but managed with Roman efficiency. They were attacked. They defended themselves. They honoured the fallen. The second was an unprovoked attack on a people with whom they had just made friends. It was their duty to protect them. They had done so. He felt no guilt.

The men led him by a circuitous route that avoided the festivities, away from the inlet and the ships bobbing at anchor, the erstwhile *circus maximus*, as if he was some sort of naughty child being kept from a party. They brought him to the low and windowless thatched building that had served as the armoury for Crassus and Sextus. A few ageing chickens scratched around at its door. Holy chickens, Quintus guessed, otherwise — scraggy though they were — they would have been eaten.

The men pushed him inside the building. For a long moment, he assumed that he was being imprisoned, in which case his execution would follow shortly. Captives were only held in prison before slavery or death. He only knew of one permanent prison — the Carcer Tullianum on the slopes of the Capitoline in Rome, with its elevated view of the Comitium and rostra afforded briefly to the condemned before their death. Vercingetorix, leader of the Celts, had spent six years of captivity there, just so that his throttling could be an ornament to one of Caesar's triumphs.

But this was no prison. Within the dark recesses of the building were two faint shadows, the two despondent figures of Jovan and Maxim. There was little light due to the lack of windows, and the floor was dark mud and old rushes, but Quintus could see all the legionaries' gear in the corner.

Here were not only shields, armour and helms, but also spears, cloaks, and belts. There were even cooking pots, tentpoles, lengths of tattered canvas, satchels and wineskins. There was more, much more than they had brought with them. In this place all that had been cast upon the shore had been stored. The slaves had been busy. Some of the armour had been cleaned, and cloaks laid out to dry.

The Macedonians did not know how to greet Quintus, whether he had come to kill or free them. They did not even know what they were doing in this place. They had been led here after the battle, loaded with gear. They had then waited as various pieces of armour, weaponry and other flotsam had been brought in for them to store. They had been left alone in the dark, with no explanation and no knowledge of the Britons' tongue. In anticipation of the worst, they dropped to their knees.

One of the men escorting him poked his head through the opening. '*Omnes*,' he stated gruffly, waving his arm to encompass both slaves and gear, followed by something in his own tongue.

Quintus understood. It was all to go, on the command of Aucissa. There should be no trace that they were ever here. He turned to Maxim and Jovan.

'Up,' he ordered. 'On your feet. You are not yet condemned. Nor, luckily, am I. But we are banished, all of us, and ordered to take our gear, to erase all memory of our presence. Aucissa orders it.'

The slaves looked at the pile of gear and at Quintus, knowing that they would never be able to carry everything that was there.

'The men will help,' Quintus said, understanding their hesitation. 'You can begin to sort it into usable piles — a cloak each, a satchel if there are enough of them, a spear, a helmet, a shield, tent poles, canvas and ropes. There are six of us now, and you can carry the rest.' He turned to his escort. 'My men,' he said, in what he hoped was a tone of command. 'Where are the others, my companions?' He could not think of a way to indicate what he meant with gestures, but waved his arms around anyway. He showed them six fingers, praying that this was not some sort of insult.

Realisation dawned on the face of one, who spoke rapidly to his companion. They seemed to understand and indicated that he should follow them. They again took him on a roundabout route, a route that brought him down the hill to the table where his men sat. Clearly, he was not to be allowed contact with either of the tribes.

He was filled with despair when he saw the parlous state that his comrades were in. The Atrebates could have killed them all with little effort. Tan could have done it, Tan's girl even, for all the resistance there seemed to be in them.

Rufus' bright head was fully laid on the table, his folded arms providing a pillow. Crassus and Sextus had their arms around each other's shoulders, each with a cup in their hand, their eyes glazed and misted. Cato was alone, staring into the distance with unfocused eyes, seeing nothing but pain and loss in his future. Tullius, Quintus thought, was the worst. He sat on the floor beneath the trestle, repeatedly stabbing the ground with his dagger, all the while muttering furiously to himself.

Quintus gave an order, but only Cato came back from wherever his mind had been wandering, lifting his dark head. He gave a weak smile. 'So, you are back,' he said, ignoring what Quintus had actually said. 'I hope she was worth it.'

Quintus might have been moved to anger on another occasion, but he could see that such an emotion would not work with his friend — not with any of them. He decided to do the only thing he could, and adopted the harsh voice of the parade ground.

He snapped, 'Cornelius Cato Petronius, legionary, to your feet, soldier. Up.'

Cato was at first confused, but then, as he rubbed his eyes and they swam back into focus, he slowly pulled himself to his feet. His fist went to his chest mechanically, with no real conviction. 'Reporting for duty,' he said.

'And the rest of you, sober up, cheer up, get up. We are leaving.'

Crassus and Sextus looked at him questioningly. Tullius at least stopped stabbing the ground, but Rufus barely moved.

Quintus raised his voice to a harsher pitch. 'Legionaries of the Ninth, Roman citizens. Up, we are leaving.'

He would have kicked the table with his heavy sandals to dislodge Tullius, but his footwear had caused him enough trouble today, and the look of defiance the legionary gave him made him think that the knife in his hand might be turned on him if he continued. Instead, Quintus moderated his tone and offered his hand. 'Come,' he said.

As decanus of the contubernium, he was the nearest thing that the men had to an officer; they had chosen him themselves, and obedience had been drilled into them. Though they moved slowly, at least they moved, even helping each other.

Quintus explained their situation as they stood and glared at him, shoulders slumped. 'If we do not leave, and soon, we either drown or burn — it seems Rome does not have the monopoly on painful and bizarre methods of execution. If you want to die fettered to a post as the sea pours down your throat on the rising tide, or to feel your flesh shrivel and crisp as you burn in a flaming effigy, then stay.' He paused for effect. 'Otherwise, move. We must also take everything from this place.' He saw looks of curiosity cross the faces of Rufus and Tullius. 'Yes, Maxim and Jovan are safe, and they are with a great pile of gear — enough to turn us once more into fighting men.'

'Why would they let us go?' Crassus began to ask. 'Why would they let us arm? What have you agreed?'

'I thought that we were welcome here,' Sextus added.

'We were. No more. The queen blames herself for welcoming us, for letting us protect her.' He shrugged. 'She blames herself for the deaths on the bridge. She acknowledges our help but does not want to judge us — it is best for her, and us, that we just vanish. And not just us, but every trace of Rome.'

XXIII: CANTIACI

'That is not the whole story, is it?' Sextus cocked his head to one side like a thrush listening for worms in the grass. He pursed his lips and narrowed his eyes in doubt. 'You coupled with her — did that not break some law?'

'I have done nothing to offend these people,' Quintus answered, 'but the Regni tribe have taken offence, and they are allies of the Atrebates. We have walked into politics.'

'I will find out, Macilentus,' said Sextus darkly, using the nickname to make his promise more personal. 'There is more to it, I know. You know that I will find out.'

'Then I will tell you a tale when we are away, and safe. But for now, we have no time. We must be gone.'

'Into the midst of this forsaken lump of wet rock?' Rufus sulked, making to sit down again.

'Perhaps to the coast, and back across the sea to our own lands, if we can find a ship — but we must be quick,' Quintus insisted, taking hold of Rufus' arm. 'Once this day is over, there is nothing to stop these tribesmen hunting us down, and from what I have seen, their chariots are faster than we could ever be.'

Rufus shook him off in irritation, but he at least remained standing, looking to the others for their thoughts and actions.

Quintus seized the moment. 'Follow me. We collect the slaves and the gear and put this place behind us.' To his relief, they reluctantly recognised the call of duty, even if it was not blown by a cornicen. Their two guards, outnumbered now and wanting to be back at the festivities, brought up the rear.

The legionaries wondered, like Quintus had, about the nature of the building they were being asked to enter, but they followed his lead and ducked inside the long, low structure. As their eyes adjusted to the gloom, they saw the piles of gear, much of it neatly sorted, and the two Macedonians waiting to greet them. There was a curtain, which Crassus pulled back to reveal the stuffed straw men that had worn his and Sextus' armour.

'They had it on display,' he explained. 'They had cleaned and polished it; we think they might have been about to worship it.'

'Or sell it to the highest bidder.' Sextus' explanation was more likely.

The veterans, Rufus and Tullius, ignored the slaves and headed straight for the shadowy piles of metal and material. Cato, Sextus and Crassus at least greeted them though, in the dim light, neither master nor slave could read the expressions on the other's face. The two men that were Quintus' — and now the squad's — guards waited dutifully outside.

Rufus and Tullius were first to put on the armour — senior men, who knew what was good and what was not. The lorica laminata they initially flung to one side — some of it was battle-scarred and other pieces were shiny, apparently never worn, probably packed in the hold of one of the ships. Both men had hoped to find shirts of the traditional ring mail, rather than the new issue. Though he had worn it, Tullius had always cursed the new armour, calling it cheap and tawdry. He far preferred his own chainmail shirt, which had belonged to his uncle before him and had been worn with pride when he had served under Marcus Antonius with Legio XII Antiqua in Parthia. The earring he wore was in memory of an earlier repair.

Rufus, too, had been happy to take the expensive iron rings from a dead man after what had turned out to be the final battle against the Cantabrians, fought beneath the melting snows of the Picos in Hispania. He had gained permission to do so from General Agrippa himself. Both now harrumphed and held up several plated shirts to the weak light before deciding on the ones that they preferred. The new armour was lighter and more efficient than the heavy shirts. They knew that it was easier to wear and preferred by the emperor Augustus for his army. Both men pretended otherwise and summoned a slave apiece to help them with the ties even whilst they still complained.

The other legionaries may have looked on with a touch of disapproval, but they understood the veterans' preference for armour that had done them good service in the past. Crassus saw it as akin to wanting to mend a favourite hammer rather than forge a new one; Sextus as still lusting for a particular woman, even though her maiden's bloom had faded; Quintus as keeping an old horse, though its work days were over.

Crassus and Sextus found their own armour, while Quintus found a set discarded by the veterans, scratched and dented but cleaned by Maxim and Jovan, and Cato found himself in unfamiliar gear.

Jovan produced a helm, also dented, but polished bright. Diffidently, he offered it to Sextus who, looking inside, was delighted to find his own initials and 'DVF' inside it — exactly where he had expected them to be. '*Deducere Velatos Fortuna*', 'bring the wearer luck' had, he smiled, been an effective prayer once again. It was the second time in two days that the helmet had found its way back to him.

To feel the weight of the armour once more was familiar and reassuring, and they, along with the slaves, assisted each other with the ties. In addition to armour there were cloaks, helms and spears. Cato's own helmet, with its own history inscribed within it, was at the bottom of the ocean, but he was happy to accept a replacement. Rufus and Tullius tried the wineskins, but each was poured out on the ground as undrinkable.

'Yet keep the skins,' they commanded the Macedonians. 'They can be used for water.'

Satchels were emptied and anything useful kept, before each legionary slung one over his shoulder. There were even entrenching tools. Tullius offered to take charge of the canvas on his already laden crosspiece, but Rufus determined that there was not enough of it to make a tent — what could be found was ripped and beyond the skills of the Macedonians to mend. The tentpoles might be useful, and these they shared between them, leaving the canvas in a heap. There were more than enough shields, but the slaves could not be expected to carry the extra ones, not in addition to the bundles they had made. They propped them in a corner with other stuff that could not be disentangled or in some cases, even recognised.

As they finished loading themselves, Tan appeared, on his own and out of breath; clearly he had come at a run. He spoke to the guards, apparently ordering them back to the festival. They left happily.

He was still panting. 'I know you are leaving.'

'We have no choice,' Sextus told him, pointing at Quintus. 'This man is, apparently, once more our officer. He commands it.'

'The queen also commands it,' said Tan, his voice carrying more authority than his young face conveyed. 'She also commands that I travel with you. She commands that I tell no others, but she wishes you gone by the fastest route.' He turned to Quintus, adding, 'I think perhaps she still has a soft spot for you after all.' He then faced the other legionaries. 'Also, I have news for you, something Aucissa did not share, but which Elrik of the Regni shared with me. News that I think you may want to hear.'

'Good news?' Quintus asked.

'I think so. I will tell it on the way, but you must — we must — move.'

'Tell it now if it is good news,' Quintus instructed, hoping that it would motivate his men.

'I will tell it briefly, then,' said Tan, lowering his voice. 'I think your other comrades may have been seen.'

Cato at once jerked his head up. 'Tell us,' he pleaded. 'Tell us that Marcus and Lux live.'

'This is what I know. A group of Regni boys witnessed a curious happening on the beach,' he said. 'It sounds like it was legionaries, rather than tribesmen. Some of the boys were killed; some were thrown on a fire and burned. It is a strange tale.'

Quintus was at once despondent. He sighed deeply, ready to put an end to their hopes, then realised that Tan was still speaking.

'The boys, as they ran from their attackers and back to their fathers, saw two others of the same stamp, wearing tunics like normal men, but recognisable as foreigners by their lack of proper facial hair — also by their strange footwear, something Elrik realised when he demanded that you remove yours, my friend. Until then, he had not made the connection.'

'Two others,' three of the legionaries echoed.

'Two others,' Tan confirmed. 'They described them as a fair one and a fierce one. They clung on to each other, driven in by the waves, floating on some sort of square piece of wood…'

'The hatch cover,' said Cato excitedly. 'Publius was holding on to the hatch cover.'

'As you say,' said Tan, slightly taken aback by the obvious enthusiasm of the dark legionary. He picked up his thread. 'They had little but their tunics, belts, swords and daggers. They wore no helms or cloaks, and carried no other weapons. They seemed to recover quickly, the big one dragging the fair one along with him. The boys said that they did not follow the coast, but went straight inland, heading for woodland, no doubt seeking food and shelter.' He addressed Quintus directly. 'It is not many days, and they will have been weak and hungry. I think we should be able to find them or find news of them. They are strangers, so they will stand out. Other tribes — some of which are our allies — will have seen them.'

'Then we head inland? Agreed?' Quintus asked his contubernium.

They nodded or grunted assent, some with more enthusiasm than others. Cato and Sextus were most keen, Tullius and Rufus the least. Though they recognised the obligation to save lost comrades, as veterans they still thought that perhaps comrades should not find themselves in need of rescuing.

'Inland, then,' muttered Rufus, without excitement.

'I suppose so,' Tullius morosely agreed.

Tan looked into the hut to make sure that it was empty. It wasn't. 'This cannot be left here,' he said, seeing the stack of shields and the pile of discarded equipment. 'Dump it on the road if you must, but my orders are that nothing remains.'

Crassus and Cato looked at the veterans and sighed. They knew who would be carrying extra weight, for Jovan and Maxim were already heavily laden. The two legionaries reluctantly hoisted the shields, intending to carry them just as far as they must to satisfy the youth, whilst Sextus called Rufus to him to assist with the pile. Tullius looked on disapprovingly as Rufus complied. The men did not know why the Atrebates were so keen to let them go armed as for war, rather than keeping the weapons for their own use, until Tan explained that Commios had thought the weapons cursed with ill-luck, even the ones worn on the bridge.

Sextus, who believed in fates, reading entrails, augury and the futures written in the stars, told the others that Commios was wrong, that these things had proved lucky for the Romans, even though the spot where they were stored was probably unlucky. Quietly, having nothing to sacrifice, he offered a warding prayer to Dis and the guardians of the underworld, and another to Neptune. But a seed of doubt had been planted and Tullius, in his perceived role as *Fortuna mala*, the bringer of bad luck, let his head drop.

The men left, discarding the extra shields and equipment into a thicket of brambles as soon as they were able. Once clear of the settlement, Quintus was given the choice of a fast pace on a clear track, the way the Regni chariots had come, or the scrambling climb up a steep cliff path, down which they and the Regni foot soldiers had arrived. Tan advocated the former. Quintus chose the latter, explaining, 'I would rather be chased by men on foot than driving chariots.' Though the way was harder, the men made their agreement known.

No human watcher could have seen them through the thick swathes of trees that covered the land, but the pair of mewing goshawks that danced in the air above the woodland cloak observed with curiosity the strange parade of shadows that marched rapidly, picked out in black against the deepening hues of the sky. Tan led the way along the ridge that snaked away north, following the line of the river as it climbed away from the sounds and salt scents of the sea. Quintus was on his heels. Cato ran to catch up with them, asking, 'Where are we going?'

Tan pointed. 'North, away from the country of the Atrebates and its allies, towards the lands of the Cantiaci, where we think your comrades are.'

'For how long?'

'Until the light fails.'

'Then we keep going,' said Quintus. 'Lead on.'

The sun finally set, although the half-light lingered as the goshawks mewed their last, returning to the tall trees. Still, the relentless march continued, the legionaries barely noticing, apart from Crassus, who trailed at the rear. The injury to his back had been aggravated by the contest with the Regni, as well as the brutal battering that he had received in the storm. Now it felt like the one hurt that lingered and, because it was damage to the great muscles of his lower back, it affected everything he did. He found it difficult to sit comfortably, he could no longer squat, and he could not bend without uttering an involuntary cry of pain. He found marching painful and awkward, though after sufficient paces the wickedest bite of the pain was lessened and it subsided into a gnawing ache. He longed to rest, but he could not ask his comrades to stop. No-one, it seemed, was tired except him and the Macedonians. Maxim and Jovan would keep going until they dropped, for that was their duty. He would do the same.

Luckily, Quintus was not as blind as the blacksmith had thought him to be. He had noticed the involuntary cries during the rope pulling contest, he had seen the wincing as his friend sat down, and he noticed now how he began to lag behind. He had been there when the original attack, a cowardly thrust from behind, had landed his amicus in the surgeon's tent.

He sought a place to halt and make a temporary camp, not just for Crassus — they all needed rest.

XXIV: FORTUNA BONA

There was a dip in the ridge, as if some giant hand had scooped out a fistful of earth. In the centre of it, still water glistened darkly, a tarn. Beyond this, the ground rose once again, this time disappearing into a mess of jumbled boulders at the foot of a ragged clump of trees. Quintus thought that the track they marched on was dangerously exposed; this was the first cover that they had encountered, the first place where they could make a defendable position.

They traversed the dip, the flat and open land leaving them feeling vulnerable, and hurried towards the trees. As they reached them, Quintus called a halt and addressed the men. 'We should camp,' he said, 'at least for a short while. The slaves are flagging — and there is some cover, though we will have to improve it.'

Jovan and Maxim were about to protest — they did not want to be blamed for any delay, but Crassus interrupted them.

'Good idea,' he said, laughing. 'We do not want to wear them to nothing.'

'Are we being pursued?' Quintus asked Tan, taking him to one side as the men began to divest themselves of their baggage.

'Not yet.' Tan shook his head. 'Though the sun has set, the day is not yet over. They will wait until they are convinced it is the following day — the stars will tell them — then they will sacrifice. Then they will pursue.'

'So we have a few hours, at least?'

'I would say so.'

'And will they definitely pursue?'

'I believe they will.'

Quintus turned away in frustration — he had hoped that chasing after a small group of legionaries, stranded in their own vast country, would not have held any attraction for the Regni. He had hoped that Aucissa would tell them the truth of what had happened — that it was an accident, followed by an attempt at a respectful send-off. He had also hoped she would tell them that the legionaries were long gone and not worth chasing after.

The slaves had piled up the gear that they had been carrying and were beginning to collect firewood.

'No,' said Quintus. 'No fire. They would see the smoke for miles. There will be other work for you.' The two slaves backed away deferentially.

Tan had carried little and now seemed eager. 'I should take my turn on guard,' he offered.

'There will not be time,' Quintus replied flatly. 'We are here for a short while only; this will be but a brief rest.'

He had an idea of when the moon would rise, and how much light it would give, and Sextus seemed to know these things by instinct. Most of the squad could easily have continued the march in the dark, but Quintus knew that Maxim, Jovan and Crassus would have collapsed with exhaustion. He thought about speaking to his amicus about his injury, but he knew that this would only result in a bout of temper and a determination to show how uninjured he was by taking on extra weight or extra work. Quintus sighed; he could not risk this, though he wanted to comfort his friend.

Instead he issued orders to all and then watched with pain of his own as Crassus did his duty through gritted teeth. 'Basic defences — we will not be here long. We need a rampart of stones to the north and south — any attack is likely to come along the ridge — and a ditch behind it. We will also need to keep watch to the east and west. Tullius, Rufus, Sextus, you take the first watch. The rest of you sleep. We will be on our way again once the moon is risen. Sextus, I trust you will know when to wake us, when to change the watch.'

'I will have an idea,' Sextus replied. 'You will get little more than an hour and a half.'

'It will have to do,' said Quintus. He looked at the Macedonians, squatting in the place where the fire should be. 'Food and fresh water: fill the skins,' he commanded. 'Do you have needles still?'

'From amongst the rescued gear, yes,' said Jovan.

'Then see what needs mending — you will have to sew whilst we wear the garments.'

'Of course.' Jovan bowed his head.

'Then you too should rest,' he added, almost as an afterthought.

The camp was soon enough constructed. Though the defences were not ideal, they were better than any other army's would have been. Quintus was still uneasy, he believed in open country, sight lines, foreknowledge of an attack. The first watch went to their places, low conversation began then faltered. Jovan approached to set about mending their clothes.

Tullius and Rufus waved him away — he was not coming near them with a needle in the dark — and Sextus did the same. If he had mending to do, it would be in daylight. Cato was talking to Tan, trying to see if there was any more information about Publius. Crassus already slept. Quintus also refused Jovan's offer, settling himself with his back against a tree with his gladius across his knees. The Macedonians filled the skins with water from the tarn, feeling horribly exposed as they did so, even though Cato and Tan accompanied them as guards. They took it back to the men, then settled down to sleep.

Cato left Tan and came to squat next to Quintus. 'Tell me why we are being pursued,' he said. 'Tell me the truth. Sextus and Crassus seem to know, but will not say. Tan has told me about the boys on the beach — that legionaries murdered children, then set fire to them. Tell me that was not you. Tell me that was not the reason for our oath to that woman.'

'It may have been the reason,' admitted Quintus with a sigh, 'though that is not the truth of it.'

'I have spoken with Maxim also, and found out what he knows.'

Quintus started, his eyes now fully open.

'No, no. Do not be vexed at him. He had no choice. I can be very persuasive — especially when I have part of a story and merely need someone to fill in the details. I fooled him. He is only a slave and a Macedonian, after all. What happened?'

'We were exhausted and unprepared.' Quintus made the excuses first. 'Two attackers came at us. We reacted instinctively…'

'We?'

'I had given — lent — Jovan a blade in order to protect his cousin from wild animals. Maxim was unconscious. We had no idea where we were or what dangers might await…'

Cato was shocked. 'A blade — to a slave — when there were two of them and one of you. Do you not know of the Servile Wars?'

'I know of Spartacus, yes,' snapped Quintus. 'Jovan is no gladiator, no *murmillo*…'

'But he was a soldier before he was taken.' Cato was insistent.

'He was a factor before he was a soldier. He is no Spartacus,' said Quintus with exasperation. 'I trusted him with a blade. And Maxim was dead to the world. It was my decision.'

'And the result?'

'We were equally to blame, I with my gladius, he with my pugio. Two attackers fell.'

'Attackers?'

'They turned out to be children.' He held up a hand to stop Cato from interrupting. 'We did not know. We were taken by surprise. We struck instinctively…'

Cato was squatting in front of Quintus and rocked back on his heels. He bit his lip and shook his head. 'It sounds unavoidable — an accident,' he said slowly.

'And so it was — you would have done the same…'

'But the fire — why the fire? Were you trying to destroy evidence?' His tone betrayed incredulity.

'No. It was made out of respect to them — it was a funeral pyre.' Quintus looked at his feet. 'It did not work — the wood was too damp. We placed Charon's obol in each of their mouths to pay for their passage. We did all we could.'

There was a silence between them, each avoiding eye contact with the other.

Cato settled back down. 'And the woman knew this?' he asked.

'She knew. I explained. But the dead were of the Regni tribe. They attacked the Atrebates without thought, thinking that Aucissa sheltered us. She did, but the way they came they gave us no choice but to defend ourselves — and the Atrebates.' He shook his head again. 'It was all a mistake. To prevent war, she will let the Regni men follow us, but not until the religious festival is over.'

'The gods laugh at us,' was all Cato could say. 'They sport with us. Maybe Tullius is right. Maybe we have failed in our duty to them. Mistakes and accidents are made by men, but they are caused by the immortals. None of us have made the correct sacrifices since we landed. We have done nothing to ward off ill luck. By Neptune and Dis, we have not even yet thanked the gods for our safe arrival.'

Quintus did not reply. There was nothing to say. Cato was right.

Cato muttered to himself and walked off into the trees on his own, drawing his sword, half hoping to find something, anything, that he could sacrifice to the gods. Quintus watched him with half-closed eyes and an expression of resignation on his face.

'The gods laugh at us,' he repeated Cato's words to himself, 'at me.' He felt for the package that contained Ursus' treasures. 'I have not failed yet,' he hissed in defiance, 'nor will I, whatever you do.'

Sextus would have been horrified at such a challenge to the gods, but he was not there to hear it, and fortunately nor was Tullius.

A noise alerted Quintus. He looked towards the woodland. Cato was returning, dragging a body, which Quintus thought at first was a beast, a sacrifice to the gods. He started when he realised that it was no animal.

The men were all awake and eager to know what had happened, what latest disaster had befallen them; even Maxim and Jovan were here, though standing well back. Cato stood facing the rest, gladius and pugio both drawn and bloodied. Behind him he clutched the body of Tan, his chest and midriff exposed and streaked with dirt, his tunic stained red, bunched around his neck where the legionary was using it to drag him. He somehow looked even younger than he had when alive, like, Quintus thought with a churning of his stomach, a child.

The men all spoke at once, asking questions and cursing, voices tumbling over each other like a river over rocky rapids. Quintus put up a hand and waited for quiet, demanding in a low but insistent tone, 'What happened?'

'This you must know first,' said the dark legionary urgently. 'We are in great danger. Whatever this boy said, the Regni men have set out already in pursuit. I am certain they will be here shortly. He has told them where we are.'

'Rufus, Tullius, go back and guard the southern approach. Raise the alarm if you see our pursuers,' Quintus ordered. 'I will relay what Cato says as soon as I am able.' He turned back to Cato. 'Why have you killed this boy?'

'Not a boy,' spat Cato, 'a man — and a liar and a traitor. He confessed before he died.'

'Confessed?' Sextus asked.

'Confessed,' Cato confirmed with a hiss. 'He is a friend, a cousin even, to Elrik's woman, and thus family to the Regni chieftain. He has been a spy in our midst ever since we first met him. He has told the Regni where we are and —' his voice rose with indignation — 'he has told me where to find Marcus and Publius. He knew all along, and he intended to lead us into a trap.'

The men again began talking all at once. Quintus once more raised a hand for quiet. 'Is the enemy close, Cato?'

'They were close enough to see this boy's signal,' the legionary replied.

'How was the signal sent?' Sextus asked. 'From how far away would it be seen?'

Cato looked up at the sky. 'A long way, comrade. He used the birds.'

'Tell us how,' said Sextus, the flight of birds being one of his specialities for forecasting the future, as it was for the College of Augurs.

'I sought an animal to sacrifice. We have had such ill luck that I thought that something, anything — even a squirrel or a fox — would help to show the gods that we have not abandoned them, and that they should not punish us.' He wiped perspiration from his forehead. 'Instead, I found the boy. He was on the ground — I thought he had fallen and was perhaps injured, but then he crouched, clearly unhurt, and I wondered what he was doing. I stopped and hid myself as he stood up. There was a long, straight branch in his hand, which he struck against the bole of a tree, making it ring with the force of his blows. There was a noise, cawing and complaining — like fishwives on the banks of the Tiber — then dozens of rooks rose, flapping and calling harshly above the trees. I had not realised what he was doing until he turned and saw me. "Too late!" he shouted. "I have done it." The rooks were meant to reveal our position.' Cato glared down at the corpse. 'His face, this innocent face, was bright with sweat, and his voice was full of triumph. "What are you doing?" I asked. "Sending a signal, a message — you Romans will not last the night," he told me. The expression on his face was twisted with such hatred. He was never a friend — he was an enemy, always.' He let the body fall and hawked at it in disgust.

'The signal would have been visible for miles,' said Crassus.

'Then perhaps they are not close,' Quintus said. The others nodded in mute agreement. 'We may have time to set a trap of our own. There is no point in running; they will just run after us.' Turning to Cato, he asked, 'What else did he tell you? What about Marcus and Publius?'

'He has known where they are all along and is leading us into an ambush with the tribe that has captured them. He means to put paid to us with either the enemy behind us, or the one in front. If the Regni warriors catch up with us, they will deliver any left alive to these captors. If we are all dead, he would be there to witness the deaths of Marcus and Publius.'

'Do you know where?' Crassus asked.

'With my knife at his throat, he told me.' Cato turned to his decanus. 'Quintus, I would have kept him alive, brought him here to question, but he fought so fiercely, with his hands tight around my neck, that I had to kill him.' He touched the red weals on his neck where his focale should have been tied. 'You took his plan from him, Quintus. He intended the fire as a signal; he did not know you would forbid one.'

Quintus nodded thoughtfully and looked at Cato. 'Luck, perhaps?' Both involuntarily glanced in the direction of Tullius, on guard duty.

'*Fortuna bona* for a change?' Cato said.

'I hope so.'

XXV: COGINUS

Cato had finished his tale and Quintus nodded his approval of the legionary's actions. He thought briefly, then turned to Maxim and Jovan and said, 'This spy may yet be of use to us. Bring him now.' As the slaves lifted Tan's limp body, Quintus grabbed spears from where they were stacked against each other then led them to the spot where Tullius and Rufus kept watch.

'Any sign of them?'

'I see no movement on the ridge,' said Rufus, 'but it drops beyond the tarn, and would easily hide men.'

'At least they cannot use chariots,' said Tullius. 'It is too steep.'

It was quiet and the moon had yet to rise. The dark waters of the tarn could be seen below them, a deeper black patch in the starlit grey of the short grass. Quintus spoke quietly, his voice carrying clearly in the still night air. 'Cato tells us that they come. The boy told him at knifepoint, so it is likely to be true. He also told him where Marcus and Publius are, that they live still. We could rescue them. All we have to do is defeat the Regni warriors.' He gestured to Maxim and Jovan, who carried the boy's corpse by its shoulders and feet. 'He will help,' he said.

It was immediately apparent that the attackers had not expected any resistance. The signal, the message, from Tan had been clear and unequivocal, though it was not the fire signal they had agreed. Still, the flight of rooks, suddenly taking off from the dark grove of trees on the skyline, was clear. They could not know that Tan had been discovered and was dead. Even had he not been, the Regni tribe were unaware of the almost religious zeal of the Romans when it came to defence — even in friendly country, the men were trained to build a defensive position, even if only stopping briefly. Legionaries gave it no thought, the actions were ingrained.

Quintus had only called a halt when they had found a position that could be defended. To east and west this bluff of higher ground was flanked by steep rock gullies. To the north it reared up in a knotty formation of rock and tufty grass, topped with a scrappy collection of determined trees. Any attack would have to come past the rough and boggy ground below.

From their raised position, the legionaries could see a long way south, to where the ridge first widened, enfolding the tarn in its arms, then flattened and tapered, with just a narrow path running along it. Of course, where their camp was sited, the Romans had built a wall of sorts, providing both a defensive line and a vantage point.

Quintus watched as the attackers approached quietly, casting many shadows in the starlight and signalling to each other. They carried long swords or axes, balanced with small, round shields. The legionaries' own shields Quintus had ordered laid flat, so that they did not catch the light and reveal their presence.

Quintus recognised the outline of Coginus at the front — tall, broad, and with a halo of spiky hair. Light glinted from his upper arms and wrists, he grasped a war axe in one hand and a long spear behind the shield in the other. Others were ranged behind and to either side of him; though Quintus could only make out a dozen or so, he thought there must be more.

After a hurried conference, they divided to go around the dark patch of water, stopping and reforming when they reached the other side. Their whispering voices rose and fell in the stillness of the night. One pointed in the legionaries' direction, where a single torch was lit, flickering sullenly at the top of the rise. The outline of a Roman could be seen behind it, armed and helmed, the discipline of his immobility admired by the Britons.

As they approached the torch, the Regni warriors ducked down but continued to slowly move forward. They waited, but all that disturbed the air was the gentlest of breezes in the grass. The only sounds were the sputtering of the flame and the distant bark of a fox.

Suddenly, at a sign from their leader, the tribesmen rose as one and shouted — defiance, insults, a wall of noise that was meant to frighten the enemy, to sow panic. But the legionary didn't move, not until a spear thudded into him, piercing his chest and sending him reeling backwards. The torch dropped at his side, still burning feebly.

With a great shout of victory, the tribesmen breasted the little wall, knocking the structure aside with their shields, before, with a cold shock of comprehension, they realised that this single guard had been dead already, propped up by a pair of spears. As the figure tumbled backwards, his helm had come away from his head, and the torch revealed the youthful face and long hair of Tan — a face that would now never grow the moustache that he had so craved.

Coginus shouted a warning, but it was too late. They had been caught in the jaws of the trap, and spears flew out from further back in the darkness, catching some men in the chest, some in the belly, some in the thigh. The chieftain took a spear in his shoulder, where it stayed as it spun him round. It had gone straight through him, the point sticking out of his back, the haft stopping him from moving. He tried to lift the arm holding his axe, but it was this side that the spear had pierced, and his hand, though it still gripped the weapon, refused to respond. He dropped to one knee, his shield cutting into the ground, then managed to turn to face his nemesis, these demons in the dark. With a strangled curse he pitched forward onto his face, the spear snapping beneath him.

Some of the others were injured, but still they kept moving forward, swords, axes and shields held high. Gradually they became aware of the fate of Coginus, causing them to waver. Without their chief, they were in disarray. Contradictory orders were shouted by those who, from different places, saw different things. As yet none saw an enemy other than the one they had felled, and he was no Roman. Quintus had ordered his men to stay and let the enemy come to them, to meet them as a line of sharpened death rather than fight them face to face, or tangle with them in the open.

The spears had done what they were intended to do: they had broken the discipline of the attackers. Mars and Fortuna had been with them in that they had taken out the leader of the Regni tribe. The others now did not seem to know what to do. They shouted challenges into the dark, but of course, the legionaries could not understand them. Even if they could, they would not have reacted.

'Cato, Sextus — can you pick them off?'

The legionaries nodded, each with a spear in hand.

'Rufus, Tullius, how about you?'

The veterans each touched a fist to their chests in the traditional salute. With their swords in a firm grip, they lifted their rectangular shields.

'Crassus, with me — I want none to escape. Loose, men, and forward!'

Cato and Sextus pitched the spears, finding two targets, as the other four, with Quintus at their head, attacked.

As the legionaries took the fight to the tribesmen, the moon rose over their right shoulders — a half-moon, but enough that the shadowy forms of the enemy could now be clearly seen. *Contendite vestra sponte*, Quintus thought, though he did not give the order for general engagement. His comrades knew what to do. His own sharp blade found a home in the flesh of one of the tribesmen, a dark and broad-shouldered man with an axe raised high, exposing his chest and belly. Bizarrely — at least to the Roman — he wore no garment on his upper body, not even a leather jerkin to give him some protection.

It meant that there was nothing to prevent Quintus slicing across his belly and moving, in two steps, on to the next. He swept his shield backwards, sending the man, already off balance, to the ground. The warrior's cry of challenge was at once cut off and his free hand automatically went to his opened flesh. He could not bring the axe to bear, and was instead smashed to his knees by Quintus' shield. He let out a long and unearthly groan; he would die in that spot and would take an age to do so. The legionary had already moved on, this time to one who had been injured at the same time as his chieftain — one who still carried the broken shaft of a spear in his thigh. Though he tried to rise, he could not, and received Quintus' blade at the side of his neck, an executioner's blow, the point driven down and deep into his heart.

Crassus had also picked out an opponent, this one with spiked hair and a long moustache. His mouth was wide open and his head tipped back as he howled like a wolf to the risen moon. It seemed to be some sort of ritual. Crassus moved forward, severed the man's exposed windpipe and sidestepped the fountain of blood that resulted, using his shield to protect him.

Quintus looked eagerly for more enemies in the silver light, but was disappointed. No more of the tribesmen stood, but nor had any fled. Cato and Sextus were pulling their spears out of the men they had targeted, also looking round for further victims. Crassus was struggling to unsheathe his sword from one of the warriors. It was lodged on something — the man's ribs, probably — so Crassus had to push his boot against the man's back in order to pull his weapon free. The victim moaned as he was pushed into the dirt and tried to rise, but Crassus placed his foot firmly on his neck and, with a sharp downward movement of one of his studded caligae, broke it. The moaning ceased.

Rufus and Tullius appeared to have despatched the rest of the party, some of whom had been injured by the spears. They were standing warily now, back to back, weapons and shields ready. The noise of combat had ceased and the legionaries were rooted, watching the tribesmen for any movement. They wanted to be sure that none survived. Quintus took a long step and bent down to slit the throat of his first victim, whose eerie moans, like the wind in the reeds, died with him. The silence that followed was profound as they all looked south in anticipation of more foes.

Each legionary had automatically moved to be close to his partner. They all expected another attack, Cato and Sextus with spears poised, the others with their swords in one hand and their daggers in the other.

But no immediate second wave came, and there was no sound of advance.

'To me,' ordered Quintus, and the four men quickly came to stand by him and Crassus, all close together in a semi-circle, still wary. Their backs were to their own little rampart and the prone figure of Tan, the slaves crouching in fear by his body.

Quintus held his hand up. 'Silence,' he ordered, 'listen.'

There was nothing. No sound. Even the wind in the grass and the rustling of the leaves was stilled. Even the death-rattles and whines of the victims had ceased. The bark of the distant fox had long since died on the air

The legionaries stiffened as the moon sailed behind a cloud and the scene was plunged into sudden darkness, but still no assault came. Instead a fine rain began to fall.

Tullius wiped his nose with the back of his hand. 'There are no more,' he said.

'I think you are right,' said Rufus. 'I hear none.'

'And I feel none,' Sextus added.

'Yet keep your guard up,' Quintus whispered. 'Back behind the wall. Keep in formation.'

The six legionaries stayed close to each other as they stepped backwards, away from the tarn and back towards the trees. Quintus and Crassus were in the centre, Sextus and Cato were on the flanks, and Tullius and Rufus filled in the gaps. Even as they stumbled over the broken rock wall, they stayed together and stayed silent. Only once they had reached the confines of their camp, did they lower their weapons and start talking quietly amongst themselves. They were not given time to relax.

'Crassus, Cato, guard duty,' Quintus ordered. 'I cannot believe that this is all that was sent after us. We must stay watchful.' He looked around the clearing in the damp gloom. He was trying to pick out the figures of the Macedonians. Seeing them huddled by the slain spy, he said, 'You two, take anything of use from the boy, and tip him over the wall with his friends. I would not have him defile our camp any longer. Do not light a fire. Dawn will not be long.'

He was right. Though the cloud had obscured both moon and stars, he could feel the warmth and light growing in the west, even whilst he cursed the continuing rain. 'It is supposed to be summer,' he grumbled, 'high summer at that. In Rome, we would be gasping from the heat. The rich would have run for the coast.' He breathed in the damp air. 'At least it smells sweet, and does not stink like the city in the heat.'

Even the clouds, which had become darker and heavier with rain, could not hold the dawn at bay for long, and soon a pale light shone on the still bodies of the enemy. A morning mist softened the scene, blurring the edges and making it ghostly. A rustling at the edge of the clearing told them that animals had discovered them already, and a fox could be seen moving as a shadow amongst them.

None had slept and, whilst Crassus and Cato had officially taken guard duty, no-one had dropped their watchfulness, all peering towards where the ridge dropped away. Their eyes searched past the disturbed surface of the tarn, punctured by spasmodic raindrops, expecting more Regni warriors or their allies.

'How many did we kill?' Quintus asked Cato.

'I count around a dozen, I think, maybe more. Some we took with javelins to start with. They are the ones over there. Their chieftain, the first to fall, is lower down the slope.'

A body lay twisted, face down, the sharp point of a spear protruding from its back.

'Coginus,' said Quintus, recognising him. 'An important man.' He looked around, still expecting further enemies to emerge from the morning — but none came.

XXVI: VELITATIO

Cato continued his tally. 'After the chieftain had fallen, Sextus and I speared two more. You got two, Crassus, including the one running away. I suspect he will not be welcome in whatever halls the dead of this island inhabit. Quintus, you took two — one carved in half, but it still counts as just the one.' He smiled a grim smile, then continued to count. 'Four at least taken by Rufus and Tullius…'

'And the spy.' Crassus moved his gaze to just beyond their makeshift wall. 'I am sorry for the boy. I liked him.'

'As did I. But I had no choice. Even with my knife at his throat, he tried to kill me. I could not quieten him — he had to die.'

Quintus nodded. He understood. 'Perhaps he will be welcome in their lands of the fallen. I hope so.'

Crassus looked again at the scene. 'We took no more than a dozen, we think, perhaps a few more. It was no more than a skirmish, a *velitatio*.'

'And are they all dead?'

'As far as we can tell. Look.' Crassus pointed to the ghostly figure of the fox moving amongst the dead. It did not seem afraid.

Smiling, Quintus realised that the beast had invited its family. A vixen, he thought, for now two or three cubs could be seen, exploring the remains for themselves. 'None live,' he pronounced, 'or the cubs would not be here — but before we move, we need to know if any more follow.'

'Do we wait, or carry on?' Cato looked up at Quintus pleadingly. He had not asked the question that he wanted to ask, and Quintus knew this.

He put a hand on Cato's shoulder. 'We will carry on soon — I know we have comrades to rescue. But for now we wait. I want to know if more enemy follow on our heels.'

Leaning against tree stumps, they half slept as they waited for the sun to fully rise and burn off the mist. Quintus wanted to send a man down the slope, through the boggy ground by the tarn to look south down the ridge, the way they had come. They could not do this until the weather cleared; they could not light a fire until they knew they were not pursued.

Cato chafed, wanting to get on with the rescue; Crassus also hated the delay; Tullius and Rufus, as old campaigners, understood that sometimes unpleasant things came from the decisions of commanders, so could cope with a little damp — at least the decision to wait would not cost them their lives.

Tullius, as ever, passed the time polishing his equipment, whilst Rufus had begun to carve some dice from a promising piece of wood.

They had a small supply of hard biscuit, rescued from the bags that the Atrebates had stored in the hut, but, for anything else they carried, Jovan would need fire and water to make it edible. Quintus knew that the Macedonians would be better off if they were occupied, so he sent them — with little hope of success — to find fresh food of some sort.

They brought back acorns, wild strawberries, a soft green fruit that Maxim had found to be bitter, and a few other poor berries that might or might not have been poisonous.

Rufus and Tullius were now up by the wall, while Cato and Crassus were talking with Quintus. Sextus was lying on his back, with his helmet off and his head beneath the trees in a vain attempt to keep off the rain. His hair had never looked so dishevelled. 'Is it food?' he demanded, looking at the berries.

'We don't know,' Maxim replied. 'Unless we see a beast eat it without harm, we don't know.'

As he lowered his head, a small patch of blue sky appeared above them, seeming to grow and push the dark clouds apart. The clouds first became lighter and then, like an early frost, melted away. The sun blazed out and the rain first lessened then swiftly stopped.

Quintus looked south along the ridge to where the shadows were melting away, to where the colours of summer, bright greens and yellows, were once more shining out. The surface of the tarn blazed silver and gold. Some few great raindrops lingered at the edges of leaves, but soon dried and wisps of steam arose from the damp ground. Suddenly, the legionaries were warm.

'Once we have made sure that we are not followed, we light a fire and eat.' Quintus stepped over the wall, seizing the two spears that had been used to hold Tan's body upright. Crassus and Rufus followed. He handed them to his comrades whilst drawing his own sword. 'Take anything that may be of use.'

Rufus was first to the fallen Regni chieftain — he had seen the belt of bronze rings before and coveted it, though he would never be allowed to wear it once he returned to the legion. Quintus was not about to stop him from taking it. Other booty included weapons, torcs and rings. Their clothes and footwear were left alone; the footwear did not seem sturdy, and the clothes were strange and impractical. They did not protect, and the long, loose undershorts the tribesmen wore would be a liability in battle. Between them, the legionaries turned over each of the bodies that were not already face up. They recognised none of them except Coginus.

Crassus turned the last one over with his foot and seemed disappointed, shaking his dark curls. 'I thought Elrik — the ship's captain — would be with them.'

Quintus considered, then said, 'I think Elrik is honouring his own gods. These men must have set off during the festivities; they must have left before the holy day was ended.'

Rufus looked with professional detachment at the remains. 'Perhaps that is what cursed them?'

Quintus pursed his lips. 'Perhaps — only the gods know. We must be sure that we are not followed. Give me the spears. I will take both of them, just in case, but I will go alone.' He knew he was probably the swiftest of the legionaries at present. Tullius had his moods, Crassus his injury, Cato his anxieties, Sextus his hair. He could have taken Rufus with him, but he decided that the men needed him more. 'Rufus, I will not be long. Can you get them organised? Stay here and dry yourselves, your weapons and your clothes in the sun.'

Rufus smiled — he had received such temporary promotions before. 'Can we light a fire on your return?'

'As long as it is clear, yes.'

'Then I will organise our camp as if it is clear.'

Quintus handed his helmet to Crassus, with the admonition to look after it, and his shield to Rufus, then set off at an efficient trot down the slope. He would have to skirt the tarn, and the bog that had temporarily grown with the rain, and this was where he would be at his most vulnerable, with no cover, especially if an enemy had decided to approach from east or west. It was a ridge, yes, but hardly a dragon-back, it would not be impossible to climb the bank — especially at this point. He kept as low to the ground as he could, glancing into the shallow valleys to his left and right, even across to the river snaking its way through the flat land to the east, but the priority was speed.

Quintus ran down the gentle slope, keeping his profile as minimal as possible, the spears held parallel to the ground, his knees bent. He felt the ground begin to soften beneath his feet and moved to the eastern edge, skirting the dark waters of the tarn and seeking dry land. He stumbled a couple of times, but quickly righted himself. Once more on firm ground, though closer to the lip of the ridge than he wished, he continued.

He glanced back at their little camp on the skyline, marked by the sparse trees. He saw that a fire would have provided a signal obvious from many miles away, and acknowledged the cleverness of Tan in disturbing the rooks instead.

Reaching the point where the ridge rose slightly, before sweeping back down, he sank into a crouch. If Regni warriors, Atrebates or others had been close, they would have concealed themselves here. He flattened himself to the ground and peered over the edge into the shallow. There was bracken and coarse grass, spindly bushes and gorse, the narrow track winding between small outcrops. There was no one there.

Looking south, down the rolling length of the ridge up which they had travelled, Quintus could see no sign of any pursuit. To the east, running in tandem with the ridge, the surface of the river was smooth, reflecting the sunlight in shimmering silver. It vanished and re-emerged from the trees several times as it meandered down its shallow valley, but he could see no boats on it, no sign of fires beside it, though the thick cloak of trees would be more than enough to hide an entire army. He looked for dust thrown up by horses' hooves, and for birds disturbed from their normal places, but there was no sign of anyone tracking them.

He wanted to be absolutely sure. He waited for what seemed an age, long enough for the sweat to dry on his neck. There was no noise or movement, no pursuit that he could see — and he could see a long way. He relaxed at last, giving silent thanks to Jupiter and to his own household gods, but still he did not stand, knowing that, just as he could see for many leagues south, his tall figure would be visible, silhouetted against a bright blue sky that had decided it was high summer after all, to any watchers scanning north.

He began the journey back up the slope in high spirits. From what he could calculate, he was sure that, had Elrik set out at all, he would by now be able to see him. Whilst the rain would annoy those — like them — who had no fire and little shelter, it would not have stopped anyone intent on a march. He thought that, before they continued north, they would at least have a chance to rest. He hoped that, if Tan's information was accurate, they would have enough time to find their comrades and to plan a rescue for them.

His return to the others was greeted with a barrage of questions, to all of which he replied, 'No sign of anyone, of any pursuit. For now, we are safe.'

The men had moved the bodies of the Regni warriors, piling them in the undergrowth, close to the treeline. 'More convenient for the foxes,' Rufus joked.

'Maxim, Jovan,' Quintus ordered, giving his pugio to the latter, 'cut a trophy from each corpse — a thumb, a scrap of cloth, an ear, whatever is easy.' He was going to ask Crassus for his blade, but, seeing the look on his friend's face, he decided not to. 'Then make a fire and lay the trophies beside it,' he added.

The legionaries began to lay out the various packs in the sun, wiping excess water away. As if they were on campaign, each of them fashioned a crosspiece, from which bags and equipment would hang. Each had a satchel also, rescued from the sea. The rest of the gear they split up so that each of them carried the same.

'Master, we have kindling,' Jovan told Quintus.

'Then make fire,' Quintus said. 'It will burn long enough for us to eat and sacrifice, no more.'

Maxim and Jovan had found dry kindling in the sparse woodland, underneath the thick layer of fallen leaves that had lain undisturbed for months. The further down they delved, the drier the material. With difficulty, they started a fire and then, once it was coaxed into flame, they were able to feed larger boughs into it. Maxim finished taking the trophies, then stacked his grisly haul on a flat stone.

As the fire crackled Quintus gathered the men, pulled his cloak over his head and spoke to Janus, god of beginnings. 'Hear us, Janus, we would make offerings.' He indicated the pile of thumbs, ears and cloth scraps. 'Take one, throw it in the flames. It is all we have to offer the gods, and it is better than nothing.'

The men complied, either covering their heads, or putting a hand to their foreheads as the fire sizzled and smoked. Each of them offered a prayer of thanks as their eyes followed the path of the smoke up into the heavens, now clear of cloud. Each of them included their own household deities as well as Jupiter, Mars and Mithras. The smoke at least showed them to be devout.

With salvaged grain, though much of it was wet, Maxim managed to make a sort of coarse flour, which he wrapped around green sticks and cooked over the hottest part of the fire. The legionaries enjoyed the food and the sun, and they dreamed of being at home, but Quintus was still nervous, especially of the smoke.

'Quench the fire,' he ordered, as he walked across to squat down next to Cato. 'Well, Nox. Where are we going?'

Cato wiped his hands on the grass and looked ahead. 'We continue to the north for a day, perhaps two — it was difficult to understand much of what the boy said. He kept lapsing into his own language. Even when he was dying, he was exulting in his victory, cursing all Romans, switching from Latin to his own tongue and back again. In amongst this, I heard him say "your friends" and then laugh horribly. I thought he meant you, and then I realised...'

'Publius and Marcus?'

'So I took it to be. I grabbed him after he had sent the rooks soaring. First he kicked and hissed and cursed, then punched, then bit, then managed to wrestle his hands into a grip on my throat. I managed to draw my knife and stab him, only then could I prise his fingers from my neck for still he would not let go. I managed to pin him down, my knee on his neck, my knife at his throat, but he was dying already from the belly wound I had given him. I could see no way to force him to speak.' He lowered his head and looked at the ground. 'He was convinced that he was going to their version of the underworld. "I will be a hero to my people," he boasted. "I will have honey and wine aplenty."'

'So what did you do?'

'I made up a story. I warned him that the gladius was a magic sword, that death from it would deny him entry to the underworld and would condemn him to wander as a shade forever. I told him that this is what happens to all of Rome's enemies. I held his jaw in my hand and looked into his eyes, his soul. I told him that all our swords had such magic, that he had been caught in its web when he had licked blood from the blade.'

'You knew of that?'

'He had boasted of it.'

'And he believed you?'

'I saw the fear grow in his eyes and felt him go limp beneath my hand. I lifted my knee from his throat — I needed him to survive a little longer. "Tell me where they are," I said.' Cato let his fist relax. 'That's when he told me. I believe him.'

XXVII: COMPITALIA

Quintus gently steered Cato back on course. 'Just repeat what Tan said. We will sort out the detail afterwards.'

'North, two days. We will reach a crossroads. At the crossroads we go east for a day or half a day — not too long, anyway. A tribe of the east have Publius and Marcus. They will sacrifice them at the end of the celebrations for the solstice. They intend to burn them alive, Quintus.' Cato was almost sobbing.

'Did Tan say when the celebrations will end?'

'I don't know — it could be just a day. The start, I think, must be marked by the sacrifice of the horse, the sacrifice that we saw — and that is two days since already.' He bowed his head, black locks falling across his brow, hiding his tears. 'If that is as long as it lasts, we are already too late.'

'But it may last longer,' Quintus insisted. 'It may depend on the portents. Festivals in Rome could be anything from a day to a week.'

'We must pray that this is the same — several days, or even open-ended.' Cato grasped for an example. '*Fors Fortuna* in summer was open-ended. It didn't finish until all the food and drink had gone. We still have hope.'

Quintus put a consoling hand on his comrade's shoulder. 'We will not abandon them, Cato. As long as we do not know that they are dead, then they live. Let us have faith that Fortuna is with us for once.'

Cato lifted his head. Beneath his dark brows, his eyes looked less bright than usual. Whilst he had been euphoric over the information regarding his friend, he had clearly taken no pleasure in killing Tan — spy though he was.

'At least Publius is with Marcus,' Quintus said, trying to lift Cato's spirits, 'a man of substance, a legionary who has been both optio and centurion, probably the most experienced and best qualified soldier of us all. If he had to be wrecked at sea and taken captive by barbarians, he would have chosen Marcus as his companion, for the best chance of survival and escape.'

'I think he might have chosen me,' said Cato quietly.

'You are right. Of course — he would have chosen you.' Quintus spoke softly, with affection.

The tall decanus moved away, issuing orders to the men, readying them to move out swiftly. The fire was already extinguished, its remnants smothered with damp leaves and soil.

'The dead?' Crassus asked.

'Leave them for scavengers.'

As the men hoisted their packs and readied to move out, Quintus decided that it had not been an entirely unprofitable halt. They had defeated an enemy, and in the process delayed pursuit. They had taken some rest and made an offering to the gods. In addition, they had rooted out a spy and, thanks to the favour of the gods, they had discovered where their comrades — the last two missing members of their contubernium — were being held captive.

Quintus should have been exhilarated, happy in the knowledge that they had appeased the gods and were now on a mission of rescue. But he was not. Something was pricking at the back of his consciousness — a niggling thought that he had missed something; that he had been told something and not attached sufficient significance to it. It was not just that his comrades might have been sacrificed already; it was something more.

He clutched the packet containing Ursus' will and gave it a squeeze — he might yet fulfil his destiny. But, as he marched, leading the men along the ridge and away from the camp, he could not winkle the thought out into the daylight.

Then it came to him.

Tincomarus was Tan's uncle. That much he at last remembered being told. Tincomarus, according to Aucissa, could have been the chieftain. Maybe he even should have been — Quintus did not know how these things worked — so what did that make Tan? An heir, a prince? Certainly more significant than they had thought.

A spy, thought Quintus.

Tan was a spy, yes, but a spy that was related to one of the senior men of the Atrebates — one who could have been king and was possibly even related to its queen, though he had never established as much. Certainly, according to Cato, Tan was also related to the Regni tribe. Quintus was pulling the threads together. Tan was not just dead, but ignominiously so, dumped with those whom he was spying for in a little wood on a forgotten ridge — on one of their holy days.

Then there was Elrik: not just a chieftain amongst the Atrebates, but a friend and a cousin to Coginus — that was the fact that had been hiding from him. That was the realisation. At the celebrations, Elrik had sat with Coginus. He had sat with the Regni instead of his own tribe because he was Regni, because he was part of Coginus' family. And his woman — his widow — had been related in some way to Tan; maybe she was even a sister, making the boy a relative to the man. Thus the death of Tan in itself was significant, but the death of Coginus

— chieftain, charioteer, husband, cousin — was enough to start a blood feud. Once the man failed to return, or Tan failed to report, Elrik would follow, if he was not doing so already, and he would have hot and righteous rage in his heart.

If they were going to effect any sort of rescue of Marcus and Publius, and escape afterwards, they needed not only speed but probably allies as well. By great Jupiter, Quintus cursed to himself, they could not even speak the language; they had relied on Tan for that — Tan, Tincomarus and Aucissa. One was dead, and the others would most likely be implacable enemies when they heard of his actions.

It made the country around them — the soft country of fields and trees and river — at once deadly. If word spread of their deeds, of the wounds that they had inflicted on the tribes of the coast, they would face death from any that they met — and not a quick end.

'Double time,' Quintus commanded. 'We do not know how long we have. The sooner we find our comrades, the better.' As the men picked up the pace, he turned to Crassus, who jogged at his side. 'You spoke with Tan. You exchanged words. Did you learn much of their tongue?'

'Little enough,' said the blacksmith. This jog-trot was what they had become used to, moving almost as fast as the cavalry. The pace did not even really make them breathe any harder — apart from Crassus, whose injury had settled into its familiar dull ache. He hid it well.

'Enough to pass for one of them?'

'I think not. What I did learn from the boy would not be of much use — how to curse, which gods to call on for greatest effect, how to impress a maiden…'

'It may have to be enough,' Quintus insisted. 'Drop back and let Sextus take your place.'

The manoeuvre was neither difficult nor unusual and, within moments, Sextus was beside him.

'You spoke with the woman?'

'Annaig?'

'Yes. Did you learn much of the language?'

'I learned a little — mostly parts of the body, and intimate terms for such things.' Sextus' smile warmed.

'I might have guessed. Still, you and Crassus are the only ones who speak any of it. You should share your knowledge.'

'And your woman, the queen?'

'We spoke only Latin,' Quintus replied flatly.

The path widened as the legionaries once more exchanged places, this time so that Sextus and Crassus could be side by side. They began putting their various words together, trying to build a vocabulary out of very little, like trying to build an arch with no keystone and no idea of the width to be spanned.

The ridge was no longer worthy of the name, having flattened and widened as they went, to the relief of Crassus and the Macedonians. They were now moving gradually downhill as the track moulded itself into the broad lands on either side. To the east was the river, narrower now, but still meandering in great coils, beds of reeds and tall grasses nestling in islets and peninsulas. To the west, as far as the horizon, were deep woodlands of oak and elm, the different greens of their wide canopies fading into a single dark colour in the distance.

The treeline ran alongside the wide path that they occupied, as if some god, or some sort of natural phenomenon had cut it off — their route remained hard, strewn with rocks. Quintus guessed that the roots of plants and trees could get no purchase here. There was no sign of other roads — though of course they might weave beneath the trees — no sign of settlements, of villages, of smoke from fires. It would remain light long after sundown, and the legionaries would camp late and rise early. Perhaps they could reach the crossroads faster than Tan had thought possible.

Rufus now marched alongside Quintus. Like the others, he had been unable to stop himself from becoming unkempt. He had already sported a moustache that would have rivalled Elrik's, and now the rest of his face was surrounded by red and gold fur, so that he looked like a bear in a helmet.

'You must be old enough to remember the way the Compitalia was celebrated in the city?' Quintus asked the veteran.

'The festivals at the crossroads? Riots and murders? Robbers and prostitutes and scenes of violent behaviour? Before my time, Quintus.'

'But you were born in the city?'

'I was, yes,' Rufus replied, 'under the Servian Wall. My father became a citizen by serving as a guard on the Viminal Gate. I suppose my birthplace is now beneath the camp of the Praetorian Guard. He had no trade. He was a thug who worked for the *collegia* when they were in the ascendant, for private clients when they were not. Although the son of a freedman, he had always wanted to be a soldier, ever since he saw Pompey's Triumph as a boy, but he didn't like the discipline.'

Quintus nodded in understanding — his own father had preferred meting out discipline to accepting it. 'We celebrated the country version. There were no riots — we just honoured the Lares, the spirits of the fields, marking the end of the cycle of seasons and the start of a new farming year. My father persisted in the placing of a wooden plough and mannequins to represent his household in the cleaning, sweeping and washing ceremonies that followed.'

'And though you know I like to talk, why is this relevant?'

'Because we are going to a crossroads to find Marcus and Publius.'

'Crossroads have never done me any harm,' said Rufus. 'In fact, I quite liked them. I haunted the crossroads near the Viminal when I was young — the Viminal road met that from the Esquiline right in the Suburra. What boy would not want to know what went on in those dark streets?' He smiled in remembrance. 'But the Compitalia itself, the winter festival honouring the neighbourhood spirits, had been all but legislated out of existence in Rome during my father's time. The patricians did not like something that they could not control.'

'Nor does anyone,' mused Quintus, 'and I cannot control our fate. Now that Tan is dead, and the Regni warriors that caught up with us, I think the die is cast.'

Rufus did not at once reply. He had been close enough to death enough times that he feared it no longer. He shrugged. 'We either find them or we don't. It is all in the hands of the gods.'

The light did not last as long as Quintus had hoped. As they dropped down onto the gently undulating land at the foot of the descent, they found themselves first level with, then under, the trees. Their great branches stretched across the track forming a tracery — like veins on the back of an ancient hand — as if reaching out in fraternal harmony for brother trees on the other side. They did not meet, the path, though narrower than it had been, was still too wide for those questing fingers to join, so the blue sky still showed above them. But shadows could span the divide, and as the day waned, they grew longer.

Whilst mountain tops would still be red and gold with evening, and meadows bathed in amber, here there was the gloom of dusk.

They stopped to investigate path junctions several times, thinking that here were the crossroads that they sought, finding instead only winding trails, small streams or animal tracks. The tramp of their heavy feet was the only sound on the path, the breeze having ceased to stir the trees. Whatever animals there were seemed to have withdrawn, being rightly frightened of this squad of strangers.

As soldiers, they were used to stopping early, whilst enough of the afternoon light remained, so that they could build a camp; they therefore expected to pause soon. But not this day. Quintus would not call a halt without constructing some kind of defences, but did not intend to camp for long enough to require much detail. So, as night gathered, they marched on.

Quintus knew when the sun had finally set — they all did, though they could not see it through the trees. The temperature dropped suddenly and quickly; this land, unlike Italy or even Hispania, seemed incapable of preserving any of the heat of the day. If they had been at home, the legionaries knew, a day with the sun as bright and high as this day would have kept the stone warm, so that dinner could be taken after dark, on a rooftop or terrace, comfortable and homely under the stars. Here the earth retained no warmth, and the air soon gained an edge to it.

Above them, great flocks of rooks and crows argued noisily over who should occupy which bit of sky. By the time the agreements were made, and the skies were once more silent, it was fully dark.

Conversation had ceased as they trudged along, and each man inhabited his own world. Quintus let his thoughts wander, but he wished he hadn't when the sight and sound of the crows and rooks triggered something in his memory, conjuring up an image of an impossibly youthful Tan having his eyes violently pecked out, whilst an unbelievably enraged Elrik looked on in horror and sorrow. Somehow the vision of the youth became melded with that of the ship's boy, the two combining to produce a frightening apparition of salt and bone and blood and flesh.

He shivered, then shook the fog of hallucination from his eyes; of course they had not bothered to close the eyes of the spy. Of course they had not placed coins in his mouth for the Ferryman, for he had proved to be an enemy. Quintus shook his head again, knowing the visions came because he was tired. Still he did not wish to stop.

Just a little longer, just a little longer, he thought, but Cato had once lost his footing, Jovan had stumbled, and Crassus and Sextus had dropped back. When Tullius tripped on a root and only just remained upright, cursing, Quintus knew that he had to halt. He counted a hundred paces more, for he did not want Tullius thinking that he was the cause of the halt.

'We camp here,' he said, as he completed the count in his head. He had looked left and right and found one of the many small streams that seemed to run on either side of the path without ever crossing it. He waved an arm at it, then turned to the slaves. 'I think we might manage a small fire, Jovan, in amongst the trees. The branches will hide and disperse the smoke. You can boil water — you have barley. Then we can eat.'

Jovan dipped his head and, touching the bandana that hid his slave mark with his fingers, moved away. The men stopped, grateful to be able to lay down their packs. The drum beat of their tread upon the ground was replaced by the sounds of gear being deposited on the earth and the beginnings of conversation.

XXVIII: VIA ROMANA

Maxim approached Quintus apologetically. 'Master, we have some barley and some other grains, many of which were damaged by saltwater. We can feed the men, but not well.'

'I understand,' Quintus nodded, then looked for the conjurer to whom he turned in such cases. 'Sextus, we need to eat. Can you magic something up?'

'A chicken, perhaps?' Rufus asked, as he leant his carrying pole and pack against a tree.

'Or maybe a roast pheasant?' added Crassus, rubbing surreptitiously at the sore spots on his back.

'I hear they stuff fish with pearls now on the Bay of Naples,' said Rufus.

'And somehow manage to make pies from the tongues of larks,' said Cato.

'I can make no promises, Cato,' Sextus replied, smiling at this last request, 'but I will see what I can do. Come with me, Maxim. I know you cook — let's see if you can hunt.'

The slave fell in beside him and they set off into the forest, following one of the winding tracks that seemed to run parallel with the stream. The rest of the legionaries were making ready to construct the simplest of marching camps.

'We will not be here long,' said Quintus, 'so basic defences will do. I do not believe that we are being followed — at least not yet — but we need eyes behind us in case. Crassus, take the first watch, a hundred paces down the road.' He looked up and down the straight track and at the trees above them. 'It is straight enough, so you will still be in sight. A shout will carry in this tunnel.'

Crassus gave the traditional salute — a fist to the heart — and picked up a shield, helm and javelin. The next hour, both he and Quintus knew, would be characterised by hard labour. He was glad to be out of it, but could not show any appreciation of Quintus' concern without showing weakness. As he turned on his heel, the others were already making a start. Jovan had disappeared to collect firewood, and Rufus had found a trenching tool and was swinging it at the ground, the ringing noise making Crassus look back briefly.

'Perhaps in the trees might be better,' Quintus said to him. 'The ground may be easier to work and the trees themselves could form part of our defences.'

'I agree,' the redhead nodded, 'but that is not why I am striking this earth. Look.' He ran the sole of one *caliga* back and forth across the surface. 'I was just checking. It is, as I thought, a Roman road. Forty years old it may be, but look — that is why no trees grow here.' He still had his trenching tool in his hand and swung it at the crown of the track — a crown, Quintus only now noticed, that caused water to be drained into the trees and the ditch on either side. It explained why the treeline stopped so suddenly. The tool barely broke the surface, chipping off a little earth and a couple of stones, which Rufus bent down to pick up. 'Look. This road was built by legionaries.'

'Another good reason for not camping on it,' grunted Tullius, who had joined them to see what they were doing.

'So the great god Caesar came this way,' marvelled Cato, giving a mock bow. 'We tread in noble footsteps.'

Tullius was not amused and looked around him as if someone might be listening. 'Do not make fun; our emperor is the son of Caesar, remember.'

Cato did not reply, but continued to untie his pack, eventually finding a trenching tool before looking at Quintus. 'Where?'

'In there, I think.' Quintus pointed into the surrounding woodland. 'The trees are not so close together, and there is room to build a fire.'

'Stakes?'

'Stakes will be enough.'

Cato called across to Tullius, and the pair of them began to cut down and sharpen branches that were about the circumference of an arm. Rufus and Quintus both joined them, clearing underbrush and establishing sight-lines to the road both north and south. Between them they would form a simple palisade with a ditch behind it, the trees doing the job on the forest side. They knew they would not be here long and would sleep in shifts, but only for an hour or so each at most.

Jovan started a fire, and soon there was warmth and a little light. After about half an hour, Sextus announced his and Maxim's return with a low whistle. Maxim carried two wood pigeons, their necks broken. 'And a bonus,' Sextus said, revealing a clutch of four eggs wrapped in the folds of his cloak.

Quintus praised their skills, then detailed Maxim to prepare and cook the birds. The eggs would be added to the grain broth he already had boiling.

'Save a little for me,' he said, getting up. 'I am going to relieve Crassus so that he may eat. I am not yet hungry.' He walked down the track to where Crassus, proper as ever, stood stiffly on watch, but did not dare to do any more than formally relieve his friend of duty. He could not ask after his health, or his injury, not when he was playing the commanding officer on a night camp — and anyway, he knew that Crassus would not thank him for the interest.

Left alone with his thoughts — as he had wanted to be — he tried to build some sort of plan in his head. He was fairly sure that they were being followed, probably on foot, with Elrik perhaps no more than a day behind them. He would follow with extra urgency if he found Tan and Coginus.

Somewhere ahead, there was a crossroads, which might not be clear or obvious, and a turn to the east — to what? The river ran from the north to the sea on that side; would they have to cross it? However they came to it, ahead were their comrades, captured and probably already killed. If not killed then awaiting slaughter at some indeterminate later date, whenever this festival of midsummer ended. Guarded, heavily or not? Injured or wounded? His mind began to spin with the grim pictures that he could conjure up. He had seen enough death and mutilation to have no trouble forming the images.

He shook his head; these visions had to be sent back to wherever they had come from. One thing was certain: there was no way that they could not attempt a rescue — these were citizens of Rome, after all. *Civis Romanus sum* guaranteed his people fair treatment anywhere in the world. But this place was not in or of the world, he reminded himself, it was outside the bounds of the great Ocean Stream, afloat in a sea of fog, and his thoughts once more plunged into despair.

The light of the morning was not yet bright, but three of the legionaries were already squatting by the stream, washing and shaving as best they could. Foolishly, Quintus had not told anyone to relieve him, so as the dawn light crept upon him, he found himself standing with his back to a tree, his head on his chest, his arms braced across the top of his shield, dozing. He was not sure how or when he had got there. He had been derelict in his guard duty, and back in the army he would most likely have been sentenced to flogging or *fustuarium* — being cudgelled to death — both punishments he had witnessed once in Hispania. It would have been at the whim of his commanding officer.

Quintus shivered at the thought, straightened up, shook the cramp from his limbs, and looked north up the track to his comrades. The men by the stream looked up as he approached. Someone should have relieved him, but none had taken responsibility. They should be striking camp, not seeing to their beards, and they should have been ready to move out. Quintus was ready to demand discipline and loyalty, but then he looked around and smiled.

Three sat by the stream, talking, laughing and helping each other with the chore of staying smart. In the area cleared and flattened, Cato was sitting by the fire with Crassus, each eating one of Maxim's specialities — a thick snake of grainy dough wound around a green stick and charred on the embers. Maxim was cooking another. Jovan at that moment emerged from the forest, adjusting his tunic. It was a homely scene that could have been taking place by any little stream in Italy, except the day would already be warm at this time of year and set to become hot. Here there was still a faint haze clinging to the trunks of the trees and the ragged growth of the understorey.

Quintus could not be angry with them — there was camaraderie here, the best discipline of all. Anyway, it was his own fault that he had not named a relief, and he had committed the worst crime — falling asleep on duty.

Maxim handed him the green stick he had just finished, as well as a bowl with at least half a pigeon sitting in grain porridge. 'We saved you some,' he said.

'As you asked,' said Cato. 'We did not wish to disturb you; we knew you would be thinking. Do you have a plan?'

'I have,' lied Quintus, as he looked at the oversized portion that they had kept for him. 'Of course I have.' Quintus looked around at the relaxed state of the little camp. 'We need to hurry,' he added gently. 'Collect your gear and put out that fire. We should have started with the first of the light.' As several of the men began to speak, he lifted his hands to silence them. 'I know, I know, it is my fault entirely. It is I who should have made sure someone was ready to wake us with the dawn. It is not your fault; there is no need to grumble. Nevertheless, we should be quick. I still believe that Elrik may be hot on our trail, though I have not seen any sign of pursuit. But even if we are not followed, we need to make good speed. We do not know when this festival of theirs ends — but we *do* know that it is likely that the end is celebrated with this pagan rite of burning captives and enemies. We have to find the crossroads and head east, down towards the river.'

'I hope we don't have to cross it,' said Crassus. He was no great swimmer.

'So do I, but only because it would slow us down. We are quite capable of swimming across a little stream such as this — even you, my friend,' Quintus said, laughing.

They struck camp swiftly, Maxim making sure that the fire was out and the evidence of its presence hidden with leaves and branches. Most of the stakes were left where they were — they would not be carrying them or re-using them. Some half a dozen, chosen for their straightness and sturdiness, were packed away by Rufus and Tullius. Crassus considered taking some, then decided against it. His back had eased a little, and he had no desire to make it worse again.

Once more they lifted their gear on to their shoulders. Some had made running repairs, replacing rescued ship's rope and ivy with material, including the belts and hair-ties of their fallen enemy. The bags that hung from the crosspieces contained everything that might be of use — they had no mule, of course, so a tent was out of the question — but the stakes were added to cooking pots, flasks, trenching tools, spare weapons and food. Their shields were tied to their backs, while the cloaks they had used as bedrolls were coiled up and tied across their shoulders. They kept their javelins in their hands. Maxim and Jovan also carried heavy burdens — though, of course, no weapons.

They were soon climbing, and had not realised they were heading uphill until they found themselves above the treeline, on a bald patch of heathland, populated by scrubby bushes and sharp-thorned thickets of holly and bramble. The road beneath their feet remained clear, but it was now narrower, so that they proceeded in single file.

As they reached the brow of the hill, they could see a long way down the valley to their right, their eyes following the line of the river, seeking any sign of pursuit. The Roman road on which they had travelled plunged under the trees behind them, so any pursuit that came this way would only be revealed by dust or fire smoke, neither of which could be seen. Ahead the road widened and vanished into a flat area of earth, much beaten down, before emerging again twenty paces on. Into the same area another track, winding and irregular, approached from the west and disappeared down what appeared to be a steep slope to the east.

'Here,' Quintus said, calling a halt. 'This must be it.'

They rested their packs on the ground and surveyed the wide area with curiosity.

'Your plan, decanus?' Tullius asked Quintus as he stood thinking, trying to make sure that this truly was the crossroads that they had sought. He hesitated, not knowing how to answer him.

He was saved by Sextus shouting across before he could respond. 'Look, an altar!' He pointed to a flat stone — ancient, but with the remnants of offerings on it: straw dolls, twists of corn or grass, even tiny animal bones. They were whitened, the other things tattered and weathered. It seemed it had not been visited recently and was no part of the midsummer festival.

'Then this is definitely the crossroads?' Cato asked dubiously, the route to the east looking difficult and dropping steeply.

'These are offerings, I would say,' said Sextus, 'to the gods that guard this place. Crossroads must be as sacred to them as they are to us.' Having said this, he looked around with trepidation, for crossroads in Rome were usually marred by violence and crime.

Quintus was brusque. 'The plan is still to find where our comrades are held with all speed, my friends. I can say no more than that — we don't even know what we face. It could be a village, or even a town, if such things exist here. Our job may be harder than we think, but we must try.'

'Once we have rescued them, we will then need to rescue ourselves,' added Rufus. 'Somehow, we have got to get off this benighted land and across the angry waves to Gaul or Frisia. That is where the rest of our cohort ended up, I believe. If we don't rejoin them, then we are all dead, not just Publius and Marcus.'

Tullius and Crassus both nodded in agreement, whilst Cato's face betrayed his anxiety.

'Lux is not dead,' Sextus told him softly, putting his hand on the legionary's shoulder. 'I have not seen it — and I cannot feel it. Marcus neither.' He had seen the upturned chin, the query forming on Tullius' lips. 'They live, I am sure of it.'

'Then we carry on with at least this part of the plan. We go east, down here.' Quintus looked over the edge at the sharp and rugged decline. There was a path there, but it vanished quickly behind rocks and scrubby plant growth, descending rapidly.

Below them, he could see the river winding down the valley like a great serpent, much of it hidden beneath spreading leaves, its sharp reflected light appearing now and then. It rose somewhere away to the east or the north, coursing towards where they stood. It then swung round in a great arc, before beginning its journey south, meandering over the flat lands where the legionaries now looked. Quintus turned his head and searched the east for their own path, spotting it emerging from the trees below. Their way, it seemed, went down to the water, but not across it.

'Crassus!' he called. 'You will be pleased to know that, if this is our road, it looks like we do not need to swim across the river.'

Crassus and the other legionaries were crowded at the edge. They could see that the path, though steep and winding, vanished into trees then came out on the north bank of the river. Providing it did not wander north again, and providing they reached their goal before it did, they had no need to cross.

'See, Tullius, the offering to the gods worked,' said Sextus, in an effort to lift the veteran's spirits. 'Fortune is with us once more.'

Tullius, grunted, unconvinced, then turned to look back to the south again. His right arm straightened, a finger accusing the gods as he spoke angrily. 'Fortune, you say? Well, we have company!' Where he pointed, they could see puffs of dust rising up in the distance, escaping from the forest and marring the clear sky.

XXIX: ELRIK

Immediately, several voices were raised.

'Who is it?'

'What is it?'

'Are they on horseback? How do they make such speed?'

Between the gaps in the trees, they could see evidence of the pursuit. Chariots, the fast two-wheeled vehicles of the Atrebates and the Regni, lightweight and manoeuvrable, flashed across. There were many of them, each appearing briefly and then swiftly vanishing beneath the cover.

'Elrik,' Quintus concluded quietly. 'He is following neither ridge nor road nor forest; he knows this country better than us.'

'Not so well,' said Sextus excitedly, shaking his head. 'Fortune is still with us. Look, he is on the wrong side of the river. He must cross it to reach us, and cross it with chariots.'

He was right. Elrik and the racing chariots were on the east bank of the river, the furthest away, meaning that the great sweep of the river's bend blocked their northward passage.

Tullius shook his head, stroked the long scar that ran down his right cheek and divided his beard. He did not yet believe that their fortune had changed. 'There will be a bridge or a ford,' he said pessimistically.

'Or not!' Rufus slapped him on the back.

Sextus was still optimistic. 'If we are up here and they are down there, we know where they are, but they do not know where we are. Surely that is better fortune, Tullius?'

'Maybe. But our path is downwards, steeply downwards, so that is one advantage ended — we will soon join them on the plain. And they may have seen us against the skyline.'

Sextus sighed and made a face, though he made sure that Tullius could not see it. Quintus peered to the east, shading his eyes with his hand. The air was clear, the sun high. He could see for a long way, many miles perhaps, though he had no way to estimate the distance.

'I can make out features a long way down the river, bends and islands, but I see no bridge or ford. If there is one, it would seem to be more than a day away, even for them. Our own path runs into the grove of trees below, but that is all — hopefully beyond that we will find our friends.'

'They are definitely the wrong side of the river.' Cato was standing at Quintus' shoulder, and spoke in support of Sextus. 'They follow the line of the ridge. Tan told them he would lead us along the ridge; he told Elrik that he would take us to where the captives are held. I think these chariots are heading straight there. If so, I think Elrik will still be seeking a signal. Even better, they will not have found our camp nor the dead we left behind.'

'Then there is a way across,' Tullius insisted. 'They must know it.'

'But our way is shorter. Believe that our fortunes have changed, Tullius.' Quintus gripped the man by his upper arms and smiled at him. 'Do it for me — it makes the journey shorter.' Tullius shrugged off the uninvited touch and harrumphed, but did not speak. Quintus then looked for Jovan and Maxim to test the descent. 'You two first — you are only lightly laden.'

'Master,' they both acknowledged.

They rose, hoisted their packs onto their shoulders and reluctantly began to pick their way down the steep and rocky descent, dodging gorse and thistle, dislodging pebbles that tumbled towards the bottom. They were sometimes forced to jog-trot a few steps because of the severity of the slope, and sometimes had to turn to face the rock and proceed backwards. They were relieved that, after just a few steps downwards, the sun no longer beat down on their heads, but the rest was hard work.

Though they were not as heavily laden as the legionaries, they were nevertheless carrying plenty. In addition they had poorer footwear, with less grip than the caligae of their masters. They tripped and stumbled, but were relieved to find that the worst of the descent was the first twenty feet or so. After that, the slope was not as steep and, as the path wrapped itself around rock and outcrop, there were many parts where the trail was all but flat — in some cases even a little uphill — and easier to traverse. They shouted this information up to the men that followed them, along with other helpful directions.

Halfway down, they began to encounter more obstacles. There were trees growing at the base of the descent, the start of the grove they had seen from above, and their upper branches scraped against the rock and attempted to catch on the climbers. They slowed Maxim and Jovan, and Rufus was the first of the legionaries to catch up with them, cursing them for not making sufficient speed.

It took a long time, and many oaths and imprecations were thrown at the gods, the thistles and the rocks in equal measure — as well as at Jovan and Maxim — before the men found themselves at the foot of the cliff. A rope slung from the top would have been useful. It was steep and difficult, hardly a path at all. As he looked at it, he wondered if he had made a huge error — if this was not, after all, the path that they had sought or, even worse, that the spy, even in the throes of death, had remained an enemy and given them false information. He sighed and decided that the space they had seen, with its beaten ground and offerings, *had* to be the crossroads. They had seen no other like it. He just had to trust that Tan had told the truth. The path on which they stood at least struck east through the trees, and was obvious.

Crassus was last down. He had brought up the rear so that he would not hold up any of the others, and was some way behind them, his back suffering a dull and throbbing ache that sapped his spirit. Quintus wanted to move off straight away, whilst they still had the light, but in consideration of his friend, he allowed the squad to rest. The ground they were on was sandy where the path led, damp and grassy to either side, and was at least flat and firm.

'Did the boy say how far to the village — or whatever it is?' Tullius asked.

Cato shook his head. 'He did not give any distances. He did say half a day or less from the crossroads — but I do not know if that included that descent or not.'

'Then we will not be there before nightfall?'

'I doubt it,' said Tullius. 'Another day lost, another day nearer disaster.'

'Half a day,' Quintus said, ignoring his tone. 'If we hurry, we might yet make it before dark.'

He ordered Crassus to lead, hoping that this would help the injured legionary to moderate his own pace. Instead he set off in rapid double-time and soon the base of the cliff was lost to them as they marched through the trees. To Quintus' relief, they began to thin, letting in much more light, and bright green turf appeared between them. Suddenly, Crassus put his hand up to halt the column, calling out at the same time.

'Ahead,' he said in a whisper, 'there are voices.'

Quintus could hear them too.

The road dipped and bent round to the west, curving around a hillock. A stand of elm jostled for light on top of the rise in the crook of the turn. There were green leaves crowding its crown, and tangled ivy and holly at its base. The other side of the track was flat, with long coarse grass and sparse bracken dropping away to marshland, providing little cover. They could see no-one, but Quintus could hear the conversations clearly enough.

There were several voices, speaking a language that he did not understand, but which might be a cousin to that of the Atrebates and the Regni. For a panicked moment he thought that it might be the charioteers that pursued them, that they had somehow been overtaken and an ambush was being planned. But he shook his head — he had convinced himself that there was no shorter route than the way they had come, and that was too rough, too steep, for chariots to pass.

Keeping silent, he gestured to Rufus to go and look. Rufus tapped his breast automatically and crept forward, leaving the road and climbing the hillock quietly, slipping between the trunks of the trees, parting the brambles and young holly that filled the space at their base, vanishing into the greenery.

Quintus signalled to the other men to close up on him, to put down their burdens, which he waved at the slaves to take away from the track. He expected the men to have to defend themselves against this group, expected the speakers to be foe — and armed. By the time Rufus reappeared, they were all ready, but the voices were already fading into the damp air.

'A small party, probably foraging,' hissed Rufus, 'though for what in this god-damned land, I do not know.' Tullius looked daggers at his comrade. He respected the gods too much to curse them. 'Their backs were to me, but I counted just five, three men and two women, carrying baskets. They were laughing and joking — wherever this is, wherever they are going, they feel themselves safe.'

'Then we disabuse them of that idea.' Tullius waved his gladius — he was all for following them and killing them.

'They do not yet know we are here,' Quintus spoke quietly and showed Tullius his raised palm. 'Let's keep it that way for now.' Tullius looked disappointed but made no further move. 'Rufus, is the passage through the trees easy?'

'It is — just brambles and thorns that might trip and scrape you.' He smiled and rubbed at the scratches on his calves. 'Nothing deadly.'

Quintus put his finger to his lips — they still needed to be quiet. The foraging party might have gone, but they could easily return, or there could be other parties. 'Follow Rufus,' he commanded, pointing the way to the trees. 'Keep silent.' With a further gesture, he made sure that the slaves and the gear stayed where they were, in short scrub a little way back from the trail.

Rufus moved off the way that he had come and the squad followed him in single file. They wanted to cut down the thorns and brambles, but did not dare in case it made too much noise, so they used their shields to push them out of the way. If they were wealthier, they would have greaves. But none of them were wealthy, Quintus regretted as a thin branch of holly whipped back into his shins.

They kept low as they passed the trees, then from the crest of the hillock they could see the track, but there was no-one on it, nor anyone to be seen on the open land beyond it. The track made a detour to the west, then only ran a short way before it turned again, vanishing out of sight to the north.

Cato happened to be nearest to the turn. 'Cato, go and see what lies ahead,' Quintus commanded, still in a whisper. The legionary scrambled down the bank — steeper here than the other side, and ran along the track. Reaching the bend, he peered around it for the shortest of times and then returned just as quickly, using the helping hands of Rufus and Crassus to pull himself back up the bank. He was breathless, but not just with exertion. He was excited.

'It is a settlement of some sort, a shallow hill, which could well be man-made, with a stockade around its base. The track leads to a gate.' His eagerness was palpable. 'I think it must be the place we're looking for.'

'Is the gate guarded?' Quintus asked.

'I could see no guards, but I would think that it is. We could climb the stockade. It is rough-hewn timber, poorly constructed, and the earthen slope before it is not too steep. If we work our way around to the other side, we could climb it and see what it holds.'

'In daylight?' Tullius asked.

'There may be another gate on the other side,' said Crassus. 'I would want an exit as well as an entrance if I were building such a thing.'

They had come across fortified villages in Hispania — stockades or hills or a combination of both. They usually had a way out as well as the main gate, and often also had ditches in front of the stockade. As Quintus pondered whether this compound would be similar, the moist air finally gave way to a soft rain. The foragers had seen the clouds and had clearly known that rainfall was coming — that was why they had been hurrying back.

'We do not have time to wait,' Cato urged them. 'We do not know when this festival ends, when the executions begin…'

'I know your concerns, Cato,' Quintus answered. 'We will use the daylight to see if this is the place we seek.' He put a hand on Cato's shoulder. 'When we know it is the right place, we can see where and how our comrades are kept and plan how we may rescue them.' He turned his attention to Rufus. 'Rufus, we need more information — we need to see how this village is defended. Be thorough, but don't dawdle.'

Rufus signalled his obedience as Cato turned to Quintus in annoyance, shrugging off his hand. 'I have told you what it looks like.'

'Nox, my friend, you but glanced at it.' Quintus shook his head gently. 'You found what you wanted to find. You know you did.'

Cato did not reply. Rufus gave him a little smile and a wave as he slipped away down the bank.

Quintus signalled to the men to lower themselves until they squatted in a semi-circle facing him; they could see the rain through the gaps in the leaves, but the canopy was thick and it had not yet penetrated to where they were. 'Now, we wait,' he said.

XXX: CAVÉ

Though it felt like an eternity, in truth they did not have to sit long before Rufus returned, his hair and beard wet and straggly. He joined the semi-circle.

'It is as you said,' he said, nodding at Cato. 'There is a wooden fence, erected on a mound, with a ditch in front of it.' He drew a circle on the ground with a stick and pointed to it as he described the village. 'The mound is man-made — I would guess it was constructed using the earth taken from the ditch. Where the road meets the fence, there is a gate, and there are men — presumably on guard, though I could see no weapons. To the east, I could just see the sun's reflection on the river, snaking north in a great arc. There will be water meadows there within its curve, and the river as extra defences.' He drew another line. 'The stockade continues unbroken to the west, though in places it is in poor repair — as is the ditch. Here —' he stabbed at the ground — 'around a hundred and fifty paces to the west — so out of sight of the gate — beasts have been allowed to go down to the water to drink.'

'The ditch is full of water?' Crassus asked.

'Not now. Despite this weather, it is summer, and the ground there, though wet with rain, looks hard and cracked beneath.'

'In the winter there would be water?' asked Quintus.

'I think so. There are hoofprints, dried out now, but clearly made when the ground was muddy, and the bank has collapsed where the animals have trodden. The ditch is shallow, so it will be easy to cross. The stockade here is not well maintained and, rather than aiding the defence of the place, it provides easy hand and footholds for any who wish to climb it. There are gaps in it that I could see through.'

'And what did you see?' Cato was eager.

Rufus shook his head gently. 'No prisoners, Nox,' he said, not unkindly.

'But that does not mean they are not there,' added Quintus quickly. 'What did you see?'

'It is big, not big enough to qualify as a town, though there are many huts, but it is a big village. It appears big enough to have purveyors of food, a forge, and even a butchery, with joints of something laid out on a block, the flies still buzzing despite the rain.' He sounded bewildered. 'There was nothing I recognised.'

'They eat fish,' said Sextus simply. 'Once, in another lifetime, I read portions of divine Caesar's *De Bello Gallico*. He says that the Britons keep geese, chickens and hares, but eat none of them, preferring fish. To them, these animals are like the dog and cat to Romans and Egyptians — pets, companions, spirits even, but not food.'

Quintus thought about his conversation with Aucissa, her contention that much of what Caesar claimed for the inhabitants was false, or based on poor or incomplete information. They were already a good way from the sea and, though the river still ran to the east, he did not think that fish could sustain a population this far inland.

Rufus sat back and resumed his description, no longer using the diagram in the earth. 'I would say that it is bigger than the coastal settlement of the Atrebates and better fortified.' He shook his head again. 'We could not conquer it by force; it would be stupid to try. If our friends are there, we can only rescue them through cunning and guile.'

259

'Then not in daylight.' Crassus was adamant.

'We rest and wait,' Quintus sighed, agreeing with the blacksmith, though not yet sure what they were going to do. He needed more information. 'Sextus, bring up the slaves and the gear. We rest here — it is as good a place as any.' He looked up at the intertwined leaves. 'It might even stay dry.'

'I could look further round to the west and gain more information,' Cato pleaded.

'Rufus, is there more to see? More that we should know?'

'There is, if we took more time.'

'Then I will go and look with you, Rufus,' Quintus declared, cutting off Cato's budding protests. 'I need you here, Cato. I need your touch with the slaves — you know how Tullius feels about Macedonians…' Tullius did not even treat Quintus to a sneer; he was once more in that other place to which it seemed he could retreat at will.

Crassus put a hand on Cato's arm. 'Stay,' he said. 'Your eagerness will get you caught and killed.' He winked. 'If Maxim and Jovan bring up the gear, we might even eat.'

The two legionaries set off before Sextus had returned, Quintus trusting that the common sense of Sextus and Crassus would prevail over Tullius' thirst for blood and Cato's rashness. He did not like leaving them, but he had to see what lay before them for himself before he could make any plans.

Rufus led Quintus down the bank. They jogged warily, bent low, along the edge of the track, one behind the other, in case anyone came out of the gateway and raised the alarm. At least it was not far before they turned west, and could no longer be seen. They slowed then, to more of a fast walk, Rufus taking them to the place that he had described, where the ditch had been collapsed by beasts. They crossed the shallow channel, the hoofprints leaving edges still as sharp as when they had dried and, as quietly as they could, they clambered up the bank. There was a narrow strip of grass at the base of the fence, long and yellowing now, but probably what had attracted the animals. The stockade itself, made of rounded timbers lashed together, was broken and rotten in places, and here and there overgrown with ivy and brambles.

They moved sideways, crab-like, along the narrow ledge, until they could see through the fence, each of them finding a gap at a comfortable height. Any noise they made was covered by the incessant music of the rain, pattering on canvas or some other hard surface within the compound. The rainfall was now steady and, to the Romans, surprisingly cold. On the other side of the fence Quintus could hear spitting and crackling — a fire in a battle with the heavens. He put his eye to the gap and looked, Rufus following suit beside him.

Inside, a fire burned close enough to the fence that they could feel its heat. It was sufficiently large for there to be an animal —unrecognisable in its blackened state — spitted across it, being turned by a surly-looking boy with a shock of unruly black hair, paying more attention to his feet, drawn up in front of him, than to the rapidly charring chunk of unrecognisable meat.

'They do eat meat,' Rufus muttered to himself.

Others moved around, some men, some women, all dark-haired, all dressed similarly to each other in unbelted short-sleeved tunics and bare feet; they did not seem to mind the rain. There were not many of them — this did not seem to be an important part of the settlement, the nearest hut being a good forty paces away. Here there were pens or storage crates of some sort, the rain pinging off their taut coverings.

'What are they doing?' Rufus asked hoarsely.

'I do not truly know, but I am guessing that they are slaves, seeing to the chores of the day. Otherwise, why would they be out in this weather? *Cavé.*'

Quintus' warning to beware made Rufus duck instinctively. A small party of men had come into view, walking rapidly towards them. They were better dressed, clothed in animal skins that were hemmed and belted. They also wore fur boots, their cloaks pinned with brooches at their necks. There was jewellery on their wrists and at the braided ends of their long moustaches. They all had the same jet-black hair as the boy beside the spit. One of them cuffed him and scolded him — the legionaries heard but did not see, and understood the tone if not the words.

'Are they Atrebates?' Rufus asked, as they waited until the voices died away so that they could go back to their peepholes.

'I think that these are the Cantiaci,' Quintus hissed in Rufus' ear. 'They are cousins to the Atrebates and the Regni, and sometimes enemies. Tincomarus did not trust them — he says that they came across the sea, that they are Gauls, not Britons, that they betrayed the Celts at Alesia, for they came too late.'

Rufus knew of the last stand of the Celts — in a fortress such as this one, only bigger and high on a hill. His uncle had taken him into Rome when he was but five years old to see the triumphs of the divine Julius, as well as the wild beasts. They were not able to stay for all of the triumphs — Caesar had many — but they did at least see the execution of Vercingetorix. Rufus remembered his long black hair and moustache.

They listened carefully until the voices could no longer be heard, then gingerly put their eyes to the gaps again. The slaves, if that was what they were, still moved around. There were many low structures of some sort, animal pens, perhaps, along the far side of the clearing. Quintus and his father had used such things to take beasts to market, but not to confine them on the farm; there — at least for the most part — they ran free. The surly boy now stood upright at his post, although he was still burning the meat in the spitting fire.

'This ground is well used,' noted Rufus, 'well beaten down. Many feet have passed this way.'

'There are horses too, there.' Quintus pointed to the rear of the line of pens, half hidden in shadow. The backs of a number of animals were side by side, as if tied in a row.

Rufus was more interested in what was happening in the foreground. 'What's that, over there? Where that woman is bending? What is she doing?'

One of the slaves had gone across to the animal pens and lifted the corner of its covering — some sort of dried hide on which the rain beat a desultory tattoo. Beneath it they could see the sides of a box. The woman had something in her hand.

'It is just more animals,' said Quintus. 'I think that is food in her hand. She is feeding livestock.'

'Sacrificial animals, do you think? For this ceremony of theirs?'

'More likely animals kept for food.' He smiled wryly. 'Although the boy appears to be dedicating that meat to the god of charcoal.'

'That is no animal,' exclaimed Rufus as he stared at the creature in the pen that the slave had revealed, shock and horror in his voice. 'I would recognise that blond head anywhere. It is Publius, bent double in a cage.'

'Shhh.' Quintus put his finger to his lips and they both froze. None of the slaves seemed to have heard Rufus, but the boy paused his spit-turning. Cocking his head, he looked at the fence quizzically, then shrugged his shoulders and returned to his task.

Quintus had seen it too, the sudden burst of straw: like the flare of a torch in darkness. He had only just managed not to cry out himself.

The woman finished whatever she was doing and straightened up, though they could still not make out exactly what it was that she held. She let the leather covering fall back down again, hiding once more the bright flash of golden hair.

'It was him? Lux? Without a doubt?'

'Who else has such hair? It was him.'

Quintus and Rufus looked at each other with astonishment.

'Does he live, do you think?' Rufus asked. 'I saw no movement.'

'No need to cage him if he does not breathe — no need to feed him either. He lives.'

'Then perhaps Marcus is there too, in one of those other crates?'

'Perhaps. For now, we watch, we wait, we hope to find him. It is likely that, if Publius is here, Marcus is also. They were together. There is much of the day left and much that can happen. We need to somehow get word to Publius that we are here.'

'I just wish this god-cursed rain would stop,' Rufus complained, wiping water from his face with the back of his wrist.

'Be careful what you wish for, my friend. They may be waiting for the rain to cease to light their sacrificial fires. The sun's light could be the signal they need from their gods to send our comrades to Elysium.' *Then, at least*, Quintus thought darkly, *they could avoid the weather.* For had Homer not written that in Elysium there is no snow, nor storm nor even rain?

The comrades settled down to watch and wait.

XXXI: DUM SPIRO SPERO

The day drew on past noon, the rain finally easing and weak sunshine breaking through the clouds and casting hazy shadows on the scene. The fire where the boy stood died down, until only red embers were left, blown to life irregularly by the fitful breeze. Deciding that he could burn the meat in his charge no more, the boy took the spit and its contents and wandered out of sight, accompanied by two of the women.

Just two female slaves remained and went about their tasks methodically, taking food to each of the covered pens in turn, lifting a corner of the covering and pushing whatever it was they carried inside to the occupant. There were many pens — sometimes a noise came from within, revealing geese or ducks, and in one case the plaintive bleating of a goat or lamb. Sometimes the noise could have been the grunt of a human. The slaves were in no hurry, stopping from time to time to chatter, or leaning against a pen to make comments on whatever lay within.

One pen, other than that which contained Publius, also definitely contained a human captive, revealed when the covers were flung back. He was a plump man; judging by his look and the remnants of his clothes, he was no Roman. His head was bald and brown and they could see it moving as he spoke to the slaves, obviously familiar with their tongue. At first his tone was soft and pleading, but when one of the women replied sharply, he became animated, shaking the cage and, Quintus guessed from the tone, throwing out insults. The slave spat at him and cursed back, quickly pulling the cover back over. She then slapped the top of it violently whilst saying something in a sing-song voice, almost like scolding a child. The man inside must have understood, for he went quiet.

The two slaves had an excitable conversation with each other, with many gestures and much pointing at the crate. The content of what they said could only be guessed at, but the tone was plain.

'He is not behaving,' said Rufus.

'A brave man,' replied Quintus. 'No Roman, but I wonder who he is?'

It looked to the legionaries as if this was the last of the crates that the women were going to deal with, and that, therefore, they would soon be gone. It was also a moment of disappointment. They had not seen Marcus, nor heard anything that sounded like his voice, which was remarkably soft for such a big man.

'If they have Marcus, he is elsewhere,' Quintus said with regret.

Rufus nodded, but still thought about the captive they had seen. 'If they go, we may be able to get a message to Publius,' he suggested hopefully. 'I think that we could easily make a gap in this fence.'

But the slaves did not go. Instead, they both armed themselves with sticks as they approached the pen on the end. As they reached it, they shouted and banged the sides and top of the container with their weapons. They each took hold of a corner of the covering and threw it back, jumping back as if a wild beast was within and ready to pounce on them.

They were not disappointed. A roar of rage came from the cage and long fingers poked out through the bars, fingers which the women were keen to strike with their sticks, though always keeping a wary distance. The maledictions and curses were loud, clear and, to the delight of the watchers, in Latin.

'Marcus!' they both exclaimed.

They could see now that this was, for the slaves, some sort of game. They had taken the sticks to goad or tease this prisoner, and now took it in turns to try and poke him through the bars at the side. This was a dangerous pursuit, for the cage did not look particularly sturdy or well made, and the man inside was large and increasingly angry. But the women, it seemed, knew that the cage was just sturdy enough, otherwise they would not have risked inciting this prisoner's temper.

'He looks fit enough,' said Rufus.

'And he sounds it. He is giving them trouble enough from inside the cage.'

The women tired of their game quickly enough and stood back, still waving the sticks and jeering, but no longer poking the prisoner. One lifted her tunic and waved her backside at him; the other made crude gestures with her fist. The watchers could see more clearly now.

'He is dirty, but does not look injured,' Rufus said.

'He is also naked,' added Quintus matter-of-factly.

'He is,' agreed Rufus, then pointed at the captive's footwear, 'though he still wears his caligae. I wonder why?'

'Maybe they have been unable to work out how to untie them?'

'Maybe they have made him walk?'

Quintus agreed. 'Maybe. He looks strong, does he not? Why take his clothes, I wonder?'

'A search for concealed weapons, I would say. A thorough search. Though not one that has injured anything other than his pride.'

It was true. Though his hair was streaked with reddish brown mud, his body smeared with more of the same, his muscles did not look wasted, nor did anything seem broken. He wore a rough beard, straggly and unkempt, which diverted attention from his broken nose. His hair had been crudely cut, with what remained made stiff by the mud.

'He looks like a cat caught in a thunderstorm,' said Quintus.

'Do not let him hear you say so,' warned Rufus, although he smiled at the image.

As they whispered, the two women became bored, for their victim was no longer responding. Instead, Marcus had slumped down in the cage, curled in a foetal position, his hands covering his ears. The women spoke to one another and then approached circumspectly, reaching for the covering and pulling it back over the top of Marcus. They did not appear to have fed him.

They discarded their sticks, picked up the bags and utensils that they had been using and, like a pair of washerwomen going down to the Tiber with their arms full of laundry, they strode off, chattering and laughing.

'Now is our chance,' said Rufus, already beginning to loosen the board where he stood.

'Wait,' hissed Quintus. 'Let them leave.'

But it was already too late. As the women left, they must have opened a gate or given an instruction, as immediately two huge hounds appeared in the yard, sniffing at the ground, dangerously quiet.

'Stand back, otherwise they will see you or catch your scent.' Quintus pulled Rufus a little way from the fence — the board, luckily, was still secure.

The dogs did not head straight for them, so had heard nothing — nor did they seem to recognise any new odours. Perhaps the stench of the prisoners, animals and men, neither of which had any sort of latrine, had masked all else. As it was, the first of the dogs cocked its leg against the crate containing the man they did not know, who let out a muffled cry of outrage, whilst the second sniffed at a number of the pens then jumped up and lay on top of the one containing Publius, its tongue lolling out.

Quintus crouched down and, as quietly as he could, made his way back across the dry ditch, signalling for Rufus to do the same. Only when he thought that they were far enough away not to be heard by the dogs did he speak in a low and urgent voice.

'We need a plan,' he said. 'We *will* rescue them — or die in the attempt.'

Rufus nodded and they withdrew stealthily from the vicinity of the fence, returning to the men underneath the trees, taking care to stay low and silent.

'*Quo vadis?*' a voice hissed from the undergrowth.

'Amicus,' Quintus replied, pleased to be challenged by Crassus as they approached the temporary base. At least his comrades had had enough discipline to put out a guard.

'I thought it was you,' said the blacksmith. 'What have you found?'

'We have found our comrades,' Quintus told him quickly, 'and now we must free them.'

'Both of them?' Crassus was amazed.

'Both of them,' Rufus confirmed, 'and they both look well.'

Crassus led the way back and excitedly told the others that Publius and Marcus had been found, though he could add little else.

Rufus filled in the detail. 'They are being held captive like wild animals. They are in pens, caged in darkness alongside birds and beasts — geese, ducks, maybe goats — and another man, a barbarian tribesman by his look and speech. The whole menagerie is guarded by two black mastiffs. We could only see when the slaves came to feed them and lifted up the coverings. Publius we at once recognised by his hair, but he made no movement or sound...'

Quintus stopped Cato with a gesture before he could interrupt. 'We are sure that he lives, my friend. They were feeding him, and they would not do so unless he lived. In fact, they do not seem to have harmed him — his hair is untouched, and he wears a tunic. He lives, Nox, but he did not look likely to come and tease you any time soon.'

Cato, though loath to admit it, missed the practical jokes that his friend was always playing on him. At the moment, he would happily have accepted another frog in his helmet or lizard in his bedroll if it meant that Publius was nearby.

'Marcus, on the other hand,' continued Quintus, addressing Tullius directly, 'has been stripped naked and had his hair cut. I suppose he resisted capture, or they may just have been searching for weapons. But I can tell you —' he put a hand on Tullius' shoulder — 'that he is definitely alive, and full of life; he was spitting, cursing, shouting and shaking his cage when the slaves came to feed him.'

'So not only is it our duty to rescue them,' said Sextus, 'but now we have found them, it is our destiny.'

'What do you see?' Cato asked anxiously.

'Nothing, my friend, nothing. Perhaps I am just too far from home. The mist has yet to clear. I could not even see if we would find them. I cannot see if a rescue will succeed, and I do think the mist is hiding unhappiness — but that could just be because they are held prisoner. I don't know how to explain it, but it does feel that way.'

'We will trust in the gods,' said Cato, dismissing Sextus' pessimistic assessment. '*Dum spiro spero*. Whilst I breathe, I hope.'

Sextus nodded. 'I cannot help how it feels.'

'But you can keep your auguries to yourself,' insisted Tullius curtly, making Sextus bridle, though he said nothing. Tullius then turned to Quintus. 'What do we do?'

'We pool our skills, make use of what we have, and devise a plan to rescue them. I think that it will have to be tonight, which means in the dark, or we will be too late. Sextus, will we have light?'

Sextus shook his head. 'I do not know. I do not know the habits of the moon in this land.'

'Think,' urged Crassus. 'What did it do last night? How large was it? When did it rise? Where? It will not be a lot different tonight.'

The previous night they had been under trees. They had been tired, and Sextus had slept. Quintus had stayed awake but failed to note the rising and setting of the moon.

'Master,' Jovan offered diffidently, waiting for permission to speak. Quintus waved a hand at him. 'Master, last night when I went to relieve myself, I found a clearing. It was a three-quarter moon, pale and hazy. It had risen late and will only have set, I think, during the day.'

'Is he right?' Quintus demanded of Sextus.

'I think so,' nodded the seer, his reputation hanging by a thread.

'Then we rely on starlight,' Crassus concluded. 'We cannot wait for it to rise.'

'Come,' said Quintus.

The men once more arranged themselves in a semi-circle, the Macedonians, to the disquiet of Tullius and Rufus, also waved in and included. Quintus saw the look of disapproval on their faces. 'We need manpower, and these are men. Their status can be ignored for now.'

Neither Rufus nor Tullius truly agreed with this but recognised that sometimes need could be a fiercer driver than their own prejudices. They grunted acquiescence, but made sure that they were not squatting next to the slaves. Quintus saw that Maxim and Jovan had brought up all the gear and stacked it neatly — shields, spears, helms, supplies, and even spare blades. He nodded at them.

'Though such diligence is praiseworthy, I do not think that we will need all of this anymore. The only way that we will rescue our comrades is through stealth, and the only way we will escape ourselves is through speed.'

He looked to the semi-circle for agreement. Cato nodded eagerly, Tullius barely dipped his head, and the others were noncommittal. Quintus sighed; he had hoped for more enthusiasm. He knew that what he had to say next would be hard for his comrades to bear.

'I will not give up my armour or my sword, nor my cloak, but shield and spear, I fear, must be left behind, along with satchels, stakes and tools. We should only take the food we need, and we will leave no weapons behind, unless they are broken — I am not about to arm the enemy.' He smiled grimly. 'If we do not reach the coast swiftly, and find a ship, I do not think any amount of supplies will help us. We will be fugitives from at least three sets of enemies. The tribesmen know the land, the dangers, the places for ambush; they have horses, chariots and even spies. We must be swift, or we will be dead.'

'Then perhaps we should forget stealth and attack the settlement,' Tullius suggested. 'We have seen no armament, they foraged without guards, and the fence is in poor repair. They are at peace. We could surprise them and free our friends.'

'Or all become sacrifices to their gods,' muttered Cato.

Quintus made a great play of considering Tullius' plan and only rejected it after sagely weighing up the advantages and disadvantages. 'Stealth,' he concluded.

There were many signs of agreement, though Tullius still offered alternatives. 'I might carry my shield as well. What if there are bowmen?'

'If we are swift, we will outrun their arrows,' Crassus said.

'If not, we will die,' added Rufus.

'Then we travel light,' Quintus continued, 'light and swift. Rufus and I saw what stands in our way. There are things that will not trouble us — we can access the cages through gaps in the fence. It is, as Tullius says, in poor repair. The cages themselves are not so sturdy, so we will be able to break them open. I don't think it would help our comrades much if they knew we were coming, and anyway I see no way of getting a message to them.'

'And the things that will trouble us?' Cato asked.

'The dogs,' Rufus offered.

'I can handle the dogs if I am close enough that they can hear me,' said Sextus.

'Really?' Tullius was doubtful.

'Really,' said Sextus, though his reputation for magic and soothsaying was somewhat tarnished.

'If they come after me, I will have your balls for ornaments after I have cut theirs off,' growled Tullius, half drawing his pugio. 'Rely on it.'

'They will not,' Sextus assured him. 'The temple dogs that guarded the Vestals were ever my friends and at my beck and call, though they would have happily torn the flesh from any man that had come nigh. I know what to do.'

'The men — and women — of the settlement are our second problem,' Quintus went on.

'If they think they are being raided…' Crassus began uncertainly.

'It is what we did at the battle in Hispania,' interrupted Cato. 'We create a diversion. In Hispania, it was slaves with fiery torches. Here, it could just be a fire.' He was excited now. 'Jovan, Maxim, can you light a fire here? Is there enough dry wood?'

The Macedonians nodded.

'If they think they are being raided, or that an enemy camps here, they will investigate — moving away from our comrades.'

'And then the escape?' Tullius asked.

'The hardest part,' said Quintus, 'not only from here, but from this land altogether.' He stroked his stubbly chin. 'I think I can at least get us away from here. As for the rest, it is in the hands of Mars and Jove and, above all, fickle Fortuna.'

XXXII: NON MULTUM AD PARTICIPES

It was time. The moon would not yet rise, but there was enough starlight in a clear summer sky to cast faint shadows on open ground. The legionaries were eager to carry out the plan as soon as they could. Cato's tension showed in an inability to stay silent. He wanted to talk to someone, to tell them how much he missed his friend, to go through the rescue plan again. Only Quintus would listen, and he with only half an ear, urging his comrade to keep his voice down. Jovan had only realised the seriousness of their plight when three of the contubernium asked him — separately and privately — to keep their wills, thrusting small packages upon him whilst he and Maxim collected brushwood for their part in the rescue. He knew that this meant these comrades thought that they might not survive.

The other men waited, wrapped in their own thoughts. Rufus and Crassus were quiet; Sextus was repeating chants and incantations to himself. Tullius, as usual, sat there sharpening his weapons with meticulous care; he had decided to conform with the rest of them and leave his shield behind, though reluctantly. As Quintus rose, ready to give the order to begin, Tullius came across and whispered something to him. Quintus acquiesced with a nod, then called the men together.

'A prayer,' he said.

The men gathered, solemn. Tullius had caught a creature in the underbrush, a mouse or shrew, grey and furry and squeaking plaintively.

'We have nothing else to sacrifice to the gods,' said the veteran. 'This will be our offering. It is all we have to show them that they are not forgotten, and that we need their help if we are going to succeed in this madness. Or at least not their hindrance.'

As they watched, Tullius raised his hands to the sky, the tiny rodent clutched between them, its head sticking out above his fingertips.

'I dedicate this life to you, oh Mars, and to you, Jupiter Optimus Maximus. And to you, Dis: should I arrive in the underworld without an obol for Charon, I pray you let me cross.' He looked quizzically at Sextus, who had assured them in Hispania that the Vestals were paying the Ferryman for those who died in battle. 'Are we still paid for, even in this land?'

'We are still soldiers,' was all that Sextus would commit to.

Tullius nodded in mute acceptance, lifted his arms high and squeezed. With a final squeak, the sacrifice expired.

'*Non multum ad participes*,' muttered Quintus with a smile, picturing Mars, Dis and great Jupiter dividing the tiny beast between them. He knew better than to let Tullius hear him, or the other men — most believed in the influence of the divine or, if not, did not actively disbelieve. They each sent up a silent prayer of their own as Tullius placed the body of the tiny creature on the brushwood — an oversized pyre for such a small offering. Sextus stroked the bulla that hung at his neck, dedicating it to the Vestals, whilst Quintus once more felt for Ursus' copper armband — won for bravery — and dedicated it to Dis in remembrance of the optio, and to Ceres and his own household gods, remembering his promise to Ursus that he would rescue their comrades or die in the attempt.

Oblations over, Quintus said, 'We can do no more. We must go.' The men slipped away from the camp.

Jovan's prediction that moonrise would not be until late had prompted Quintus to make a start as soon as he thought the settlement would be at rest. In this foreign land, he did not have a precise enough idea of when Luna's horned chariot would make its appearance, nor when the inhabitants would retire. It was perfectly possible that they went to their rest as soon as the sun did — or equally that they stayed up all night singing songs around fires — he just did not know. The action in the mountains of Hispania — ultimately a successful action — had owed its success to both local knowledge, and to the amazing timing device that the prefect had squirrelled away in his tent. They now had no such knowledge and no such device, no way of knowing that they acted in concert. He could only hope that the timing worked.

Rufus had suggested that they make the noise of an owl when they were in place — but the woods already had their own avian inhabitants, owls who called to each other as night fell. Also, Tullius pointed out fearfully, the cry of an owl was a presager of death. Had not divine Caesar been assassinated following the cry of an owl? He was already praying that the owls he had heard in the dusk were predicting the deaths of others, not himself. Quintus also did not wish to unwittingly alert the tribesmen to their presence with some amateur and out-of-place noise. They would have to rely on timing.

So now he waited. The only way to be confident that everyone had managed to reach their position was to give more than enough time for them to do so, and then for them to wait. On Quintus' signal, the brushwood that the men had piled up would be lit by Maxim and Jovan. That would then be the signal for the others.

Crassus and Cato would leave the group first, then Sextus, then himself with Rufus and Tullius, ready to take up station by that part of the fence where the ditch had collapsed. Crassus and Cato had the job of working their way around the perimeter until they reached the horse lines, or stalls, that Quintus and Rufus had observed. Had Crassus thought that his friend was protecting him from any fighting, he would have been furious, but Quintus had insisted that the task needed someone with speed and certainty — and a sharp mind to do what he had to do. They would of course also have to take care of any guards or grooms that they found.

Cato protested against his posting; he wanted to be the one to actually free Publius and would have argued had Quintus not cut him off brusquely, reminding him of the hierarchy. He also felt it vital that Cato's nervous energy found an outlet in action sooner rather than later. The work needed more time than the others, so they needed to begin it before the fire was lit; they needed to be in place before the rescue could even start. They slipped away together into the gloaming.

They had been gone Quintus knew not how long, but he gauged that by the time the moon had ridden clear of the trees, his task would be complete. So he watched as the horned goddess extricated herself from the branches and took up station alongside the stars.

He prayed that he had allowed enough time, but did not dare wait any longer — the more he delayed, the greater the chance of discovery. Leaving Rufus and Tullius in place, gently loosening planks, he ran back down alongside the ditch, keeping low. Then, where the track met the palisade, he stood and looked south, waving his arms and hoping that Maxim and Jovan could see him in the half light. He could have waved a torch, of course, but here he was almost in line with the gate, and a torch would almost certainly have been seen by the enemy.

Three, four, times he jumped up and down and waved his arms, though he knew that Jovan should be on the lookout for him. He ducked down, ready to return to the gap in the fence, but hesitated, thinking about signalling once more. Though he decided that the Macedonians must have seen him, he returned much more slowly along the way that he had just come, wondering whether he should return and make certain. Without the fire as a diversion, there was no way the plan would work. It was unlikely to work anyway, he thought ruefully, but at least with the fire it had a chance.

Then, with relief, he saw the first bright flashes amongst the trees and the first wisps of smoke. It was small, but it was definitely there. He quickened his pace. As he returned, he passed Sextus, hidden in the ditch, and hissed, 'Now, my friend, we are relying on you.'

The dark shadow that was Sextus rose up, climbed lithely onto the bank, reached up and pulled an already loosened plank away from the fence. It was enough that he could get most of his face into the gap, though he would not have been able to put his head through. This was but caution on his part, in case his plan did not work — though if that were the case, he would have to choose between having his face ripped off by a mastiff or his balls cut off by Tullius. The three-quarter moon cast enough light for him to clearly see the lumpy shapes of his quarry, both lying flat in the yard.

He put his face through the gap and whistled softly, then began to recite what sounded like an incantation, with a tone and cadence that was insistent and repetitive. He puckered his lips and whistled again, slightly louder, repeated the incantation, then whistled once more.

The dogs did not run, nor bark, nor even growl, but they did prick up their ears and turn their heads to look in the direction from which this strange summons came — for it was, to them, undoubtedly a summons. The furthest one from Sextus seemed satisfied, and, incurious, dropped its head once more to its paws. The nearer one rose slowly, scratching its ear with its back leg and walking a slow circle around the other hound. It, too, was about to settle back down when Sextus whistled again, just a little louder.

It was enough to make the mastiff change its mind, lift its muzzle and sniff the air. It rose and stretched, sniffed and gazed in the direction of the sound. Sextus was desperate to have it fix its attention solely on him, but he did not dare whistle any louder. He instead continued with the chant, which became a little more strident than it had been. It had always worked on the dogs in the temple of the Vestals — that was where he had been taught the trick. He had practised often on the even bigger dogs in the temple of Capitoline Jove when he had needed somewhere to sleep. He needed it to work again now.

Quintus carried on and reached the other two legionaries. They were crouching in anticipation by the palisade, next to where the ditch had been filled. Tullius was keeping a lookout, while Rufus stood ready to remove the planks they had been working on.

'The fire is lit,' Quintus told them. 'Do it.'

They had already prised the timbers loose — enough so that a man could get through — and now swiftly pulled them away, praying that the dogs had been neutralised. Tullius, watching the yard through a knothole, was holding his breath.

'They have risen and are looking towards Sextus, but they have not approached him. We cannot risk entering yet.'

The dogs had paused, clearly torn between the curiosity of the gap appearing in the fence and the summons coming from the other direction. But the spell being woven by Sextus proved to be the more compelling attraction. Without even casting a backwards glance at Rufus, his shadowy form now clearly outlined in the gap, they wandered towards the siren sound.

'Now,' hissed Tullius urgently, 'now.'

Quintus, Rufus and Tullius went through the gap, shoulders first, both glancing in the direction of the dogs and the village. The dogs were by the fence, the village quiet. It was dark, but their eyes had adjusted, and the sky, full of stars, was clear.

'I will free Publius.' Quintus went straight for the cage where he had seen the captive earlier, lifting the cover to reveal its occupant. 'Rufus, you and Tullius free Marcus.'

Rufus nodded and waved Tullius towards the end cage.

Quintus found Publius curled up, seemingly asleep, looking tiny and vulnerable despite his soldier's frame, instantly recognisable by his bright blond hair. Quintus' gladius was in his hand and he used it to cut the leather thong that kept the cage closed; he could see that it was built more like a laundry basket than a prison, and was able to easily lift off the top. He reached down and shook his comrade, but he did not move, and immediately Quintus feared that he no longer lived. His entreaties were in a voice that was hoarse, both with urgency and emotion.

'Lux, Lux, it is I, Quintus. Wake up.'

Publius moved slightly and moaned, but no amount of shaking could rouse him. 'Help me,' Quintus pleaded to the others.

But they were busy themselves, reaching Marcus' crate, where they threw back the covering. Marcus was not sleeping; he immediately let out a curse and a yell, compromising their efforts at stealth. Tullius leaned in and silenced him with a hand across the mouth and a curt obscenity. All the men immediately froze, holding their breath and turning their eyes towards the settlement and the dogs. Publius sniffled and subsided, his chin dropping to his chest. The dogs had looked up, then been drawn back by the spellbinding chant. No-one came running from the village.

They began to breathe again, their hearts pounding.

Tullius removed his hand slowly. They persuaded the naked legionary, as quietly as they could and in as few words, that they were here to rescue him and that they were not slaves or servants come to taunt him — difficult when both had blades drawn. Finally, throwing off the fog of his rage, Marcus recognised them. Of course, he had questions.

'Not now,' Tullius insisted, as he helped him out of the crate. Tullius was primus amicus to Marcus — he felt guiltily that he had not protected him well enough. At least he was fit enough to be able to help free himself, despite the marks of the lash on his back — marks that shocked Tullius. Quintus was still trying to extricate Publius. 'He cannot move; we must lift him,' he commanded.

'What is happening there?' Marcus demanded, now fully alert. He pointed towards the settlement, where now there was increased activity. The noise and light from the huts had grown, and people were shouting from one side of the village to the other. Torches were being lit; there were shouts of what might have been command, as well as cries tinged with fear — but it was fear of an attack, not an escape, and their attention was on the outside, on the fire in the trees, not on the prison. The smoke from the fire could now be seen and Quintus fancied that he could hear it crackling. Still no-one came to investigate the prisoners, the intended sacrificial victims, for the dogs had sung out no warning.

'The hounds,' said Marcus. 'Where are the hounds?' His eyes, adapted to seeing in the dark by his time in the crate, could pick them out. As he spoke, one of them turned and half rose; then, to his surprise, it lay back down again, and its mate laid its head on its back.

'So, Sextus' magic has worked,' Tullius said with surprise. 'Now we just need Crassus and Cato to succeed.'

'Sextus is here?' asked Marcus.

'Using sorcery on the dogs.' Tullius gave Marcus a thin smile. 'Crassus, Cato? Who else?'

'Everyone, my friend, everyone. Only you and Publius were missing.'

'We were resting up,' Marcus grinned, his teeth white in his dirty face, 'deserting, no doubt. Publius is here somewhere — have you found him?'

'We have him.' Tullius nodded towards the other crate.

'Lend me your knife,' said Marcus, holding out his hand. Tullius did not know why, but complied.

Quintus and Rufus had managed to get Publius out and he now hung between them. His eyes were open but vacant, and dribble crept down his chin. They were almost ready to move. With the dogs seemingly asleep, and with no interference from the village, their rescue had gone smoothly so far.

'There is another man, a tribesman, in the pen next to mine,' Marcus said, as he cut at the covering on his own crate with the pugio. 'Free him if you can; he is a human and does not deserve to burn.' He turned his attention once more to his task and succeeded in cutting away a large square of material, wrapping it around himself like a tribesman's animal skin. He passed the knife back with a grunt of gratitude.

'Burn?' Tullius asked, shocked.

'Burn. That is what they plan,' said Marcus.

Tullius threw back the cover on the crate and, with a finger to his lips, he urged its occupant to silence. The man's eyes widened in terror, but he stayed quiet. Tullius cut the leather bindings on the top and helped him out. He seemed relieved and pleased to see Marcus, pawing at him as if to make sure that he was real.

'We are leaving,' Marcus told him simply. 'Just follow.' The man nodded enthusiastically like a puppet on a string, still grinning inanely. He had understood the meaning, if not the words. Marcus pushed him towards the gap, Tullius already at it, Quintus and Rufus half carrying, half dragging Publius.

They shouldered their way through the fence, Tullius hanging back, both blades drawn. But the dogs were still, and all the activity beyond seemed to be aimed towards the supposed threat from the outside. He shepherded the captives and their rescuers through the gap, took a last look towards the settlement, and followed them, crossing the ditch and running north. Hearing footsteps behind, he turned, ready to fight, but it was Sextus who came towards them.

'Come on,' Tullius called, still low and hoarse. 'We have them.' As Sextus caught up, he added, 'It seems your magic worked on the hounds.'

'Later.' Sextus was hurrying, more interested in escaping than explaining. 'I will tell you later. Who are they carrying?' He pointed towards the silhouette of the slumped figure between two others.

'It is Publius; he is injured. The sooner we are away from here, the sooner we can see to what extent.'

'And him?' He indicated the tribesman.

'A friend of his.' Rufus jerked a thumb at the strangely garbed man accompanying them.

'Marcus!' Sextus exclaimed at the unusual costume of the legionary. 'Is it Lupercalia already?' As a city boy, Sextus knew all the festivals that involved young men and women and free food and drink. Lupercalia had the added benefit of young people chasing each other naked — the state he had noted Marcus was trying to cover. Unable to do anything else whilst they hurried, Sextus touched his fist to his heart. 'I bid you welcome.'

Marcus nodded and together they jogged behind the others, constantly looking back to see if they were being followed. The plan had worked so far. They just needed the last piece to fall into place, and that depended on Crassus and Cato.

XXXIII: ERICTHO

At the side of the settlement, they stopped and crouched, breathing heavily. Here, beneath the spreading boughs of a solitary beech, was their meeting point; here the palisade once again turned, this time to the north. The noise of shouting faded as they put distance between themselves and the tribesmen fighting the blaze. Until it was extinguished, no enemy would follow.

Gently, they laid Publius down with his back against the tree. He breathed, but his breath was ragged and rough; his eyes were open, but did not appear to see. He could barely keep his head upright, and his chin lolled on his chest. A thin line of dribble still leaked from the corner of his mouth, meandering down to his chin. His hair, amazingly, seemed clean, combed and shining, unlike the matted mess sported by the other captives they had freed. There was no sign of any injury upon him, no break or cut or bruise, but still he failed to properly wake.

Quintus knew the legend of Erictho, the witch employed by a son of Pompeius to bring a slain soldier back from the underworld to prophesy for him. Publius seemed like such a ghost. Shaking his head to rid it of the image, Quintus told Marcus, 'He must remain here.' Then, looking at the way the big man had half-clothed himself, he added, 'You'd better stay and look after him. And your friend.' He indicated the little man. 'Sextus, can you tell him he is safe?'

Sextus spoke some halting words in the tribesman's tongue.

Quintus thought that Marcus might object to the role he had been given, but he just nodded and said something to the man, who nodded in turn and moved across to Publius.

'We'll be back soon enough,' Quintus said. 'Keep safe. This is the meeting point. The slaves should find you here.'

'Our slaves?' Marcus asked incredulously.

'Our very own,' replied Quintus. 'Believe it. It is they who lit that fire. They have done well.'

'They helped? You freed them?' Marcus asked. 'Have they done enough to earn that?'

'I do not have that power,' said Quintus quickly, shaking his head. 'You know I do not. I am only decanus of our squad, and only by the leave of its members. I am no centurion or tribune, no great officer that could make such decisions.'

'Perhaps it does not matter if we do not treat them as slaves,' suggested Marcus.

'Perhaps,' agreed Quintus, though he was doubtful. 'They will join you soon; treat them as you see fit.' He and Sextus waved a brief farewell and joined the veterans, following the line of the palisade, its shadow stretching across the ditch as the dawn broke red in the east, the smoke from the fire visible now.

The four legionaries reached the gate where Crassus and Cato had entered even as the sullen morning sun shone eerily into the settlement like spilled wine. The light highlighted an opening in the palisade, a break in the long shadows where timbers were missing for, as Rufus had predicted, there was a second entrance to the compound. There were no hinged gates hanging open — as might be expected — but instead a narrow gap across which wooden poles had been mounted on hurdles. They were not so high that the men could not clamber over them. The opening was wide enough for two horses, or a single chariot, little more. It was not, Quintus thought, designed to keep enemies out, but to keep livestock in.

The line of the ditch here was also broken, a narrow portion of it covered with boards. The state of the ground at either end of this makeshift bridge pointed to a lot of coming and going, the evidence of a much used track winding away up into the low hills to the west, following the line of the forest as it petered out into little more than scrub. The slopes beyond it were pale with long grass, punctuated with round grey stone outcrops. It would seem that this particular tribe, Cantiaci or no, were either at peace or unafraid of any encroaching neighbour.

Not far inside the opening they came across four bodies; men dressed in the native garb of tunic and trews, sprawled two to each side, two of them with their throats cleanly cut, the other pair more hacked about. Next to them on the ground were the torches, extinguished now, which they had no doubt been holding. The morning's flies had already moved from horse manure and rubbish pit to a new feast, congregating on the opened flesh, rising in clouds from the places where blood was already blackening as the legionaries passed.

'Move those poles,' Quintus ordered, in as quiet a voice as possible, in case other tribesmen were on guard nearby. Rufus and Sextus took one end each of the nearest pole and lifted it from its hurdle, turning it ninety degrees and laying it on the ground. Tullius took one end of another pole and dragged it around so that it was parallel to the first. Neither barred the gap any longer. Sextus and Rufus quickly rejoined Quintus, whilst Tullius bent over one of the corpses, pugio in hand.

'This is no time for trophies,' hissed Quintus.

'Not a trophy,' the veteran replied over his shoulder, holding aloft the dead man's tunic, neatly slit down the back, and stuffing the dead man's long sword into his belt. 'For Marcus.' He placed the tunic over one of the hurdles then rejoined the others. Together they moved stealthily towards where they knew the horses had been tied.

Crassus and Cato had, as far as they were concerned, drawn the most difficult task. The first part of it was easy; they knew where the horses were kept. The second part was more difficult. They needed to get to the horses and bring away five or six beasts to ride. They knew there would be no saddles, for these animals were used to pulling chariots rather than being mounted, but they hoped that they could find bridles or something that would enable the horses to be ridden. Their only tools were their blades and a couple of lengths of thin rope that had been amongst the stuff taken in their expulsion from the village of the Atrebates. Their mission was crucial. Without the horses, they knew that their escape would have to be on foot, and therefore almost certainly doomed.

They expected to have to deal with tribesmen, with ostlers at least, if not armed guards. But the four men they had killed had been dicing and laughing instead of keeping watch. It was obvious that no attack had been expected, and the legionaries were amongst the horses, setting about their task without any further disturbance.

Now, however, something had been discovered: the settlement had erupted into noise and uproar. There was shouting and wailing — a scream as if someone had discovered a dead body, although the only bodies that the legionaries knew of were yet to be found. There were sharp shouts, the tramping of feet, the cries of women, the light of torches bobbing around then being extinguished, the dawn turning from red to bright oranges and yellows as the sun escaped the horizon. Quintus could see the smoke from the fire in the wood, and knew that this would be what had initially roused the tribesmen, but they now seemed to have discovered that this was not the only evidence of a raid. The sounds of geese honking and dogs barking, mixed with a noticeable increase in the level of fury, told him that the escape of the prisoners had been discovered, for there had been geese and other animals caged beside their friends.

Quintus led his men onwards past the bodies, speed now even more essential. Still they did their best to conceal themselves, crouching low, with only the protection of a woven willow fence to hide them from the turbulent village. The sound of horses' hooves and whispering voices ahead made Quintus raise his hand to halt them; then, with relief, he realised that the hissed conversation, which came from the direction of the settlement, was in fact between Cato and Crassus. They came into view quietly leading four horses, two each, using halters made from thin rope. These were small but sturdy beasts dappled brown and white, and behind them two smaller ponies followed, seemingly of their own volition.

Quintus was impressed. Though his heart had dreamt of success, his head had been repeatedly telling him that it was a foolish wish, and that his idiot plan would not work. Now the sight of the two legionaries with the horses gave him hope. Rufus and Sextus at once helped with the lead horses, whilst Tullius got himself behind the loose beasts and urged them on. The horses could not, of course, crouch as they had done, so the willow fence was no longer of any use in hiding the party.

'Run,' ordered Quintus, repeating the order. 'Run fast!'

As they fled the compound, the decanus straightened up and took up station alongside Crassus, all attempts at stealth or concealment abandoned. This was now flight.

'You did it,' he said excitedly, clapping Crassus on the shoulder. 'Well done indeed!'

Anger could be heard bubbling up behind them, a crescendo of complaints, shouts, indignation, rage, horror — there was no need to understand the words of the language; the tones were sufficient to glean their meaning.

'What did you do to the rest? Will we be followed?' Quintus asked breathlessly.

'You said we should hamstring them, I know, but Cato and I thought not. We thought they would scream and attract attention. So we hobbled them. We tied their back legs together and to each other. They will free them unharmed, but not quickly.'

Quintus disapproved, but said nothing. Crassus being soft-hearted with the horses meant that the tribesmen could pursue, and probably a lot faster than his friend thought. A sharp knife would make short work of any knot, however well tied; Alexander himself had proven that in Phrygia.

For Crassus, the guards he had killed were the enemy, not innocent beasts. He had spent the whole of his youth caring for, and being comforted by, horses. He had lived and breathed horseflesh since he could walk, and would not have knowingly caused one of the animals pain.

Now that there was definitely no longer any question of stealth or subterfuge, Quintus and Crassus shouted to the others to wait. Cato was struggling to keep the horse he was leading from turning to reach its foal, and Sextus had little control of his beast, which kept shaking its head as if to throw off the rope at its neck. Tullius' arm-flapping just seemed to be scattering the younger animals.

'We will take them,' Quintus said.

Both he and Crassus knew horses well, the one a farmer, the other a blacksmith. 'Go, go!' he shouted as he ran around to relieve Cato. 'You have done well,' he said to his comrade, 'but let me take them now.' As he grabbed the rope halters from Cato and Sextus, both happy to let go of the animals they were handling, he turned to Crassus. 'The loose ones?'

'They are scions, yearlings,' Crassus said, indicating the two animals. 'They will follow their dams. I freed no stallions, so these others should be docile enough.' He turned to Sextus for help. 'Make me a step. I can ride.'

Despite his back injury, he managed to step into Sextus' clasped hands and climb aboard one of the mares, controlling her with his knees whilst still clutching the halter of the one who fretted alongside. Rufus saw and offered a similar step to Quintus, who also managed to pull himself onto the back of a horse, snatching at its mane as he almost slipped all the way over, and only just succeeding in righting himself. He, too, took a second rope. Gaining control, the two legionaries urged their mounts forward and both loose horses and the remaining men followed, Crassus passing through the gap first, followed by Quintus and his two charges. The loose horses were herded through by the other men, clapping and encouraging them.

Behind them Rufus and Tullius took the initiative and pulled the poles back across the entrance. It would not hold the enemy tribe once they came, but would delay them at least a little. Tullius was last, pausing briefly to grab the tunic he had left behind. The horses' hooves clattered across the boards that spanned the ditch and those on foot struggled to keep up as the pace of the mounted men increased.

Behind them the risen sun had revealed several seats of chaos — woodland fires, dead guards, mounts stolen, broken fencing, missing prisoners, hobbled horses — as if an army of raiders had descended in the night. For now, panic held the inhabitants in its grip as they ran to and fro, trying to control the blaze, the wind carrying sparks dangerously close to the palisade and the turf roofs of the settlement. Some took to cursing the slaves, as if it were they who had let the prisoners free, and others tried to mount a pursuit but found their horses' back legs tied up and fell over each other in confusion.

Quintus urged both his ride and his men on. He would have whooped with joy like a child if they were not still in so much jeopardy.

His heart thumped as they approached the corner where the palisade turned and he heard men calling and shouting just beyond. He pulled hard on the halter, slowing his mount first to a walk and then bringing it to a standstill, and Crassus followed suit. The men on foot caught up quickly, breathless, swords already drawn in anticipation of a fight.

'What is it?' Rufus asked hoarsely.

'Is it the enemy?' Tullius demanded.

'I think so. Stand ready,' commanded Quintus. 'Listen.' He, too, had drawn his sword and was ready to fight. Then a grim smile cracked his face, and he shook his head disbelievingly, making his cheek pieces jangle. 'I hear Latin,' he said in mock horror, but in reality full of relief. 'The insubordinate oafs have disobeyed orders; they are our own.'

'I see them now!' Cato was overjoyed. 'And I see Publius, alive and uninjured and upright. I see my friend.'

He ran headlong towards the limp figure of Publius and grabbed him around the chest, not realising that it was only through the help of Marcus and Maxim that he was upright.

'Hold,' said Marcus sharply, pushing him away. 'Your reunion will have to wait.'

'Marcus?' Cato said foolishly. He was torn, stepping back from Publius in response to his brusque order.

'He is not well,' Marcus told him, in as kind a voice as he could muster. 'Leave him for now.' He addressed Quintus on his horse. 'Let's get out of here. There will be time for explanations.'

'There will,' Quintus agreed. 'Get Publius up here in front of me. The rest of you, spread yourself around the other mounts, the foals. We need to head back down the track, back the way that we came.'

'No,' said Marcus firmly shaking his head. 'Not that way.'

Before Quintus could respond, bridling at this attack on his authority, the little tribesman looked at Marcus and said something.

'He says he does not ride, Quintus,' Marcus swiftly explained. 'More importantly, he says do not follow the track. That is why we have come this way. He says to follow the fence, then turn east, down into the valley.'

'Past our pursuers? Past the gate we have just left?' Quintus asked incredulously.

'Or back into the fire and the enemy behind us. The slaves did well — too well; the fire is almost impassable at the moment. We could not go that way. The villagers will have it out soon enough, but will then defend the track.' Marcus pointed to the tribesman. 'This man's boat is on the river, and back the way you have come and down the hill is the fastest way to it.'

Quintus was reluctant. It felt like he was again taking orders from the man who had once been his superior. He hesitated, but Sextus was already organising the others onto horseback and Marcus had turned away to speak to the little man. No-one but he noticed his hesitation as, with a nod to himself, he accepted the sense of what had been said. He knew that his dead captain and friend, Ursus, would understand.

Marcus lifted the small man and placed him in front of Crassus. Though he was frightened, he complied. Publius was more difficult, as it seemed as if his bones had turned to rubber. After a brief struggle, Quintus ordered that he be slung across the horse like a sack of flour. Sextus had mounted one of the other horses and now helped Rufus up behind him, whilst Cato, also mounted, held his arm out to Tullius.

Tullius shook his head. 'Take him; he cannot run wearing that,' he said with a half-smile, indicating Marcus and his strange dress. 'I will run alongside with the slaves. We have neither the skill nor the time to catch those other two.'

The yearlings had stood a little distance away, unwilling to be parted from their dams, but equally unwilling to be too close to the men and their noise. Cato helped Marcus aboard and Tullius shoved the tunic into his hands. 'Take this. I think you may need it.' He laughed and set off the way they had just come at a jog, waving at the slaves to join him.

As they all rushed back towards the danger they had just escaped, Publius let out a long, low moan. The image of the witch and the ghost sprang into Quintus' mind, and a shiver ran down his spine. Publius was unmoving but not dead; Quintus could still feel the warmth of his body. There was no time to check on his condition; they had to move.

XXXIV: INTER MALLEUM ET INCUDEM

The group that cantered off did not look like the raiding party of dozens that the Cantiaci thought had descended upon them; if anything, they looked like a motley troop of vagabond actors fleeing a city where their performance had not gone well.

At the front was the little tribesman clinging on to an armoured rider; next came a tall legionary in a metal helm with what looked like a dead body slung across his pony in front of his long legs, which seemed to almost reach the ground. Alongside rode one who looked bizarre, like he had escaped from some sort of play; he had dirty hair and a wild beard, and was dressed in a kind of rough leather cloak. He was sitting awkwardly, his arms around the waist of a man much smaller and darker skinned than him. On the final mount, a bright red bushy beard was the most marked feature of the pair, who, as with the others, seemed too large for such small beasts. Three more came with them on foot, one armed and fierce, two others empty-handed. They were all of necessity rushing headlong towards the danger that they had only just left behind.

As they approached the plank bridge over the ditch and the narrow gap in the fence, this time intending to ride straight past, they could see horses milling in the yard, riders attempting to mount them. The enemy were making ready to pursue.

But they could also see that there was no discipline. Men were shouting and cursing, tripping and pushing each other in their haste to clear the gate, whilst behind the barrier too many beasts were in too small an area, the horses bucking and biting at each other. Some men had been determined to go back towards the main part of the village, as that was where the enemy seemed to have struck. Others wanted to leave the yard via the gate, and some were even attempting to harness chariots, men and horses and intentions all getting in the way of each other. Quintus had been right; it had not taken long to free the horses, hobbled or not. But in the confusion, even the simple task of removing the hurdles and poles was taking time.

Suddenly a single voice roared, and others joined it, and many fingers pointed as the tribesmen saw the strange troop galloping past. Here were the raiders, or at least some of them; here was a focus at last for their anger. As if the distinct voice had finally given them purpose, the tribesmen surged towards the opening, some now mounted, many on foot.

They began to cross the plank bridge as the poles were finally cleared, but the narrowness of the opening worked against them. The mounted men struggled to pass through the crowd. They hampered each other as each tried to reach the enemy first and the moment was lost.

At once the Romans were past, leaving the shouting in their wake, galloping and running along a well-used track. Following the counsel of the tribesman they had freed, they turned east at the corner of the settlement. The palisade on their right was tall, with no breaks in it, and plunged down the steep slope into the valley. The riders urged their ponies on as the men on foot caught up with them, and they were all forced to navigate the precipitous descent. The settlement was built on a man-made hill, but on this side the defences had also made use of the scarp that dropped down to the crook of the valley.

Quintus could see the great sweep of the river below, flat water meadows to either side, the morning sun turning the smooth surface of the water to silver. If they could but reach the river, and the little man's boat was there, they would be safe. He could also see the continuation of the track that led across the front of the settlement and knew that, if the tribesmen realised the nature of their escape plan, they could be easily cut off by chariots issuing from the main gate. They would be caught between a hammer and anvil, *inter malleum et incudem*, and crushed.

The ponies slowed, having to pick their way down, unused to the burdens they were carrying, whilst Tullius and the two slaves jumped from tussock to tussock, heading straight down rather than using the narrow winding path that the horses followed.

'They are making better speed,' Sextus yelled into Rufus' ear.

'I see it,' Rufus replied. 'I never was one for cavalry.' So saying, he slid off the pony. He landed on his backside but quickly rose to his feet and followed Tullius and the slaves on foot.

'Nor I,' said Sextus, dismounting much more gracefully than his comrade. He landed on his feet and broke into a run. The pony, unfettered by any passengers, immediately slowed, then continued picking its way down towards the water.

Crassus, with the terrified tribesman clinging on to him, could not make this choice. Nor could Quintus, bearing the dead weight of a barely conscious Publius, but Cato could.

'I will run,' he told Marcus, laughing. 'You stay here, or you will trip over your dress.' He slipped off the back of the horse and, like a goat on a mountain, vaulted and leapt the rocks and tussocks with his comrades.

There was no time to issue orders, or to try and make this anything other than a headlong flight down the hill, but there was no need either. As long as no-one fell or stumbled — and fear was lending swiftness to their feet — they would all be together on the riverbank. The runners leaned their bodies forward, which forced their legs to pump ever faster to keep themselves upright. Their downhill rush was so desperate that their breath came in great gasps and their muscles burned with the effort.

Quintus dared to look behind. The pursuit had already reached the top of the slope, and heavily armed men were dismounting and starting to descend. It seemed that they would not risk their ponies. As he watched, a spear thudded into the ground ten paces behind him, another quickly beside it. They were out of range for now, but he thought it would be only a matter of moments before one whistled past his ear or buried itself in his spine. The loose horse, still finding its way more slowly down the slope, would prove a hindrance, but not enough to halt the chase.

'Find the boat!' he shouted at the men running ahead, as he urged his mount on down the twisting path. 'Without it, we are lost. Crassus, get him down there as fast as you can.'

Crassus was not only at the front, but also had the most expertise with horses. He had the least heavy of the burdens and managed to guide the horse down some of the slopes between the turns of the path, following the lead of the runners. They had already passed the end of the palisade, where the track crossed the meadow, and, as the slope flattened out, they slowed to catch their breath, lungs and legs on fire. As soon as Crassus' pony reached level ground, it picked up speed, and it was clear that it would overtake the runners and arrive at the river before them.

Quintus and Marcus hit the flat ground at almost the same moment and soon overtook their comrades who were on foot. They were now able to see back towards the main gate of the settlement.

Though there was much movement by the gate, many people milling about, there was no sign of anyone on horseback and as yet no evidence of pursuit. On the slope above them tribesmen had paused to fling spears, but the range was still too great and the enemy could not match the speed of men who were in fear of their lives.

'They are on foot. I think we can outrun them.'

'You are right!' shouted Quintus. 'I think we might make it yet!'

'Our friend will make it.' Marcus waved his arm at where Crassus had dismounted from his horse at the side of the river and was helping the little tribesman down. The man gesticulated towards a tall growth of reeds and the pair, looking back to make sure they were followed, set off for the spot.

'They are coming from the gate!' shouted Quintus. 'They have seen us!'

Sure enough, the confusion and chaos on the track in front of the gate had resolved itself into some form of order, with chariots and runners now streaming towards them. A quick glance told him that they were running short of time; the men careering down the hill were closing in on them, and those on the track were now also determined. He urged the pony onwards, swiftly reaching Crassus' horse, and dismounted. As Marcus too leapt from the back of his mount, dam and foal were once more united.

'If I was armed, I would hold them!' Marcus shouted. 'But we do not even have shields!'

'We travel light out of necessity,' Quintus responded. 'Come, we do not want to lose you now, not after all the trouble we have taken to free you. Come and help me with Publius instead — he cannot walk.'

Marcus hastened across. Seeing what they were doing, Cato also rushed to lend a hand with Publius, gently slapping his cheek in a fruitless attempt to bring him back to this world. All he achieved was a long sigh and eyes that opened without seeing, then rolled back.

'Drugged in some way, I think,' Cato said.

'Or bewitched. They practised sorcery, I know it,' said Marcus.

Sextus and Rufus also caught up. 'I think he is injured in some way,' Sextus said, 'though I don't dismiss the possibility of magic.' He lowered his voice. 'Tullius has been like this before, without either injury or sorcery — it could be that...'

Tullius and the slaves were about to catch them up — Tullius very much alive and roaring with rage. 'Bastards tried to throw spears at us!' he complained loudly. 'Rufus, Marcus, let's stand and take a few out.'

'Like this?' Marcus raised his arms to show that he was unarmed. He still clutched the tunic that Tullius had grabbed for him, whilst the loose square of leather he had used to clothe himself hung awkwardly from his shoulders, barely covering him.

'We are supposed to be escaping, not dying,' said Rufus. 'Look, the boat.'

From out of the reeds, the beak of a sturdy wooden craft was emerging; it was high-sided, with a sharply pointed prow rearing to the height of a man above the water. Crassus was reaching up, holding on to the edge of the planking and, with difficulty, dragging it out of the rushes. The tribesman was nowhere to be seen.

'Help me!' Crassus shouted. 'Help me get it into the water!'

Tullius and Rufus immediately ran to help, whilst Publius slumped between Quintus and Marcus. Maxim and Jovan also took up position behind the legionaries, their combined effort managing to free the boat from the bank and shove it into the water. The tribesman could be spotted now, standing in the stern, tiller in hand. He shouted something at the shore, something that sounded panicked.

'What is he saying?' Quintus demanded of Marcus.

'I do not know…'

'I do,' interrupted Sextus. 'He is telling us to get aboard quickly. It must have snapped its mooring. I doubt he can hold it by the shore for long; there should be a crew.'

'There should be oarsmen,' agreed Quintus, seeing the ports along the side. He and Marcus dragged Publius to where the others were and heaved him up half into the boat, so that his head vanished inside and his feet dangled down, folded like a scrap of laundry on a line; still he made no noise.

'In, in,' ordered Quintus. 'We can help him once we are aboard.'

Between them they climbed and scrambled, making steps for comrades with their clasped hands, so that they could heave themselves over on to the decking, then reach back and pull those same comrades in after them. Quintus and Crassus strained to hold the boat steady, all the while glancing fearfully at the approaching enemy then, with everyone else aboard, helped each other up, Quintus making a step for the blacksmith, and the blacksmith and Rufus then dragging the tall legionary aboard.

Publius was the last to be dealt with — he appeared safe enough doubled over the side as he was, until the first of the spears rattled the timbers. The men rushed to bring him fully into the boat and, as they succeeded, the ship turned gradually into the current, its prow heading out towards the middle of the slow-moving river. Missiles — slingshots, spears, axes even — embedded themselves into the timber or bounced off the decking. Quintus thanked the gods that these people did not seem to have bows and arrows. He clutched Ursus' armband and mouthed a silent prayer of gratitude.

XXXV: FRISIA

The tribesman, bald head still below the edge of the craft and weathered hand clutching the tiller, was shouting instructions in his own language. There were three of them now who could pick out the odd word or phrase; Marcus had learned a little, as had Sextus and Crassus, whilst no-one else understood anything he was saying.

'Quiet,' commanded Quintus, putting a finger to his lips. 'We need to work out what to do ourselves.'

The man looked affronted, but stopped shouting. The bottom of the boat was full of water, a good hand's breadth of dirty brown liquid swilling around, with a few oars scattered in it — not enough for a full crew, but usable. Quintus picked one up.

'Tullius!' he called to the man nearest to the stern, handing him the wet timber. 'Take this oar and push us off.'

Tullius grabbed the oar and, regardless of the risk of being struck by one of the missiles, he raised his head and shoulders above the stern boards and fed it through his hands until it made contact with the bank. As he gave it a shove, Rufus joined him, also with an oar, and the boat lazily swung away from the shallows as the first of the men who had followed them down the hill approached the bank. Some even waded into the water — but they were too late. The craft was free of its moorings, free of the pull of the bank and floating further and further into deep water. Though they shouted and cursed and threw spear after spear and slingstone after slingstone, they had lost the race.

For the legionaries, most of whom were slumped on the boat's rowing benches, their feet in the filthy bilge water, the closeness of the escape was such that they could almost feel the angry breath of the pursuers on their necks.

Publius lay awkwardly in the boat, his feet and lower legs in the brown water, his tunic torn and wet. His head lolled on the folded material of the boat's sail, which flapped where it had freed itself from the ropes that had once tied it to the mast. Only his hair still shone, catching the light of the sun. The mast lay along the length of the boat, one end of it in the bilge at the stern, beneath where the little ship's captain manned the tiller, the other raised on a short crosspiece in the prow. The sail had been wrapped around it, but some of it had come free. The mast was a sturdy tree, Quintus noted; there was no way that this man could have lifted it himself.

Marcus wet his hands in the brackish water and wiped his face as clean as he could, at the same time attempting to flatten his hair. He then took up station beside the bald tribesman to help if needed, whilst the others congratulated each other on their narrow escape. Even the Macedonians received claps on the back and words of praise, though they did not seem sure how to take this unaccustomed inclusion.

Quintus shook himself into action; they were not free yet. There were just four oars, the two that Rufus and Tullius had used to shove them off, and two others half floating in the bottom of the boat. 'The far bank,' he ordered. 'Take the oars, Tullius, Rufus, and you two.' He indicated Maxim and Jovan. 'Marcus, are you fit? Can you help with steering? We have many pursuers. I will explain later.'

'I am fine, just a little exposed.' Marcus managed a weak smile as he held his arms open, revealing his naked body. 'This will be useful,' he added, waving the crumpled rag — the tunic that Tullius had rescued. Tullius managed to respond with a languid wave as he settled onto one of the rowing benches, facing the stern of the boat. He swatted away Jovan, who sat on the bench next to him.

'Go elsewhere,' said the dour legionary gruffly, who did not like Macedonians. Jovan shrugged and took the seat behind.

The shouts of the tribesmen were already muted as they progressed down the river, putting the stand of reeds and bulrushes in which the craft had been hidden between them and the bank. By the time they were clear of these, they were in open water, in the centre of the river, and could see beyond to the wooden palisade, the hill with its dwellings and to where the smudges of smoke against the blue sky bore witness to their escapade.

Quintus turned to Cato. 'Nox, look after Publius. Get him out of that water.'

'Help me,' Cato pleaded, turning to Sextus. 'Help me to get him upright, away from the oars.' Between them, they propped Publius up. The men detailed to do the rowing had had to step over his prone body, but now were able to start pulling on the oars in earnest. Again the tribesman bobbed up and down, this time addressing Marcus, his speech accompanied by many repetitions and hand gestures.

'He says not the other bank!' Marcus yelled from the stern. 'I think he says that there is nowhere to land. There is marsh. He says there may also be enemy there.'

'Then how far down?' Quintus asked, squinting along the course of the river from his vantage point in the prow. His sweating comrades were now striking up a rhythm, Cato stamping his foot to provide a beat, whilst cradling Publius' golden head in his lap.

The tribesman spoke again, and Marcus shrugged. It was Crassus who understood. 'All the way, he says, all the way to the sea. His own men are lost, his trading goods also.'

'The boat is all he has,' Marcus added. 'It will take us away from this cursed land, across the ocean; it will take us to Frisia.'

Quintus looked up at the sun, then at the silver serpent of the river, then at the dark water swirling in the base of the boat. Though he clutched Ursus' armband hidden beneath his tunic, and prayed, he did not truly believe it possible that they would reach the sea.

As the hypnotic swish of the blades in the water continued and the boat glided down the river. Quintus took a turn himself as the men on the oars spelled each other, all apart from Tullius and Rufus, who turned down offers to relieve them and seemed determined to do more than their share.

He noticed that the Macedonians, too, were not happy being idle. Maxim had found a needle and thread from somewhere and was sewing up the tunic that Marcus had come away with, whilst the legionary made further efforts to clear his hair and face of mud. Jovan was helping with the bailing as the men used their helmets to empty out the bottom of the boat, although their captain seemed unconcerned at the water sloshing in the bilge.

Cato also did not row. Instead he tended Publius, trying to make him as comfortable as possible. He had managed to keep his own helmet throughout the flight, and now, leaning precariously over the side, he filled it with river water, which he brought to Publius' lips. But he could only pour it in; Publius, though he breathed still, made no effort to help himself. Cato tried to rouse him a couple of times, but with no success.

At first they glimpsed the enemy tracking them through the reeds and bushes of the bank from which they had embarked.

There were horses and chariots, and many men on foot, but the woodland and the stretch of water between them muffled their shouts.

When Quintus looked ahead, there was also no sign of Elrik or any of his fellow warriors approaching. He looked at the water behind them — he could see for many leagues down the flat valley — but there seemed to be no water-borne pursuit either. Perhaps these people did not use boats, even though they lived by the waterside. It was not unknown.

The track could not follow the great meanders of the slow-moving river, so that the pursuers inevitably fell behind. In the crooks of the bends were marshlands, bog and reed, full of the croaks of frogs and the cries of water birds, flapping above the rushes, trailing water from their wingtips. When the river bent back the other way, the track — and the pursuit, still seen through a screen of trees — came dangerously close and lent urgency to the arms of the rowers.

As they passed a tall stand of bulrushes, shaded by ancient willows, and the river once again bent to the east, the trees diminished alongside the track, becoming first a low hedge and then vanishing altogether. The tribesman had pushed the tiller hard over and pointed urgently towards the far bank. Fearing enemy, the men stopped rowing, ready to pick up weapons, but at this the man became more animated, miming furious rowing. Marcus was the first to realise what he meant.

'Row!' he shouted, as he lifted his own oar. 'It is a fork in the river. We need to row to stay in our own course.'

At once the men picked up their oars, now seeing the river dividing, a pointed island or spit of land protruding into its centre before them. Their branch was heading south, the other taking a more westerly course, the track no doubt following it. Crassus made a shape with his hand, fingers together, and showed it to the tribesman, whilst using a word he had learned as they had defended the Atrebates. The tribesman shook his head enthusiastically.

'No bridge. That will put paid to any pursuit on foot,' said the blacksmith, lowering his hands with satisfaction.

'Will it also trap Elrik on the other bank?' Sextus asked, not having forgotten their other pursuers.

'We can only hope so,' Quintus replied.

The tribesman made more gestures with his hands and spoke some guttural words. Crassus seemed to understand. 'I think we have left the territory of the Cantiaci,' he told them. 'This fork must mark their borders.'

As the boat entered the channel on the left, the man turned to the rowers, smiled and pushed both hands, palms down, towards the deck, in a gesture that the men knew to mean 'slow down'. One after the other they shipped oars and allowed the boat to drift downriver, though the man still kept hold of the tiller and made sure they did not run aground.

Suddenly they were all exhausted — hungry, thirsty and aching, lacking even the energy for conversation. As the oars were brought inboard, the men seemed to deflate before his eyes.

'Can you men find out if it is safe to camp here?' Quintus asked Marcus, Sextus and Crassus, hoping that between them they could interpret. 'Perhaps on the eastern bank?'

The three legionaries looked at each other for a moment, then elected Marcus to talk to their boatman. 'I will try and find out,' he said.

He climbed up to the base of the little platform reserved for the helmsman and, in a combination of hand gestures and simple words in both of their languages, now and then asking for assistance from the other two, he managed to convey the state of the crew and their need for food and rest. At first the man shook his head, but as Marcus theatrically pointed out the state of his comrades, he relented, pointed downstream and held up two fingers.

'I think he means two hours, though I do not know how they calculate the time,' Marcus called back to Quintus.

'Do we need to row?'

Marcus turned and mimed rowing to the man, who shook his head. 'I think the river will take us,' he concluded.

Quintus was about to congratulate his comrade but decided it would be awkward. Officially, as decanus, he was senior to Marcus, but the legionary had been senior to him once, an officer, and he still felt it. Instead, Quintus grunted, a sound that he hoped conveyed approval.

As he looked around at the state of the group that had shipped from Hispania with such high hopes, he decided that he had failed in his duty. Publius lay comatose, his head on Cato's lap. Sextus sat next to Cato, talking softly, squeezing the leather casing of his bulla. Tullius and Rufus were sprawled across the rowing benches, staring at the open sky.

Marcus, wrapped in his improvised cloak, was kneeling on the step of the helmsman's platform, his hands and shoulders slumped across the side of the boat, his head tipped so that he could watch the slow passage of the riverbank. Crassus sat awkwardly on one of the benches, leaning forward. Quintus realised that he was easing the pain in his back — an injury that they had all forgotten about in the heat of the flight.

'Crassus...' he began, but his amicus just raised his eyes to him and gave a slight shake of his head, the meaning of which was clear. Once more, he felt the loneliness of command. He knew that his comrade would accept no sympathy, nor any lighter duties, and that any admission of pain would be seen as a sign of weakness.

Quintus turned his attention to the last of their party, the two slaves, who were huddled together at the back of the boat, having run out of tasks to do. He sighed again, thanked the gods for their safety and the success of the rescue, then closed his eyes, hoping for visions of green fields and golden corn.

XXXVI: PIACULUM

He was startled out of his reverie by a shout from Marcus. The helmsman was pointing to a spot on the eastern bank where there seemed to be a sort of beach, sloping down to the water. Quintus' eyes had been closed for longer than he had realised — the sun was much lower in the sky, and the right-hand bank had once more receded.

'Is this the place?' he asked, shading his eyes from the suddenly bright light.

'It is!' called Marcus. 'He will steer us; we may need to row.'

When he looked, Tullius and Rufus were already manning an oar each and, between them, one rowing, the other creating a backwash by reversing his oar, they had turned the boat sharply towards the beach. As Quintus looked, the bright lightning plumage of a kingfisher flashed across in front of them — a harbinger of better luck, he hoped.

Everyone on the boat stirred, except poor Publius, as they ran it aground on the gently sloping sand. The tribesman was lowered down by Marcus, and fixed the painter to a piece of timber, then wedged the wood behind a rock before turning to help the others out. Marcus had already followed, moving with surprising agility considering the nature of his captivity. The men did not seem to mind getting wet, and helped each other climb down — an undignified scene had anyone been around to see it. Tullius tripped and sat flat on his backside in the water, but managed a weak smile. Crassus grunted, though none but he could have said whether in pain or effort. Sextus jumped down and helped Cato with Publius, Rufus taking over

313

the task from the bank, leaving Cato free to swiftly clear the small stones away from a section of the beach with his foot.

'Put him here,' he said, 'carefully.' They laid Publius gently on the cleared space. He looked for all the world as if he slept peacefully, his hair still bright and fair, and longer than he usually wore it. His chin was smooth, and his nails were clipped and painted red. Where Marcus had been dirty and unkempt, Publius had been kept clean — even his tunic was still reasonably white, bearing only the marks of his escape.

'Everything but a garland of flowers around his neck,' said Sextus, clearly disgusted.

'What do you mean?' Cato asked.

'That he has been dressed as an offering, a *piaculum*, for sacrifice,' said Quintus.

'They were going to burn us all.' Marcus had walked across to where Publius lay. 'They took his clothes, as they did mine, but then washed him thoroughly and gave him a clean tunic, whilst merely confining me to a cage. They seemed to have some sort of fixation with his hair.'

'The colour,' offered Sextus. 'The brightness of his hair could have been precious to them.'

'Or to their gods of fire,' said Quintus.

'The slave girls washed and combed his hair and shaved his chin, but they also made him drink something that seemed to take the spark of life from him,' Marcus said. 'He was also visited by some sort of priest or shaman, all furs and skins and ornaments of bone. They were placed here, here, and here.' As he spoke, he showed them where the ornaments had been — around his neck, wrists, and upper arms, and in his hair and ears. 'It was he who painted his nails. The poor lad has not spoken in days, not since the priest, or whatever he was, was with him.'

314

'If it is a potion, we should seek a cure,' said Cato.

'Even if it is a spell, it can be broken,' Sextus added.

'If we find out how it was cast,' said Quintus doubtfully. 'For now, we rest; we all rest. He may even come out of it on his own; Maxim recovered from something similar.'

The slaves set to work finding kindling and building a fire, once the tribesman had indicated that this would not be a problem. Once it was lit, he gave them a crooked smile and signalled for them to lift him back into the boat, where he scrabbled about and then reappeared with a cooking pot, not large but sufficient to boil water. He threw it over the side and then ducked down again towards the stern before emerging with a wet bundle held in his arms. He tipped it over the side where it landed with a splash, and then followed it into the water, picking it up and holding it out to Jovan and Maxim like a trophy whilst pointing at the river.

'A net,' said Maxim, taking it from the little man's hands.

'And a river,' Jovan grinned. 'I think he is encouraging us to catch dinner.' He turned to Quintus. 'Master?'

'Of course,' Quintus laughed, 'fish away.'

Unlike Publius, both Marcus and the tribesman were filthy. They had not had access to water with which to wash, nor even to proper latrines, for many days. The tribesman had on a tunic that had once been light, but which was now stained with spit, blood, and waste. Marcus had rubbed off some of the dirt from his face and head, but there was much dried filth beneath his improvised cloak.

Where they had landed, the shingle beach sloped down to the water, and the tribesman was first to wade in and begin to clean himself. Marcus followed, carrying his newly acquired tunic but still wearing his makeshift cloak, so as to clean it at the same time. The little man ducked his head beneath the water, rubbing his bald head vigorously, and then began pulling at his tunic to take it off. Marcus waded across to help and managed to drag it over his fellow captive's head. Freed of the wet cloth, the man used it to sponge himself with the water. Marcus threw off his covering too and scrubbed thoroughly. The two men chortled and splashed each other, laughing breathlessly, acting like young children let out of lessons early. Quintus was shocked to see the marks of the lash still fresh on Marcus' back.

The other men, whilst not as filthy, still carried sweat and grime beneath their tunics. They therefore followed suit, leaving weapons on the beach, helping each other out of armour, and wading into the water. Crassus and Sextus were first in, washing their tunics whilst they wore them, then helping each other to remove them.

'Jovan!' shouted Crassus. 'Here.' He held out his soaking tunic.

'And this,' added Sextus, holding out his own, 'and boil some water — we all need shaves.'

Jovan ran down to the water's edge to collect the garments. He washed them vigorously in the water, wrung them out and then hung them to dry over the side of the boat and along the stretched length of the painter. Other legionaries called him as they finished rinsing their own tunics.

Quintus, as the tallest, had to wade further out in order to submerge himself and now strode back into the shallows. He had left Ursus' package with his belt on the shore — other packages were left with other belts, the wills of the men, returned by the slaves once they were out of immediate danger, so it did not look like anything special, although Sextus had eyed it curiously.

Quintus stood up to his knees in the water, hands on his hips, and hooted as he surveyed the collection of gear. 'Look at us, a full squad, fully armed, prepared for war over the water.'

The men followed his gaze and saw the sorry state they were in with regards to equipment.

'Where is the quartermaster when you need him?' Rufus joked.

'And the armourer,' added Tullius.

'And the barber,' complained Marcus, from within his spiky mass of hair. 'Tell me, decanus, how do we all find ourselves here? What has happened since the storm?'

'That needs a fireside and a flask of wine,' said Quintus. 'Soon, I hope.'

As they looked at the collection of rags and remnants lying on the sandbank in the bright sunshine, Quintus could not help but start to chuckle. Soon most of the others had joined in, all laughing as they looked at what was left of their gear — all but the tribesman, who looked confused.

On the strand were swords, daggers, belts and aprons for half a dozen at most, along with incomplete sets of armour. There were also tattered cloaks and four helmets, but no spears, no shields, no water or wine skins, and no standards. No-one had removed their caligae.

'I have my costume for Lupercalia,' laughed Marcus, who had climbed out of the water, and wrapped his tunic round his waist. He performed a swift twirl, hand to his chin in a coquettish manner, the delicacy of his pose spoiled by his behind peeking out from the folds.

He struggled to pull the damp tunic over his head, wriggling into it whilst Maxim held his breath at the strain put on his stitching. The garment that Tullius had cut away was now clean, apart from the brown stain at its neck where its previous owner had met his end.

One by one the men returned to the fire, sharing the cloaks. The fire provided welcome homeliness as well as warmth, and the slaves had soon netted their supper, which they now charred on spits over the flames.

Cato was the only legionary who had not joined in with the jollity in the water, instead sitting by Publius' side and praying for some movement or spark. Quintus ruffled the curly hair. 'Go, wash yourself,' he said kindly. 'I will watch over him.'

Reluctantly, and with none of the merriment that had infected the others, Cato took off his arms and armour and went down to the water. He sat morosely in the shallows and struggled to extricate himself from his tunic.

'Jovan, help him,' Marcus ordered, taking the skewered fish from his grasp.

Jovan would have sighed had he dared, but instead waded in once more to assist one of his masters. Cato was wrapped in his own dark thoughts and did not even acknowledge the assistance, instead washing himself carelessly and inadequately and hurrying back, wet tunic in hand, to take up his vigil again.

Jovan returned to the fire and squatted in his own thin, wet tunic, allowing it to dry on his back and obeying orders mechanically. Surreptitiously, he studied the might of Rome — reduced to a few half-naked men spitting out fish bones. He had removed his thin leather shoes, and washed his hair and beard, but no amount of scrubbing would remove the letters 'RRE' inked on his forehead — *Res Romani Exercitus*: property of the Roman army.

'I have my own helmet still,' said Quintus proudly, as he dressed, 'thanks to Jovan.' He gave a mock bow in the direction of the Macedonian that had rescued the less than shiny headgear from the sea and seen the initials, 'JQQ', inscribed within. Jovan nodded an acknowledgement, but still rubbed at his tattoo.

'Come, Jovan, work to do,' said Tullius, tugging at his hair and offering a pugio, haft first. 'You will need a blade.'

'Me next,' laughed Marcus and Sextus in unison.

'Maxim, you must help,' Jovan said, realising that nearly all of them needed grooming.

That night, with the murmur of the river as a lullaby, they slept soundly, though discipline demanded that they mount a guard — especially since Publius needed to be protected. At all times at least two of them were awake, talking in the flickering light of the fire that they kept alive. Though he fought hard against it, Cato's head finally dropped to his chest.

He woke with a start, immediately guilty at his lack of vigilance, and saw the slaves leaning over Publius. At once he drew his gladius and shouted, ready to run them through if they were doing his friend harm. Both of the Macedonians stood back quickly, hands out, each of them grasping something in one fist. Cato grabbed Maxim's wrist, and made him drop what it held, then stopped as he realised that it was just a cloth that fell, not a weapon.

Publius lay on his back still, but with his tunic bunched up to his waist. His hair had not been cut, but was tied back, away from his face, making him look even more pale and vulnerable.

'Explain,' commanded Cato, picking up the cloth and brandishing it, furious enough to do them harm.

They both looked at the ground meekly, in fear of their lives. 'Master,' Jovan said softly, 'he has … soiled himself. In the night. We have washed him and are now making him comfortable.'

At once the rage went out of Cato like air from a punctured bladder. He was embarrassed — but these were slaves, and had no right to see his shame. 'Finish, then,' he barked, throwing the cloth back at Maxim, then stamped off towards the river, leaving Jovan and Maxim looking at each other in shock.

'Do as he bid you,' said Quintus with authority, but no trace of rancour. He had witnessed the little scene and himself had — momentarily — jumped to the conclusion that the slaves meant Publius harm. He shook the thought from his head. Of course, they were only doing their duty.

In the early morning light he walked towards the water, where Cato stood, now with Sextus' arm around his shoulders. Thanks to Maxim and Jovan, all the men were tidier now. Marcus had ordered Jovan to shave his head, his hair was such a rat's nest, and Jovan had found a belt of sorts amongst the gear in the boat, which Marcus used to gather his tunic. He was also now armed with the long blade that Tullius had taken for him.

Seeing that the boat appeared to sit much further up the beach than it had done, Quintus scratched his head, wondering where all the water had gone. Then he realised that they had reached the tidal part of the river. Though Cato had laboured in the wharves by Tiber island, he had never noticed the waters rising and falling. In that part of the world tides were small, meaning that both he and Quintus were only vaguely aware of them. Each had only once sailed on the open sea, each had only once seen ships raised by the waters.

Quintus looked further afield as the sun lit up the camp. Beyond the river the land was flat and featureless, sweeping on for what seemed an eternity. It was peppered with stretches of water, now seen as bright islands of light. All across it the mournful cries of seabirds were mixed with the squabbling and shrieks of others, wheeling and diving for whatever morsels were hidden in the sand. It seemed bleak and endless, the sky somehow wider and emptier than it had ever been. But there was no other sign of life — no boats, no chariots, no pursuit. He tasted salt on the tip of his tongue: the sea, the sea and home.

XXXVII: KENEIL

Breakfast was, of course, yet more fish, caught before dawn by the slaves, who now moved carefully around the legionaries, treading as if they walked on hot coals, even though they had done nothing wrong.

Tullius, Rufus and Crassus sat together, talking quietly as they ate. Marcus, Sextus and the tribesman were squatting by the flames, laughing intermittently at some ribaldry or other. Quintus was curious, and went to join them.

'We are learning wicked words,' laughed Sextus.

'Useful,' scoffed Quintus, raising an eyebrow.

'Better than nothing.' Marcus allowed himself a smile.

Quintus squatted with them, chewing on the skewered and charred fish he held. 'I think our story is too long for now,' he said. 'But tell me yours. How did you all come to be captives together?'

'We were thrown up on a beach, Publius and I. He was in a worse state than me. I thought we needed to get inland, to cover, so I dragged him with me. Only when I thought we were safe did I light a fire.' He sighed at his foolishness. 'I should have known that it would attract enemies. We were surrounded at night by tribesmen.' He spat into the fire. 'They seemed to be in awe of Publius — but it did not stop them knocking us both senseless. When I awoke, I was bouncing in one of those chariots of theirs, bound and gagged.'

Quintus knew that it took a lot of courage to admit to this — being captured was almost as much of a disgrace as desertion. With a single gesture, he dismissed the shame and encouraged Marcus to continue.

'I was confined in a cage and found this man next to me, though I cannot pronounce his name.' He looked at the man and made a sound in his throat, at which the man just laughed, and repeated a similar sound, whilst pointing to himself. Marcus smiled, then continued. 'He had come to trade, but they stripped his boat of almost everything and beached it where we found it, probably intending to come back later for the oars and the sail. He had a crew — he does not know if they were killed or imprisoned, or if they fled.'

'Why the cages, the animals, the birds?'

'I learned some of his language, and he already knew some of mine. He told me they build a great wheel for the solstice, and burn in it many sacrificial victims. They burn them alive — including humans. I think Publius was to be the central attraction. They worshipped his hair.'

The tribesman interrupted, speaking in a serious tone. He used a mixture of Latin and his native tongue. Marcus interpreted.

'He says it is a holy ceremony, that Publius would have been made into a god. He seems in awe of it.'

Quintus laughed a little, finding the man's accent impossible. 'And you can understand him?'

'We were held together for long enough that we can — barely — understand each other.'

'And you? Also a god?'

Marcus laughed, though no amusement reached his eyes. 'I think I was but fuel. They stripped me naked and scourged me when I resisted.'

'I saw the marks... I wondered at them.' Quintus chewed thoughtfully, pulling a fish bone from between his teeth. 'Can he get us across the ocean? Is he able?'

Marcus shrugged. 'He says he does it often — he calls it the narrow sea. I believe him.'

'Then so will I,' Quintus said, rising to fetch himself more fish. 'We should give him a name.'

The man looked and puffed out his chest, pointing to himself. 'Keneil,' he said. This did not sound like the name he had said earlier, which none of the legionaries had been able to pronounce.

Quintus realised this, but pointed to himself anyway and spoke his own name. The man shook his head, crossed his hands over his heart, then held them forward, palms up.

'Friendship…' started Marcus tentatively, then realised what the man was trying to say. 'I think it means "friend."' He pointed to each of the legionaries in turn and repeated, 'Keneil, keneil.'

The man nodded and smiled broadly, then tapped his own chest and said, 'Keneil.'

Marcus turned to Quintus in triumph. 'It is not his name,' he said. 'It means "friend", or something close to this, in his tongue. I think it will pass for a name.'

'Keneil it is, then,' said Quintus, smiling at the boatman, then pointing at himself and his comrade. 'Marcus, Quintus.'

Though he had trouble with the start of 'Quintus', Keneil managed both passably and grinned at his own success, returning to his boat and repeating the names to himself.

'And your own story?' Marcus asked. 'How are you here and alive?'

'As I said, it is a long tale,' Quintus replied, 'a tale for evening and firelight and wine — in a place of safety. Once the boat re-floats we must leave and seek such a place — even if it means crossing this "narrow sea".'

Marcus made a non-committal noise and turned back to Sextus whilst Quintus went to investigate Publius' condition.

Cato was once more on guard at the side of his amicus, waiting for him to wake, hoping for some witchcraft to bring him back to this world. He used a damp cloth to wet Publius' cracked lips and wipe his brow. Quintus carefully lifted an eyelid to see if there was a glimmer beneath, but there was none.

'Is it sorcery?' Cato asked fearfully. 'Can it be undone?'

'I cannot say,' said Quintus, straightening up, 'although I have seen something similar before. A medic tried to explain it to me. It is not sleep, but something else.'

'Sextus put the dogs to sleep,' whispered Cato conspiratorially. 'Do you think he could do the opposite?' Before Quintus could stop him, he called to the group by the fire. 'Sextus, have you no magic that would help?'

'Your sorcery worked on those guard dogs,' said Rufus, through a mouthful of fish. 'I did not think it would. I thought you were boasting. I was impressed.'

'It was only partly sorcery,' Sextus was forced to admit. 'I used a sort of magic to begin with, I held them in my spell for a little while. But then there was noise, movement — I heard Marcus cry out, so the dogs must have heard also. The villagers were lighting torches, calling to each other. The beasts grew anxious; it was clear that my spell over them would soon be broken. I soothed them and sang to them, repeated the incantations I had learned, but still they began to fret, to look across, anxious at the noise coming from their masters.'

The men listened with fascination. 'Go on,' Quintus encouraged.

'Then they and I both heard a clear call from the village — their names, as I took it, to which they were eager to respond.'

'Did you have stronger magic?' Rufus asked.

'I did not need it. By now there was noise everywhere. The bigger one barked and went towards its caller, the other followed.'

'So, no magic,' said Cato bitterly.

Sextus shook his head.

Keneil had been listening to the exchange and caught the gist of what had been said. He beckoned Marcus over and spoke quietly to him, clarifying points he did not understand. Eventually, Marcus turned to the waiting faces of his comrades. 'Our friend knows of powerful magic, further down the river. He thinks it may help. Come down here, Cato; listen to what he has to say.' He beckoned to Quintus, who also knelt by Publius. 'You, too — you are decanus, after all. It will be your decision.'

In obeying, Quintus knew that he passed just a little of his authority to Marcus. If it was deliberate, it was cleverly done. 'You watch him,' he ordered Jovan, 'but do not touch him.' He then went down to the fire, Cato following reluctantly.

'He will show us our position,' said Marcus, 'and what is ahead of us.'

Keneil squatted and in the sand drew a map of sorts whilst the legionaries looked on. First, he described a sinuous double line marking the river, with a cross to show their position on it, beyond the fork.

'This is us here?' Quintus asked, pointing.

'It is,' Marcus confirmed.

The fork itself Keneil drew as a straight line, heading first a short way west, then turning south to run almost parallel with its wider cousin. At the end of their course, a line drawn across both forks indicated the sea, judging by the wave shapes he marked beneath it. Above the fork, next to the river, he drew a circle and, Quintus realised with a squint, flames — the place where the prisoners had been held. Almost at the fork, he drew a line of dots across the whole map.

'Cantiaci,' he said, pointing his stick to the north of the line. Pointing to the south, he said, 'Atrebates.' He then drew a circle near the coast on the Atrebates side and spoke a word that Quintus did not recognise, but he knew what it meant.

As Marcus looked at him for enlightenment, Quintus explained. 'These are the names of the tribes — the ones who captured you, and the ones we fell in with before we rescued you. What he has marked there is their town. He must have said its name, which we never knew.'

Keneil had paused, but Quintus waved him on. Not far from the sea, he used his thumb to draw a short, straight line across the smaller river, then said a familiar word to Marcus.

'A bridge,' Marcus said.

'I think we know this bridge,' said Crassus, exchanging a glance with Sextus.

'I too,' Quintus said, 'though it seems like a lifetime away.'

'Can we ask him to mark the stone circle, to be sure?' Crassus asked.

Quintus used his hand to flatten another area of sand, and drew the distinctive shape of one of the structures. Two uprights, with a lintel across the top. Keneil smiled in understanding and showed where this lay: on the other side of the river to the settlement.

'This is a religious place,' Sextus explained to Marcus. 'We saw a sacrifice made there amidst much pomp. It is a place with its roots deep in the past. Here there is strong magic. If we could but harness it, perhaps we might find the cure for Publius?'

Marcus spoke with Keneil, who shook his head energetically. 'Not this place,' said Marcus. 'There is another. Watch.' He waved at the boatman to continue his map. In the middle of the river, where it widened out, the man marked an irregular shape, an island, then drew a track across the water from each bank.

'A bridge?' Quintus asked. 'Surely this is too long?'

Keneil swept both halves of the track away with his hand, redrew them, then swept them away again, and looked at the legionaries quizzically.

Sextus was the first to realise what he meant. 'It is not a bridge, but a causeway of some sort, only there at low tide. The river is tidal, and the path vanishes when the tide is high.' He drew the structure again and swept it away, pointing to the boat, the water already lapping at its lower planks. Keneil nodded in understanding.

'What is the significance of the island?' Quintus asked. 'Is it important?'

'He says it is the centre of their religion,' Marcus said, 'a temple of some sort, along with priests and acolytes. The word he used was "druid". They are healers as well as priests, he says. This is the place where a cure might be found. If we can but meet the priests when they are there...'

'Ask him about this temple,' Quintus instructed.

Marcus and Keneil communicated using a combination of words, gestures and drawings in the sand, Crassus and Sextus helping where they could. Finally Marcus turned back to the expectant group. 'It is occupied only on special days. There is a full moon due — it was almost full last night. That is when they will be there.' A flurry of questions was thrown at him, and he raised both his hands, adding quickly, 'There is a problem; they will need payment.'

The men were immediately quiet. How could they provide payment? They had nothing — they had been laughing about that only the afternoon before.

'Perhaps we could pay with his golden hair,' said Cato. 'They seem to value it. And he can always grow more.'

Marcus turned to the boatman and asked a question. Keneil shook his head. Again Marcus translated. 'They do not value such things, he says. They are not Cantiaci. They are, I think he said, all of the tribes.' He seemed doubtful, unsure of what this meant. 'They will take blood, a sacrifice, I think — or he could mean something that has tasted blood. It is not that I do not understand; it is that he does not know.'

Several voices were raised at once.

'A sword?'

'A knife?'

'A spear?'

'The tribesman's blade?' Marcus suggested, pulling it from his belt.

Keneil shook his head and gestured a refusal with his palm. He then stood next to Quintus, around two thirds of his height. Gently, he reached across for Quintus' blade, the decanus allowing him to pull it from its scabbard. He held it out gingerly, flat across both hands, holding it up to the group of legionaries.

'A gladius,' Sextus said, looking at the blade with something approaching reverence. 'This they would accept?'

'It is new to these islands,' said Marcus. 'Much better than this.' He tapped the native sword. Then he shook his head. 'But our friend says not this one.' He looked up at Quintus. 'I am sorry, Quintus, but he says it has to be perfect. This one has blemishes.' He looked down quizzically at the man holding the blade, who passed it back to Quintus deferentially. Quintus sheathed it, glad to have it back, whether or not it had blemishes.

Cato at once offered his weapon, but it, too, was rejected as imperfect. Sextus knew the answer, but did not know if he dared. To the legionary, the gladius was an extension of himself, as was his armour, his helmet, his belt and his pugio. Stealing a glance at Publius, white as the wing of a swan, he decided to speak. 'Tullius, it must be yours. You polish and sharpen it all the time.'

Tullius was reluctant. 'It is as one of my limbs,' he said. 'I would as soon lose an arm or a leg as let my blade go.'

Under his breath, directly into Tullius' ear so that no other should hear, Sextus spoke urgently. 'Friend, you will still have your knife and we will find you another sword, but this is your redemption. This is what will take the Furies from your back. You know of what I speak.'

Tullius' dark eyes locked with Sextus' soft brown ones. The contrast between the two men was striking — Tullius with his jagged scar and ripped ear, his earring and the appearance of being always on the edge of anger; Sextus with his smooth skin, newly shaven jaw and handsome features full of confidence.

Tullius lowered his gaze and slowly drew his gladius. 'Let it be so, then, for there is no doubt that this is the finest weapon we have.' Amidst nods of approval and admiration, and not a little curiosity about what Sextus might have said, Tullius handed the blade to the tribesman.

Keneil smiled at its perfection and said just one word: 'Yes.'

XXXVIII: ELYSIUM

Cato continued to dampen Publius' lips with a wet cloth and tried to spoon liquid into his mouth, and his chest continued to gently rise and fall, his heart to beat. There was no way that Cato could get him to eat solid food, so he could only give him a weak fish broth on a spoon. Although his condition appeared unchanged, Quintus knew that the longer he did not eat, the closer to death he would be.

As the boat began to rise with the tide, Quintus sent Sextus and Crassus to check on their pursuit. The two legionaries left the little beach and struggled north through bog and reed. In less than fifteen minutes, with both of them up to their knees in brackish water, and plagued by biting insects, they abandoned the mission. There was no way they could be followed on this bank of the river.

Meanwhile, Quintus had climbed up into the boat and stood high on its stern to see if any water-borne pursuers followed. There was no evidence of any, and no sign either of chariots or foot soldiers on the far bank. He jumped down and called for Keneil and Marcus. Marcus arrived out of breath, having been first sharpening, then drilling with his new blade.

'Keneil, do we go now, or wait for the moon?' Quintus asked, indicating the river.

The boatman pointed down the river, then spoke words in his own tongue to Marcus.

'We go,' Marcus said. 'It will take, I think, a day to reach the causeway. I suppose that by that night the moon will be full. He must cross it when the water is here.' He indicated chest height.

'I suppose that when the tide is at its highest is the only time he can cross.'

'We are putting a lot of trust in this tribesman,' said Quintus, though without rancour, for they could do nothing else. 'Keneil, we break camp,' he told him, then repeated the order loudly for the rest of the contubernium.

They struck camp efficiently, stowing their gear in the boat, dousing the fire with sand and even keeping some of the live fish in the net, dangling in the water at the stern. They laid Publius in the boat on a sort of bier, cleverly made by Jovan from woven osiers and two rigid branches to serve as carrying poles. The bottom of the boat still held water, but as Keneil did not seem to be worried, nor were they.

As the craft floated downstream, the current taking it, their comrade lying supine with his sightless eyes now staring at the sky, Quintus could not help but think of Charon's boat silently traversing the Styx. He shook his head to clear it of the image — Publius had no obol under his tongue, after all, so ought not to pass — but the vision kept returning. They rowed now and again, but most of the time they drifted with the current, Sextus and Crassus even swimming alongside the boat for a while, where they were joined by a pair of strange grey pig-nosed creatures with flippers, whiskers and smooth skins. They were clearly cousins to the creatures — dolphins, Quintus remembered they were called — that had played alongside the ship as they had left port in Hispania.

Tullius, Rufus and Marcus sat in the stern of the boat playing knucklebones with stones that Rufus had picked from the riverbank. Tullius had been in one of his deep sulks, sad about the loss of his blade and refusing to talk to anyone until Rufus had produced the means to gamble, though they had nothing with which to wager.

Their quiet progress disturbed many birds, including water birds, some of which came too close and died from their curiosity, so that at least the squad would eat flesh that evening. They debated whether the flippered animal could be eaten, and whether it was fish or meat, but found the beasts too wary to catch and did not have the words to ask Keneil, who pointed at the beasts and smiled. Perhaps they were a good omen. The sail stayed furled, presumably because the wind did not blow.

It was a fine day, with nothing but baby white clouds low on the horizon — a day that, in the valleys of Rome, Quintus thought would have been unbearably hot, with the stench of the rubbish pits, the unburied dead and the great mass of people hanging above the city like a poisonous mist. Here, the cool water, the sounds of the birds and frogs, and the occasional splashing of the oars made it the closest thing to Elysium that he had ever experienced. Even the biting insects of the marshes did not venture across the water. He looked at where Cato ministered to his friend and hoped that Publius was experiencing the same.

In the late afternoon, as Keneil had predicted, the river forked, two channels bending around a central land mass. Through sign language, Quintus confirmed that this was the island they sought. As they were steered down the eastern channel, a long sand bar appeared, preventing any further progress. It was only just visible beneath the surface of the water, but the tide had already turned and the boat could not have navigated these shallows. Two of the smooth grey creatures sat on it and watched them for a moment, looking much more clumsy on land, before diving off downstream. Quintus could now feel the salt tang of the sea in his nostrils.

Keneil turned the prow towards the island, beaching the vessel in a little bay, out of sight of the causeway. The men unloaded, carefully placing Publius on the ground, Cato covering him with his own cloak. Quintus sent Sextus and Crassus to watch for any movement on the causeway whilst the rest of them settled into their regular routine. Sextus climbed an oak rooted in a small hill, its lower branches easy to clamber on. Crassus waited at its foot.

Maxim asked Quintus if he should build a fire and he, in turn, consulted Keneil. Keneil licked his thumb and held it upwards, testing the wind, then shook his head. They could not risk the smoke leading to the discovery of the boat.

The sun set without spectacle across the flat sands and, before the moon had risen, Sextus, from his vantage point up the tree, called down that he could see lights, far to the east across the marshland. As they came closer, Crassus could also make them out. They were far away, meandering in a sinuous line. The torches, clearly carried by men, snaked around the ponds and meres, reflecting off their rippling surfaces, moving mysteriously like the fin of an eel through dark waters. They reported the sighting to Quintus.

'They come,' Crassus said. 'A couple of dozen, slowly, on foot.'

'We need to be there before them, waiting for them,' suggested Cato, 'so that they know we are no ambush and do not wish them harm. We can wait at the door of their temple.'

Again, Quintus consulted the boatman and, with the help of Marcus, determined with difficulty that this was a good idea. They tried to find out how far away the temple was, but failed to understand the answer or whether Keneil spoke of time or some measure of distance. However, he was able to tell them that they should leave straight away. He was also able to show them which path to take, but shook his head when they asked him to come. He pointed to his boat. This was his charge.

Four of the men moved to lift the stretcher on which Publius lay — Sextus, Rufus, Maxim and Jovan. 'I think not the slaves,' said Tullius, looking to Quintus for guidance. 'They should stay here with Keneil and guard the boat.'

'Agreed.'

Maxim and Jovan bowed their heads in acknowledgement and withdrew.

'Tullius? Cato?' Quintus asked.

'Not them, either,' said Crassus firmly. 'Cato must continue to watch and minister to Publius, not carry him. Tullius carries our offering, so it should be Marcus and I.' Marcus nodded his agreement and stepped into the place vacated by Jovan, Crassus to the other side. Quintus knew of Marcus' scars and Crassus' battle wound; he should have known that neither would prevent them from doing their duty.

Quintus gleaned that Keneil wanted the boat to be on the other side of the causeway, the seaward side. Keneil had pointed downriver and tried to explain this; they had conversed in a series of gestures and words in both their languages. Finally the boatman had turned to Marcus and spoken at length, talking as much with his arms as his voice.

'What is it?' Quintus was now impatient for them to leave, the strain showing on his brow.

'He wants to know if he can trust the slaves,' Marcus said.

'They are Macedonians, after all,' Tullius muttered.

Quintus glared at him with ill-concealed annoyance. He needed harmony at the moment, not conflict. 'What does he want with them?'

'He wants them to row him to the other side of the causeway when the tide rises high enough, so that our escape route is open. He fears they may attack him.' He smiled. 'Apparently slaves in his country are not always as docile as ours.'

'Tell him they can be trusted,' Quintus pronounced. 'They have had many chances to run away, and they are still here.'

Marcus explained as best he could to Keneil, who grinned and made a shallow bow in Quintus' direction. Maxim and Jovan listened to what was said about them without reacting — whilst they might crave freedom, they did not intend rebellion. 'Keneil will take them and cross with the next tide and wait for us,' Marcus translated.

'Then we take our chances — we trust him, and them,' Quintus confirmed.

The matter settled, the party with the stretcher set off down the track indicated to them, hoping to find the great temple. They did not know what to expect — a turf mound, like the temple of Romulus in the city, simple but powerful; bronze doors and a marble roof like the temple of Jupiter, or a circle of stones like the temple where the horse had been sacrificed.

Half an hour later they stood and wondered, for it was none of these, but it was surely a temple.

Here there was no studded door, for there was no building, no golden roof or portico, no steps or columns, and no circle of stones, only the majestic trees of the forest. This was their temple — grander, taller and more ancient than any wooden or stone building. The trees here stood in an almost perfect circle.

They were oaks, their broad boughs reaching out to each other to form a canopy, and their trunks were massive, pitted and scarred with seasons and storms, many of the lower branches missing or shortened by weather or the depredations of the forester. The floor of the temple was brown, crisp and deep, a hundred years or more of fallen leaves. At the centre was a single flat stone, which Quintus took to be an altar of some sort.

'These are old trees,' he said quietly to Sextus. 'The people who planted them must be long gone.'

'Perhaps the trees are tended by the ancestors of those who set them here,' offered Sextus.

The legionaries put Publius down gently on the floor. They had only just arrived ahead of the priests — if that was what they were. They watched as the men gathered here in the shadowy light of their smoking torches. The sun would only touch the central stone at noontide, when it was overhead and at its highest. The moon, even full, would struggle to penetrate to the heart of this grove. Maybe at its height its silvery light would fall on the sacrificial stone — for that is what Quintus thought it was.

The arrivals were each grey-robed and hooded, and each seemed to have an allotted place to which he all but silently moved, only the soft crunch of leaves underfoot accompanying the slow dance. They must have seen the legionaries on the edge of their sacred space, but decided to pay them no attention as yet.

One by one, they pulled their hoods back from their heads, revealing men of all ages, mostly bearded, with plaited moustaches and long hair tied in braids. There were younger men too, acolytes or apprentices, Quintus guessed, although with a shudder he realised that they might also be sacrificial victims. There were dark days in Rome's past when the Republic was threatened and foreigners had been buried alive beneath the Forum Boarium as sacrifices to placate the gods. Generals in the field had been known to turn to such practices, so Quintus held no misconceptions about such things. After all, had they not just saved Marcus and Publius from such a fate?

XXXIX: TINCOMARUS

Quintus did not know what to do. After all of their rescues and adventures, he realised that he had brought everyone to a sacred place where they were not sufficiently armed to defend themselves. He had therefore managed to put the whole contubernium at risk, and, if that was not enough, he had all but freed Maxim and Jovan and given them their means of escape. He clutched his hidden armband and recited a desperate prayer to the shade of Ursus, promising a black lamb to father Dis should they survive.

One of the grey-robed priests, who had stood holding a torch with his back to the legionaries, turned and smiled at Quintus. With a start, Quintus realised that here, outlined in the flickering light, was a face that he knew, as did others of the contubernium. An older man, balding, but with a long black moustache plaited and tied and a wise and placid countenance, though wreathed in shadows. It was Tincomarus of the Atrebates who now left his comrades and walked across to the group of soldiers.

'Quintus of the Romans,' he greeted the decanus in flawless Latin, not even showing surprise. 'I thought you had fled back over the narrow sea, or were by now dead. You look like you have found more of your brood —' he nodded in the direction of Marcus, then his soft eyes landed on the outstretched figure of Publius — 'and been in trouble.' He smiled patronisingly at the faces he knew, then turned to the circle and spoke in his own tongue. The priests remained facing the stone, but closed the gap he had left. Quintus saw one of the younger men step forward, walking towards the centre.

'A sacrifice?' Quintus asked in a whisper, not wanting to witness such a thing.

'Not at all.' Tincomarus shook his head, clearly amused by the idea. 'An education, more like. Come, follow me. You are not permitted to watch.' The tone of his voice did not brook dissent. He turned and headed down the track up which the legionaries had come.

'We follow,' Quintus ordered, waving the others on, including the stretcher, before joining at the end, the column trailing after the bobbing light. They spoke softly to one another as they made their way back towards the water, Marcus curious about this man, Rufus telling him some of the tale of their time with the Atrebates and how they knew him. They, along with Crassus and Sextus, carried Publius carefully on his litter, Tullius and Cato ahead of them. Though Tullius had his sword unsheathed, Tincomarus disregarded it. Quintus marvelled that somehow the man knew that they had not come to do battle.

Once out of sight of the oak circle, Tincomarus found a clearing, now brightly lit by the risen moon, and called a halt to the strange procession. Quintus caught up with him as the men once more laid Publius on the ground.

'What is it about you Romans?' He had to crane his neck to look into Quintus' eyes. 'Why do you think everyone wants to sacrifice everyone else?'

'He was to be burned,' Quintus said in disgust, pointing at Publius.

'He was to be a god,' Tincomarus replied flatly, nodding at the painted nails. 'He has been prepared.'

'And the youth?' Quintus twitched his head in the direction of the oaks.

'As I said,' Tincomarus explained wearily, 'an education. We are not priests of any god, we are more —' he fished for the right word — 'guardians. Druids, we are called.' He faced the rest of the contubernium and asked, without emotion, 'Who killed Tan? Who killed my nephew?'

'It was I,' said Cato, from his position kneeling by Publius' head. 'It was I who discovered his treachery; he intended to lead us all to our deaths. He fought. It was not dishonourable.'

'And my cousins of the Regni tribe, Coginus and the rest?'

'A skirmish — spear, shield and sword,' Quintus said. 'Again, an honourable death. How did you know?'

'I felt it. You just confirm it.'

Quintus cursed their stupidity. Tincomarus could have remained in ignorance.

Marcus knew a little of their adventures, but there was much he still did not know. 'Who is this man?' he demanded gruffly, unable to contain his curiosity. 'Why have you killed his nephew and friends but not him?'

'He is a senior member of the tribe that we first met.' Quintus held both palms up. '*Pax*, Marcus, there is much yet to tell.'

Tincomarus looked at the ground beneath his feet, muttering words — a prayer, perhaps. He then addressed the legionaries, his head turning first to Marcus then to Publius. 'Where I have lost, you have gained.' He knelt at the head of Publius, opposite to where Cato was already kneeling. 'You killed Tan?' he asked softly, looking into Cato's eyes.

'I did,' Cato replied.

Tincomarus seemed to accept this, and did not investigate further. 'Who is this?' he asked.

'My friend and comrade, precious to me.'

'Injured?'

'Drugged, we think, or bound by sorcery.'

Tincomarus opened an eyelid with a thumb and let the light from his torch fall on the eye. Then he put his hand gently on Publius' forehead and finally, he reached inside his tunic to measure his heartbeat. He straightened up, rearranged the material and patted the tunic flat. 'There is no sorcery here,' he said to Cato. 'There are drugs and poisons, but no witchcraft.' He stood and addressed Quintus. 'I know what you want. I cannot help.'

'But we bring an offering.' Tullius was eager, thrusting the shining gladius at him.

Tincomarus did not reach out to take it, instead holding his arms wide, palms upward in a gesture of refusal or helplessness — or both. He spoke kindly. 'Our order does not go armed. Anyway, this will take more than a mere sword, though I admire the weapon. You should keep it. This requires medicines we do not have. All I can offer —' he reached inside his robe and pulled out a small pouch — 'is honey.' He placed the bag in Cato's palm and closed the soldier's fingers over it. 'We carry it to give us strength and stamina. Perhaps if he could reach your home, there might be people who could aid him. This might help him get there alive.'

'Is that it?' Cato opened his hand to look at the tiny package. He was almost in tears with frustration and desperation.

'That is it,' Tincomarus said firmly, then offered Quintus the torch. 'Take this; go back to your boat.' He raised his eyebrows at the shocked reaction of the men. 'Of course I know that you came by water — how else? Pick him up and go. If you manage to get him home, there could be hope for him, but not here.'

Quintus took the torch, but could not stop himself from asking, 'If you could help, would you?'

'No,' said Tincomarus unhesitatingly, but quietly enough that only Quintus could hear.

'Why?' Quintus asked.

'The gods create balance and harmony,' Tincomarus whispered. 'A boy was killed. He had a family. This evens the scales.' What came next was more like a curse, hissed into the legionary's ear. 'Know that the chase is not over, nor will it ever be. You have made enemies of many tribes. You have not just freed the sacrificial beasts of the Cantiaci, you have stolen their god, whilst the Regni seek vengeance for both children and chieftain. They will hunt you through each other's territory, through fire, air and water.' He pulled his hood back over his bald head and spoke clearly so that the others might hear. 'Despite all your Roman arrogance and pride, and the death of my nephew and the king of the Regni, I send my friendship and that of Aucissa and the Atrebates to your great Caesar.' He turned his eyes on Quintus and spoke with finality. 'But not to you, never to you.' The next part was clearly an order. 'Now go.'

He did not wait for a reply, but turned and set off down the path, quickly vanishing from sight.

'Why not you?' Marcus asked Quintus, in the wake of the departure.

'I have offended,' Quintus answered wearily. 'The Furies will not let me be.'

Tullius was sheathing his sword and looked up at this. 'I thought it was only me,' he said in wonder.

'There is guilt in us all,' Quintus replied sadly.

It was a subdued group that made its way slowly back along the track. They had set off in the hope that Publius might walk back, and now their comrade felt like a burden. Quintus sent

Tullius running ahead with the torch to make sure the boat was still there, and to delay its departure if it was. He had no idea of the patterns of the tides and prayed that the vessel would be this side of the causeway still.

When they arrived, the boat was still there, though the causeway was not. The prow of the boat was still beached, but would not be for much longer, the rising water already lapping at it. The men laid Publius down on the bank and turned to Quintus for orders. Keneil joined them, jumping down with the painter in his hand. The men squatted or sat in a rough circle, Publius at its centre.

Quintus had hoped, if not for magic, then for Aucissa of the Atrebates. She had shown both wisdom and authority. He saw her as a healer and sorceress — her smile crinkling the lines that framed her blue eyes as she looked deep into his soul. He sighed, regretting that she was not one of these druid priests, that he could not borrow her skills. He tugged at his tunic, straightening it beneath his armour, and pushed a lock of hair from his forehead. Those who knew him would know the signs of a decision made.

'We go home,' he said simply, 'or at least as far as Frisia, if that is as far as this man can take us. Tincomarus says that there is nothing for us here, that he cannot help. I believe him.' He addressed Cato, still at his friend's head. 'It is not sorcery, Cato, but concoctions of some sort that have robbed Publius of sense and consciousness. His blood may purge the poisons by itself, otherwise we must look to our own medics.'

'Tincomarus cannot or will not help?' Cato asked, desperation in his voice. 'Is it because I killed Tan?'

Quintus spoke gently. 'I think "cannot". You told him you had no choice.'

'Why will he not help?' Marcus asked sharply. 'Who is Tan? What have you done here?'

'Made enemies,' said Quintus dismissively. 'There is no help here.'

Keneil had listened without understanding, but now recognised the tones of an argument brewing. He tapped Quintus' arm and pointed at the boat, which had now begun to bob fretfully on the rising water.

'Get him aboard.' Quintus indicated Publius. Crassus and Tullius took their comrade's head and feet and handed him up to Sextus and Rufus, who had climbed into the boat. As the legionaries made to help each other aboard, Keneil jumped up and down, shaking his head and both hands, waving the men out of the craft.

'What is it?' Quintus demanded.

Marcus held up a hand to silence him, then he and Keneil had one of their strange conversations, until the combination of words, tones and gestures brought realisation.

'Too much weight may mean the keel will not clear the causeway,' Marcus said. 'I suppose that, if they sail this way, the crew are made to walk whilst the boat crosses. We must walk. Only Publius and whoever rows can sail. Two rowers only.'

'You walk,' Rufus told the slaves, who still sat at the rowing benches. 'We row.' His gesture meant himself and Sextus. Cato turned to Quintus, hoping he would overrule this order so that he could stay by Publius' side, but Quintus failed to notice the pleading look. As Rufus gave Sextus a lift, the slaves complied and began to climb down to the land, turning onto their fronts to slide themselves down the side of the boat. With his feet over the side and about to let himself drop, Jovan froze and pulled himself back.

'What is it?' Quintus asked.

Jovan spoke urgently. 'A noise, sir. Master Publius made a noise.'

'Quintus! Hurry!' Cato's voice carried an authority it had never had before. He demonstrated to the tall man what he wanted him to do, clasping his hands together. Quintus understood at once and made a step with interlocked fingers.

Cato clambered into the boat in time to see Publius cough violently and spit out a wad of black bile, a foul-looking thing like a lump of putrid flesh that splashed into the bilge water and disappeared. He leaned over and put his face close to that of his friend.

'What is happening, Cato?' Quintus shouted. 'Keneil is getting anxious; the boat must leave.'

The little man was becoming more agitated next to his craft, desperate to get aboard and get going. He tugged at Crassus' arm urgently and the legionary made a step for him, almost throwing him into the boat. It was now held to the shore by nothing — no painter, no anchor, no solid earth — and it swung round, pivoting on its stern. The flickering light of Tullius' torch reflected off not just the boat's timbers, but the widening stretch of water between it and the land.

'He lives,' Cato shouted. 'He coughs up poison, but he has opened his eyes.'

'Has he spoken? Does he sit up?'

'Neither, Quintus, but he will, I am sure of it. He even looks better; there is colour in his cheeks.'

'Stay with him and row,' Quintus ordered, though both knew that he did not have a choice as the boat swung round to face downriver. 'Come on,' he commanded the rest.

XXXX: SALACIA

'Look!' Quintus pointed to where their route to the causeway was already being eaten up by water, the gap between river and the trees of the island narrowing. There was no obvious way through the forest, apart from back to the druid's circle, so they would just have to run along the bank, hoping that they could beat the tide. The causeway was no more than a quarter of a mile away, but the waters were rapidly rising and rippling unbroken across its middle section. It was no longer a bridge.

'Tullius, you lead. Keep to the bank,' he said, although the contrast between the moonlit surface of the water and the dark of the land seemed obvious.

Tullius set off at a jog, Crassus behind him. Marcus was shouting insistently at the slaves, who were trying to drag the stretcher from the water. 'Leave it!' he yelled. 'Run!' He grabbed Maxim and propelled him forward, then dragged Jovan roughly by his upper arm. Quintus did not disapprove, but instead added his own voice as they all, alternately splashing and slipping, ran along the narrowing bank.

Breathing heavily, they gained the point where the causeway met the land, then were shocked to discover that, at the other side of the spit, there was no bank, the trees coming right down into the water. They paused and looked desperately for the boat, but could not see it.

They might have panicked had not Tullius called out, his torch held high. 'There is a path of sorts in the trees!' he shouted. 'It runs alongside the river. It is the only way.'

Quintus waved the little party onwards. They ran along the dark tunnel, following the bobbing light of Tullius' torch.

There were trees crowding either side and intertwining branches cut off the moonlight above, but the path was wide enough for them, and must have been made for men, though they had to walk in single file.

'Slow down!' Quintus called from the rear. 'Keep together.' In truth, they needed to slow their pace so that they did not blunder into dangers. At least they knew that they were going the right way, as every so often they glimpsed the river to their left and, in places, the ground underfoot became wet, their steps sticking and squelching.

They ran on further than they had on the other side, long enough to drop into that efficient pace that another legionary would have recognised as double-time, long enough to slow their breathing, long enough to begin to doubt whether they would ever come out onto the bank again.

But at last, as the light strengthened, the torch ahead of them bobbed out of the trees, and they followed to find themselves on a long strand of sloping sand running alongside a shallow bay. It was already turning pink and white with morning, and they blinked as they came out of the dark tunnel. The taste and smell of salt was strong here, and the sky to the south seemed huge and endless, as if they had come to the threshold of a great cave.

The sea — which they now knew did not mark the end of their world — lapped at their feet and spread flat to the horizon, waveless and still, apart from the birds that skimmed across it.

Quintus searched for the boat, panic growing in his chest as he could not at first see it. Then a smudge appeared far out into the bay, a smudge that resolved itself into the lines of the little craft. It was heading towards them, but it seemed to take forever for the outline of the boat to solidify. Meanwhile, the waters continued to lap at their feet.

'The tide is still rising,' Quintus said to Crassus, who stood behind him. Marcus, Tullius and Rufus decided they would be more comfortable on the dry path in the tree-lined tunnel, so they withdrew. Maxim and Jovan went with them.

Quintus stayed by the shore, heedless of the water nibbling at his feet. He desperately wanted to know how Publius was, and equally desperately, he wanted to leave this land.

As the boat entered the little bay, the oars were shipped, and its own momentum brought it onward. Cato's head appeared above the prow. As soon as he saw Quintus, he began waving furiously and shouting with joy. 'Publius is recovering! He has smiled at me — he will live!'

As the sky turned from white to grey, giving the lie to the fine day predicted by the dawn, the boat at last ground to a halt on the beach and Cato jumped down. He hugged Quintus, grasping the tall legionary round the middle whilst chattering incessantly. Quintus did not quite know how to take this, lifting Cato's arms gently so as not to offend, and placing his own hands on the legionary's shoulders to put him — in as kind a way as possible — at arm's length.

Keneil threw the painter to Quintus, and Sextus' head also appeared. 'I am looking after him,' he said. 'He cannot be left.'

Cato was excited. 'He is conscious! He has opened his eyes, he has managed to swallow, and he has even tried to speak.'

'Then all we have to do is get off this god-cursed island,' Quintus laughed, 'and we are whole.' He looked around for Marcus and saw him striding out of the wood. 'Marcus, can you find out from Keneil if we can light a fire? If we can eat? Or must we leave at once?'

Marcus waved an acknowledgement and once more communicated with Keneil, who had clambered out of the boat, splashing his way to where the others stood. Quintus had his answer when the little man pointed to Sextus and made a gesture with his fingertips together, thumbs high, like a fin.

'I understand,' Sextus smiled, and disappeared into the boat, emerging seconds later with a net full of the fish they had previously stowed, flinging it to the shore.

'The tide still rises,' Marcus said. 'We must leave when it is falling.'

Quintus nodded. 'A fire,' he ordered Maxim and Jovan, 'and hot food.'

Maxim soon had a blaze going and fish turning on spits. They had decided not to move Publius, so Cato waded out with food for Sextus, climbing aboard to also try to encourage his friend to take some fish. But Publius was still not quite back in the waking world and would not eat, lying on his back and staring heavenward.

For the men on the shore, the reprieve marked a temporary return to normality — or at least a badly dressed, badly armed version of it. They relaxed, chatted and even joked. Marcus and Rufus sparred, wrestling as Crassus watched and scored points. Tullius temporarily vanished — they presumed to attend to personal business.

The noise that heralded the return of the grizzled veteran was enough to make all of their heads turn. He was not alone. In his grip was one of the flippered beasts that they had seen on the other side of the causeway. It was alive but injured, its jaw hanging slack. It had not stopped trying to escape.

'A beast,' he said triumphantly, almost sitting on it to keep it still, 'and it lives. A sacrifice to the gods to carry us safely across the water.'

'Whatever it is,' complained Crassus, his eyes narrowing, 'it is not acceptable to any of the gods above.'

'Then we sacrifice to Dis, and ask him to leave us be,' said Marcus, 'or to Neptune — is he not of the gods below?'

'Neptune requires a bull. I have seen it,' said Rufus, as he, Keneil, Maxim and Jovan backed away, putting the fire between them and Tullius.

'Sextus!' Quintus called to their acknowledged expert in the boat, and Sextus' face, chewing fish, popped above the prow. 'Is this thing a fit sacrifice? And if so, who to?'

'I don't know what it is, but it is a creature of the sea. Look.' Where Sextus pointed, there were others of the same race, swimming and basking in the shallow waters. 'If it is offered honourably, I think it is acceptable. We have sacrificed less, and the gods listened. Not Neptune, though. He is quick to take offence.' He shivered at the memory of his last sea voyage. 'His wife, perhaps?'

After a brief discussion, with no-one really speaking from a position of knowledge, the decision was made. The beast would be sacrificed to Salacia, wife of Neptune and mistress of calm seas. No-one knew her rites, or whether she would accept offerings burned on the fire. Sextus suggested a compromise: the throat could be cut over the land, so that the blood soaked into the earth; the innards could be burned on the fire; and the parts they could not eat — flippers, tail and head — could be thrown in the sea. In that way, at least something of the sacrifice would reach the goddess.

Tullius knelt, his cloak pulled over his bald head, and slit the beast's throat. 'We wish for safe passage, mother goddess, but for me, I also ask for forgiveness from the Furies,' he whispered.

Quintus heard and shook his head, sad that Tullius still felt his guilt so keenly. Pulling his cloak over his head, he offered a prayer himself. 'I would uphold my oath to Ursus; bring us all safe home,' he said.

The dead animal was tough to carve, thick-skinned, but once it was opened, Sextus put his hand inside and pulled out its innards, flinging them into the flames, where they sizzled. Cato watched the smoke rise from his post beside Publius, his position made more difficult as the boat continued to rise on the swelling tide.

The men on shore cooked joints of the beast as best they could, but its flesh proved to be chewy, salty and fishy. They were happy to fling what was left — with a final prayer — into the sea. None of them was sure whether they had done the right thing. The beast itself, the goddess they had chosen and the rites were all questionable, and the mood became fractious as the men argued the rights and wrongs of the sacrifice.

Keneil had been watching his boat carefully and now pointed to it as the painter pulled taut. He gestured for the legionaries to climb aboard.

The estuary was wide at this point, entering the sea not all at once, but in many separate channels, spread out like the fingers of an oak leaf across the bay. Within its protection, the waves were small, insignificant little things that barely managed to produce a whitecap. That this was the same sea from which they had been tossed ashore with such fury — was hard to believe. A light breeze came from the land as they rowed the vessel to the mouth of one of the channels, where the outgoing tide would carry them into the ocean.

The sail flapped sullenly; it had hardly been worth the trouble of raising it, but Keneil had insisted. Perhaps it would be of use on the open sea, Quintus thought, as he idly watched the seabirds swoop, dive and quarrel over fish and crabs.

Suddenly Keneil yelled and all eyes turned to where he pointed. The spits on either side of their narrow passage were no longer empty, the falling tide revealing land. Rushing down each side of their channel was a line of chariots, the hooves of the horses kicking up mud, sand and surf, the crunch of wheels mingling with the cries of the occupants and the slap of leather. The drivers were managing twin reins while a warrior stood at the back of each chariot, spear levelled.

The legionaries had nothing with which to defend themselves — no spears, no slings, not even shields to catch the shafts of death that would be thrown.

'Who is it?' Cato cried, rising from his place by Publius' side to see.

'Cantiaci!' shouted Marcus. 'Our captors!'

'Regni!' shouted Rufus. 'Our enemy!'

'Atrebates!' shouted Crassus. 'Our friends!'

'Britons — the same that sent great Caesar back across the water!' Quintus concluded, spitting into the sea. 'Tincomarus has betrayed us.'

They were sitting ducks. The channel was narrow and straight, and the fingers of land stretched long on either side of it. Five minutes more and they would have been clear. No-one dared to criticise the sacrifice, but all knew that had they not bothered, they would now be out of range.

Spears splashed into the wavelets to left and right of them, one passing clean through the sail, several thudding into the timbers. The legionaries bent down to avoid the barrage, hiding at the back of the mast, squatting behind tipped-up rowing benches. Keneil crouched, keeping hold of the tiller, protected by the stern boards.

A gust of wind caught the sail and pushed the little boat out towards the open sea, leaving the chariots and their warriors yelling shouts and curses. Quintus looked heavenward and clutched Ursus' armband. Perhaps the sacrifice had been worthwhile; perhaps the gods had not yet abandoned them.

More spears planted themselves in the benches and the tiller. As the gap between the boat and the shore widened, the men who had ducked them dared to raise their heads, counted their number, and thanked the gods for their fortune. Publius, of course, did not have this choice. He lay on his back, barely awake, staring at the sky. They could not move him; only the gods could protect him.

A few final spears still splashed and skimmed in the water behind them, but none any longer reached the hull. As the wind picked up and the sail filled, the noise fell further behind, until it was indistinguishable from the cries of the seabirds. The hail of spears ceased. They had seen no sign of boats, though of course knew that the Atrebates, at least, could be even now putting to sea.

The coast faded into the thinning mist that coiled across the estuary. At that moment the clouds finally parted, revealing a sultry red-gold sun, spreading warmth. It lit the weary faces of Quintus' contubernium, all of them. He looked from red-headed Rufus to bald-headed Tullius, from the solid blacksmith Crassus to the ever-smiling Sextus, from golden-haired Publius to his deeply loyal amicus, Cato. Even to the evocatus Marcus, standing in the stern with the slaves. They were all here.

'All of them,' murmured Quintus to himself. He fingered Ursus' tokens, thanking him again for watching over them.

As the boat skipped across the waves, the mysterious isle of Britannia once more vanished behind a rolling curtain of mist.

HISTORICAL NOTES

Ocean is deliberately capitalised when spoken of by the Romans. What we call the English Channel was known to the earliest classical geographers as part of Oceanus, the Ocean Stream, which connected with the North Sea and the Atlantic to encircle all known lands. Effectively, it defined the limit of their world.

Caesar's brief visit to remote and mysterious Britannia, lying on the other side of Oceanus, would have resonated in Rome like the 'conquest' of the South Pole did to the Victorians, or the 1969 moon landing with that generation.

We cannot read Caesar's mind, but we can posit that the 'invasions' of Britain were probably for political rather than military reasons. He wanted to show his enemies back in Rome that he was all-powerful. Celts, Gauls and Britons of course, as Aucissa explains, crossed the Channel often to trade.

In spite of Hollywood telling us otherwise, my Britons do not wear woad. Woad, modern scholars tell us, streaks easily, is ineffective as a skin dye and is caustic, producing scarring (that is not blue). You can dye material with it. Caesar's original phrase, in *De Bello Gallico*, his first-hand account of the Gallic Wars (Book 5, Chapter 14) is '*Omnes vero se Britanni vitro inficiunt, quod caeruleum efficit colorem*' which roughly translates: 'In truth, all Britons dye themselves with glass (vitro), which produces a blue colour.' A mistake by Caesar, or a reference to a coloured glass of Rome? We can interpret, but not make absolute sense. (There are rabbit holes on the internet that you can explore to your heart's content.)

On the other hand, *De Bello Gallico* also claims that Britons 'raise hare, chicken and goose for their own pleasure' and that it is against their religion to eat them — and archaeological evidence — animals buried whole — supports this assumption that they were kept as pets. It also supports the sacrifice of the horse and burial of its head.

A NOTE TO THE READER

Dear Reader,

I cannot thank you enough for taking the time to read the second novel in the Quintus Roman Thrillers series. I hope you enjoyed it. The next book in the series, *Optio*, resumes the adventures of Quintus and his comrades in a new land. I hope you will continue to follow them.

Caesar's 'invasions' of Britain have always puzzled me. There was nothing in the country of any use to Rome — except perhaps a few surly slaves — certainly no gold or silver, and no military advantage to holding the territory. While some scholars have claimed his aim was to stop tribes assisting their brothers on the continent, I think this unlikely. The might of the Celts had been irrevocably smashed at Alesia in 52 BC, which surely marks the destruction of the Celtic 'nation'.

It is more likely that Caesar was demonstrating his awesome power to his enemies in Rome. 'Look at me,' he was saying, 'I can cross even great Oceanus, the limit of our world.' Having been rebuffed (he barely even landed the first time) he returned, better prepared and better armed, less than a year later. He still achieved very little, if anything.

Augustus could also see the political value in crossing Oceanus, and himself prepared for a great invasion of Britannia. A disgraced cohort — such as that to which Quintus belongs — could easily have been sent to reconnoitre, its loss going unrecorded.

While I try my best to be accurate, if you find any errors I shall be delighted to hear from you and, if you're right, correct future editions. I can be found on **Twitter at @NeilDenbyAuthor** and **Facebook at NeilDenby-Writer**.

Reviews by knowledgeable readers are an essential part of a modern author's success, so if you enjoyed the novel I would be grateful if you could spare the short time required to post a review on **Amazon** and **Goodreads**.

Neil Denby

Sapere Books is an exciting new publisher of brilliant fiction and popular history.

To find out more about our latest releases and our monthly bargain books visit our website:
saperebooks.com

Printed in Great Britain
by Amazon